ROSEMARY ROGERS

SCOUNDREL'S HONOR

HQN™

Recycling programs
for this product may
not exist in your area.

ISBN-13: 978-1-61664-964-7

SCOUNDREL'S HONOR

Copyright © 2010 by Rosemary Rogers

This edition published by arrangement with Harlequin Books S.A.

® and TM are trademarks of the publisher. Trademarks indicated with ® are registered in the United States Patent and Trademark Office, the Canadian Trade Marks Office and in other countries.

Printed in U.S.A.

Thank you always, new readers and old.
—RR

SCOUNDREL'S HONOR

CHAPTER ONE

THE VILLAGE OF YABINSK in the Volga River Basin near Moscow was the typical cluster of low, sturdy homes scattered near a wooden church. On the distant hills the wealthier citizens built their redbrick mansions to overlook the lesser folk, while small fishing boats painted in cheerful colors lined the meandering river.

On the very edge of the village, a three-storied coaching inn with attached stables squatted next to the narrow road leading to Moscow to the south and St. Petersburg to the north. With a tile roof and recently painted shutters the building managed to appear respectable, if not prosperous. It was an image that was enhanced by the meticulously clean foyer and the small chambers upstairs that smelled of wood polish and dried flowers.

Behind the stables was a small wattle-and-daub cottage nearly hidden behind the stone wall that divided the property.

It was little more than a kitchen, a front parlor and two bedchambers in the attic, but it was sturdily built to keep out the worst of the Russian winters and filled with delicate birch and cedar furnishings that were more suitable for the palaces of St. Petersburg.

In truth, Fedor Duscha had been a master craftsman before his untimely death and in great demand by many of the finest noble families. The furniture was worth a tidy sum of rubles, but his daughter Emma Linley-Kirov would have starved before selling it off. It had been wrenching enough to convert her father's precious workshop into the coaching inn for a means to make money for her and her younger sister, Anya.

On this cool autumn day, however, she barely noted the scrolled settee set beneath the window of the parlor or the hutch that held her mother's English china.

Instead, she paced the threadbare carpet, her stomach knotted and her hands shaking as she smoothed them down her plain gown of brown kerseymere. At last she turned to meet the concerned gaze of Diana Stanford, who was currently seated on the settee.

Although nearly ten years older than Emma, the English nanny was her dearest friend. Emma's own mother had been raised in England and after her death there had been a comforting familiarity in Diana's companionship.

A traditional English rose, Diana possessed fair hair and blue eyes that lent her an air of deceptive fragility. Emma on the other hand had inherited her father's honey-brown hair, which she kept pulled into a knot at the nape of her neck, and a pair of hazel eyes that regarded the world with a grim determination that tended to intimidate any who hoped to take advantage of a woman forced to stand on her own.

A necessity for keeping her inn profitable and for raising her sixteen-year-old sister, but decidedly detrimental to her relationship with the local villagers. Most of her neighbors condemned the mere thought of a lady attempting to run her own business, let alone raise an impressionable girl. A proper, well-behaved female depended upon a man. Only an overly forward tart would dare to toss aside convention and remain independent.

The others found her a source of amusement, whispering behind her back and ensuring that she felt suitably unwelcome at the local gatherings.

Until today, she rarely allowed their opinions to trouble her.

"No, you must be mistaken," Diana said, breaking the tense silence. "Anya might be stubborn and occasionally impulsive—"

Emma snorted. "Occasionally?"

Diana smiled wryly. Emma's younger, far more beautiful sister was a volatile mixture of absurd fantasies and caprice.

"But she is not utterly bird-witted," her companion continued. "She would never leave her home with two strangers who have no family connection to her."

Emma reluctantly handed over the crumpled note she had found on Anya's empty bed when she had awakened that morning.

"She would if those two strangers happened to be wealthy noblemen who promised her a career upon the stages of Europe."

Diana read through the short missive, her brows drawing together.

"An actress?"

"You know how Anya has always dreamed of a glamorous life far away from Yabinsk."

"Fah. What young lady does not fill her head with such nonsense? Every girl in the village has dreamed of attracting the attention of a handsome prince who will carry her away." With a rustle of her pale peach gown, Diana slowly rose to her feet. "Yourself included, Emma Linley-Kirov."

Emma shrugged. Any dream of handsome princes and tender romance had died along with her mother.

"Yes, but most of us put aside such fancies with our dolls. Anya, however, refused to accept there were no such things as fairy tales." She wrapped her arms around her waist, shivering at the cold sense of dread that held her captive. "I blame myself, of course. After father's death I did not devote nearly enough attention to her."

"Good heavens, Emma, you have sacrificed everything to provide a home for your sister. You should take great pride in all you have accomplished."

"Ah, yes, my accomplishments," Emma said, her voice thick with bitterness as she glanced toward the nearby inn. "They are quite amazing."

"Yes, they are, my dear," Diana firmly said. "You were barely more than a babe when your poor mother died and you were forced to assume the duties of the household, not to mention caring for Anya. And then to lose your father." The older woman clicked her tongue. "Well, any other girl would have fled such burdens, or at least have depended upon the charity of others. But not you."

"No, I was determined to stand on my own, no matter what the cost."

"Which you have done with remarkable success."

Emma shook her head. Her friend was too loyal to mention the fact that Emma's accomplishments had barely provided the essentials for her sister. And that she had managed to ostracize them both from local society.

"At the cost of Anya."

"Absurd."

Emma breathed in deeply, inanely astonished by the familiar scents of wood smoke and freshly baked bread. Since she discovered Anya's disappearance, she had felt as if the world had become a strange nightmare.

"I convinced myself that I was teaching Anya the importance of being self-sufficient," she rasped. "Now I have to wonder if I was merely being selfish."

"Selfish?" Diana wrapped a comforting arm around Emma's shoulders. "You are the most generous and kind-hearted young lady I have ever known."

Emma reluctantly forced herself to overcome the pained embarrassment that had held her silent since her father's death nearly four years before.

"No, Diana, I could have accepted Baron Kostya's offer."

"Offer?" The older woman dropped her arm and stepped back in shock. "He proposed?"

"Not marriage, although his arrangement did include having me in his bed." Emma grimaced, the memory of the night the baron had arrived on her doorstep with her favorite apricot-and-honey sponge cake seared into her mind. God almighty, she had been so stupidly naive. He had assured her that he was there to ease the burdens she was carrying and she had wildly imagined that he intended to invest in her coaching inn, or even to offer Anya a position as a maid at his mansion overlooking the village. It had never entered her mind that he would shame her with the demand that she become his mistress. Or his threat to make her life a misery if she did not accept. "No. He wished to offer me carte blanche and he was prepared to be remarkably generous."

"Good heavens." Diana pressed a hand to her impressive bosom. "That certainly explains his odd behavior. One day he was singing your high praises and the next—"

"He treated me as if I carried the plague," Emma finished, not needing to add that his cruel attitude had only encouraged the villagers to turn their backs on her.

"Why did you not tell me?" Diana breathed.

Emma plucked at the frayed hem of her sleeve, a familiar sickness rolling through the pit of her stomach.

She had been horrified by the baron's offer, but more than that, she had been deeply hurt.

Once her family had been highly respected in the area, and she could have chosen from a number of eager suitors. The very fact that the baron had felt free to offer such a shameful arrangement had revealed just how far she had fallen.

"It is hardly something I wished to discuss," she muttered. "I was desperate to avoid any further gossip."

Diana regarded her with sympathy. She better than anyone understood the sacrifices a woman on her own was forced to make.

"Well, I must admit that I would have counseled you to decline such a scandalous offer, but there is no denying that he is quite wealthy and I do not doubt his offer to have been generous."

"Generous enough to ensure I could have devoted myself to Anya rather than to keeping a roof over our head."

"Yes, I suppose so, but that is no assurance that Anya would not have had her head turned just as easily."

"We both know it would have been far less likely." Emma waved a hand to encompass the barren room. "Not only would she have possessed the small luxuries she has always desired, but I would have had the opportunity to look after her properly. She spent far too much time alone."

Without warning, Diana reached to grab her hand, her eyes dark with concern.

"Hear this, Emma. You are not to blame."

"But I am." Emma heaved a sigh. "I could not bear to sacrifice my virtue, and now Anya is paying for my foolish pride."

"If you must blame someone, then it should be those horrid strangers for taking advantage of a silly young girl. What sort of gentlemen would do such a thing?"

Emma's aching fear was replaced with a flare of pure fury.

When the two elegant travelers had first arrived at her coaching inn she had been delighted. They were not only swift to pay their bills, but they were lavish with their tips. She had already begun to imagine the small Christmas gifts she could purchase with the extra funds.

Now she would give everything she possessed if they had never come to Yabinsk.

"No true gentlemen."

Diana blinked. "You believe they were imposters?"

She gave a restless shake of her head. "I am not certain what I believe, but I know I must do something."

"What can you possibly do?"

That was the question, was it not?

When she first discovered Anya missing, she had been too shocked and bewildered to consider what should be done. She simply couldn't accept that her sister had truly allowed herself to be carried off by strangers.

Eventually, however, the fierce determination that had allowed her to survive any number of disasters had her thrusting aside her pained sense of guilt and considering how to rescue Anya.

"Patya overheard the men in the stables speaking of their return to St. Petersburg. At the time he thought nothing of it, but when I went to the stables to discover precisely when the gentlemen had snuck away, he conveyed their conversation."

Diana's grip on her fingers became positively painful as she regarded Emma with disbelief.

"You intend to follow them?"

"Of course."

"Emma, please do not be hasty," Diana pleaded. "You cannot possibly travel to St. Petersburg on your own."

"I will take Yelena with me," Emma assured her, referring to the aging maid who assisted at the coaching inn. "If we catch the stage this afternoon, we should be in St. Petersburg within two days."

"But—"

"I am quite determined, Diana, and you know it is a waste of effort to argue with me," Emma firmly interrupted the looming lecture.

The older woman pressed her lips together in disapproval. "Always assuming you manage to arrive in St. Petersburg unscathed, how do you propose to find Anya? St. Petersburg is not a quiet village where neighbors are well-known to one another. You could search for weeks and never cross her path."

Emma smiled wryly. She might be a provincial old maid, but she was not without a measure of common sense. She had known from the moment she'd made the decision to travel to St. Petersburg that she could not expect to stumble across Anya.

"I intend to request Herrick Gerhardt's assistance."

"Gerhardt? The emperor's advisor?"

"Yes. He is rumored to possess mysterious powers that allow him to be aware of all that occurs in the empire. There are those who refer to him as the 'Spider' for his ability to spin webs that capture even the most clever of traitors."

Diana stepped back, studying Emma as if she feared she'd taken leave of her senses.

"Whatever they may call him, Herrick Gerhardt is one of the most powerful gentlemen in Russia. You cannot just arrive on his doorstep."

"As a matter of fact, I can."

"Emma."

"Do not fret." Emma held up a slender hand. "He is related to my mother—a distant cousin I believe—and he sent a very kind letter after Father's death inviting me to call upon him if he could ever be of service to me."

Diana did not appear particularly reassured. "I do not approve of this dangerous scheme."

Emma did not particularly approve of it herself.

Unfortunately she had no choice.

"Anya is all I have left in this world," she said, her voice raw with suppressed emotion. "I will not fail her again."

Blessing the full moon that washed the elegant study in silver light, Dimitri Tipova knelt beside the mahogany desk. He had finished his search through the papers and journals in the drawers, now his slender fingers ran over the carved panels in hope of discovering a hidden compartment.

What gentleman did not have secrets to hide?

And Pytor Burdzecki had more to hide than most.

Intent on his self-imposed task, Dimitri nearly missed the soft footfall just outside the door, and it was only his swift instincts that had him straightening and moving to stand casually near the bay window. Wisely, he had opened it before beginning his search; a successful thief always had a ready escape prepared.

The door to the study was slowly pressed inward and Dimitri cast a downward glance to ensure his black jacket and silver waistcoat were properly buttoned and as crisp as could be expected, considering they had recently been tossed on a bedroom floor. A searching gaze would no doubt detect his cravat was hastily tied and the raven hair pulled back in a queue was still rumpled from feminine fingers, but with luck the darkness of the room would conceal such imperfections.

And if not…well, he possessed the means to keep his presence in the St. Petersburg town house a secret.

Reaching into the inner pocket of his jacket, Dimitri closed his hand over the pearl handle of his small pistol, prepared to kill until a slender, obviously female shape stepped over the threshold.

"Pierre?" the woman called softly.

Dimitri swallowed an impatient sigh. He had hoped to slip away before Pytor Burdzecki's young bride, Lana, realized he was gone.

The pretty woman with auburn hair and wide blue eyes had been easy enough to seduce. He had only to pretend to be a visiting French diplomat who occasionally crossed her path at the opera, or at the Gostiny Dvor where she would shop with her maid. Within a handful of days she allowed him to escort her to the nearest coffee shop with giggles and inviting glances.

She had no reason to suspect that he was the infamous Beggar Czar, ruthless leader of the underworld, or that his interest in her was merely a means to enter this palatial home that was heavily guarded by trained soldiers.

Loosening his grip on the gun, he smoothly stepped toward her.

"*Ma belle,* I thought you were asleep."

She glanced about her husband's private study with a frown. "What are you doing?"

"Preparing to leave, I fear."

"Did you lose your way?"

With another step he was close enough to tenderly tuck a dark curl behind her ear. She was a vain, self-absorbed little creature, but she was harmless. Which was more than her husband could claim.

Or Dimitri, for that matter.

"I prefer to slip away unnoticed by the servants," he murmured, speaking the perfect French all Russian nobles favored. He was also fluent in Russian and English, and could comprehend several of the Germanic dialects. He was an excessively well-educated thief, thanks to his mother's insistence that his bastard of a father pay for his schooling. "I would not desire such a beautiful creature to be the source of ugly gossip."

"Oh." She batted her lashes, eager to accept his smooth lie. "Must you leave so soon?"

"Hardly soon. I risk being castrated by your husband if I linger any longer."

She pouted, grasping the lapels of his jacket as she pressed against him in unspoken encouragement.

"He never returns before dawn, if he even bothers to

return at all." She kissed the tip of his chin. "If we are fortunate, we could enjoy the entire day together."

Dimitri narrowed his whiskey-gold eyes. "I never depend upon luck, *ma belle*."

"But, when will we meet again?"

"Who can say when fate will be kind enough to cross our paths again?"

"Tonight—"

"We shall allow destiny to unfold," he interrupted, firmly removing her hands from his maltreated jacket and lifted them to his lips. "Return to the warmth of your bed. You shall find a small token of my esteem tucked beneath your pillow."

As expected, Lana was readily distracted. "A present?"

"*Òui.* I hope you will think of me whenever you wear them."

"Wear them?" Her blue eyes sparked in anticipation. "What are they? Gloves? Earrings?"

"Why do you not go and discover for yourself?" he urged, smiling wryly as she giggled and hastily skipped from the room.

Despite the fact she was wed to a sexual deviant more than twice her age, Lana was little more than a *jeune fille* in many ways. Nothing like the women in his world who were rarely allowed a childhood.

Listening to the sound of retreating footsteps, Dimitri slid through the open window and dropped into the garden below. He had not yet finished his search of the house, but Lana was certain to have attracted unwanted attention among the guards, and he could not risk being caught.

He landed with the ease of an avid sportsman, his hand reaching for his pistol even as he straightened. The instinct that had kept him alive more times than he could recall was prickling in warning.

"Come out," he growled softly.

A lean form draped in a heavily caped coat detached from the shadows of a marble fountain.

"I must admit to my own share of curiosity," an aggravatingly familiar voice taunted. "What did you leave beneath the pillows?"

Dimitri's lips tightened, realizing the open window had allowed this man to hear his entire conversation with Lana.

Of course, Herrick Gerhardt did not need to lurk beneath open windows to discover the information he desired, Dimitri ruefully conceded. Although he did not believe the advisor to Alexander Pavlovich possessed mystical powers as some did. He was, after all, intimately aware his methods were more mundane.

"A pair of diamond earrings," he grudgingly confessed.

Herrick arched a brow. A gentleman of Prussian descent, he possessed a gaunt countenance, a thick crop of silver hair and piercing brown eyes that held a cold, ruthless intelligence.

"A rather generous gift for a female you bedded for the sole purpose of searching her husband's study."

Dimitri shrugged. "Lana might be a shallow tart with the soul of a merchant, but she still deserves better than being bartered to a husband twice her age whose sexual perversions cause even me to shudder in disgust."

Herrick deliberately glanced toward the neoclassical palace looming behind Dimitri.

"No doubt most of society would consider her well compensated."

"Only because their lives are as cold and empty as the marble crypts that await their deaths."

"A philosopher, Tipova?" Herrick demanded.

"A simple criminal."

Herrick's chuckle floated on the chilly October breeze. "As if I would ever be foolish enough to underestimate you. What did you discover?"

Dimitri folded his arms over his chest, his expression guarded. Since he had come to the attention of Herrick Gerhardt and the Duke of Huntley several weeks before, he had reluctantly become Alexander Pavlovich's most secret weapon against the traitors who stirred discontent. One did not say no to the Emperor of Russia.

His presence in Pytor Burdzecki's home, however, was personal business he did not intend to share with anyone.

"Nothing that would be of interest to Alexander Pavlovich."

"You would be surprised at the emperor's vast interests," Herrick countered.

"The emperor or his most trusted advisor?"

"It is one and the same."

"Is that why you are here?" Dimitri demanded. "To discover what I might find among Burdzecki's papers?"

Herrick waved a dismissive hand. "Actually I am here to discover you."

Dimitri stilled, his eyes narrowing with suspicion.

"And how, I wonder, did you know I would be here?"

"You are not the only gentleman with the ability to gather information."

"Yes, but—" Dimitri bit off his words. "Never mind, I shall eventually uncover the traitor." He waved a hand toward the empty flower beds and the marble fountains that had already been covered in preparation for the brutal Russian winter. "If you wished to meet with me you had only to send a message. There was no need to creep about in damp gardens."

The smile faded from Herrick's face, his eyes hard with the ruthless resolve that lurked just below his charm.

"You do not promptly respond to my summons."

"I am not a toady of the empire."

"No, but you are a loyal citizen, I trust?"

Dimitri dropped his arms, his hands curling into fists. Despite his considerable power, he never allowed himself to forget that Herrick Gerhardt need only speak the word and Dimitri would disappear into the nearest dungeon.

"Are you threatening me, Gerhardt?"

The silver head dipped in apology. "Forgive me, Tipova. You have proven your devotion to Czar Alexander more than once."

"As if I had a choice," Dimitri grumbled. "What do you want of me?"

"On this occasion I believe we can be of mutual benefit to one another."

"I have no need of the royal coffers."

"My business with you is of a personal nature and I offer something far more intriguing than money." Stepping to the side, Herrick glanced toward the sleek black carriage that was waiting in the mews. "Will you join me?"

Dimitri paused, studying Herrick's impassive face. Then, with a sigh, he conceded defeat. The older man would not leave him in peace until he had his way.

"Why do I sense I am going to regret this?" he muttered.

CHAPTER TWO

DIMITRI REMAINED SILENT as Herrick led him to the carriage and they settled into the soft leather seats. There was a small jerk as the driver urged the horses into motion, then they were traveling through the streets of St. Petersburg that were still crowded despite the late hour.

"Brandy?" Herrick inquired, pouring two glasses of the amber liquid and pressing one into Dimitri's willing hand.

Taking a cautious sip, Dimitri lifted his brows in surprise. There was no mistaking the smooth ease with which the liquid fire slid down his throat.

"You must be anxious for my assistance if you are willing to share from your private cellar," he said.

Herrick leaned back in his seat, his gaze hooded as he studied Dimitri.

"As I mentioned, I think our arrangement will be mutually beneficial."

Dimitri could not prevent a small flare of curiosity. Herrick Gerhardt had devoted his life to Alexander Pavlovich. What private business could he possibly have?

"I am willing to listen to this…arrangement."

"First I must bore you with a bit of family history." Herrick swallowed his brandy and refilled his glass. "As you perhaps know I was born in Prussia to a respectable, albeit poor family. I was fortunate enough to travel to St. Petersburg to finish my education when I was just seventeen and eventually to capture the attention of Alexander Pavlovich. My elder cousin, on the other hand, chose to seek his fortunes in England where he wed and produced several children."

"Fascinating."

"One of my cousin's daughters became a governess to a Russian family to teach the children English. She in turn wed a local furniture maker and had two daughters before she died."

Dimitri tapped his finger against his glass, his brows pulled together in a frown.

"I presume this tedious story has an end?"

"As I was saying, there were two daughters, Emma and Anya Linley-Kirov," Herrick continued, ignoring Dimitri's growing impatience. "After their father was tragically killed by a poacher, Emma transformed her father's workshop into a small coaching inn."

Dimitri's frown deepened. He adored women. All women. And it was well-known that any man who mistreated a female beneath his protection was a certain means to a brutal beating, if not death. Still, he could not deny he preferred to avoid those women with more spirit than sense.

In the end they not only brought misery to themselves, but those who cared for them.

"How very unconventional of her."

"It was quite admirable of her," Herrick corrected, easily sensing Dimitri's lack of approval. "Unfortunately her considerable courage did not protect her from the nefarious gentlemen who stayed at her coaching inn for several days."

"Nefarious?"

"When they left the inn they took Anya with them."

Dimitri stilled, his attention fully captured. "The sister?"

"Yes."

"How old is she?"

"She just turned sixteen."

Draining the last of his brandy, Dimitri carefully set aside the glass, silently considering the unexpected revelation at the same time he accepted that his personal investigations were not quite so secret as he believed them to be.

"And Emma Linley-Kirov is certain she was taken by the gentlemen?" he demanded.

"Quite certain. Anya left a note explaining she was to become a famous actress."

Dimitri was careful to keep his expression unreadable, even as his heart gave a jolt of recognition at the familiar ruse used by his father and his cohorts to lure young females from their homes.

"Did the note also mention the gentlemen were traveling to St. Petersburg?"

"A groom overheard the gentlemen discussing their return to the city."

"And the woman is certain she would recognize them if she were to see them again?"

"Yes."

Dimitri casually glanced out the window, not surprised to discover they had made a circuit of the Upper Nevsky and were nearly back to Pytor Burdzecki's palatial home. There was never a moment when he was not acutely aware of his surroundings.

"What made you believe that I would have interest in your tragic, though not uncommon, tale?"

"It has not escaped my notice that you keep a very close watch upon Count Nevskaya and his associates."

Dimitri absently studied the Anichkov Palace that had once housed Catherine's favorite lover, Prince Potyomkin, and had been recently refurbished by Giacomo Quarenghi to house the Imperial Cabinet. Unlike many, he preferred the classical colonnade to the earlier, more flamboyant style.

Not that Czar Alexander had requested his opinion.

Grudgingly he turned his attention back to his companion.

"As you have no doubt surmised, the count is my father."

A smile touched the older man's lips as his gaze deliberately studied the elegant lines of Dimitri's features, lingering on the aristocratic thrust of his nose and high, Slavic cheekbones.

"It is difficult to overlook the resemblance."

Dimitri's jaw hardened. He often used his considerable male beauty to his advantage, but he cursed the resemblance to the man who had brutally forced himself on a young, defenseless female.

"We share the same countenance, but make no mistake that is where the similarities end," he said, his voice colder than a Siberian winter.

Herrick dipped his head in acknowledgment. "That is difficult to overlook as well, which is why your constant surveillance of the count piqued my interest. It was obvious you were searching for particular information."

Dimitri was not pleased. He spied on others, they did not spy on him.

"You have an annoying habit of meddling in my private business."

"It is my duty to meddle in the business of others."

"You play a dangerous game, Gerhardt."

Herrick shrugged, unperturbed by the threat in Dimitri's soft voice.

"And you are intimately familiar with dangerous games, are you not, Tipova?" he asked. "The count would be most displeased to realize his bastard son suspects he is involved in illegal activities."

Dimitri briefly considered the pleasurc of tossing the older man into the nearby Fontanka Canal, then disregarded the notion. As pleasant as it might be to see Herrick's impervious calm rattled, it was not worth the loss of his head.

Besides, there were more important matters to consider at the moment.

"What would you have of me?"

Herrick leaned forward, his dark eyes glittering in the moonlight.

"Meet with Emma Linley-Kirov. I truly believe the two of you are searching for the same answers."

"I knew I was going to regret this meeting."

PEERING OUT OF THE carriage window, Emma studied the pale stone building built with a columned portico in the center and two wings that spread along the canal. Although newly arrived in St. Petersburg, she would presume that the far side of the building was devoted to gentlemen lodgers. Why else would the small cluster of men be standing on the paved walk and keeping such a close watch on the passing traffic? On the other side was a more familiar coffee shop with several small tables and a back counter that held trays of tempting pastry that made Emma's mouth water even at a distance.

"There it is," she said, turning her head to meet her maid's sour expression.

Yelena had firmly disapproved of Emma's decision to meet with the Beggar Czar, Dimitri Tipova.

Of course, the elderly maid with a thatch of gray hair and slender body wrapped in a black cloak had disapproved of traveling to St. Petersburg, of accepting Herrick Gerhardt's surprisingly warm welcome, and even of being sheltered by Herrick's dear friend, Vanya Petrova in her beautiful mansion beside the Fontanka Canal.

Emma, on the other hand, was deeply grateful to the older man who had greeted her without a word of condemnation of her forward behavior and had promised he would do whatever possible to help her locate Anya.

"It does not appear to be a den of iniquity," Yelena at last muttered. "Are you certain this is the proper address?"

Emma wrinkled her nose. "Appearances are too often deceptive, as I have so painfully discovered. It is rather public, however."

"I should think it is public." Yelena folded her gnarled fingers in her lap, her lips pinched together. "You cannot meet with a strange gentleman in private without so much as a proper introduction."

Despite her raw nerves, Emma couldn't contain her sudden chuckle. "I am about to request the assistance of the most renowned criminal in all of Russia and your concern is our lack of a proper introduction?"

The older woman sniffed. "I have a great number of concerns."

Instantly contrite, Emma reached across the elegant carriage that Vanya had kindly insisted she use during her time in St. Petersburg, and patted her companion's hand. Yelena was one of the very few people who had stood by her through the years.

"Forgive me, Yelena. I fear my nerves are in tatters. I did not mean to snap."

Yelena's expression immediately softened. "The past week would try the patience of a saint."

Surely truer words had not been spoken, Emma acknowledged with a sigh. She did not wish to recall the grueling journey to St. Petersburg, or her sick trepidation as she had approached Herrick Gerhardt's beautiful home to beg for his assistance.

It was enough to concentrate on today's troubles.

Perhaps more than enough.

Pretending that her stomach was not cramped with fear, Emma managed a smile as the uniformed groom pulled open the carriage door.

"Remain here."

Yelena frowned. "Emma—"

"We have been through this," Emma interrupted. "The message was quite clear that I come alone. Besides, if I do not reappear then I shall need you to storm the fortress and rescue me."

The maid pressed a shaking hand to her bosom. "Dear Lord."

"I am merely teasing, Yelena. All will be well." Keeping the strained smile intact, Emma allowed herself to be assisted from the carriage and headed for the door of the coffee shop. "Please God, let all be well," she muttered beneath her breath.

Entering the coffee shop, she took the seat closest the window as the message had demanded. Thank goodness she had wrapped herself in a sturdy gown of dark gray that buttoned to her chin and brushed the wooden floor past her sensible leather boots. And that her honey hair was covered by a wool scarf her mother had knit. There was a roaring fire across the room, but so close to the door there was a distinct chill in the air.

Settling uncomfortably in the wooden chair, Emma cast a swift glance about the wide room, relieved that many of the tables were empty. There were two elegantly attired gentlemen playing chess by the fire, and a group of more roughly dressed men at a table that ran the length of the far wall, but she was quite alone in her corner.

Her appreciation for her solitude, however, began to wane as an hour passed, and then another. Where the devil was Dimitri Tipova? Had he invited her here just to see if she would risk her reputation by meeting with a notorious criminal? Was this a mere hoax at her expense? Or were

Beggar Czars so busy they found it impossible to keep their appointments?

Tapping an impatient finger on the table, Emma found her anxiety hardening to a simmering anger.

She was accustomed to being treated with disrespect. She was even accustomed to being ignored by others who thought themselves above her. But she could not afford to waste an entire day on some ridiculous game. If Dimitri Tipova did not wish to be of service then he should at least have the decency to send his regrets.

On the point of rising to her feet, Emma was caught off guard when a large man approached her table and settled in a chair at her side.

"Well, well. Such a tender little morsel," he husked, his face with its heavy jowls and beady blue eyes far too close. "I wonder if you taste as sweet as you look."

Emma tilted her chin, shifting away from the hulking body attired in a faded green coat and the heavy boots of a laborer.

"Please move along."

A cruel smiled curved his lips. "Perhaps I do not want to move along. Perhaps I intend to take you to the back room and sample your wares."

Emma should no doubt have been terrified, but at the moment her temper was fully aroused and in no mood to endure the man's rude behavior. Even if he was twice her size.

Grasping the cup of coffee she had bought in an effort to pass the time, she narrowed her gaze.

"Either you leave me in peace or I will pour this exceedingly hot coffee into your lap," she warned. "Perhaps that will teach you not to impose your vile presence on unfortunate maidens who might cross your path."

The intruder blinked, as if stupefied by her threat. "You…"

His lips had barely parted when another man joined them, this one far more slender, although the scar running down his cheek from his eyebrow to the edge of his mouth made him appear far more sinister. Her companion seemed to think so as well, as his face paled and sweat beaded his forehead.

"Semyon, return to the docks and make certain that the ship that arrived this morning is properly unloaded. You know how our employer dislikes unnecessary attention to our business."

"Yes…of course."

Stumbling to his feet, the man performed an awkward bow and headed for the door. Emma straightened from her seat as well, her temper not appeased.

She had been ignored for hours, and then rudely insulted by that brute. She had endured enough.

"Emma Linley-Kirov?" the man demanded.

"And you are?"

"Josef. I am here to escort you."

Her lips tightened. So, Dimitri Tipova could not be bothered to greet her in person.

"Escort me to where?" she demanded.

The servant waved an indifferent hand toward a door at the back of the room, clearly unimpressed with his current duties.

"Merely to the private rooms upstairs. There is no need to be afraid."

She squared her shoulders. "I am not afraid, I am furious. Do you know how long I have been waiting?"

A startled silence filled the entire room as Josef regarded her with astonishment.

"Dimitri Tipova is a very busy man," he said, his tone chiding. "You are fortunate he agreed to meet with you at all."

Emma sniffed, refusing to be intimidated. "Ah, yes, you

cannot imagine how honored I am to be graced with a few moments of the Beggar Czar's precious time."

With a muttered curse, the slender man headed toward the back of the room.

"This way."

Stiffly, Emma followed in his wake, acutely aware of the hard gazes trained in her direction. Josef pulled open the door and led her up a narrow flight of stairs, then reaching a landing, he motioned her toward a small room with a brocade sofa and two scrolled chairs set beside a marble fireplace.

"Wait here."

Not bothering to turn, Josef continued toward a door on the opposite side of the landing, shoving it open and stepping through. Ignoring good manners, Emma remained poised on the landing, blatantly attempting to overhear the low conversation between Josef and whoever was waiting in the room.

"She arrived?" A man that Emma presumed was Dimitri Tipova demanded, his dark voice sending an odd tingle down her spine.

"Regrettably," Josef muttered.

"Why regrettably?"

"The woman is sour enough to curdle milk."

"No doubt she is concerned for her sister."

"It is not concern that makes a woman into an overbearing shrew. She is the nasty sort who tosses out orders and expects them to be obeyed."

"Naturally." The gorgeous male voice held an edge of resignation. "I should have known Gerhardt would take pleasure in plaguing me with his old maid cousin. No doubt he is seated before a warm fire, relishing his peace while I am stuck with the harridan."

Emma winced, then gritted her teeth, pretending she

wasn't wounded by the familiar mockery. She had not traveled to St. Petersburg to charm the local thieves.

Stepping over the threshold, she had a brief impression of a small study with bookshelves lining the walls and a porcelain stove set between two leather wing chairs. Then a tall man lifted himself from behind a heavy walnut desk and her mind abruptly refused to function.

He was just so absurdly beautiful.

Her stunned gaze traced the bronze perfection of his features. The wide, intelligent brow. The slender nose and full, sensual lips. The slash of his prominent cheekbones. The chiseled brows that were the same raven-black as his long hair pulled into a tail at his nape.

It was his eyes, however, that stole her breath.

An astonishing gold that shimmered in wicked temptation, they were surely the eyes of the devil.

Or perhaps a fallen angel.

All Emma knew for certain was that he was a compelling combination of lethal power and male sensuality that would make any poor woman go weak in the knees.

An odd, heated excitement fluttered in the pit of her stomach as that golden gaze flared over her tiny form. An excitement that was swiftly replaced with hollow disappointment as his lush lips twisted with a familiar male disapproval.

What did she expect, she mocked her temporary insanity?

That Dimitri Tipova might be unconventional enough not to judge her bold manner? That a man forced to survive in a harsh world was capable of understanding the need for her to do the same?

Thrusting aside the inane thoughts, Emma conjured the icy composure that was her only protection.

"I may be an old maid, but I at least possess a few manners," she stated, her gaze never wavering from the unnerving golden eyes. "Something sadly lacking among you and your loathsome band of cutthroats."

DIMITRI SHOULD HAVE been amused.

The tiny female wrapped in layers of wool barely came to his chin and weighed less than his wolfhound. To have her burst into his room and chide him as if he were a naughty child rather than the most dangerous man in St. Petersburg was absurd.

It wasn't amusement he felt, however, as his gaze rested on the honey curls that peeked from her scarf to lie against the purity of her ivory skin and the steady hazel eyes that held unwavering strength.

There was something about her that challenged him at his most primitive level.

He wanted to loom over her until she dropped her bold gaze in silent defeat. He wanted to bluntly inform her that he was an unrepentant tyrant who expected immediate obedience from others.

He wanted to haul her against his body until the defiance faded from her beautiful eyes and her lush lips softened in invitation…

Thankfully unaware of the currents of prickling awareness that swirled through the air, Josef folded his arms over his chest.

"What did I say? Curdled milk," he muttered.

Dimitri never allowed his gaze to stray from Emma Linley-Kirov's stubborn expression.

"That will be all."

"Are you certain? There is nothing more dangerous than an angry female."

"Thank you, Josef, I believe you have done quite enough," Dimitri dryly assured his friend, waiting for his servant to leave the room before he rounded the desk and perched on the corner.

His lips twisted as her gaze skimmed down his tailored, cinnamon jacket that he had paired with a cream satin waistcoat. He had tied his crisp cravat in an Oriental knot and a diamond the size of a thimble winked in the perfect folds. Clearly the woman had expected him to be a savage rather than the sort of sophisticated gentleman who could appear comfortable in the finest home.

"There is a saying that listeners rarely hear good of themselves," he at last broke the silence.

An indefinable emotion flared through her eyes before she was jutting her chin in silent condemnation.

"I am indifferent to your opinion of me, sir—"

"Dimitri," he smoothly corrected.

"I beg your pardon?"

"I am no gentleman as you have so graciously implied. You will call me Dimitri."

Her lips tightened, whether in disapproval at the informality or at being given an order, it was impossible to determine.

"If you insist," she grudgingly conceded.

"I do."

"Can we please discuss my sister?" she snapped. "I have wasted enough of my day."

Dimitri narrowed his gaze, shoving from the desk and prowling toward the woman regarding him with an imperious scowl. A surge of male satisfaction raced through him as she instinctively backed away from his approaching form, even as his more civilized nature was shocked by his fierce reaction to the delicate slip of a woman.

What the hell was wrong with him?

Herding her until she was pressed flat against the bookcase, he reached to grasp the shelves on either side of her shoulders.

"Perhaps we should discuss the nature of our—" his

brooding gaze lowered to the tempting curve of her lips "—relationship, Emma."

Heat flared beneath her ivory skin, but her eyes shimmered with rebellion.

"There is no relationship, merely a set of unfortunate circumstances that have forced us to join our resources for the time being."

He pressed closer, caught by surprise when a raw awareness of her slender body seared through him. It was inconceivable. He enjoyed his women soft and vulnerable. The sort who depended upon him to offer support and protection. Not aging tartars who smelled of soap and starch.

"Then let me clarify the *joining of resources.*"

Her color deepened at the hint of huskiness in his voice. "What do you mean?"

"You desire my assistance, then you will have to follow my rules. Otherwise you can turn around and leave now."

A tense silence filled the room he had recently converted into his private office, then without warning, Emma was shoving him away and pacing toward the window that overlooked the street.

Dimitri couldn't deny a grudging respect for her courage. He knew only one other woman who would not have fainted or fled by now.

His mother.

The realization did nothing to ease his potent need to tame the prickly female. His mother's courage had put her in an early grave.

"Fine." Slowly turning, Emma regarded him with an unflinching gaze. "What are these precious rules?"

"The first is that I will not tolerate an ill-tempered termagant in my presence. If you cannot control your sharp tongue, then I will discover a means to tame it."

Her eyes widened. "Tame? If you think I will tolerate being beaten by—"

He was moving before he could halt the impulse, his hands holding her face steady as he lowered his head and covered her mouth in a soft, coaxing kiss. He had intended to teach her a lesson in controlling her shrewish tongue, but at the first taste of her honeyed innocence his passions stirred, his body hardening. His hands tightened on her face as he deepened the kiss.

Just for a moment she softened against him, her lips parting in a sweet surrender. Then, with a choked moan, she jerked back, her eyes blazing with a fury that did not entirely mask her startled desire.

"Why, you…"

Well versed in the ways of women, Dimitri easily caught the hand she lifted to slap his face, bringing her fingers to his mouth.

"The second rule is no striking your master," he could not resist taunting.

Flecks of gold smoldered in the hazel eyes. "Master?"

He kissed her slender fingers. "You are in desperate need of my assistance, which means that while you remain in St. Petersburg you are in my power."

"I will not be treated as if I am a serf."

"You will do precisely as I say and you will do so without complaint."

She jerked her hand from his grasp, marching toward the door with her chin high and her back stiff.

"This is absurd."

"If you walk out that door, Emma, I can assure you that you will never find your sister."

CHAPTER THREE

EMMA HALTED AT THE soft threat.

Dimitri Tipova was not at all what she had expected. She had been prepared for a rough, ill-mannered oaf who used his fists, not his wits, to control the underworld. Certainly, she had never dreamed he would be a sophisticated, well-educated gentleman who was as beautiful as an angel and as wicked as Lucifer.

And that kiss…

No. She hastily thrust aside the feverish memory of her first kiss.

She was suitably rattled without the distracting thought of Dimitri's warm, seeking lips and the potent heat that speared through her body.

Slowly turning, she met his ruthless gaze. "You know where she is?"

"No, but—"

"Then I will find someone less offensive to help me."

He strolled forward, the scent of sandalwood and warm male skin teasing at her senses.

"There is no one in all of Russia who has devoted the time and resources that I have to uncovering the habits of those noblemen who prey on children." Halting directly before her, he cupped her chin, his gaze briefly dipping down to her mouth before returning to meet her wary gaze. "And more important, I have only to whisper in the requisite ears and there will be no one in St. Petersburg willing to lend you help."

"Herrick warned me that you had your share of

arrogance, but you cannot possibly believe you possess the power to influence every citizen in St. Petersburg."

"So naive," he mocked. "Tell me, Emma, how many merchants would be willing to speak with you once it became known that the goods they purchase from my warehouses were about to double in cost? And how many servants would agree to speak with you once they learn you are a suspected spy for Alexander Pavlovich in search of traitors to the crown? As for society…" His soft chuckle brushed over her cheek, causing her stomach to clench with a startling excitement. "Well, even presuming they would be willing to meet with a commoner, they would have you tossed in the nearest dungeon for daring to implicate a noble in such a wicked crime."

She clenched her hands, wanting desperately to walk away from the conceited beast and never look back. Unfortunately, she suspected his words were not empty boasts.

Could she truly risk the opportunity to find Anya just because this man threatened to drive her to madness?

"Why are you being so cruel?" she demanded.

"Not cruel—efficient," he corrected. "As you said, for the moment we have need of one another. I have no intention of spending the next days, perhaps weeks, being flayed by a shrill-tongued harpy. If you behave as a lady and do as I say, we shall rub along quite nicely."

"So I am expected to be a proper lady while you are at liberty to behave as an ill-mannered brute?"

"You are at least intelligent." A slow, wicked smile curved his lips. "Do we have a bargain?"

Emma sucked in a sharp breath, not for the first time wishing she had been born a man. How delightful it would be if she possessed the power to knock the arrogant toad onto his backside.

"Do I have a choice?" she gritted.

"Of course." He peered deep into her eyes, almost as

if willing her to obey his words. "You can return to your home where you belong."

"I will not leave St. Petersburg without my sister."

"Even if I give my word I will do my best to discover her whereabouts and return her to you?"

"And why would I trust the word of a—" Her insult was sharply interrupted as his head swooped down and he kissed her with a seeking demand that made her heart skip a beat. Dear...Lord. After the death of her father she had resigned herself to becoming an old maid. At the time she had regretted the loss of many things, most notably the lack of a companion who could share her joys and fears and the mundane events that were all a part of life. It had not occurred to her that she might rue the lack of a man's touch. Not until Dimitri had revealed just how potently addictive that touch could be. Arching back, she struggled to breathe. "Stop that."

He studied her from beneath his thick tangle of lashes. "I did warn you that I would tame your unruly tongue."

Emma grimly stiffened her spine, refusing to dwell on her tingling lips or the restless, achy sensation that gripped her body. Obviously she was coming down with a chill.

"I cannot believe that Herrick would request that I meet with you," she muttered. "Do you make a habit of attacking helpless females?"

"Helpless?" His sharp burst of laughter echoed through the room. "I have hired savage, fully-armed bandits who inspire less fear than having to face your expression of cold disapproval."

She turned her head to stare at the leather-bound books lining the shelves, determined to hide her reaction. What did he expect? Simpering and batting her lashes was not going to save Anya from disaster.

"You have already assaulted me, there is no need to mock me, as well."

With a surprisingly gentle touch he forced her face back to meet his searching gaze.

"It was a simple kiss, hardly an assault," he murmured, his arm wrapping around her waist. "You have been kissed before, have you not, Emma?"

"Release me."

"What an odd contradiction you are," he breathed, the golden gaze searing over her face with a disconcerting intensity. "You wrap yourself in fire and brimstone, but beneath that armor is a bewitching innocence."

Her heart fluttered and she abruptly shoved away from his disturbing touch.

"I came here to discuss my sister, not to indulge in foolish games."

For a tense moment she feared he might haul her back against his chest. And more important, she feared she might not protest.

Then, with a rueful shake of his head he waved a hand toward the wing chairs.

"Have a seat, and I will order tea."

She stubbornly remained standing in the center of the floor. "Do not pretend to be civilized on my account."

He leaned against the desk, the late afternoon sunlight slanting over his elegantly chiseled features.

"Most of my guests find my manners exquisitely polished and my hospitality without equal."

"Indeed?"

His lips twisted. "It is only you who seems to rouse my more barbaric nature."

"Do you intend to assist me or not?"

"Tell me of the gentlemen who you believe abducted your sister."

Unprepared for his abrupt question, it took Emma a moment to gather her scattered thoughts.

"They were obviously noblemen."

He arched a raven brow. "How can you be so certain? Even the most common criminal can mimic his betters with enough wealth and the proper training. I possess a number of employees who could attend a ball at the Winter Palace without stirring the least curiosity."

She grimaced. "It was not their fine clothing or their elegant speech that marked them as nobles."

"Then what?"

"It was their utter contempt for those they considered beneath them, and how they expected others to bow to their every whim."

He seemed surprised by her explanation. "You are very perceptive."

"Obviously not perceptive enough," she said, her voice edged with bitterness. "I should have suspected that such elegant gentlemen would never willingly remain at my modest coaching inn without some nefarious purpose."

"What explanation did they offer?"

She shrugged. "They claimed to be searching for a small estate to purchase that would be suitable for a hunting lodge."

Dimitri nodded, as if he'd expected a similar story. "What names did they use?"

"Baron Fedor Karnechev and his younger brother Sergei."

"And you would recognize them?"

A cold, dangerous smile curved her lips. When she found the men who had taken her sister, she intended to rip out their hearts with her bare hands.

"Without a doubt."

Amusement smoldered in the whiskey-gold eyes as Dimitri watched fury ripple over her face.

"Does your sister resemble you?"

"There are some similarities, but Anya's hair is lighter

in color and her eyes the shade of a summer sky." A wistful smile touched her lips. "She is quite beautiful."

"I was referring to her temperament, not her physical attributes."

Emma frowned in puzzlement. "What does her temperament matter?"

"Gerhardt divulged the fact that Anya went willingly with her captors, believing she was to become a famous actress." His gaze swept down her tiny form before returning to study the stubborn line of her jaw. "I find it difficult to imagine you ever allowing yourself to be so easily persuaded."

She shifted, feeling awkward beneath his relentless scrutiny. "She is very young and gullible."

"More likely she is vain and spoiled."

She jerked at the unexpected attack. "You know nothing of Anya."

"I know that a young lady with the least concern for her family does not abandon her home and allow herself to be carried off by the first gentleman to turn her head with a bit of flattery."

The very fact he was right did nothing to ease her flare of anger. In truth, she was horrified that Anya had been so easily led astray, but she did not blame her younger sister. No. Any blame should be laid directly at her own feet.

"I have endured enough." Blinking back hot tears of shame, Emma once again headed for the door. "I do not understand why you agreed to meet with me, but it is obvious you have no interest in helping me."

She had managed to reach the hallway when a pair of warm, ruthlessly strong arms wrapped around her waist and tugged her back into the room. Bending his head, Dimitri spoke directly into her ear.

"You truly must learn to control that temper of yours, *milaya*."

FOR A CRAZED MOMENT, Dimitri savored the sensation of her feminine body pressed against his arousal. Then with a curse at his deranged reaction to an ill-tempered spinster, he quickly released his tight grip, not at all surprised when she spun around to stab him with a furious glare.

"Are you going to rescue my sister or not?"

If he possessed a shred of sense Dimitri knew he should have allowed the woman to stomp away. Herrick Gerhardt could not expect him to force himself on an aggravating woman who was too foolish to appreciate his assistance. Instead, he met her glare with a ruthless smile.

"First we must discover the identity of the gentlemen who abducted her."

Her glare remained, but she gave a grudging nod. "I can describe them if you wish."

"There is a more practical means. You will accompany me this evening."

"Accompany you where?"

"I own a number of gambling establishments that cater to the aristocrats of St. Petersburg. If the gentlemen who visited your inn are truly noblemen and they have returned to the city, then they will eventually make an appearance at one of my clubs."

Her mouth fell open. "You intend to escort me to a gambling club?"

Thoroughly enjoying her shock, Dimitri shrugged. "I intend to escort you to several gambling clubs."

"You must be jesting."

"Tell me, Emma, when you came to St. Petersburg did you expect to discover your sister being kept hostage in a church?" he taunted. "Or perhaps awaiting you in the throne room of the Winter Palace?"

The ready color crawled beneath her cheeks. "Of course not."

"Then why the maidenly outrage?"

There was a tiny pause before she was jutting her chin in a stubborn angle, her magnificent hazel eyes hardening with determination.

"I was merely caught off guard."

With a silent curse, Dimitri spun away, disturbed by Emma's combination of vulnerability and determination.

"If you wish to capture the dregs of society you must hunt them in the gutters," he said, his voice unnaturally harsh. "Are you prepared to do what is necessary?"

"Yes."

"We shall see." Sucking in a deep breath he turned back to meet her guarded gaze. "Where are you staying?"

"Vanya Petrova was kind enough to offer her hospitality."

Dimitri nodded, already having suspected that Herrick would turn to his dear friend to provide Emma a home.

"Then I will collect you at nine this evening."

"Very well." With a stiff nod, the woman headed for the door.

"Emma," he called softly.

She froze, her hands clenching before she forced herself to turn and meet his brooding gaze.

"Yes?"

"Staid spinsters do not visit gambling clubs. If you wish to avoid unwanted attention you might consider a gown that does not smother you in wool."

Her eyes flashed with the sort of fury that made Dimitri relieved that there was no knife at hand.

"I am not the one who needs to fear being smothered."

EMMA PEERED OUT THE window of the carriage, allowing her maid's incessant lecture on what happens to females who spend an entire afternoon in the company of known criminals to flow past her. She did not need to be reminded she had been a fool to meet with Dimitri Tipova. Or that she was an even greater fool to have agreed to his outrageous suggestion that she allow him to escort her to his gambling clubs.

For goodness' sake, if she were recognized she would never overcome the scandal.

Whatever the dangers she fully intended to travel from one den of iniquity to another until she located the men who had abducted her sister. There was no point in dwelling on the insanity of her behavior.

Instead, she studied the overwhelming beauty of the city around her.

Over the past two days she had been too occupied with her troubles to truly notice its magnificence. Now she allowed herself to appreciate the stunning palaces that lined the narrow canals.

How odd to realize that such glory could rise from such brutality.

Her lips twisted as she recalled her history lessons. The cold-hearted Ivan and his private army, the *oprichniki,* who had terrorized the boyars until the Tatars attacked Moscow. Ivan had ordered any number of bloodbaths to maintain his ruthless rule until he had tumbled into utter madness and he was at last murdered by his own heir.

As much a monster as Ivan had been, however, the period of chaos that followed his death had proven the need for a strong leader to rule the vast empire. It had been the desperate Cossacks and outspoken *Streltsi,* and even a group of more prosperous peasants, that had demanded the *zemsky sobor* be called to name a new czar.

Eventually, Peter had come to the throne, his life already scarred by being forced to witness his closest family butchered when he was just ten years of age. Not that his years of being condemned to the remote hunting lodge on the Yauza River had been wasted. Indeed, they had offered him a rare opportunity for self-education.

Left to entertain himself, he studied with the local craftsmen to acquire skills in everything from blacksmithing to carpentry. He also gathered devoted friends who assisted him in mock battles and discovering the best means of drilling an infantry. Long before acquiring an army he had practiced besieging a scale-sized fortress and could calculate the ranges for his artillery.

Perhaps most important, he developed an obsessive fascination with sailing.

With remarkable foresight he had realized the future of his country depended upon opening itself to the world, and with a cruel efficiency he conquered a path to the Baltic Sea and then set about building a city that would rival Versailles.

There was a clatter of hooves as the carriage crossed the Fontanka River over the Semyonovsky Bridge and Emma realized they were nearing Vanya's home.

Tugging the scarf more tightly around her neck, she was prepared as the carriage halted in front of the imposing mansion with its columned balcony and massive jade lions that guarded the double doors. Leaving the carriage she climbed the steps and entered the marble foyer.

There was an awkward moment as the uniformed servants scurried about her, attempting to perform small services before Emma waved them away. She would never become accustomed to having others wait on her.

Hovering uncertainly by a rosewood table that held a delicate Chinese vase, Emma was relieved by the sudden appearance of a strikingly beautiful woman with silver hair and a tall, curvaceous form attired in a morning dress of lavender silk.

"At last. I was becoming quite concerned," Vanya murmured, a hint of worry in her pale blue eyes.

"I am sorry." Emma removed her scarf and tossed it aside. "The impossible man kept me waiting for near two hours. As if he were royalty rather than a common criminal."

Taking Emma's hand, Vanya led her up a curved staircase. "I should never consider Dimitri Tipova common," she said with a small sigh. "He is sinfully handsome, is he not?"

A dangerous sensation fluttered in the pit of her stomach. "I suppose he is handsome enough, although that does not compensate for his utter lack of civility. He is the rudest man I have ever encountered."

Vanya allowed a mysterious smile to curve her lips as she led Emma into a private salon with emerald wall panels and gilt cornices. The furniture was a dark mahogany with gold velvet cushions and the wooden floor covered by an Oriental rug. The overall atmosphere was one of rich sensuality.

A perfect setting for Vanya.

"Odd." Vanya settled on the sofa and pulled Emma down next to her. "I have always thought him to be surprisingly gracious."

"You are well acquainted?"

Leaning forward, Vanya poured two cups of tea from the tray left on the low table, adding a generous amount of milk and sugar before handing a cup to Emma and leaning back into the cushions.

"He performed a great service for a dear friend of mine," she explained, sipping her hot tea. "I consider myself in his debt."

Emma hastily tempered her words, far too polite to insult a man her hostess held in high esteem.

"No doubt it is my fault." She took a reviving sip of tea, hoping it would help the lies tumble from her lips. "He did mention that I stir his more primitive nature."

"Did he?" Vanya's smile widened. "How very intriguing."

Intriguing? Emma found it utterly vexing. As if she were to blame for his irritating lack of manners.

"Let us hope our time together is of short duration."

"Did he agree to assist you in your search for poor Anya?"

"Yes."

"Thank goodness." The older woman reached to pat Emma's arm. "Whatever your opinion of Dimitri there is no gentleman more suited to helping you."

Emma battled the urge to roll her eyes. "So he has told me."

Vanya's smile faded, her fingers gently squeezing Emma's arm.

"Emma, do you prefer that I find another to lend you assistance?"

Her lips parted with a cowardly urge to agree to Vanya's suggestion. Dimitri Tipova was arrogant and provoking and…

Dangerously attractive.

Then, she hastily swallowed the ridiculous words. If both Herrick and Vanya considered Dimitri Tipova the most suitable man to help her rescue Anya, then she would be inexcusably selfish to turn him away just because she… what? Feared him?

"No, of course not," she said, her tone brisk. "Indeed, I need your help to prepare for the evening."

"You have made plans?"

"I am to accompany Dimitri Tipova to several of his gambling establishments in the hopes I will recognize the gentlemen who lured Anya to St. Petersburg."

If she was shocked by Emma's revelation, then Vanya hid it well. Indeed, she nodded as if it were perfectly reasonable for a young, innocent maiden to allow herself to be escorted by a renowned criminal to his wicked clubs.

"Ah."

"I shall need a means to disguise myself," she firmly insisted. "I cannot risk being recognized. Who can say what the odious creatures will do to Anya if they realize I have followed them?"

"Do not fear, my dear." A gleam that Emma did not entirely trust sparkled in Vanya's blue eyes. "I shall ensure that not even your sister will recognize you."

CHAPTER FOUR

THE SUNKEN ROSE GARDEN was thankfully wrapped in shadows as Dimitri strolled past the Italian sculptures and marble fountains. Despite his connections among the most elite members of the Russian court, he was still a bastard. Which meant he entered the fine homes by the servants' entrance.

He was moving toward the narrow door at the back of the garden when his instincts prickled and he turned to discover a statuesque woman stepping into the garden from the French windows.

"Dimitri."

Hiding a smile at Vanya Petrova's imperious tone, Dimitri followed the flagstone path to halt before the older woman and perform a deep bow.

Vanya was one of the few aristocrats he truly admired.

"Vanya, as beautiful as ever," he murmured. "I trust Richard Monroe appreciates just how fortunate he is to have captured your fair hand?"

A warm smile curved her lips at the mention of the Englishman who had been her devoted suitor for the past twenty years. Much to the surprise of St. Petersburg, Vanya had at last agreed to Monroe's proposal.

"I presume he does." She touched the large strand of pearls that encircled her neck. "The wedding is less than a month away and he has not yet bolted."

"If I were not a dedicated bachelor I would attempt to steal you away."

Vanya allowed her gaze to roam over his jacket in a pale blue-and-silver waistcoat that he had matched with black knee breeches. She smiled, almost as if she suspected he had taken particular pains with his attire.

"Every gentleman is a dedicated bachelor until he encounters the perfect woman."

He clicked his tongue. "I did not expect such a predictable response from such a delightfully unconventional lady."

"I intend to be even more predictable when I warn you that I am depending upon you to protect my young and decidedly innocent guest."

"You have no need to fear. I promise that Emma Linley-Kirov will not leave my side."

Vanya narrowed her eyes. "That does not entirely relieve my unease."

Dimitri frowned, pretending that he had not spent an inordinate amount of time dwelling on his encounter with the bothersome female.

"For all my sins I am no debaucher of the innocent. Especially not when that innocence is wrapped in such a prickly package."

"Do not allow her indomitable spirit to deceive you. Emma has taken on responsibilities that would have broken a lesser woman," Vanya chastised. "Underneath all her pretense of courage, however, she is a young maiden who is terrified for her sister."

His expression hardened. He was unaccustomed to being lectured as if he were a school lad. Not even the most cut-throat villain dared to question him.

"I will attempt to keep that in mind."

There was the sound of footsteps and they both turned to watch Emma step from the house.

"Ah, here she is," Vanya murmured.

Briefly caught in the candlelight from the house, Emma's

honey curls tumbled freely about her shoulders, but Vanya had cleverly hidden the young maiden's face with a charming hat made of gold feathers and a diamond-encrusted veil that ended just above Emma's lush lips. It added a hint of provocative mystery that would stir a man to investigate more. With the same masterful touch, Vanya had wrapped Emma's slender body in a long cape of black velvet trimmed with matching gold feathers.

There was not a soul who would recognize her.

"Well done, Vanya," he murmured. "I knew I could depend upon you to be rid of the nasty wool."

The older woman chuckled, as if she harbored a secret. "You have no notion. Good luck, my dear."

Moving toward the house, Vanya paused to kiss Emma on the cheek before disappearing through the French doors. Dimitri traced her footsteps, halting at Emma's side to offer an arm.

"Shall we go?"

She hesitated, and Dimitri sensed her silent battle to overcome her fear. Then, with that courage he knew beyond a shadow of a doubt was destined to lead her into trouble, she laid her hand on his arm and allowed herself to be led to the carriage Dimitri had left next to the mews.

Assisting her into the vehicle, Dimitri placed the heated bricks at her feet before settling at her side and tugging the rug over both of them. The night air was crisp enough to be uncomfortable.

He waited until the driver had set the matching black horses into a brisk trot before he reached into a drawer built beneath the leather bench and retrieved a silver flask and two small crystal glasses.

Pouring them both a measure of the potent spirits, he pressed one of the glasses into Emma's unwilling fingers and lifted his own glass in a toast.

"Za vas."

She cautiously sipped the expensive liquor, predictably choking as the fiery liquid slid down her throat.

"Good Lord. What is it?"

"Cognac." Dimitri took a far more appreciative sip, savoring the nutty flavor of the well-aged spirit. "It will help keep you warm."

She frowned, but she took another sip, perhaps hoping to ease her nerves.

"Is it a great distance to your club?" she demanded.

"No, it is quite close." Dimitri refilled her glass, studying her brittle expression. She appeared ready to bolt. Clearly a distraction was in order. "Is this your first visit to St. Petersburg?"

"This is the first occasion I have ever left our tiny village." A rueful smile touched her lips, her hazel eyes shrouded in mystery behind the gossamer veil. "I suppose that makes me impossibly provincial?"

"I refuse to be baited, Emma Linley-Kirov. Do you wish me to point out the more historical buildings we will pass on our journey?"

"I…" She paused, then offered a small dip of her head. "Yes, I would be very interested, thank you."

Scooting closer to her, Dimitri glanced out the window as the carriage turned onto the Nevsky Prospekt.

Within moments the stunning Our Lady of Kazan Cathedral came into view. The domed church was an impressive sight with its sweeping colonnade that framed a small garden complete with a fountain.

"Perhaps you know Emperor Paul intended the structure to imitate Saint Peter's Basilica in Rome despite the church officials' outrage at having a replica of a Catholic church."

As he had hoped, Emma's tension eased as she pressed her nose to the window, obviously eager to enjoy the spectacular view.

"My father told me that Alexander Pavlovich had commanded the church become a memorial to the defeat of Napoleon."

"Yes," Dimitri agreed dryly. The emperor had been quite eager to ensure that his victory over the Corsican monster was suitably commemorated throughout the city. "The great Mikhail Kutuzov is laid to rest in the cathedral and the keys from several European cities and fortresses were placed in the sacristy in honor of Russia's victory."

The carriage rattled onward and Dimitri pointed out the Stroganov Palace with its massive entrance arch supported by two Corinthian columns. Like much of St. Petersburg it had been designed by Rastrelli. Turning eastward they passed the Admiralty and headed toward the Palace Square. It was, of course, the crowning jewel of the city with its lavish facade painted a pale green and trimmed in white. Massive statues lined the roof and at one end an onion dome dominated the skyline. Next to the palace were the Hermitage houses that held Catherine's vast collection of paintings as well as the theater built for Catherine by Giacomo Quarenghi.

Dimitri hid his smile as Emma pointed toward the passing buildings, asking endless questions and unabashedly enjoying the short tour. It had become fashionable to pretend a jaded indifference to the world, and he could not deny it was refreshing to be in the company of a woman willing to reveal her emotions.

Her eyes widened in fascination as she spotted the Peter and Paul Fortress on the northern bank of the Neva, she sighed at the beauty of the summer gardens, and shivered at the forbidding Mikhailovsky Castle, a fortress built by an insane Emperor Paul where he was later to be murdered.

It was almost a disappointment when they crossed the bridge leading to the lower Nevsky and turned onto a narrow street lined with unpretentious elegant buildings.

Emma turned to him in surprise. "Why are we slowing?"

"I prefer not to leap from a moving carriage unless absolutely necessary," he informed her dryly.

She sucked in a sharp breath, her gaze taking in the building painted a brilliant yellow with a wide entrance that was guarded by two servants. Although it was early, there was already a steady line of opulently clad gentlemen climbing the stairs and producing their gilt-edged cards that marked them as members.

"This is your club?"

Ridiculously, Dimitri discovered himself offended by her shock. "Did you expect a hovel in a dark alley?"

She drained the last of her cognac before setting aside the empty glass.

"I have never given much thought to gambling establishments. Now I realize they must be quite profitable."

He shoved open the door, assisting her onto the paved walk. "Sin is not without its reward."

"Spoken by an unrepentant sinner."

"Of course," he agreed.

As the bastard of a nobleman he had received a fine education, but was forbidden to take his place among society. At the same time, he was too cultured to be accepted among the peasants. With no true place in the world, he had turned his ruthless willpower to creating an empire of his own making.

Leading Emma up the stairs, he nodded toward his guards and entered the large octagonal vestibule that was tastefully decorated with a black-and-white-tiled floor reflected in the silver-framed mirrors that lined the walls.

At their entrance a tall servant with a regal bearing approached to offer a deep bow.

"Vladimir will take your wrap," Dimitri informed his silent companion, his brows lifting as she clutched the velvet cloak with a white-knuckled grip. Did the chit fear his servant intended to make off with her clothing? "I promise you it will be returned."

"Very well."

Her chin lifted as she tugged off the cloak with a swift motion and handed it to the waiting servant. In a heart-beat, the crowd came to a captivated halt as all eyes turned toward Emma.

It was not that her gown was particularly shocking. Indeed, it was a deceptively simple sheath cut to reveal her shoulders and gathered beneath the gentle swell of her bosom. It was more the shimmer of the gold satin that molded to her slender body. And the tiny diamonds that glittered along the low-cut line of her bodice that drew attention to the perfection of her ivory skin.

Combined with the satin tumble of honey hair and the promise of her sensuous lips, it was enough to make every male in the club crave to have her in his bed.

Including Dimitri.

Muttering a startled curse, he grasped her upper arm and hauled her through a nearby alcove, tugging her down the short hall until he could thrust her into the privacy of his office. It was a plain room, with cream walls and parquet floor. The desk set near the fireplace was a pale cedar that matched the rest of the furnishing and the draperies were a soft shade of rose.

Slamming shut the door, he turned to glare at his com-panion in the muted light of the fireplace.

"What the devil are you wearing?"

With a sharp tug, she freed her arm from his grasp. "You were the one to insist I dress in an appropriate fashion."

Clearly, he had been out of his mind, he acknowledged, searing a hungry gaze over the delectable curve of her breasts.

"Appropriate, not designed to create a riot."

"It is no more revealing than those gowns worn by the finest ladies in St. Petersburg," she protested.

"Then why did Prince Matvey nearly knock himself senseless by walking straight into a wall? And why did one of my most trusted servants drop an entire tray of champagne?" he growled.

"You are being ridiculous. I witnessed women wearing far more daring gowns before you so rudely hauled me away."

A voice of reason whispered that he was overreacting, but Dimitri was in no mood to listen. Not when his entire body burned with the need to haul her to the nearest bed.

"Perhaps more daring," he husked, "but none so enticing."

She nervously licked her lips, the unwitting gesture making Dimitri groan in frustration.

"First you complain my gown is too prudish and now you complain it is too revealing. Are you never satisfied?"

Unable to resist temptation, he stepped close enough to trail his fingers along the elegant line of her shoulders. His body stirred, hardened; responding to her with a near painful intensity.

It wasn't uncommon for him to desire a woman.

He was a healthy male with all the normal appetites.

But this biting ache combined with a fierce possessiveness was utterly unfamiliar.

And equally unwelcome.

"Ironically I was quite satisfied until my peaceful existence was disrupted by an intimidating spinster who is far too fond of her independence."

She shivered as his fingers traced the plunging line of her bodice.

"Dimitri."

He stepped closer, breathing in the tantalizing scent of warm woman and clean soap.

"I never knew such skin truly existed," he rasped. "It is as soft and perfect as fresh cream."

"We are supposed to be searching for the gentlemen who took Anya."

"In a moment." Wrapping one arm around her waist, he carefully lifted the veil, his gaze sweeping over her pale, beautiful features. "First I must taste you."

"No—" Her protest fell on deaf ears as he captured her lips in a branding kiss. He wanted to wrap her in his arms until she melted with soft compliance. He wanted to mark her with his touch, his scent, his desire. He wanted to ensure that every man who caught sight of this woman understood that she belonged to him. Only him. "As sweet as honeyed almonds," he muttered, his tongue teasing her lips until they slowly parted in invitation. "Yes, *moya dusha,* open for me."

She groaned, her hands clutching at his shoulders as if she struggled to keep herself upright.

"The cognac…" she muttered.

He gripped her hips, pressing her against the blatant evidence of his arousal.

"It is not the cognac that is causing your head to spin and your heart to race."

She arched back to stab him with an angry frown, but Dimitri did not miss her small shiver of awareness.

"You believe yourself to be irresistible?"

"It is the hunger that burns between us that is irresistible," he corrected, his voice hard. He had made his fortune on catering to other's weaknesses. He had never dreamed he might himself become a victim. "I always thought this sort of craving a myth. Now I do not know whether to have you locked in my dungeon or hauled off to Siberia."

She licked her lips, and Dimitri swallowed a groan as his cock hardened with tormenting anticipation.

"Do not say such things," she breathlessly commanded.

"Even if they are the truth?"

An unmistakable fear darkened her hazel eyes as she lifted her hands and pressed them against his chest.

"I may be attired as a tart, but I assure you I am a lady," she gritted.

His lips twisted. "I am painfully aware you are a lady, Emma Linley-Kirov, and for the moment you are under my protection."

"Then release me."

His gaze lowered to her honeyed lips that could drive a saint to sin.

"Is that what you desire?"

"You must."

"Damn." Pushing away from the delectable heat, Dimitri shoved his hands through his hair and struggled to regain command of his rebellious body. "You should never have come to St. Petersburg."

AT ANY OTHER TIME, Emma might have been dazzled by her surroundings.

Who knew that a den of iniquity would be a sprawling honeycomb of ivory-and-gold rooms with crimson carpets and marble columns that soared up to the vaulted ceiling painted with Greek gods playing among the clouds? Or that the massive chandeliers would cast a blazing light over the elegant gentlemen who weaved their way among the card tables and flirted with the women dressed in low-cut gowns?

She had assumed the place would be dark and cheap with furtive men hunched over their cards, or tossing dice in the corner.

Which only proved she truly was naive as Dimitri claimed.

Dimitri...

She covertly glanced at the man walking at her side, a dangerous excitement fluttering in the pit of her stomach. Even elegantly attired, there was no disguising the ruthless predator that lurked just beneath Dimitri's polished exterior.

Not that his dark beauty and experienced touch was an excuse for the manner in which she had melted beneath his kiss. Or the prickling awareness that continued to torment her. She was supposed to be a sensible female of advanced years, not a giddy maiden who dreamed of being rescued from her life of drudgery by a handsome prince.

After all, she was quite reconciled to being a spinster, and even if Dimitri were a prince rather than the Beggar Czar, he was not interested in making her his princess. Just like Baron Kostya, Dimitri considered her worthy of a quick tumble, but nothing more.

She felt an odd pain knife through her heart, but before she could consider the cause, a tall, silver-haired gentleman in a burgundy jacket and gold-striped waistcoat that did nothing to flatter his rotund figure deliberately stepped in their path.

"Tipova," he said, his beady eyes skimming over the veil that once again hid Emma's face before latching on to the swell of her bosom. "As always you have managed to create a sensation."

Dimitri wrapped an arm around her shoulders, shielding her from the rude leer.

"I fear I cannot take the credit on this occasion, Prince Matvey."

"Do you intend to introduce me to your companion?"

"Actually she is visiting from Moscow and prefers to keep her privacy." His smile was one of sheer male possession. "Is that not so, *moya dusha?*"

She huddled in the protection of Dimitri's arm. "Yes."

"Ah." The prince licked his fat lips. "A mystery."

"Have you seen Count Fedor?" Dimitri demanded.

"Tarvek?" The prince glanced around the crowded room. "Not this evening, although I encountered him at the Winter Palace last eve."

"Then he returned from his journey?"

"Yes, I believe he returned with Sergei last Sunday. Do you have a particular need to speak with him?"

Emma sucked in a sharp breath, her suspicious gaze studying Dimitri's cold expression.

"I am a businessman at heart and I make a habit of knowing where to locate those who are in debt to me," Dimitri drawled.

"Yes, of course." The prince blanched and tugged at his elaborately tied cravat, as if it were too tight. "If you will excuse me?"

Dimitri smiled. "Certainly."

Waiting until the prince had vanished among the crowd, Emma struggled to put a measure of space between them.

"You told me that you did not know who had taken Anya—"

"Shh." He lowered his head to speak directly in her ear. "I had a suspicion when you said their names. It seemed a strange coincidence that the men arrived at your inn claiming to be brothers and possessing the names Fedor and Sergei, but I cannot be certain since they at least had the sense to alter their title. It would be dangerous to leap to conclusions."

She stilled, ruefully accepting the truth of his words. "Very well."

Pulling back, he regarded her with an unreadable expression. "We will take a turn through the dining room to ensure we have not overlooked our prey and then take our leave."

"How many clubs are we to visit this evening?"

A muscle clenched in his jaw as he steered her toward an arched doorway.

"One has been more than ample."

"I do not understand."

"My nerves are quite shattered," he drawled, the golden eyes blazing with an indefinable emotion as he glanced down at her puzzled expression. "I intend to return you to the protection of Vanya."

"But—"

He placed a silencing finger against her lips. "Do not play with fire, Emma, unless you wish to be burned."

CHAPTER FIVE

THE MANSION THAT COUNT Fedor Tarvek shared with his younger brother Sergei was not the finest in St. Petersburg. Situated on the banks of the Neva, it had once been a grand structure with an ornate frieze carved over the front entrance and tall windows that overlooked the formal gardens. Unfortunately, time and neglect had stolen the original charm, and there was no hiding the growing shabbiness of the estate.

Slipping silently through the cavernous rooms, a portion of Dimitri deplored the rotting floorboards and the mold marring the once handsome furnishings even as he appreciated the lack of servants. He preferred to invade another's privacy without interruption.

Intent on his search through the upper bedchambers, he nearly missed the slender man who silently approached the house through the kitchen garden.

With a lift of his brows, Dimitri hurried down the stairs.

He had sent Josef to keep watch on Count Fedor and Sergei, knowing the brothers would attend Czar Alexander's inspection of his troops that afternoon. They might secretly despise the emperor, and even attempt to undermine his rule when possible, but they dare not publicly ignore his summons.

It seemed the perfect opportunity to discover if the Tarveks were hiding any nasty secrets.

Silently leaving the house by a side door, he gestured toward his servant and headed for the back of the stables, not surprised to discover Josef had hidden his horse next to his own dappled-gray mare in the overgrown bushes.

They had spent a number of years working together. Perhaps too many, he ruefully acknowledged, watching the wiry man round the edge of the stables. They were both reaching an age where they should be considering an occupation that did not include a noose or firing squad.

"That was speedy," he muttered. "The drills cannot have ended yet."

"Oleg is keeping watch on Tarvek and his brother." Josef's expression was sour. "I thought you would desire to know that Vanya Petrova was among the crowd."

"Alone?"

"Nyet. She has a young female companion with her."

Dimitri tensed, telling himself it was anger that made his stomach clench and his heart miss a beat. After all, he had specifically commanded Emma Linley-Kirov to avoid being seen when he had left her at Vanya's the night before. He had told her he would contact her when he decided what was to be done next.

"A female companion with honey hair and hazel eyes?"

"That is more than a mere man can say." Josef shook his head in disgust. "She is wearing one of those foolish bonnets that make it damned well impossible to know what's beneath the tangle of ribbons and feathers, but I would bet my last ruble it's the dragon from Yabinsk."

As would Dimitri.

Emma was stubborn enough to flaunt herself beneath the noses of the men who would kill her without hesitation.

"Damn. I'm beginning to believe she was sent to St. Petersburg to punish me for my numerous sins," he muttered, untying the reins of his horse from the bush. "Come along."

Josef grimaced, twisting the scar that ran down the side

of his face. The disfigurement terrified many, which suited Josef, but Dimitri knew he had received the wound protecting his sister from his drunken mother.

"I will remain and search the house."

"That will not be necessary. There are no females being held hostage in the cellar or convenient map to reveal their location. Although…"

Deliberately allowing his words to trail away, Dimitri mounted his horse and headed toward the narrow lane that led out of the estate. He knew his companion's curiosity would overcome his reluctance to mix among the nobles.

There was a muttered curse, then the sound of scrambling as Josef retrieved his horse and urged the beast to match Dimitri's steady pace.

"What did you find?"

Dimitri reached beneath the black multicaped coat he had chosen to cover his plain attire and riding boots. With a crowned beaver hat pulled low on his forehead and a heavy muffler wrapped around his lower face he was impossible to recognize. Even his stocky mare was unremarkable.

Being a successful criminal meant blending into the background when necessary.

"I found this in Tarvek's bedchamber," he said, pulling out a folded piece of parchment and handing it to his companion.

"Katherine Marie," Josef read out loud. "Friday at noon." He glanced toward Dimitri with a frown. "An assignation, no doubt."

"Quite possible," Dimitri readily agreed, urging his horse into a trot as they reached the paved street leading toward the Winter Palace. "But I recall finding a similar message in Pytor Burdzecki's desk."

Josef easily kept pace. "Katherine is a common enough name."

Which was precisely why Dimitri had dismissed

Burdzecki's note as inconsequential. The aging roué was known to keep several mistresses, not to mention the brothels he visited on a regular basis.

"Yes, but for both gentlemen to have an assignation on the same day, at the same time, with a woman with the same name defies the odds."

"You suspect this Katherine is a female they have abducted?"

"Or intend to abduct."

Josef was swift to realize the importance of Dimitri's words. "Then we can follow them. If they do snatch a female they will have to take her to their hidden lair."

Dimitri nodded, his expression grim as the traffic thickened and he was forced to slow his pace.

"That was my thought, as well. We need to keep a close guard on the men we suspect are involved with my father."

They traveled in silence as they weaved through the elegant carriages and small groups of pedestrians who were battling to make their way to the Palace Square. It was not that the crowds possessed an interest in the military drills or the poor soldiers expected to stand for hours in the cold as they prepared for the event.

But, it had become a rare occurrence for Alexander Pavlovich to make a public appearance over the past few years and the entire city was determined to catch sight of him.

"What's troubling you?" Josef abruptly demanded.

Dimitri smiled with wry amusement at his servant's perception. Yes. They had most certainly been working together for too long.

"Katherine Marie," he muttered, annoyed by a vague memory teasing the edge of his mind. "The name is familiar."

Josef shrugged. "As I said, it's common enough."

"Yes." Dimitri shook his head in frustration and abruptly

turned down a side street that would lead to the Summer Garden and the Field of Mars beyond. He knew a few tricks to avoid the worst of the traffic. "This way." Intent on reaching Emma, it took Dimitri a moment to realize his companion was beginning to fall farther and farther behind. He glanced over his shoulder with an expression of impatience. "Josef?"

The servant shifted uneasily in his saddle. He hated being in the finer neighborhoods. Understandable, of course. One misstep and a man could find himself rotting in the nearest dungeon.

"You wanted those noblemen to be watched. I'll find—"

"I have need of you," Dimitri firmly interrupted, returning his attention to the road.

"I knew that woman was going to be trouble the moment she threatened to geld Semyon with scalding coffee," Josef muttered, grudgingly returning to Dimitri's side.

Dimitri scowled. He was not pleased when he discovered Emma had been troubled by one of his own servants.

"Semyon should have been gelded, although I believe the flogging I gave him should be lesson enough in how to treat a lady."

"What do you intend to do with her?"

"That is a question that kept me pacing the floor most of the night," Dimitri said dryly.

Josef shook his head in sad resignation. "A wise man would pack his bags and flee at this moment."

"No doubt."

"And yet you intend to pursue her."

Dimitri shifted in his saddle, balking at the accusation. He took women beneath his protection and sheltered them from the cruelties of the world. He did not *pursue* them. Especially not those women who flouted his authority and deliberately placed themselves in danger.

"I intend to make certain that she does not ruin our opportunity to capture the bastards," he snarled. "If they recognize her, then they will become even more cautious. We will never be able to follow their trail."

Josef snorted. "And you are not at all fearful she might be in danger?"

Dimitri ignored the question, slowing his mount as they neared the Palace Square. Over the heads of the crowd, he caught sight of the soldiers marching past the emperor, who watched on horseback, his once handsome features lined with fatigue beneath the pale autumn sunlight. The duties of the crown sat heavily on Alexander Pavlovich's shoulders. At the czar's side was Herrick Gerhardt, his eagle gaze missing nothing of the milling crowd.

With a grimace, Dimitri turned his attention to the carriages that lined the square.

"Where did you last see them?" he demanded.

"Near the end of the Hermitage." Josef pointed across the Square. "What do you intend to do?"

He gritted his teeth, refusing to give in to the impulse to charge across the parade grounds and toss Emma over his shoulder as if he were a barbarian. Not only was it a ridiculous notion, but he would attract precisely the kind of attention he was hoping to avoid.

"You will ensure a note is delivered to Vanya that she is to return home without delay," he commanded.

Josef narrowed his eyes. "And you?"

"I will be waiting."

DISCREETLY STANDING behind Vanya, Emma attempted to concentrate on the passing crowd. She had, after all, been the one to plead with the older woman to discover a means she could catch sight of Count Fedor and his brother, Sergei. And she had promised faithfully she would do nothing that would allow others to believe she was other than a maid who was there to fetch and carry for her mistress.

But while she was desperate to discover if the count was the same Fedor who had stayed at her inn, she could not help being distracted by the stunning beauty that surrounded her. Over and over her gaze strayed to the imposing Winter Palace with its magnificent Corinthian columns and the statues that seemed to peer down at her from the roof. Almost as dazzling was the handsome emperor seated on his horse less than a stone's throw away, his large form attired in military splendor and his brilliant blue eyes seeming to regard his passing troops with a wistful gleam, as if he were wishing he could join the precise lines of soldiers and march away from the crowd that pressed around him.

For a woman who had never been more than a mile from her forgotten village in the wilds of Russia, it was a breathtaking vision she knew she would never forget.

With a shake of her head, Emma sternly returned her attention to the elegant women with their fur-lined capes and the gentlemen in their military finery as they jostled to gain a place near the emperor. None paid her the least amount of attention as she stood in the shadows, her face hidden beneath the oversized brown bonnet and matching cloak that fell from her chin to the tips of her toes. To the nobles she was a meaningless servant beneath their notice.

She was attempting to get a better view of the two gentlemen crossing toward an older man with silver hair and arrogant expression when a tiny boy dressed in ragged clothing stopped next to Vanya and shoved something in her hand.

Emma instinctively moved forward to protect the older woman, but she had barely taken a step when the urchin darted away, weaving his way with ease through the people.

"This is odd," the older woman murmured, glancing down at the crumpled note she held in her hand.

"What is it?" Emma asked.

"I suppose we shall soon discover. Will you be gravely disappointed if we leave?"

"Certainly not." Emma winced as a rotund woman nearly knocked her to the ground. "I doubt I could recognize anyone in such a crowd."

Vanya offered a comforting smile as they moved toward the waiting carriage.

"Do not fear, my dear. We shall find another means to cross paths with the gentlemen you seek."

The trip back to Vanya's home was speeded by the servants who walked ahead of the carriage and cleared a path, and within half an hour they were pulling to a halt. Allowing Vanya to be assisted by the waiting groom, Emma stepped onto the pavement behind her, unprepared for the ruthless hand that seemed to come from nowhere and clamp about her upper arm.

With a startled gasp, she whipped her head around to discover a man looming beside her, his face hidden behind a muffler.

"A word in private, Emma Linley-Kirov, if you please," he growled, his dark male voice and smoldering golden eyes all too familiar.

Dimitri Tipova.

She pressed a hand to her thundering heart. "Good Lord, you near scared the life from me."

Ignoring her chiding words, the exasperating man began hauling Emma toward Vanya's private rose garden.

"If you will excuse us, Vanya?" he belatedly tossed toward the older woman.

Vanya arched a silver brow. "Do I have a choice?"

"Not on this occasion."

Shocked by Dimitri's unexpected arrival, Emma allowed herself to be pulled through the gate and into the small stone grotto that hid them from view. It was only when he spun her to meet his furious gaze that she jerked her arm free of his slender fingers.

"You truly must overcome your habit of manhandling me, sir—"

"Dimitri," he bit out, removing his hat and muffler and tossing them on a nearby marble bench.

A chill inched down her spine at the hard expression on his beautiful face, but she held her ground, refusing to reveal her unease.

"I will not be bullied."

"Be happy that I have not turned you over my knee as I long to do," he snapped.

"I beg your pardon?"

"I suspected that you were headstrong and impulsive and inclined to follow your heart rather than your head, but I did not realize you were without sense."

"I do not have to remain here and be insulted by a—"

Her proud words were brought to a sharp halt as he reached up to tug the bonnet off her head, disregarding her angry protest as he dropped it on the ground.

"Did you truly believe that ridiculous concoction would protect you if you encountered the men who abducted your sister?"

"As a matter of fact, I do," she said, tossing back the thick honey hair that tumbled about her shoulders. "No one took the least notice of me."

"My servant recognized you from across the square."

"More likely he recognized Vanya Petrova and assumed I was her companion," she argued. "The men I am seeking have no expectation of seeing me in St. Petersburg and certainly not in the company of a noblewoman."

He stepped forward, his hands clenched at his side. "You took an absurd risk."

"I am quite at liberty to take whatever risks I desire. It is none of your concern."

"Emma, do not be a fool," he rasped. "Those men may hide among polite society, but beneath their fine clothing and excessively large homes they are no better than animals. If they decide you are a threat to them they will not hesitate to put you in a grave."

Emma bristled at his unwanted lecture, but there was something in his voice that tempered her fury.

It was understandable for any gentleman with the least amount of decency to be outraged at the thought of innocent young girls being abused. But there was something personal, perhaps even intimate, in Dimitri's anger.

Tilting back her head, she studied the chiseled perfection of his aristocratic features. This man was proving to be disturbingly complex.

"Herrick insisted that you were the best suited to assist me in finding my sister, but he did not reveal what connection you possess with these men."

His eyes darkened. "Do you wonder if I am a partner in their crimes?"

"No. Certainly not."

"I have confessed to be a sinner."

Without thought, she reached to place her hand on his forearm. "You might be a sinner, but you are not evil."

His gaze lowered to where her fingers lay against his coat. "There are those who would disagree."

She shrugged off his warning, bitterly aware that the opinion of others rarely had anything to do with the truth.

"Besides, if you were involved in their ghastly business you would hardly be eager to bring them to justice."

"Not justice." A terrifying anger burned in his golden

eyes. "I want them destroyed. I want their foul deeds exposed to the world so that they flee to the wilds of Siberia to hide from their shame. I want them to die alone and in complete despair."

Emma shivered at the stark pain that she sensed beneath his fury. "They hurt someone you love. Your sister?"

His jaw hardened and she thought he intended to ignore her question. Then, with a sharp movement, he turned away to gaze out the small window overlooking the nearby fountain.

"My mother."

Her heart squeezed with sympathy. "They abducted her?"

"There was no need. My mother was the daughter of a simple cobbler." His voice was as hard and frigid as the Siberian winter. "One day Count Nevskaya walked into my grandfather's shop and had his servant collect my mother and carry her to his waiting carriage."

"He just…took her?"

"He tossed a few coins on the counter in payment."

She swallowed the bile that threatened to rise in her throat. "And your grandfather did nothing to stay him?"

"It was a different time and the count was a close friend to Emperor Paul." The lines of his shoulders were rigid, his hands clenched at his sides. She had obviously stirred his deepest demons. "My grandfather could not risk the wrath of a nobleman when he had several other children to support."

Emma wrapped her arms around her waist, feeling cold to her very soul.

"How old was she?"

"Just turned fifteen."

It was worse than Anya. Dimitri's mother had been taken as if she were no more than an object that had been bought by a handful of coins.

"Where did he take her?"

"He owns a home near Novgorod. He kept her there for near six months, then…"

She unwittingly moved to his side, studying the bleak lines of his profile.

"Then what?"

"It became obvious she was with child so he dismissed her."

Her breath tangled in her throat as she abruptly realized she had been absurdly blind. She should have suspected the truth from the moment she had caught sight of his lean, noble features. Or at least after he'd attempted to bully her. That sort of arrogance had to be bred into a man.

"You are that child?" she asked softly.

He slowly turned to face her, his expression guarded. Emma sensed how difficult it was to speak of his past, as if the wounds were still raw and bleeding.

"I am."

She hesitated, unwilling to further his pain, and yet needing to know what happened.

"Did your mother return to her family?"

"They refused to take her back into their home. She was, after all, ruined in the eyes of the world. They could not hope to marry her off with a bastard child in tow."

Her cheeks heated with outrage. "But she was taken against her will."

Leaning against the fresco painted on the stone wall of the grotto, Dimitri studied her flush beneath his half-lowered lashes.

"You are not that naive, Emma."

No, she was not.

So long as women were kept powerless they were at the mercy of men, society and even fate that too often treated them with a ruthless cruelty.

"What happened to her?"

"What happens to most women forced onto the streets," he said harshly. "Once she gave birth to me she entered a brothel. Does that shock you?"

His wary gaze skimmed over her face, no doubt accustomed to others condemning his mother for the choices she was forced to make. Emma, however, felt only sympathy. And admiration.

"On the contrary, I admire her," she said with a steady sincerity. "She was obviously a woman who did whatever necessary to survive."

"From what I could discover she became reconciled to her fate and soon learned that her considerable beauty could provide her the necessary funds for a modest home." He grimaced. "A pity she could not be satisfied."

"What do you mean?"

"She was determined that I would have a proper education."

"It is what any woman would want for their child."

His features might have been carved from granite in the sunlight slanting through the grotto window.

"I did not ask for her sacrifice," he growled.

She frowned, puzzled by his lack of gratitude. Surely he must understand a woman was willing to sacrifice anything for the people they loved?

"Dimitri?"

His eyes grew distant, the muscles in his jaw knotted as he recalled his past.

"One morning she attired me in my finest clothes, which meant they did not yet have holes in the knees and elbows, and we walked for what seemed to be miles until we at last came to a magnificent palace. I will never forget marching up the front steps and ringing the bell as if we were welcome guests." His lips twisted. "I was terrified."

Emma smiled in understanding. Approaching Herrick Gerhardt's elegant home mere days ago had taken every bit of courage she could muster. And she was supposedly a mature woman.

"How old were you?"

"Eight, or perhaps nine." He shrugged. "Certainly old enough to realize we were not where we belonged."

She ignored the urge to reach up and stroke the sleek raven hair pulled into a ribbon at his nape. The wounded boy that lurked deep inside Dimitri made him no less dangerous. Indeed, the wave of tenderness that swept through her was far more disturbing than the potent attraction that tingled within her.

"Were you turned away?"

"No, my mother was quite determined, and my unmistakable resemblance to my father managed to get us over the threshold and into the count's private study." Shoving away from the wall, Dimitri paced to the center of the grotto. "I understood very little of the conversation beyond the fact my father did a great deal of shouting and my mother refused to leave. It was only later that I learned she had threatened to approach the count's wife and inform her that he had forced himself on a mere child if he did not see to my education."

Emma carefully considered her words. The tension in the air was tangible.

"Clearly her threat was successful."

His breath hissed through his clenched teeth. "It was successful in the sense I was sent to school in Moscow, but my father was far from pleased to be outwitted by a mere whore and set about destroying her life."

Emma winced, already suspecting that the poor woman had suffered for her bold courage.

"What did he do?" she husked.

"He had her evicted from her home, and then he ensured her wealthy patrons would no longer seek her companionship. It became more and more difficult for her to earn a decent living and she was forced to take rooms in the sewers of St. Petersburg." The golden eyes darkened with a bleak loss that tore at her heart. "It was only a matter of time before she had her throat slit and her body left in the gutter."

CHAPTER SIX

AS THE WORDS ECHOED through the grotto, Dimitri wondered what the hell he was doing.

He never shared his mother's tragic story. There were a handful of people who knew his mother had been a whore, and that she had been left to die in the gutter. And, of course, there was no denying his connection to the count.

But the sordid, intimate details…those he kept buried deep inside.

Until this woman. Emma Linley-Kirov stirred emotions he'd struggled for years to forget.

There was a rustle of wool and the light touch of slender fingers on his arm. Dimitri sucked in a startled breath. When had he developed an addiction to the scent of soap on warm, feminine skin?

"What happened to you?" she demanded.

He searched the wide hazel eyes, finding nothing but gentle understanding. Not that he was particularly surprised. While most women would be shocked by his mother and the life she had been forced to lead, Emma appeared almost…admiring.

And why would she not?

She possessed the same reckless courage and stubborn determination to risk her foolish neck for those she loved. His gut twisted with that same white-hot anger he had felt when he'd discovered she had been prancing about St. Petersburg for all to see.

"I was too far away to realize what was happening and

it wasn't until I fled the school when I turned fifteen that I realized she was dead," he snapped.

Her eyes widened at his blunt explanation. "You must have been devastated."

"I was infuriated." He grasped her shoulders, glaring down at her pale, fragile face. "If my mother had never confronted the count then she still would have been alive."

She met his gaze without flinching. "And you blamed her for leaving you on your own?"

"I blamed her for taking a stupid, unnecessary risk," he gritted, refusing to recall the endless nights he'd cried himself to sleep when he discovered his mother was forever gone from his life.

Emma frowned. "She loved you and wanted to do whatever she could to provide you with a future. You should be proud of her."

He tightened his grip, his eyes narrowed. "Do you think your precious Anya would be proud to learn you had died attempting to rescue her?"

She stiffened and met his glare with her own.

"I have to do this."

"For your sister?" he snapped. "Or for your own selfish need to be a martyr?"

She paled, her eyes suddenly appearing too large for her face. "So I am not only a bitter spinster, but a tedious martyr. It is fortunate your opinion means nothing to me."

Dimitri growled in frustration. "My opinion is that you are a stubborn minx who has mistakenly convinced herself that accepting help from others makes her weak. Return home, Emma, and allow me to search for your sister." He leaned down, whispering against her lips. "Or better yet, come with me and I will ensure your protection."

He heard her breath catch. "I doubt protection is what you offer."

Dimitri pulled back, his gaze sweeping possessively down her slender body.

"Once you are known to be mine there is no one who would dare harm you."

A frantic pulse fluttered at the base of her throat. "Except you."

Unable to resist, Dimitri skimmed his lips down the curve of her neck, lingering on that revealing pulse.

"I swear I would treat you with exquisite care." His voice thickened, his anger altering to a blaze of desire. "You would want for nothing."

She moaned, briefly melting against him before she abruptly stepped away to regard him with a leery frown. Her body might recognize that she belonged to him, but her mind was not yet ready to concede defeat.

"What I want is to find my sister and to return to our home together."

"Emma—"

"No." She shook her head, her hand pressed to her throat. "Do you believe your father is involved with the gentlemen who abducted Anya?"

Dimitri grimly restrained his need to yank her back into his arms. His experience with tender virgins might be limited, but he did know when a female was on the brink of bolting.

"Yes." He shoved his fingers through his hair, his body hard and aching. A distressingly predictable sensation when he was in the companionship of this frustrating woman. "His debauched taste for young girls has never diminished."

"Why did you not kill him when you discovered he was responsible for the death of your mother?"

Dimitri lifted his brows, startled by the blunt question. "He was a powerful nobleman and I was a mere boy," Dimitri reminded her, his tone dry.

"I cannot believe that is what deterred you."

"You think I was born a bloodthirsty criminal? Or perhaps you assume all bastards are without morals?"

A blush stained her cheeks, but she refused to be cowed. An unfortunate habit.

"I think you loved your mother and would move heaven and earth to avenge her death." She narrowed her gaze, studying him with unnerving perceptiveness. "So why do you hesitate?"

"Because death is not enough," he roughly admitted. "I want to make certain that Count Nevskaya and his cronies publicly suffer for what they have done."

The hazel eyes darkened. "And how many girls have been hurt because you were more concerned with humiliating your father rather than making certain he was unable to abuse helpless children?"

For perhaps the first time in his life, Dimitri Tipova was struck speechless as Emma turned on her heel and left him standing alone in the grotto.

THERE WAS A HEAVY, gray chill in the air as Dimitri left his horse in the shadows of a high hedge, and walked toward the plain black carriage that waited on the elegant street corner.

Wrapped in a heavy coat and muffler that served as his disguise, Dimitri cast a sour glance at the brooding clouds. Although St. Petersburg would always be his home, he often wondered if Czar Peter regretted his fierce determination to create an empire out of this wet, frozen landscape. The emperor had, after all, sacrificed an enormous number of his people, not only to the cold and disease and wolves as the city was being built, but also to keep his throne from a land-hungry Charles XII as well as uprisings from the Cossacks and even his own son, Alexei.

With a shake of his head, he dismissed his inane thoughts

and paused at the side of the carriage. Covertly glancing up and down the quiet street to ensure there were no prying eyes, he tugged open the door and climbed inside.

He settled on the leather seat across from Josef, who kept his gaze trained on the window that offered a perfect view of Pytor Burdzecki's town house.

"Well?" he demanded.

Attired in rough wool clothing more suitable for a dockhand than a man who had acquired a small fortune over the past years, Josef grimaced.

"Not so much as a leaf has stirred."

"And there has been no word from the others?"

"Nothing."

Damn. He had commanded two dozen of his most trustworthy cutthroats to keep watch on the homes of those gentlemen he suspected were involved in his father's nefarious amusements. The notes he had stumbled across had specifically mentioned noon, but unwilling to take any chances, Dimitri had demanded his employees hide themselves near the various homes before the crack of dawn.

"You made certain the household servants were to be followed?" he demanded.

With an offended expression, Josef reached for the nearby bottle of vodka and a large glass.

"You do not pay me because I am careless."

Dimitri could not argue. Josef possessed a meticulous cunning that had made him a successful thief long before Dimitri had taken him beneath his wing.

"Forgive me, Josef. I had convinced myself we could catch the bastards in the midst of their foul deeds." He clenched his hands, needing a means to vent his simmering frustration. "Now it seems they are to elude me yet again."

Josef gave a lift of his shoulder. "The messages you

discovered had no date. It could be they mean the next Friday."

"Or a Friday long past and once again I am too late," he snapped.

"Here." Pouring a large measure of the vodka, Josef shoved a glass into his hand. Dimitri swallowed the potent liquor, grunting as he lowered the glass and Josef leaned forward to refill it. "Another."

He arched a puzzled brow. "Is there a reason you are plying me with vodka?"

"I hoped it might sweeten your foul mood."

Dimitri scowled. "Of course my mood is foul. I do not appreciate being outwitted by a collection of aging reprobates."

"Those aging reprobates possess enough power to alter the course of history as they have too often proven," Josef said, his voice harsh with disgust. Many of the noblemen were personally responsible for squashing Alexander Pavlovich's attempts at reform in the early days of his reign. "Keeping a handful of peasant girls hidden would be a simple matter with a dozen estates and serfs who are too terrified to reveal the truth." Josef leaned back in his seat, his gaze watchful. "And your mood has been foul since you last met with Emma Linley-Kirov."

Dimitri grimaced, swallowing his instinctive denial. Why bother? Anyone unfortunate enough to cross his path since Emma had abandoned him in Vanya's grotto was painfully aware of his vile temper.

"She holds *me* responsible for her sister's abduction."

Josef sucked in a sharp breath. "Is she daft?"

Dimitri polished off the last of the vodka. He had spent the night trying to comfort himself with the notion that Emma Linley-Kirov was a provincial spinster who was too naive and too stupid to comprehend the complexities

of his revenge. A wasted effort. Nothing managed to ease
the nagging sense of guilt.

"She is annoyingly stubborn, headstrong and beautiful beyond reason, but I would never consider her to be
daft."

"She must be if she would accuse you of harming
children."

"She did not suggest that I personally forced a child into
my bed, but rather that I stood aside and allowed others to
continue with their loathsome deeds."

"What would she have you do?"

"Kill them."

Josef blinked, staggered by the thought of a sweet, innocent maiden harboring such bloodthirsty desires. Then
he lifted the flask to take a large swig of the vodka.

"If she is so anxious to be rid of the bastards, then why
does she not tend to the duty herself?" he muttered.

Dimitri's brows snapped together, a chill shivering
down his spine. "Good God, do not say such a thing in
her presence. She is quite capable of attempting murder if
she thought it would save her precious sister."

"Perhaps she would discover it's not a simple matter to
rid society of its vermin."

Dimitri tossed aside his empty glass, casting a jaundiced
glance out the window of the carriage.

"Not simple, but not impossible, either."

"You have allowed the female to rattle your wits."

A humorless smile twisted his lips. Emma had rattled
more than his wits. His long night of pacing the floor had
not been solely due to her accusations. He had been hard
and aching to bed the wench since she stormed into his
office.

"Rattled wits or not, she was not mistaken. My
desire for revenge has allowed my father to continue his
debauchery."

Josef muttered his opinion of overbearing spinsters and the stupidity of men who allowed them to interfere in his business.

"The count is the villain, not you," he at last snapped. "How many women have you taken under your protection over the years? Only an arrogant ass would believe he could rescue them all."

Dimitri turned back to meet his loyal servant's scowl. "I can always depend upon you to keep me humble, Josef."

"I assume that is why you have kept me in your service for so many years."

"Well, it most certainly is not for your charm." Dimitri reached for the door of the carriage. It was obvious his hopes of discovering how his father and his associates kept the women they abducted hidden was doomed to failure. At least for today. "Return to your home, old friend."

Josef frowned as Dimitri stepped out of the carriage. "What of you?"

"Alexander Pavlovich is unveiling his latest portrait at the Hermitage this afternoon."

"God almighty, another one?"

Dimitri chuckled. Czar Alexander had avoided many of the Romanov's tendencies, but he was as vainglorious as his grandmother.

"Vanya Petrova is certain to attend and I do not doubt she will be brazen enough to bring her mysterious young maid with her."

Josef drained the last of the vodka, his expression sour. "You should be pleased. It is possible the female can be of service. People tend to be more willing to speak with a pretty young maid than a cutthroat."

"Pleased?" Dimitri clenched his fists, a dark fear churning through him. "If she has put herself in danger I intend to lock her in my cellar and never release her."

"You were right, Tipova," the scarred servant jeered. "Emma Linley-Kirov is not daft, you are."

EMMA FELT AS IF SHE were in a dream when Vanya's elegant carriage swept through the archway and halted in the courtyard before the vast Winter Palace.

How often had she dreamed of traveling to St. Petersburg and encountering a charming prince when she had been young and still naive enough to believe in childish fancy? Or of being draped in rich satin as she entered the vast palaces and curtsied before Czar Alexander?

Instead, she was dressed in the drab clothing of a proper maid and struggling not to stumble over her feet as Vanya led her into Jordan Hall with its grand columns and vaulted ceiling lavishly painted and rimmed with gilt moldings. She had a brief glimpse of the elegantly attired crowd sweeping toward the Jordan Staircase before Vanya pressed her toward a side hall, jolting her out of her brief moment of madness.

Maids did not belong in the upper rooms.

Which suited her perfectly, Emma sternly told herself, traveling through the spider web of corridors and shrugging off her sense of unreality.

Her journey to St. Petersburg was more of a nightmare than dream, and the sooner she found Anya so she could return home the better.

Besides, she was discovering that beneath the breathtaking beauty of the city and the grandeur of the nobility, there was a pervasive rot that lurked just beneath the surface. There was evil in shadows.

Shuddering at the unpleasant thought, Emma hurried toward the servants' quarters. The air was thick with a smothering heat that was no doubt necessary for the exotic plants she had glimpsed in the various salons and drawing rooms she passed, but hardly pleasant for the servants that scurried about their tasks. Ignoring the sweat that trickled down her spine, she followed the scent of baking bread, occasionally stopping to chat with the other maids that crowded into the kitchens.

She would question as many of the servants as possible before returning to the vast entryway and finding the best place to hide and watch as the guests departed the palace. If the men who had abducted Anya were attending Czar Alexander then she would see them leave.

But first…

Reaching the far end of the kitchen that overlooked the small enclosure with a handful of cows, she was nibbling on a plum and almond tart when one of the palace maids cautiously sidled next to her, a wary expression on her plump face that was framed by a halo of red curls.

"What is your interest in Count Fedor Tarvek?" she whispered, her gaze warily darting about the bustling room, as if terrified they might be overheard.

Emma slowly set aside the tart, careful to hide her flare of hope. The woman was as skittish as a dormouse, clearly uneasy at the mention of the man's name. She did not want to startle her into flight.

"My younger sister is seeking a position in his kitchens," she said, keeping her voice equally soft. "She is anxious for a job, but I have heard rumors—"

"You should warn your sister to seek a position elsewhere," the woman hissed.

"What do you know of him?"

The dark gaze again darted about the bustling kitchen, ensuring that no one had noticed them speaking.

"Nothing."

"Please." Emma reached to lightly touch the woman's arm. "Anya is young and headstrong and unless I can offer her more than vague warnings she is certain to ignore my fears. Did you work for the count?"

"No." She bit her bottom lip. "It was my cousin."

"What happened to her?"

"No one is certain. She told my Aunt that she was offered a position as parlor maid, but when she did not return home that night my uncle went in search of her."

A sick dread curled through Emma's stomach. "What did he discover?"

The woman's freckled face hardened with an impotent anger that Emma easily recognized. It was the same helpless frustration that had plagued her since discovering Anya was missing.

"She had simply disappeared. The count claimed that she had never arrived at his home, but my uncle was certain he found a ribbon belonging to my cousin in the hedge surrounding the estate."

"Dear Lord." Emma pressed a hand to her stomach. "You never heard from her again?"

"Nyet. And I have heard whispered she is not the only female to disappear."

"Do you…" Emma's words were cut short as the maid abruptly grasped her hand and nodded toward the window.

"The devil himself," she whispered.

Her breath was lodged in her throat as she leaned forward, staring at the two gentlemen who strolled past the window.

They were both elegantly attired in dark tailored jackets and breeches with high glossy boots that she would bet her last quid were worth more than her cramped cottage. Beneath their tall hats she could catch a glimpse of gray hair and lined countenances. That, however, was where the resemblances ended.

One man was short and stocky with a heavy jowl and an unmistakable paunch under his charcoal-gray jacket. The other was tall and lean with an autocratic profile and air of haughty superiority that annoyed her even from a distance.

Her gaze lingered on the shorter man, her heart skipping a beat as she recognized the debauched face.

"That is Tarvek?" she rasped.

"Yes. Filthy murderer."

Emma clenched her hands at her side. So, Dimitri's conjecture had proven right. Count Tarvek was the man who had stayed at her inn and snuck away with her sister.

She had a name for the bastard, now what did she do with the information?

"Who is that with him?"

"Count Nevskaya," the maid said, her eyes widening as Emma mouthed a startled curse as she realized she was staring at Dimitri's father. "Is something the matter?"

"I shall return in a moment," she muttered, heading for the nearby door.

The maid scurried behind her. "No, listen to me," she pleaded softly. "They truly are dangerous men."

"They will never know I am near," Emma promised, tossing the woman a reassuring smile before she slipped from the kitchen and headed for the back gate.

Count Tarvek and Dimitri's father. Two men who both possessed an evil lust for young girls.

It could not be coincidence they were together, clearly attempting to avoid others as they strolled along the paved lane.

Emma followed behind the two men, careful to keep a cautious distance. Despite Dimitri's low opinion of her intelligence, she had no desire to put herself in danger. But neither was she willing to ignore an opportunity to discover more of the men responsible for her sister's disappearance.

Staying in the shadows of the looming buildings, she shivered as the breeze tugged on her woolen cloak. After the oppressive heat of the palace, the chill of the gray afternoon was even more noticeable. Or perhaps it was a reaction to being led farther and farther away from the guests.

With her heart lodged in her throat, Emma followed the men through a stone archway, nearly stumbling over her feet as they came to an abrupt halt. Thankfully, neither glanced over their shoulders and she was able to scurry behind a bush as they stood closely together, pretending to study the nearby flow of the Neva River.

"The ship has sailed?" Tarvek demanded, his voice pitched low.

The tall, slender gentleman nodded, turning to regard his companion, and Emma's breath tangled in her throat. Good God. There was no mistaking he was Dimitri's father. It was in the chiseled perfection of his profile and arrogant thrust of his jaw.

Not that he could claim Dimitri's stunning beauty, she decided. There was a frigid lack of emotion in his eyes and a repellent sneer that twisted his thin lips. He reminded her of a snake. Cold, lethal and willing to strike without remorse.

"It departed on schedule," he was assuring his companion. "Soon it will arrive in London with our tender cargo."

Tarvek rubbed his fat hands together in a gesture that Emma remembered with a quiver of disgust.

"Tender, indeed," he husked. "I hope that our English friends were fortunate in their hunting. The last lot they delivered was barely tolerable."

Emma frowned in puzzlement. Tender? Hunting? Were they transporting live game? And if so, why would they go to such an effort to discuss their business so far from the other guests?

Dimitri's father shrugged. "They were not of the finest quality, but they brought a tidy profit."

"For you, perhaps," Tarvek growled. "My allotment was not nearly so generous."

"It is my ship that hauls the cargo and my crew who protects our investments. It was agreed I should have the larger profit." The older count slashed his hand through the air in a gesture of disdain. "Besides, you contributed only two of the females for our last shipment."

Tarvek shifted uneasily. "I cannot always control Sergei."

"It is unfortunate, but not my concern," Nevskaya said, his cold voice sending a chill of horror down Emma's spine.

With a gasp, she grabbed at the bush, feeling her knees threaten to buckle.

God almighty. The cargo was not wild game.

They were speaking of girls. Sweet, helpless children they considered of no more worth than animals.

And what did Tarvek mean that Sergei could not be controlled? Her stomach rolled at the mere thought.

"You should at least be pleased with my latest offerings," the villain said, a nasty smile of anticipation curving his lips. "Those were three of the most succulent females I have ever captured. It's a pity that they will be wasted on a boorish Englishman. Any man who would willingly live on that soggy island is barely more than a savage."

Emma's disgust was overwhelmed by a tidal wave of fury. Was Anya one of the three women? Was she even now being hauled far away from Russia? Her hands clenched. If she had a gun she would have shot both the monsters in the back.

Nevskaya laughed, unaware of the woman behind him plotting his imminent murder.

"So long as they fulfill their part of the bargain then I do not care if they mold in their dreary homes."

Lost in her violent imaginings, Emma was unaware of the shadow looming behind her, or the faint crunch of gravel beneath an approaching boot. It was not until a hand clapped over her mouth and a masculine arm wrapped around her waist that she realized the dangers of her distraction.

CHAPTER SEVEN

IGNORING THE FRANTIC struggles of the woman held tightly in his arms, Dimitri hauled her away from his father and Tarvek. In truth, she was fortunate that the need to avoid attention kept him from tossing her in the nearby river.

He ground his teeth, his temper still smoldering at the sight of her crouched behind the bush, mere steps away from two of the most savage creatures to roam St. Petersburg's streets.

The aggravating wench was clearly determined to put him in an early grave.

"You will not be satisfied until you have managed to get that lovely throat slit, will you, *moya dusha*," he rasped close to her ear, rounding the corner of the palace where his horse and carriage waited.

With a jerk of her head, she managed to dislodge the hand he had clamped across her mouth.

"How dare you follow me?"

Dimitri conveniently ignored the fact he had not only followed her to the palace, but that he had scoured the damned place from the attics to the cellars before he had at last caught sight of her behind the bush.

He was not prepared to admit how desperate he had been to find her, not even to himself.

"Such vanity," he mocked. "Do you believe I am so taken with you I must trail behind you like a hungry stray?"

"I think you are the most irritating, arrogant, utterly vexing man I have ever had the misfortune to meet," she hissed.

He tightened his arms around her slender body, taking grim pleasure in the feel of her squirming form pressed against him. He was angry, not in his grave. Just having this woman near was enough to stir his desire.

"Careful, Emma, you will quite turn my head with such flattery."

"How did you find me?"

"I was searching for my father when I recognized a luscious backside where it did not belong," he glibly dissembled. "I knew it was only a matter of time before you were discovered."

"And so you charged to my rescue?"

"It is an unfortunate habit I seem to have acquired."

"And one you can leave off at any moment," she tartly informed him.

"Ah, if only it were that simple." He caught the gaze of his waiting driver and gave a nod of his head. Instantly, the carriage rolled forward.

"It is," she challenged. "Put me down."

"I have not yet completed my rescue," he said, reaching to yank open the door and tossing his wiggling bundle inside. Then, with a smooth motion, he was on the leather seat beside her, slamming shut the door.

"What are you—" Emma's angry words were forgotten as the carriage jerked into motion, racing over the cobblestones at a brisk pace. "Stop this carriage at once."

His lips twisted at her imperious tone. "I realize you are accustomed to giving commands in your isolated kingdom, Emma Linley-Kirov, but I am not one of your subjects."

Anger flashed through her magnificent eyes, but she was wise enough to realize he would not be bullied. Instead, she nervously shifted into the corner of the seat, as if that paltry space could dim the awareness prickling between them.

"Please, Dimitri," she stiffly pleaded. "Vanya will be frantic with concern if I disappear."

He shifted to face her directly, his leg stretched outward to prevent any attempt at escape. God knew she was idiotic enough to risk throwing herself out of a moving carriage.

"Word will be sent to Vanya that you are in my care."

Her lips thinned. "And that is supposed to reassure her?"

"Certainly it is preferable to having you left to your own devices, creating chaos among the fine citizens of St. Petersburg."

She muttered something beneath her breath that Dimitri suspected was comparing him to midden heap and glanced out the window, her brows drawing together at the elegant shops of the Gostiny Dvor they passed at a shocking speed.

"Where are you taking me?"

"I merely wished to speak with you in private." He diverted her question.

"Why?"

"What did you overhear between Tarvek and my father?"

She jerked, her eyes widening at his abrupt question. "You lecture me for being a reckless fool and now you desire me to share the information I have discovered?"

A slow smile curved his lips. "I do admire your intelligence."

With a snort she folded her arms over her chest. "I have no intention of telling you anything."

He leaned forward to whisper directly in her ear. "You will if you truly desire to find your sister."

Her hands lifted to press against his chest, but Dimitri didn't miss her revealing shiver. Or the leap of her pulse that fluttered at the base of her neck.

"Fine," she rasped. "I very much fear that Anya has been sent to England."

Dimitri reared back, his breath hissing between his clenched teeth.

"What did you say?"

Emma hesitantly repeated the conversation she had overheard, her wary gaze never straying from his grim expression.

A heavy silence filled the carriage as he considered the shocking information. How many years had he searched to find a trace of the women he suspected were being abused by his father and his associates? Christ, he had spent countless hours hidden in frozen gardens and dark alleys attempting to discover the truth. And worse, he had stumbled across the truth and he had been too blind to realize he held it in his hands.

"Dimitri?"

Shaken out of his dark thoughts, he clenched his hands with self-disgust.

"I have been unforgivably stupid," he gritted. "The *Katherine Marie*. I should have recognized the name."

"Who is she?"

"Not who. What," he corrected. "The *Katherine Marie* is my father's private ship."

"My God," she breathed, her face pale and her hands trembling as she folded them in her lap. "Then it's true. They have taken Anya away from St. Petersburg."

Dimitri resisted the peculiar desire to cradle her in his arms and offer her comfort. He protected women. He bedded them. He even supported a few. But there was something unnerving in the tug of tenderness Emma Linley-Kirov inspired.

Besides, she was as likely to slap him as to thank him for his effort. Emma was not a woman who appreciated having others witness her vulnerabilities.

"It would explain a great deal," he admitted.

He heard her draw in a deep, steadying breath, her chin tilting with the stubborn determination that was certain to give him nightmares.

"Such as?"

"I hire a vast number of people to keep me well informed. It seemed impossible that I was unable to discover more than vague rumors that young girls, and occasionally boys, were disappearing. I assumed they must take them from St. Petersburg, but it never occurred to me they would actually ship them abroad."

"I do not understand. If they—" she faltered, a flare of color staining her cheeks "—desire these girls, then why would they send them to England?"

He scowled, cursing the missing Anya for dragging her elder sister into the muck. For all her courage and tenacious strength, Emma possessed an innocence that was remarkably rare.

"Leave it be, Emma," he said roughly. "You have been forced deep enough into this sordid business—"

"I need to know."

"Emma."

She laid a pleading hand on his arm. "Please, Dimitri."

His gaze shifted to the window, absently noticing the aging palaces were being replaced by the classically designed homes preferred by Alexander Pavlovich's architect, Carlo Rossi.

"It would be my guess they transport the women to a select group of gentlemen in England who, in return, send back the females they have lured into their trap," he grudgingly revealed his suspicion. Now that he understood how his father had rid himself of the local females, it was a simple matter to deduce the remainder of his nefarious scheme.

Her brow wrinkled in confusion. "But why go to such a bother?"

"They did not in the beginning, as my presence in St. Petersburg is ample proof." He restlessly tugged off his hat and muffler, tossing them into the opposite seat. His gloves followed. "But Alexander Pavlovich has become remarkably pious as the years have passed and while he is not foolish enough to truly believe he can command his court to put aside their wicked pleasures, he has insisted they become more discreet."

"I still do not understand."

He reached to take her hand, not surprised to find her fingers were stiff with cold. Where the hell were her gloves? And her scarf? The foolish wench. She could shoulder the responsibilities of her business and her sister, but she was stunningly incapable of caring for herself.

Clearly she was in need of someone to protect her, regardless of her prickly independence.

"Allow yourself to imagine a very young and frightened English girl being smuggled into St. Petersburg," he said, studying the shadows that darkened her beautiful eyes. "She would be a world away from her family and friends, she would have no money and no ability to speak the language. She would be utterly at the mercy of her captors."

"She would not dare try to escape."

"Precisely."

She worried her lower lip with her teeth, too intelligent not to realize the dire fate awaiting such women.

"They cannot hold them captive forever."

"No. Once they…" He rubbed a hand over his face, hating the necessity of discussing such a repugnant subject with Emma. "Wearied of the girls, they no doubt sell them to brothels in Novgorod or Moscow."

She swayed, her face ashen. "Anya," she breathed. "I have to find her."

"Emma, we cannot be certain she was on the ship."

She met his gaze with an implacable expression that made Dimitri's gut twist with dread.

"There is only one means to discover."

HER WORDS WERE STILL ringing through the air when the carriage was pulled to a halt in front of a newly constructed house.

It was a home any gentleman would be proud to claim.

Built of pale stone, it boasted five bays with a central bowed projection that was most notable for the Venetian glass he had imported for the windows that flanked the double doorway. A sweep of stairs led to the wraparound terrace that overlooked the sunken garden arranged on both sides and the high brick fencing that offered a rare privacy.

For once, Dimitri did not experience the flare of pride at his creation. He was far more intent on scooping the startled Emma into his arms and climbing out of the carriage.

Predictably outraged at being carried through the gate and up the stairs, Emma smacked his chest, a stormy flush bringing welcome color to her cheeks.

"Have you taken leave of your senses?" She continued with her futile assault. "Put me down."

Dimitri crossed the terrace, smiling as the door was pushed open to reveal a broad man with the corded muscles of a laborer and the weathered features of a sailor. Hardly a typical butler, despite the distinguished mane of silver hair. In truth, Rurik looked exactly what he was. A pirate. And nothing could make him appear respectable. Not even the uniform Dimitri insisted he wear.

Dimitri shrugged. He had done his best to prevent panic among the neighbors.

"Caught a feisty one, eh?" Rurik demanded, a curious

glint in his blue eyes. Dimitri had never brought a woman to this house.

"Not intentionally," Dimitri gritted, entering the marble foyer and headed directly toward the massive cedar stair-case that had been hand carved. "Now I must decide what is to be done with her."

"The dungeon is currently empty," Rurik offered.

Dimitri smiled down at the furious woman tucked in his arms.

"A temptation I must admit, but for the moment I will content myself with an undisturbed privacy. Would you ensure that dinner is prepared and kept warm in the kitchen?"

"Of course."

Emma's eyes widened as she turned her head to watch Rurik stride toward the back of the house.

"Wait." She jerked back to meet his amused expression as Rurik disappeared. "I see you have your servants trained to ignore the pleas of the poor women you kidnap."

Dimitri climbed the stairs, fully enjoying the sensation of Emma cradled in his arms.

"Rurik needed no training. He was a pirate who terror-ized the seas until he was captured by the French during the war."

"If he was captured then what is he doing here?"

He reached the upper landing and headed directly for the main saloon.

"I take exception to fine Russian citizens being tortured by that French imposter."

She made a choked sound of disbelief. "You snuck into Napoleon's prison?"

"There are few men more loyal than those who have been rescued from the guillotine. And, of course, his wife happens to be the finest cook in the empire. When she promised her services in exchange for her husband's freedom I could not resist."

Her eyes narrowed, obviously suspecting the danger Dimitri had risked sneaking into the brutal French prison despite his nonchalant tone. Thankfully, her probing questions died on her lips as he stepped into the long saloon.

A tiny gasp escaped her as she studied the coved ceiling with gilded rosettes that framed the line of crystal chandeliers. The walls were covered in emerald satin panels with marble columns set between the high arched windows. The furniture had been purchased from the finest Russian craftsmen as had the parquet floor that was inlaid with cherry and teak. In all, it was a room that spoke of refined elegance.

"What is this place?" she asked as he settled her on the gold settee beside the massive black marble fireplace.

He moved to light the logs already stacked in the fireplace, chuckling at her astonished tone.

"My home."

"*Your* home?"

Turning, he leaned against the carved mantel and regarded her with a lift of his brows.

"Despite the rumors, I do not crawl from the pits of hell each evening."

She waved a hand toward the delicate jade figurines perched on a satinwood table.

"This hardly suits the image of the Beggar Czar."

"True—" he shrugged "—which is why I have several residences spread throughout the city. Each of them serve their own specific purpose."

"And what purpose does this residence serve? Your private brothel?"

"If that were true it would be an abysmal failure."

She jerked as if he had slapped her. "I suppose that is yet another insult at my lack of attractiveness?"

He frowned, prowling toward the settee. Was the woman demented? She was the most tempting, most exquisitely beautiful female he had ever encountered.

"On the contrary, *moya dusha,* it is the highest compliment." He sat on the cushion next to her stiff body, turning to study her wounded hazel eyes. "You are the only female beyond my cook to ever step over the threshold. In fact, there are less than a handful of people who even know of this house. I come here when I desire to be alone."

"Then why have you brought me here?"

With experienced ease, he reached to unbutton her cloak, tossing it aside, not at all surprised to discover her swathed in yet another layer of brown wool beneath.

"A dangerous question, Emma Linley-Kirov."

He felt her shiver as he turned his attention to the buttons that lined the gown from her chin to beneath the soft swell of her bosom.

"For goodness' sake, what are you doing?"

His blood heated as he slowly peeled back the heavy material to reveal the satin beauty beneath.

"Attempting to understand why you would believe for a moment I find you lacking in appeal."

"You have accused me of being a shrill-tongued spinster, a selfish martyr—" Her recriminations faded to a breathless sigh when he pressed his lips to the base of her throat.

"A delectable innocent who I have imagined unwrapping from your woolen layers a hundred times."

Her hands lifted to lie against his chest, but she made no effort to push him away.

"You complained when I did not hide myself."

"Of course." He stroked his lips to the hollow beneath her ear, his fingers continuing to unbutton the body of her gown. "Only I am allowed to enjoy your most intimate beauty."

"I think you enjoy mocking me."

"If you need proof of my desire I am happy to oblige."

"That is not—" She squeaked in alarm as he effortlessly pressed her back onto the cushions of the settee, following downward to cover her with his larger body. "Oh. Good Lord."

Good Lord, indeed.

CHAPTER EIGHT

EMMA KNEW SHE WAS IN trouble as soon as he claimed her lips in a kiss that seared her to the tips of her toes. She was aware of being lowered to the cushions, and the pleasant sensation of his hard body pressed to her softer curves. More distantly, she could feel the friction of the wool gown as it was pulled slowly, yet relentlessly down her body. But the fear that should have had her shoving him away was overwhelmed by the excitement that jolted through her.

Clutching at his shoulders, she quivered as his tongue traced the seam of her lips, silently encouraging them to part. Hesitantly, she opened her mouth, shocked as he dipped his tongue between her lips. He tasted of cognac and danger, a heady combination that made her heart race.

Over and over he plundered her willing lips, his tongue tangling with hers in a beautiful dance.

She heard him groan, his hands expertly loosening her curls and gently spreading them across the cushions beneath her. His touch was tender, but she sensed the fierce hunger under the surface. It was etched in the taut muscles beneath her hands and the harsh rasp of his breath.

She shifted beneath him, her fingers biting into his shoulders. What was the odd restlessness that was plaguing her? The sense that her body was seeking a fulfillment that only Dimitri could offer?

"So sweet," he murmured, his lips drifting down the line of her jaw.

She instinctively tilted back her head, offering her throat to his skillful kisses.

"This is insanity," she muttered.

"Delectable madness," he readily agreed, his hands lowering to cup the soft swell of her breasts.

Emma shuddered in shocked pleasure, realizing her gown had been tugged down to her waist, revealing the plain shift she wore beneath. She could feel the heat of his hand branding through the thin material and when he bent his head to cover a straining nipple with his mouth, she nearly screamed. Dear Lord. The feel of the damp linen and the rough stroke of his tongue grazing her sensitive nipple were sending tiny darts of bliss through her.

She had never suspected a man's touch could offer such exquisite pleasure. Or that her body would respond with an aching need that overrode the whispers of alarm in the back of her mind.

"Dimitri?"

"Yes, *moya dusha,*" he softly assured her, his lips continuing to torment her breasts as his hands slid beneath her, subtly tugging her heavy skirt upward. "Allow me to please you."

She trembled at the heady sensations that swirled through her. She felt as giddy as if she had drunk an entire bottle of champagne.

A moan was wrenched from her throat as Dimitri's slender fingers delved beneath her skirt to stroke up the back of her legs. Lightly, he traced the top edge of her stockings, making her lower stomach clench with a sharp pang of need.

Oh, this was...astonishing.

Her eyes squeezed shut as she instinctively allowed her legs to part. She could feel the hard thrust of his arousal against her hip and hear his fractured breathing as he buried his face in the curve of her neck, but nothing mattered apart from those clever fingers.

Allowing her hands to tangle in the thick satin of his

hair, she unconsciously arched her back, seeking relief from the tension coiling deep inside.

There had to be something...

"Please, Dimitri," she choked, not certain what she needed, but sensing he would understand.

As if capable of reading her mind, Dimitri brushed his fingers upward, seeking her damp cleft. At the same moment, he shifted to cover her mouth in a kiss that smothered her shocked scream of exhilaration.

Oh, yes, he understood perfectly.

Forgetting the necessity of breathing, Emma became lost in Dimitri's touch. With obvious experience he stroked his fingers through her moist heat, discovering a small spot that seemed to be the center of her pleasure.

Relentlessly, he continued his intimate caresses, his kisses becoming more demanding as her body tightened with a tension that was near painful. Her hands gripped his hair, her hips lifting of their own volition to meet his steady strokes.

She was straining toward an elusive peak, shivering as if she were in the throes of a fever. And then, just when she was certain she could bear no more, the pressure exploded, shattering through her with stunning force.

Dazed by the unfamiliar sensations, Emma lay shuddering beneath Dimitri, distantly aware of the soothing words he whispered in her ear.

How often had she assured herself that she was missing nothing by keeping men at arm's length? That she was content to remain a virginal spinster?

Only now did she realize just how bleak and lonely the endless nights were destined to be.

She shivered, her hands shifting to press against his chest with a sense of urgency.

"Dimitri, get up."

Slowly, he pulled back, studying her flushed face with

a brooding gaze. His lips thinned as he easily read the panic threatening to overtake her. He leaned down to steal a frustrated kiss before he straightened and watched her awkwardly tug her gown back into place.

Emma was acutely aware of his unwavering attention as she fumbled with her buttons and shoved the thick tumble of hair out of her face. His dark, beautiful features were tightly composed, but it was his unyielding scrutiny that made her shift uneasily into the corner of the settee.

A tense silence filled the saloon, then with a sharp motion Dimitri was on his feet and heading toward the door.

"Remain here."

Did she truly have a choice?

Emma lowered her head into her hands, attempting to sort through her baffled emotions. She was embarrassed, of course. She had behaved as a wanton in Dimitri's arms and he had every right to consider her no better than a tart. But the regret she should have felt was decidedly absent.

Indeed, there was a traitorous part of her that savored the vivid memories of Dimitri's every touch and caress, as if they were treasures she intended to harbor deep in her heart.

The thought was more unnerving than being trapped alone in this elegant house with a lawless scoundrel who could make her melt with a smile.

With a shake of her head, Emma shoved away her bewilderment and wrapped herself in the cool composure she had forged and tempered by a life of hardship. She would have ample opportunity to dwell on her reaction to Dimitri when she returned to her home.

For all that mattered now was finding the means to follow her sister to England.

She was busy sifting through her limited possibilities

when Dimitri returned to the saloon, a large tray balanced in his hands.

Her brows lifted in surprise as he set his burden on the low table in front of the settee. Good heavens, did Dimitri's cook prepare such a massive dinner every night?

Her stomach rumbled as her gaze took in the roasted veal, the pickled cucumbers and the traditional pancakes stuffed with mushrooms and rice. To drink there was a bottle of *medovukha* that had been made with honey, and for dessert were plates of *syrniki,* fried fritters garnished with sour cream and jam.

"I trust you are hungry?" Dimitri demanded, settling next to her and filling two plates with the delectable meal. "Irina left us a small feast."

She frowned. "I cannot remain here for dinner."

"You have a pressing engagement?" he demanded, forcing the plate into her unwilling hands.

Her mouth went dry as she glanced at his absurdly handsome face. During his absence Dimitri had removed his jacket and waistcoat, revealing the fine lawn shirt that was thin enough to hint at the muscular chest. His raven hair was still ruffled from her frantic fingers and the shadow of whiskers darkened his jaw. With his eyes glimmering like liquid gold in the candlelight he had never appeared more dangerous. Or beautiful.

"Vanya will be expecting me."

"I sent word that her little chick would be returned safely to her nest."

Her teeth clenched at his arrogance, a heat staining her cheeks.

"And, of course, it did not occur to you that I might not wish to have all of St. Petersburg know that I am here alone with a man?" she asked tartly.

He regarded her with mocking disbelief. "You have

flouted every rule of decorum since leaving your home and now you are concerned for your reputation?"

"It is enough that I must be a source of amusement, I will not also be considered a—"

She bit off her words, belatedly noticing the flare of fury in Dimitri's eyes.

"A whore?" he silkily demanded.

Her gaze lowered to the plate still clutched in her hands, regretting the painful reminder of his mother. No matter how angry Dimitri might make her, she deeply respected the woman who had sacrificed her life for him.

"Please, let me go," she whispered.

He heaved an explosive sigh, ramming his fingers through his tangled hair.

"Emma, there is no need to agitate yourself," he said, his voice carefully controlled. "Vanya is quite proud to be regarded as the most unconventional woman in all of St. Petersburg. She would approve of you doing whatever necessary to find your sister. And as for my servants..." He shrugged. "They would walk through the pits of hell before they revealed my secrets. There will be no one to judge you or what we choose to do in the privacy of my home."

"I still would prefer—"

"Why would you believe you are a source of amusement?" he overrode her, studying her with an unnerving intensity.

"Surely you must realize that young, unwed females are expected to remain in their proper place, not intruding into men's business by opening a coaching inn?"

"And how do they propose a proper female support herself and her sister?"

She shrugged. "I could beg on the streets or—"

"Or?" he prompted.

"Or accept a discreet arrangement with the local baron."

A murderous anger tightened his elegant features, reminding Emma he was a ruthless bastard who was rumored to cut off the hands of his victims.

"Give me his name."

"His name?"

"The baron who insulted you."

She shivered at his frozen tone. "Why?"

"I will kill him."

Her heart missed a beat. Despite the pain that Baron Kostya had inflicted, she had no desire to be responsible for his death.

"Is that not rather hypocritical?" She deflected his question. "You seemed eager enough to take me to your bed."

"I will take you wherever you want, but only if our desire is mutual." His eyes narrowed. "I do not use sex as a price to assist a woman in need."

She believed him. She doubted there was a woman born who would not tumble into his arms if given the opportunity. Not that she would ever give him the satisfaction of knowing just how irresistible she found him.

His arrogance was quite outrageous enough.

"Do you intend to take me to Vanya's?"

"After we have finished." He cut a piece of the tender veal and pressed it between her lips. "You cannot allow Irina's exquisite creations to go to waste."

She nearly moaned as the flavor of the succulent meat exploded on her tongue. Now she understood why a man would risk a French prison to earn the services of Rurik's wife in his kitchen. She was a genius.

Of course, she did not believe for a moment that was why Dimitri had risked his neck.

For a criminal he possessed a loyalty and honor that was far superior to most supposed nobles.

With a sigh, she conceded defeat, her hunger overcoming her common sense.

"Were you never taught the meaning of the word *no?*" she asked between bites.

He set about eating his own dinner. "I can't seem to recall. Perhaps you should remind me."

She shook her head. "I do not believe you are so desperate for a dinner companion. What is it you truly want?"

The golden gaze flared down her body with a tangible heat. "Never doubt my desire for your companionship, Emma Linley-Kirov."

She shivered as a heady excitement pierced through her. Already she desired the feel of his skillful hands; his warm, seeking lips...

She abruptly set aside her nearly empty plate. "And you have no other motive?"

"We need to discuss what you overhead between my father and Tarvek."

It was, of course, precisely what she had expected. For reasons she did not comprehend, Dimitri was under the mistaken notion he was at liberty to interfere in her life.

"What is there to discuss?" She conjured a meaningless smile. "I revealed all that I heard. Do you believe I am attempting to conceal information from you?"

"I am more interested in what you intend to do."

"At the moment it appears I have little choice but to share your dinner."

He made an impatient sound, his fingers cupping her chin and forcing her to meet his searching gaze.

"What I most admire about you, *moya dusha,* is your refusal to pretend you are less than intelligent. Do not begin now."

The edge in his voice warned he would have the truth from her, no matter how long it might take. Aggravating ass. She defensively squared her shoulders.

"I told you from the beginning what I intend to do," she grudgingly admitted. "I came to St. Petersburg to find my sister and nothing has changed."

His jaw knotted as he struggled to control his temper. "Not even you can be foolish enough to believe you can travel alone to London?"

"Why should I not?" she countered. "I speak perfect English and I have distant relatives I can contact should the need arise. Besides, I am certain Vanya must possess some acquaintance who intends to travel to England or even to Europe within the next few weeks." She folded her hands in her lap, her spine stiff with determination. "I am willing to become a companion or maid or whatever they might need."

"Whatever they might need?" he rasped.

"Within reason."

His bronzed features were rigid as Dimitri studied her with an expression of furious disbelief.

"Emma, you are not stupid. You must realize how vulnerable you would be traveling with strangers?" His fingers tightened. "What will you do when a bored husband decides you will offer a convenient diversion during the long voyage? Or when one of the sailors captures you alone?"

She forced herself to meet the blazing golden gaze without flinching. Dimitri Tipova might be the unquestionable leader of the St. Petersburg underworld, but he had no authority over her.

"A woman is always at risk of being abused by men, no matter where she is or what her station."

He arrogantly peered down the length of his nose. "Not if she is protected as she should be."

"I have learned to protect myself, Dimitri."

"Only because you had no other choice." His fingers eased their grip to brush over her pale cheek. "Now I offer you one."

Her eyes narrowed. "What precisely do you offer?"

"Stay here with me."

"As your mistress?"

He gently outlined her unsteady lips. "Call it what you will."

"And my sister?"

Concentrating on his tender caresses, Dimitri was seemingly oblivious to the dangerous sparks smoldering in her eyes.

"I will send my men to follow the *Katherine Marie* and rescue your sister."

"Tell me, Dimitri, if I refuse to become your mistress will you allow my sister to become another tragic victim of your father?"

He muttered an angry curse, leaning down until they were nose to nose.

"I told you that I do not barter for sex, Emma. With or without you in my bed I intend to capture my father's ship and return it to Russia so I can expose those involved."

Her stomach fluttered as his breath brushed her lips. A distant part of her understood the danger of provoking this man. Another part, however, was hurt and angered by his refusal to accept her desperate need to take part in rescuing her sister.

"So you can have your revenge?" she accused.

"Of course."

"While my sister—"

"Will be safely escorted to her home along with any other victims," he muttered, his fingers tangling in her hair as his lips skimmed down the line of her throat.

Her heart leaped with a treacherous excitement. "Dimitri."

"Yes, *milaya?*"

"What are you doing?"

He nuzzled the pulse that hammered at the base of her

throat. "I do not particularly care for your implications that my only means of persuading you to share my bed is with blackmail."

Her toes curled in her sensible boots, her body humming with sizzling awareness. Desperately, she pressed her hands against the hard muscles of his chest. This explosive reaction to Dimitri Tipova was a danger she did not know how to battle.

"I will not be distracted."

"If you believe all I desire is to distract you, then you are even more naive than I suspected." He breathed against her sensitive skin.

"No, Dimitri." She arched away from the tormenting kisses. "It is past time that I return to Vanya's."

The golden eyes narrowed, a slash of color staining his high cheekbones.

"We have not finished our discussion."

"I did not realize we were sharing a discussion. It seemed very much as if you were issuing orders and expecting me to obey them."

His brooding gaze lowered to study her lips. "If you will recall, I also offered you an invitation."

Her pulse gave an eager leap at the memory of his words. Despite her innocence she recognized the touch of a master. Dimitri would be an exciting, skillful, wholly consuming lover. The sort of lover that women would sacrifice husbands, riches, social standing—and all they possess to claim.

He would also be forceful and overbearing and convinced he would always know what was best for those under his protection. He would demand that she give away her hard-earned independence and that was a sacrifice she was unable to make.

Not when he would soon enough lose interest and leave

her to salvage her tattered life. She had been abandoned too many times to risk yet another loss.

Before he could guess her intent, Emma was shoving him away so she could hastily rise to her feet.

"The same invitation that I have turned down from other gentlemen who promised to protect me…"

"Do not compare me to that bastard." He fiercely overrode her words, his eyes blazing with frustration.

"Then do not insult me by treating me as if I am a foolish chit who must depend upon a man to survive." Collecting her cloak, she headed for the door. As humiliating as it might be to admit, she could not trust herself when Dimitri was near. One touch and she was lost. "I am perfectly capable of caring for myself and my sister."

She had reached the door when Dimitri was blocking her path, his hands reaching to grip her shoulders.

"Where do you think you are going?"

"To Vanya's." Emma tilted back her head, forcing herself to meet his dark glower. "I will walk if necessary."

His fingers tightened, his temper at the breaking point.

"Do not be a fool. My carriage will return you to Vanya."

"Thank you."

He hauled her against his chest, swooping down to kiss her with a brazen hunger.

"I will allow you to flee in fear tonight, but make no mistake, *moya dusha,* you are destined to become my lover," he murmured against her swollen lips. "And not because you need my assistance, or because I have forced you to my bed."

Dizzy from the pleasure of his kiss, Emma struggled to think clearly.

"Then why?"

"Because I have tasted your passion. You desire me."

His hand skimmed down her back, deliberately pressing her against the proof of his arousal. "Desperately."

Her mouth went dry, her heart thundering in her chest. "Good Lord. Your conceit is astounding."

A humorless smile tugged at his lips. "No more astounding than your ridiculous attempts to pretend you do not ache to be in my arms."

It was the biting truth of his words that gave her the strength to wrench out of his grasp and scurry down the hallway. She might yearn to melt in his arms, but she was not a fool.

At least, not a complete fool.

"Goodbye, Dimitri Tipova," she muttered.

"À bientôt," he called, his voice mocking.

It wasn't until she was safely stowed in Dimitri's carriage that she realized he had warned he would see her again rather than saying goodbye.

THE ST. PETERSBURG DOCK was bustling with activity as Vanya's carriage headed toward the end of a wharf where a sleek wooden vessel swayed on the white-capped waves. Winter was swiftly approaching and soon it would be only the staunchest sailors who would brave the frigid, buffeting waters of the Baltic. In the meantime, there was a frantic pace as sailors, merchants, dockhands and passengers darted among the looming stacks of cargo waiting to be loaded on the various ships.

Emma was relieved to leave the majority of the crowd behind as they halted near the edge of the water. It was unsettling enough to board a ship and sail so far from home without adding the worry of battling through the crowds.

Licking her dry lips, she peered out the window at the waiting ship.

When she had returned to Vanya's home three nights before, she had revealed all she had learned of her sister, as well as Dimitri's suspicion that Anya was being taken to London. The older woman had been sympathetic, but surprisingly reluctant to assist Emma in finding a means of following Count Nevskaya's ship.

Then yesterday morning, she had come to Emma's private chambers and revealed she had booked passage upon a ship bound for London. Emma had been caught between overwhelming relief and a natural fear at charging into the unknown. For all her pretense of courage, she was not indifferent to the many dangers that lurked once she left the protection of Vanya and Herrick Gerhardt.

And oddly, there had been a strange sense of regret.

She tried to tell herself that it was merely a reaction to the thought of traveling so far from home, but she knew she was not being entirely honest. That bothersome ache in the center of her heart was directly connected to Dimitri Tipova.

Damn his aggravating soul.

Hastily thrusting aside the unnerving thought, Emma turned her head to meet Vanya's searching gaze, managing to conjure a smile of appreciation.

"I do not know how to thank you, Vanya," she said, reaching across to pat the older woman's hand. "You have been so extraordinarily generous. It will take time to repay you, but I swear—"

"Nonsense," Vanya firmly interrupted, seemingly embarrassed by Emma's excessive gratitude. "You are not the only one who cares what happens to those poor girls, Emma. And if I were a few years younger I would be traveling to England at your side. As it is, I know that you possess the courage and strength to do whatever necessary to rescue your sister and the others."

Emma straightened, unashamedly pleased by Vanya's words. At least someone appreciated her determination, she told herself, smoothing her hand down her thick woolen cloak.

"Thank you."

"But you must promise that you will take the greatest care and quickly return to me," she urged. "Herrick Gerhardt will have my head upon a platter when he discovers I assisted you in leaving the country."

Emma hid her tiny shiver of fear. She would be strong for Anya. She had no choice.

"I promise."

"And this is the letter of introduction I promised. I have written to Leonida, so I trust she will have ensured there will be someone awaiting you at the London docks, but in the event you find yourself in need, you can use this to call upon assistance from the Russian Embassy."

Emma unsteadily tucked the envelope into the pocket of her cloak. Seated across from her, Vanya appeared to be yet another useless lady of society with her teal merino gown and pale fur shawl wrapped about her shoulders. But she had proven to be a woman with intelligence and compassion and an ability to take command when necessary. Emma could only hope she did not disappoint the older woman.

"This is so much more than I ever expected." She bit her bottom lip as she struggled to hold back a ridiculous urge to weep. "I do not know what to say."

Vanya leaned forward to gently pat Emma's knee that was currently hidden beneath several yards of brown wool.

"You do not always have to depend on yourself, Emma," she implored. "Accepting help from others does not make you weak."

Emma frowned, puzzled by the woman's peculiar manner. "I am accustomed to taking care of myself."

"As was I, but I have discovered that my independence was not nearly so threatened as I feared it would be when I opened my heart to another." She appeared as if she desired to say more, but as they both caught sight of the large man attired in the rough clothing of a common sailor, she instead settled back in the leather seat. "I believe this young man is here to assist with your bags and to escort you to the ship."

Emma sucked in a deep breath, refusing to acknowledge the flutters of fear in the pit of her stomach.

"I will never forget what you have done for me."

"Hmm." Vanya shook her head. "I am not entirely certain that is a good thing."

"Vanya?"

"Just know that I have tried to do what I think best for you."

"Of course, I know. I could not have asked for a greater friend."

The door to the carriage was pulled open by Vanya's driver and without giving herself time to hesitate, she allowed herself to be assisted into the chill morning breeze.

"Be brave, *mon enfant*," Vanya called softly.

CHAPTER NINE

DIMITRI IGNORED THE shifting deck beneath his feet as he poured over the charts his first mate had spread across the bench.

It was not his first journey aboard his sleek Baltimore clipper. He occasionally felt the need to escape from the grinding demands of his role as Beggar Czar. There were few things more exhilarating than skimming across the water, surrounded by silence, and knowing that his duties were being left far behind.

Not that he had made such a large investment for the rare days of freedom. He was a businessman first and foremost. The ship had been built in the Americas to be the fastest on the waters and his crew had been hired in London from among the finest of all English seamen. As a result, he had made a small fortune in transporting various diplomats, noblemen, and even a few wealthy merchants who preferred to keep their travels confidential.

Which made it perfect for his current plans.

A grim smile curved his lips at the sound of approaching footsteps, and turning his head he waited for the large sailor with a thatch of black hair and weathered features to halt in front of him.

"Is our passenger aboard?" he demanded.

Andrew Simmons scowled, his hands shoved into the pockets of his wool coat.

"Safely stowed in her cabin as you ordered."

Dimitri narrowed his gaze. "You have no need to remind

me that you disapprove of having a female aboard the ship."

"Every sailor knows a wench is bad luck."

Although several stones lighter than the hulking sailor, Dimitri stepped forward, his hand deliberately caressing the handle of his dagger he had tucked into the waistband of his breeches.

"Andrew, allow me to offer a warning that you will share with the rest of the crew," he said with a lethal softness.

The man blanched. "Aye, sir?"

"Emma Linley-Kirov is an honored guest on this ship and if I discover a member of my crew has offered her anything less than utter respect they will be tossed overboard and left for the fish to enjoy. Do you comprehend?"

Sweat glistened on Andrew's forehead despite the noticeable chill in the air.

"Aye."

"Good. It would be unfortunate if there were any misunderstandings."

"There will be no misunderstandings."

"Then I believe we are ready to cast off."

"At once."

Stumbling over his own feet in his haste to obey Dimitri's command, Andrew headed toward the bow of the ship. Dimitri watched his departure as he regained command of his temper.

He had not been boasting. He would personally punish any man who dared to offer Emma an insult.

Refusing to consider why he still itched to pummel the large sailor, Dimitri at last turned on his heel and made his way to the lower cabins. With each step his annoyance transformed into a burgeoning sense of anticipation.

The past three days had been sheer hell. His empire might be made of thieves and scoundrels, but that did not make his responsibilities any less demanding. He had to ensure all his various businesses were operating smoothly before leaving the country. And of course, there had been the constant concern that Emma might foolishly attempt to slip away before he had completed his plans. The woman was as unpredictable as she was stubborn.

Most disturbing of all, however, had been the sleepless nights he had paced the floor of his bedchamber, his body on fire with the need to have Emma in his arms.

His pace quickened as he pushed open the door to his private cabin and stripped off his heavy coat, tossing it on the wide bunk. The room was built along the same sleek lines as the ship with table and chairs beneath the port hole and a chest of drawers attached to the paneled wall. He paused long enough to straighten his dove-gray jacket before heading toward the door that opened into the connecting cabin.

For a moment he stood in the doorway, his gaze unerringly finding Emma's slender body poised in front of the port hole as she watched St. Petersburg disappear into the mist. He would be able to sense her presence if he were blind.

The cabin was similar in design to his own, although constructed on a smaller scale as befitted a servant. Not that it mattered. Emma's place was at his side. And in his bed. And that was exactly where she was headed.

He stepped forward, his blood heating despite the ugly brown gown that offended his senses. He knew precisely what was hidden beneath the woolen layers.

"Surely you cannot be missing your home so soon?" he asked.

He heard Emma's gasp of horror as she spun around to regard him with an expression of stark disbelief.

"You."

Strolling forward, he flicked a finger over her pale cheek. "Yes, it is I."

Her lips parted, but it took a moment before she could speak.

"What are you doing here?" she at last managed.

"I did warn you that I intended to hunt down the *Katherine Marie*."

"No, you said you would send one of your servants in search of the ship."

His fingers shifted to tug the pins from her hair, breathing deeply of her warm scent as the honey curls tumbled about her shoulders. It did not matter if she were dressed in rags—she was the most beautiful woman he had ever seen.

"Ah, well, that was when I had hopes of a warm, delectable female to keep me distracted."

He felt her tremble, but her hazel eyes flashed with a predictable fury.

"And you wish me to believe that it was mere coincidence that you happened to choose the same ship as I did?"

"It is not so difficult to comprehend." He threaded his fingers through her hair, his body swaying in tempo with hers as the ship left the harbor and headed into open water. "This is the only ship currently bound for England that accepts passengers."

"And the cabin that connects to mine was the only one available?"

His lips twitched. "That is rather more difficult to explain."

"Yes, I can imagine it would be." She narrowed her eyes. "Not that it truly matters."

"No?"

"I will simply request that the captain offer me a different cabin."

"You believe there are an endless number of rooms aboard such a small vessel?" he taunted.

A dull flush stained her cheeks. "Of course not, but there must be one passenger who will be willing to exchange cabins."

He smiled wryly at her naiveté. "I would not be so certain."

"Your arrogance is truly astonishing, Dimitri Tipova," she snapped, her hands pressing against his chest. "You might be in command of St. Petersburg, but you have no authority aboard this ship."

He wrapped an arm around her waist and tugged her close, swallowing a groan as he accepted just how perfectly she fit against him.

"You should learn never to underestimate me, *moya dusha*."

She stiffened, a frown marring her brow. "And what is that supposed to mean?"

"It means that any pleas to the captain will fall on deaf ears."

"You cannot be that certain, unless…"

"Unless, what?" he softly prompted.

"Unless you have already bribed him?"

"There were no bribes, but considering the fact that I do pay his wages I should hope his loyalty would be to me." His gaze slowly roamed over her upturned face. "Of course, he has always possessed a weakness for beautiful women so perhaps we should not put him in such an uncomfortable position."

In the distance the sound of the rough shouts and boots pounding against the deck echoed through the air, but within the narrow cabin Dimitri was aware of nothing beyond the play of emotions that rippled across Emma's face.

"You pay his wages?"

"I pay the wages of the entire crew."

She licked her lips. "Why would you do that?"

"You know why, Emma."

The color leeched from her cheeks as she slowly began to realize she was completely and utterly in his power.

"This is your ship."

There was an uncomfortable tug on his heart as he gazed down at her pale, vulnerable face and the wide hazel eyes that were dark with apprehension. His jaw clenched with regret. Dammit, did she fear him? And why did the thought trouble him? Surely the stubborn female needed to be taught the dangers of her reckless behavior?

He shoved aside his momentary weakness and hardened his determination.

"It is."

She shook her head. "This is madness."

"My father is not the only man capable of owning a private fleet, although mine is considerably larger and far superior in design." A grim smile curved his lips. "With any luck at all we should reach London before the *Katherine Marie* docks."

"If you expect me to be impressed, then you are far off the mark."

Dimitri swallowed a sigh at her tart tone. How many women had fallen to their knees and tearfully praised him for his assistance? How many had offered whatever he desired in payment of his services?

"I am becoming resigned to your lack of appreciation for my stunning achievements," he dryly admitted, "but you could occasionally offer some well-deserved words of gratitude."

"Gratitude?" She jerked as if he had slapped her. "For what? For deceiving me? For luring me onto this ship under false pretenses?" There was a sharp pause, her hazel eyes darkening with pain. "Oh, my God."

"Now what?"

"Vanya knew this was your ship." She glared at him as

if he were responsible for the older woman's decision to conceal the truth from her. And...he was. He had insisted that no one know that he was in pursuit of his father's boat. Or that Emma was traveling with him. He would not risk alerting Count Nevskaya that he was in danger of having his sins revealed. "She was a part of your plot. How could she betray my trust? I thought she was my friend."

Gathering her hair in his fist, he tugged the satin strands until her head tilted back, revealing the flashing hazel eyes and the lush temptation of her lips.

"It is because she is your friend that she is determined to protect you," he growled.

He was tired of battling this woman. He wanted her in his bed. He wanted her beneath him as he parted her legs and sank into her feminine heat with a deep, hungry pace that would tumble them both into paradise.

As if sensing the sudden tension in the air, Emma sucked in an unsteady breath, a visible pulse fluttering at the base of her throat.

"By putting me at the mercy of a ruthless criminal?"

"At my mercy, eh?" Unable to resist temptation, Dimitri leaned down to touch his lips to that revealing pulse. "Mmm. Now that is a delicious notion."

Her hands pressed against his chest. "Dimitri."

"Yes, *milaya?*"

"I demand that you return this ship to St. Petersburg at once."

He nipped her sensitive skin, a smile curving his lips as she trembled in pleasure.

"Do you truly believe you are in a position to demand anything?"

"I mean it, Dimitri. Return me to St. Petersburg or—"

"Or what?" he challenged. "You will swim back to Russia?"

She arched her back, clearly attempting to avoid his

seeking lips. "Do not mock me. I will never forgive Vanya."

Pulling back, he studied her sulky expression, his fingers covertly unfastening the buttons that ran the length of her spine. He needed to feel the warm satin of her skin.

"Vanya is considerably older and far more experienced than you. Can you not accept she made a choice she thought best?" he coaxed. "And that she simply desired to protect you?"

"I can protect myself," she muttered.

His teeth clenched at her stubborn refusal to admit she needed him. Why did she have to be so damnably independent?

"Truly?" he rasped, easing the heavy gown down her body. "You have just admitted you are at the mercy of a ruthless scoundrel. And you have no one to blame but yourself."

Intent on their argument, Emma appeared unaware of his skillful disrobement, not even when the gown was pooled around her feet.

"I trusted Vanya," she hissed.

"You have relied upon blind luck since arriving in St. Petersburg." His gaze searing over her slender body. "And if not for the kindness of Herrick Gerhardt and Vanya you most likely would be a captive with your sister upon my father's ship or already sold to a brothel."

"And instead I am trapped with you."

Trapped? Could she possibly be more insulting?

He would prove that for all her spitting fire, she was eager to be *trapped* with him. Pressing her back against his body, he yanked at the ribbons that held up her linen shift.

"I could easily have ensured that you remained in St. Petersburg or were even returned to your tiny village," he rasped.

He heard her breath catch as his fingers skimmed the bare skin of her shoulders, her hands digging into his chest and a beautiful color returning to her cheeks.

"I was brought to this ship under false pretenses," she accused.

"Do you wish to rescue your sister or not?"

"Of course I do."

"Then put aside your ridiculous pride and accept that you are far more likely to bring Anya safely home with my assistance."

"It is not pride."

"No?"

Her lips tightened at his mocking tone. "I do not appreciate being manipulated."

And Dimitri did not appreciate desiring this woman with a consuming hunger that would not leave him in peace. If he had any sense he would have left Emma Linley-Kirov in St. Petersburg and concentrated on capturing the *Katherine Marie* so he could at last destroy his father.

Muttering a curse beneath his breath, he scooped her off her feet and headed toward the connecting door.

"It would not be necessary if you would be reasonable."

She squirmed in his arms, her eyes wide with shock. "What are you doing?"

"Taking you to our cabin."

"I have my own cabin."

He glared down at the face that had haunted his nights and intruded into his thoughts at the most inconvenient moments. He had not left her in St. Petersburg because he was unwilling to be parted from her. Annoying, but true.

"You belong with me."

With a frown, she smacked her hand against his chest. "You cannot simply decide I belong to you, Dimitri Tipova.

I am a person, not a bit of property you can collect and toss aside when you weary of me."

"How the hell am I supposed to weary of you?" He spread her across the narrow bed, his hands oddly awkward as he yanked off his jacket and waistcoat. His cravat and linen shirt followed. "You plague me no matter how I attempt to rid you from my mind."

She brushed aside the thick honey curls that tumbled across her face, her eyes widening with a wary excitement as he perched on the edge of the mattress and tugged off his boots.

"And you blame me?"

Shifting, Dimitri ran a hand over her slender foot and up the back of her calf, inching the thin shift upward and exposing the slender leg covered in a white silk stocking. Her undergarments were predictably prim, but ridiculously the sight of them made his gut clench with a savage lust.

He had tasted the delights of the most skilled courtesans throughout Russia and Europe, but while they had been delightful diversions, they had never made him so desperate to have them in his arms that he was willing to kidnap them.

"Of course I blame you," hc husked, his fingers reaching the silken skin of her thigh at the top of her stocking. He groaned, his arousal heavy with a painful need.

Her eyes darkened with an awareness that slammed into him with potent force.

"For what?"

Beyond reasonable thought, Dimitri reached for her shift, ripping it from bodice to hem with one easy motion. She muttered something beneath her breath, but Dimitri barely noticed. Instead, he was lost in the beauty of her slender, perfect body.

The air was squeezed from his lungs as his gaze swept over her, the pink-tipped mounds of her breasts, the tiny span of her waist, and the sweet honey curls that hid the source of her most intimate pleasure.

"For daring to challenge me," he managed to rasp.

"I have done nothing but attempt to rescue my sister," she breathed, her tone distracted as Dimitri slowly lowered himself on the bed beside her. "You are the one who continues to interfere despite my pleas to be left alone."

He framed her face in his hands, his lips skimming over her flushed face.

"And that is what you desire? To be left alone?"

"Yes."

He chuckled as her hands instinctively smoothed over his bare chest, her body arching toward him in unmistakable invitation.

"I do not believe you."

"I…" Her words broke off with a shuddering sigh as his mouth traveled down the curve of her throat and feathered light kisses ever lower. "Oh, Lord."

His tongue circled the straining bud of her nipple. "Tell me again what you desire."

She cried out, her fingers shoving into his hair as she shifted restlessly beneath him.

"Dimitri."

"Do you wish me to halt?"

"No. God, no."

Raw relief surged through his body. He might very well have tossed himself overboard if she'd denied him.

With a driven groan, he suckled her nipple, peeling away what remained of her shift. She tasted of soap and sweet innocence and Dimitri cursed as he battled to remove the remainder of his clothing, his hands shaking. He was infamous throughout St. Petersburg as a skilled, talented lover willing to devote hours to a woman's pleasure.

At last rid of his clothing, he settled on the mattress and smoothed his hands down Emma's back, easing her toward his aching body. She briefly tensed, no doubt unnerved by the feel of his erection pressed against her lower stomach, but with a soft moan of capitulation she speared her fingers through his hair and urged his mouth toward the tight buds of her breasts.

Fiercely pleased to comply with her silent demand, Dimitri tugged her nipple between his lips, using his teeth and tongue until she was squirming with pleasure against him. His hands slid over the curve of her buttock and down the back of her thigh. With a small tug he had her leg draped over his hip, allowing his cock to press against her damp heat.

Raw lust slammed into him at the sensation of her warm, silken skin brushing against him, stealing his breath and making him quiver. Restlessly, he turned his attention to her other breast.

"Sweet Emma," he groaned, "I need you."

"Please, Dimitri."

He chuckled as his hand softly brushed the back of her leg, edging slowly upward.

"Trust me."

"Never," she breathed, but she readily cried out in pleasure as his fingers slid between her legs.

Dimitri clenched his teeth, staggered by his need to be inside this woman. She was so soft, so delicate, so utterly innocent...

Innocent.

His gut twisted. What he knew of virgins could fit in a thimble, but he did have enough wits left to realize he would have to take care not to hurt her.

Stroking a finger through her tender flesh, he found her tiny nub, teasing it softly while he shifted to capture her lips in a deep, demanding kiss.

Emma arched against him, her hands running a fitful

path down his back. She might be innocent, but her body was eager to be tutored.

Almost as eager as he was to tutor her.

With a smooth motion he rolled Emma onto her back, settling between her parted legs and continuing his persistent caresses. He heard her choked moan as he released her lips to trail a path of fevered kisses down her throat.

He cursed, trembling with the effort to not simply plunge into her and ease his craving. What had this woman done to him? His heart was pounding, his breath coming in sharp rasps and his cock so hard he feared he might come just trying to breech her maidenhead.

Pulling back, he studied her face surrounded by the spill of honey curls. The pale, creamy skin. The fan of lush lashes that lay against her flushed cheeks. The rose-tinted lips parted in invitation.

So beautiful, he thought, a flare of savage possession gripping his heart as he positioned himself at her entrance and with a slow, steady thrust sank into her heat. For a brief moment, Emma tensed and Dimitri forced himself to pause as her body adjusted to his invasion. Continuing to fondle her, he waited for her muscles to ease and her fingers to clutch impatiently at his shoulders before he at last pushed past her barrier.

His breath hissed through teeth at the exquisite sensations that jolted through his body. She was glorious. An enticing, splendid woman who had denied her own needs for far too long.

"Emma," he husked, his hips pulling gently back before sinking back into her welcoming body. "My sweet Emma."

"Yes," she sobbed, her nails raking down his back.

The tiny shock of pain was like a spark to his very short

fuse. With a groan of surrender he lost himself in the pagan tempo that was as ancient and powerful as the sea churning beneath them.

CHAPTER TEN

EMMA SHIVERED AS Dimitri's ship slid silently through the eastern entrance basin into the Thames River.

It was a gray afternoon with a sharp breeze, but the docks were overflowing with ships vying to unload their cargo at the nearby warehouses. Tea, silk, fruit and tobacco was piled on the quays while spice merchants and pepper grinders plied their trade among the vast crowd of sailors, dockhands and passengers. It all combined to create an image of colorful chaos.

At any other moment she would have been thrilled with the sights spread before her.

How often had she lain awake at night dreaming of traveling to distant lands? Or begged her father to read her stories beside the fireplace so she could imagine being far away from their tiny village?

Now, however, she couldn't summon the proper appreciation for the busy docks, or the vast city that sprawled in the distance.

Not when her sister might be near.

Clutching the railing of the bow she leaned forward, indifferent to the breeze that tugged at her heavy wool cloak and the gray scarf she had wrapped around her head.

Too often over the past days she had allowed herself to forget the reason for her journey to England. Dimitri's fault, of course. It was not enough that he had spent their long nights seducing her with his wicked kisses and experienced touch, but he had also consumed her days, charming her with stories of his reckless youth that revealed far more of his true self than he realized.

He was loyal and protective and generous to those he had taken beneath his wing. He was also quick to guard his heart and to keep others at a distance. He would always need to be in command of a relationship, ensuring that no one was allowed to step beyond the boundaries he set.

Including her.

As if her thoughts had conjured him into being, Dimitri appeared at her side, a scowl marring his handsome face as he studied her.

"The air is brisk," he said. "You should return to the cabin."

Emma swallowed a rueful sigh, her heart fluttering with an unbearable excitement as he leaned against the railing. It was more than the elegant beauty of his bronzed face and astonishing gold eyes. Or the chiseled perfection of his male body beneath the tailored jade jacket and buff breeches.

It was the ruthless sensuality and sheer male power he carried about him with such ease.

Desperately, she fought to hide her ready response to his presence behind a cool smile. She could not make herself regret the nights she had spent in Dimitri's arms. Her destiny might be to live as a lonely spinster in a tiny Russian village, but she would have memories that would keep her warm for years to come.

Still, she could not allow the madness to continue.

Not only did she need to concentrate on discovering her sister, but she would not become a source of amused gossip once they were settled in London. It was one thing to be known as Dimitri's lover by his trusted servants, and quite another to have strangers speculating at her uncharacteristic behavior.

"And miss my first glimpse of London?" she demanded. "Do not be silly."

His scowl deepened at the cool edge in her voice. "The docks are hardly worth the risk of consumption. They are as foul and rat-infested as any other dock to be found in the world."

"Not all of us are jaded travelers who are incapable of appreciating the novelty of arriving in a city I never dreamed I would one day visit." She shrugged, ignoring the fact that she was shivering beneath her cloak. "Besides, it is no colder than it was in St. Petersburg."

With a sound of impatience, he grasped her arms and turned her to meet his searching gaze.

"You have no interest in London. You are hoping that your sister will be standing upon the docks, awaiting you to rescue her."

Her lips thinned with annoyance. It was bothersome that he could read her so easily.

"Whatever your opinion of my intellect, I am not entirely stupid," she snapped. "But neither am I willing to be hidden away when Anya has need of me."

His hands skimmed up her arms with an intimate gesture of possession.

"I will soon know if the *Katherine Marie* has recently docked. Until then I prefer no one know we have arrived in London."

With an effort, Emma shrugged his hands away and stepped back. How could she think clearly when she was distracted by the temptation of his touch?

"There is no one who could possibly recognize me."

His jaw tightened, but thankfully he contented himself with folding his arms over his chest and regarding her with a narrow gaze.

"Do not be so certain. I, better than most, know that there are eyes in the most unlikely places."

Emma didn't bother arguing. Of course Dimitri would know where danger might be skulking. It was one benefit of being a talented criminal.

"Do you intend to remain on the ship until we find the *Katherine Marie?*" she asked instead.

"No. I have requested the assistance of an acquaintance. He will be awaiting us once night falls."

She rolled her eyes at his vague explanation. "Is there any place you do not have acquaintances to offer you assistance?"

"My reach extends far beyond Russia." His brooding gaze swept down her slender form. "It is something you might wish to keep in mind."

A cold chill of premonition shivered down her spine. "Is that a threat?"

"I am not stupid either, Emma. No matter how many warnings I might offer, you will happily rush into danger if you believe it will help your sister. I intend to make certain you are not allowed to tumble into disaster."

The ship swayed as a larger vessel surged past them, sending Emma careening into Dimitri's waiting arms. For a moment she was lost in the heat and scent of the man who had taught her the meaning of ecstasy. Her mind might have decided that Dimitri was no longer her lover, but her body was eager to respond to the feel of his hard muscles pressed tight against her.

She sucked in a shocked breath as she hastily pushed away from his clinging hold. What was the matter with her? Was she truly so weak?

Grasping the rail to keep her balance, Emma glared at the man who was now smiling in smug satisfaction.

"On how many occasions must I remind you that you are not my keeper?" she said tartly. "If I wish to tumble into disaster then it is none of your concern."

He reached to cup her cheek in his hand, the golden eyes shimmering with a sinful temptation.

"As your lover it is my right to protect you. Even from your own stubborn nature."

"Dimitri, I am not, nor will I ever be a helpless female who must depend upon you to decide what is best. And you are not my lover."

"No?"

"No."

His lips twitched. "Then I imagined the nights you spent in my arms? And the taste of your sweet lips? And your soft moans when I enter you—"

Without thought she reached up to cover his mouth with her hand, her cheeks hot with embarrassment.

"Shh." Her gaze darted about to ensure the crew were scurrying about their duties. "Someone might hear you."

He stepped closer, his head lowering to whisper directly into her ear.

"Do not ever deny I am your lover."

She shivered, clenching her hands against the urge to tug the leather cord that held his hair in a tidy queue and run her fingers through the satin darkness.

"Dimitri, please," she husked. "What happened between us is a madness that must end."

His thumb gently caressed the chilled skin of her cheek. "It is too late for regrets."

"I do not speak of regret, merely a return to sanity." It took more effort than she cared to admit to knock his hand away. "I have traveled to England to find my sister, not to indulge in a meaningless affair."

His beautiful features hardened. "I assume you are deliberately attempting to stir my anger?"

She squared her shoulders, refusing to be browbeaten. "Why would you be angered? I am not the first woman who you have bedded, nor will I be the last. I should think you would be relieved that I am not so absurd as to attempt and cling to you."

"Instead you claim me to be meaningless and toss me from your bed?" His voice was as cold as the winter wind.

A treacherous part of her wanted to believe he was hurt by her rejection. Perhaps even distressed at the knowledge he would never again share her bed. But Emma was nothing if not sensible.

Dimitri had no doubt found it amusing to tutor an aging spinster in the arts of love to pass the tedious voyage. What else did he have to keep him occupied? His passionate seduction, however, had included a great deal of skill with a notable lack of emotion.

Which meant the only wound he suffered was to his pride.

"No doubt your acquaintances in England include a woman willing to take my place," she said, a matching chill in her tone.

His brows snapped together as if he were insulted by her words, but before he could speak one of the crew shouted a warning and they both turned to catch sight of the small boat being rowed in their direction.

"Emma, go below," Dimitri commanded. Then, as she stubbornly remained at the railing, he turned to grasp her hands in his. "Please, *moya dusha*."

She held his unwavering gaze for a long moment, frustrated by his continual attempts to keep her sheltered. But even as she told herself she was not going to be dismissed as if she were a mindless child, she caught sight of Dimitri's nod toward his gathering crew.

He would have the rowboat turned aside before he allowed the strangers to board the boat with her on the deck.

With a glare that warned of dire retribution, Emma spun

on her heel and marched toward the stairs that led to the cabins below.

It was not that she did not appreciate Dimitri's concern. In truth, it had been so long since anyone had considered the possibility she might need protection that she could not deny the treacherous warmth that filled her heart.

Thankfully she was wise enough to understand the danger of undermining her hard-won independence. Dimitri was a passing presence in her life. Once she had rescued Anya they would return to Yabinsk and she would once again be alone to shoulder her responsibilities.

Besides, she instinctively prickled at the suspicion Dimitri desired to transform her into a helpless female that depended utterly on him. She could never become such a creature.

Deliberately she moved through the cabin she had shared with Dimitri and into the connected chamber. She would not allow herself to be distracted by memories of being seated before the built-in dresser as Dimitri brushed her hair, or her giggling pleasure as he had slowly and thoroughly bathed her in the copper tub, or the strength of his arms as he had carried her to the narrow bed.

Pacing the floor, Emma forced her thoughts to Anya. *Dear Lord, please let her be near,* she silently prayed. *And let her be unharmed.*

A surprisingly short period of time passed before she heard the sound of Dimitri's approaching footsteps. Turning, she watched as he entered the cramped space, his dark features unreadable.

"Has something happened?" she demanded.

"The *Katherine Marie* docked this morning."

She frowned. Dimitri had been confident they could outrun his father's bulkier ship, but only days out of port they had been hit by a storm that had thrown them off course and damaged the mast. Obviously, the delays had meant they'd arrived later than Dimitri had planned, but Emma could think of nothing beyond her vast relief that the *Katherine Marie* had made it safely to harbor, and that she hadn't been mistaken about the destination.

"Then my sister is here," she breathed.

"It would seem so."

"Thank God." She frowned at the frustration that shimmered in his golden eyes. "What is wrong?"

"Huntley placed servants on the docks to keep watch, but my father's crew managed to unload their cargo and slip past the guards unnoticed. She could be anywhere."

Her brief surge of hope began to fade as she realized the daunting task of searching London for a handful of girls. It could take days, even weeks. Always assuming they had not spirited Anya out of the city.

"Surely they cannot have gone far?"

As if sensing her growing distress, he moved forward to take her hands in a firm grip.

"We will find Anya," he murmured, his warm touch and low voice enough to soothe her fears.

Emma was unnerved by the realization of how deeply he affected her. Almost as if...no. She would not even think it. Dimitri Tipova had proven he could seduce her body, she damned well would not allow him to seduce her heart.

With an effort, she tilted her chin and met his gaze squarely.

"You said Huntley. Do you mean the duke?"

"Yes." He lifted his brows. "Are you acquainted?"

She grimaced. Did he truly believe a spinster from a tiny Russian village could be acquainted with a duke? Even with her English mother such a thought was absurd.

"Of course not, but Vanya said she had sent a message to the Duchess of Huntley and that she would provide me assistance." A pang of regret twisted her heart. "I suppose that was yet another deception."

"Quite likely she wrote to the duchess. And no doubt Leonida is prepared to offer you whatever assistance you desire without informing her husband of her promise." His lips curved in a mysterious smile. "She is as headstrong and unmanageable as you."

"How do you know an English duke?"

"I performed a small service for the duchess a few weeks ago."

Emma stiffened, an odd tightness squeezing her chest. There was husky amusement in his voice when he spoke of the duchess. As if he were intimately acquainted with her.

"What sort of service?"

He shrugged. "I fear it was a private matter that I am unable to discuss."

Without thought she yanked her hands from his grip, glaring into his handsome face.

"I see."

He appeared momentarily startled by her reaction, then his smile slowly widened.

"Ah. Are you jealous, Emma Linley-Kirov?"

She sniffed. He would, of course, be arrogant enough to presume she was jealous rather than...what? Furious? Outraged? Worried. Yes, of course.

"I merely am concerned that she will be too distracted to be of service," she bit out.

With a chuckle, he leaned down to brush his mouth over her lips. "Pack your belongings. I dare not wait until sunset to begin our search."

More in an effort to hide her flushed cheeks than to obey his husky command, Emma darted past him into the main cabin.

"How will you begin?" she asked, pulling her satchel from beneath the bed and filling it with her handful of possessions.

He leaned his shoulder against the paneled wall, watching her jerky movements with a rueful expression. Almost as if he regretted the end of their voyage.

She hastily shook off the dangerous thought.

"I will have my servants visit the local pubs."

She straightened in surprise. "You think my sister might be so near?"

"No, but the crew of the *Katherine Marie* will be eager to ease their thirst, as well as their various hungers, after such a voyage," he explained. "I hope they will be willing to reveal where the cargo was taken with proper incentive."

She nodded, wryly acknowledging it was a clever notion.

"And what of you?"

"Me?"

"If I have learned nothing else of you, Dimitri, it is that you are never without a plan to take advantage of whatever situation comes your way."

Without warning the golden eyes darkened and he prowled forward to wrap her in his arms.

"I would hope you have learned far more of me than my penchant for making plans," he growled softly.

She shivered in ready awareness. But with surprising resolution she pressed her hands against his chest in unmistakable denial.

"I know you detest losing, Dimitri, but I am not a challenge to be conquered."

His eyes smoldered at her direct challenge. "No, you are a treasure. One that I have claimed as my own." His gaze skimmed down to her slender body. "And I guard my treasure with great care."

Wiggling from his arms, she returned to her packing, pretending she did not notice his searing gaze.

"What do you intend to do once we are in London?"

There was a tense silence before Dimitri heaved a sigh of pure irritation.

"I will request that Huntley introduce me to society."

She dropped the stockings she was folding into a neat square. "I beg your pardon?"

He reached to pluck the silk stocking from the bed, absently sliding it through his slender fingers.

"It would be impossible to search all of London for your sister. I must attempt to bring her to us."

"And you intend to do that by prancing through society?" she accused.

"What I *intend* is to make it known that I am a gentleman of wealth who is in England for a short visit and willing to pay an extravagant sum to sate my particular lust for young females."

She paused to consider his words. "You think the men who are holding Anya captive will approach you?"

"If I offer the proper temptation."

"But it could be days before they approach you."

He nodded, his rigid expression easing with regret. "I am sorry, Emma, we must be patient."

Her jaw clenched. How could he say such a thing? She had been patient for weeks.

She wanted to rant and rage and curse in frustration at her inability to rescue her sister.

"And what of me?" she asked instead.

"You will be my wife."

"Wife?" Her heart came to a sharp, painful halt. "Have you taken leave of your senses?"

He shrugged. "I assumed you would wish to be included in the search."

"I do, but…" She stopped, licking her suddenly dry lips.

"Yes?"

"I could be a maid," she desperately offered. "In fact, it would be far easier if I could travel about unnoticed."

An unexpected anger flared over his bronzed features, and, tossing aside her stocking, he reached to frame her face in his hands.

"You could never be unnoticed," he rasped. "And listen well, Emma, you will not be traveling anywhere without me."

"It is not your decision to make."

"Do not be a fool, there will be far more doors opened to the wife of a wealthy Russian aristocrat than a foreign maid."

It was true. Certainly she could move about the seedier parts of London as a servant, but the elegant drawing rooms where the gentlemen who bought and sold young girls traveled would be closed to her. The knowledge, however, did nothing to ease the fluttering alarm at playing the role of Dimitri's wife.

"Even if I agreed to such a ridiculous notion, no one would believe I am a refined lady," she argued.

"There is no need for modesty. Whatever your father's occupation, it is obvious you were well educated and tutored in the manners of society." His thumb absently outlined the unsteady curve of her lower lip. "With the proper clothing there would be no one to question your disguise."

"Unfortunately I do not possess your acting skills."

"Very well. You can remain upon the ship if you prefer." His voice thickened with a wicked promise. "I vow to visit each night to keep the chill away."

She grasped the lapels of his jacket as her knees threatened to buckle.

"Absolutely not."

He smiled with insolent satisfaction. "Then let us be on our way, Huntley is waiting for us."

CHAPTER ELEVEN

IN THE TRADITION OF MOST gambling halls, the Bacchus Club was a combination of opulence and depravity.

Tucked in a tiny cul-de-sac near Brook Street, the three-storied brick building was hidden behind a high fence guarded by two burly footmen. Inside, the tiny foyer led to a sweep of marble steps opening to a large, cavernous hall that was most notable for the floor-to-ceiling mirrors that reflected the light of the overhead chandeliers with dazzling zeal. A dozen small tables were scattered across the Italian marble floor, most of them already crowded with gentlemen who possessed the tense, hunted expressions that Dimitri easily recognized.

Addicts.

He had taught his servants to turn away such men. They inevitably caused trouble for his establishments, not to mention their poor families.

The Bacchus Club, on the other hand, was renowned for the debauchery of its clientele. It readily catered whatever sin might be desired.

He hid his grimace as the small steward scurried toward them. Beneath the scent of roast beef and cigar smoke was the unmistakable stench of desperation.

"Your Grace, such an honor," the man said with a deep bow. "Can I offer you a drink?"

At Dimitri's side, Stefan, the Duke of Huntley, peered about his surroundings in barely concealed disgust, seemingly unaware of the stir he was creating by his entrance.

Of course, Huntley had been creating a stir since leaving the cradle.

It was obscenely unfair that a gentleman who was born into wealth and power should also have been blessed with a tall, magnificent form and the finely chiseled features of his Russian-born mother. Combined with his dark hair and shocking blue eyes, he was a gentleman who commanded attention wherever he went.

Dimitri had become acquainted with the reclusive duke when the nobleman had been chasing his stubborn wife, Leonida, across Russia. It had only been with Dimitri's assistance that they had captured the villain who had been attempting to blackmail Leonida's mother.

"Cognac," the duke murmured.

"At once." The steward waved a hovering waiter forward and whispered in his ear before returning his avid attention to Stefan. Dimitri could appreciate the poor man's excitement. Stefan made no secret of his distaste for London society as well as the numerous gentlemen's clubs that had vied for his membership. If the Bacchus Club could claim him as a patron it would offer them an image of respectability that had been sadly lacking with their current members. "You will discover we offer whatever distraction that might strike your fancy, Your Grace. There is a light supper laid out in the hazard room and billiard tables down the hall. The cock fighting will not begin until later, but if you desire entertainment you are welcome to sample our delightful wares that await your pleasure upstairs."

Stefan waved a dismissive hand. "That will be all."

"Of course."

The servant bent low enough his pointed nose was in danger of brushing the marble floor before backing slowly away. Huntley watched the retreat, then turned to regard Dimitri with a jaundiced gaze.

"I did warn you the establishment was a sordid collection of reprobates," he muttered.

Dimitri chuckled, not nearly so fastidious as his companion.

"Did you expect a gentleman willing to rape young girls for enjoyment would choose a quiet evening at White's or Boodles reading the evening paper?"

"True." Huntley's expression hardened. He had not hesitated to offer his assistance once he discovered Dimitri's reason for being in London. "Where do you wish to begin?"

Dimitri glanced toward the curved staircase. "You mingle among the natives, I will return shortly."

Huntley arched a mocking brow, his gaze deliberately shifting to the buxom blonde who leaned over the wrought-iron railing with a provocative smile.

"I am not certain your wife would approve of such a tête-à-tête."

His hands fisted. *Wife.* It was a word that made most men shiver in fear.

Who desired to be forever tied to the same female who would no doubt consider it her duty to nag him into an early grave?

It was not fear, however, that made Dimitri shiver when he thought of Emma Linley-Kirov. Instead, it was an emotion that he refused to name.

"Then perhaps it would be best if she did not learn of it," he warned, already having endured a savage argument when Emma was forced to remain at the Huntley town house preparing for her introduction to London society.

"Women always have a means of discovering such things," Huntley drawled.

"There is nothing to discover. I am merely asking a few questions." His gaze narrowed. Huntley might be a powerful duke, but Dimitri had rightly earned his reputation as a

ruthless bastard. "And Emma will have no means of knowing unless you are incapable of guarding your tongue."

There was no mistaking the glint of humor in Huntley's
blue eyes. "As you say."

"You find something amusing?"

"I do indeed," the man admitted without apology.

Dimitri bit back his sharp words and instead heaved a
rueful sigh. Weeks ago Dimitri had taken a great deal of
enjoyment in watching Huntley being driven to distraction
by Leonida. Perhaps it was not so surprising the man would
appreciate witnessing Dimitri's bafflement when Emma
was near.

"You are a vindictive bastard, Huntley."

"And you are quite deserving of your inevitable fate."

Dimitri shook his head. "We are wasting time."

"I shall make a few discreet inquires among the guests,
but I prefer not to linger longer than necessary."

"I shall be swift."

"A wise decision," Huntley drawled as Dimitri headed
toward the stairs.

Dimitri ignored the taunt. He intended to question the
whores, not make use of their services.

Not that Emma could complain if he did, he told himself
as he climbed the polished steps. Had she not been the one
to claim their affair was at an end? As if their passion could
be so easily dismissed.

Perhaps she should be forced to consider the notion that
he had no need to beg for a woman in his bed. There were
always females anxious to enjoy his seduction.

Thrusting aside his lingering annoyance, Dimitri forced
himself to concentrate on the task at hand. He would deal
with Emma Linley-Kirov later.

He reached the top of the stairs, prepared for the garish
crimson sofas and crude paintings of naked women that
lined the walls of the saloon. The main focus was expected

to be the women sprawled upon the velvet cushions in varying degrees of undress.

His gaze skimmed over the females, barely noting the sheer gauze that revealed more of their lush bodies than it concealed or the sudden interest that brightened the heavily painted faces.

"Well, well." The blonde who had been leaning over the railing sashayed across the carpet, licking her lips as she studied the manner Dimitri's garnet jacket molded to his wide shoulders and the hard length of his legs in the black satin breeches. Or perhaps it was the emerald stickpin nestled in his cravat and the diamond on his ear that had captured her attention, he cynically acknowledged. "Ain't you the lovely one?"

"Here now, it be my turn, Edwina," a slender brunette protested, sidling next to Dimitri to thrust her bosom into prominent view.

"You never minded sharing afore," Edwina snapped.

"Be quiet." A commanding voice had both women hastily stepping back, revealing an imposing matron with her auburn hair piled high on her head and her lush curves encased in a jade satin gown striding in their direction. "The gentleman will decide which one of you he fancies." The brown eyes regarded him with a shrewd gaze. "Perhaps you would like a small sampling before you choose?"

"That will not be necessary. I prefer a few moments alone with you, Mrs.…?"

The woman's expression hardened with suspicion. "Pickford," she grudgingly supplied. "Surely you would prefer one of the younger girls?"

He conjured his most charming smile. "Not this evening."

There was a long pause as she considered the lethal danger etched onto his features. She was a woman who had seen enough of the world to sense Dimitri's feral nature. At last she gave a shrug.

"Very well."

Waving away the curious cluster of females, the older woman led him down the long corridor, pushing open the last door to escort him into a sitting room that was filled with solid English furniture and gingham curtains that were distinctly out of place in a brothel. Dimitri felt a pang of regret at his insistence. This was Mrs. Pickford's home and he was an unwelcome intruder.

"This way," she stiffly urged, waving her hand toward the connecting door.

"Actually this will do," he said gently.

The woman turned to face him, her expression wary. "What is it you're wanting from me?"

"Nothing more than information."

"A dangerous commodity."

"I assure you that whatever you tell me in this room will go no further."

She snorted at his smooth promise. "And why should I trust you?"

"Because my mother shared your profession."

Mrs. Pickford sucked in a shocked breath at Dimitri's blunt confession, her suspicions slowly transforming into a shared understanding.

"What do you want to know?"

"A number of young girls were taken from St. Petersburg and brought to London. I intend to find them and take them home."

The brown eyes flashed in outrage. "If someone told you that they was here, then you've been taken for a fool. Nothing but good English girls here and none of them being held against their will."

Dimitri held up his hand in a gesture of peace. "Be at

ease, Mrs. Pickford, I do not suspect you of dabbling in the slave trade, but you are a woman of the world."

Her ruffled feathers soothed, the older woman allowed a faint smile to curve her lips.

"I suppose that's a fancy name for it."

"You, better than anyone, would hear rumors of those gentlemen who possess a taste for children."

Her smile faded. "Such gentlemen prefer to keep their tastes a secret."

"And yet these things have a way of becoming known to those in the business."

"If your mother truly was one of us then you should know that those who don't learn to keep their mouth shut find themselves floating in the Thames." Her lips tightened. "The Bow Street magistrate can claim to have made the streets of London safe, but a nobleman can do whatever he pleases with us lesser folk."

Dimitri sympathized with her concern. Hell, he better than anyone knew what happened to whores who spoke out of turn.

"I have promised that no one will ever know we have spoken," he gently reminded her. "You have my word."

With a shiver she paced toward the sideboard, pouring herself a whiskey that she downed in one swallow.

"It's too dangerous."

Regretting the necessity of pressing the older woman, Dimitri crossed the room to turn her to face him.

"Mrs. Pickford, it is obvious you are very protective of the girls in your care."

"Someone has to keep an eye on the foolish chits. They haven't the sense that God gave a goose."

"Precisely." He caught and held her wary gaze. "So you understand my desire to protect those I consider under my care."

For a tense moment, Dimitri feared that the woman

would refuse to help, then with a shudder, she determinedly squared her shoulders.

"I can offer nothing more than rumors," she warned.

"That is enough."

"It is said that Lord Sanderson has an unhealthy interest in young girls as well as boys."

"Does he live in London?"

"He has a town house in Mayfair."

Dimitri tucked away the information. Not that he expected to discover the girls being held captive in an elegant Mayfair town house. But Sanderson was unlikely to have developed his own father's caution. There might very well be something in the Sandersons' home that would reveal his secrets.

"What of his acquaintances?" he pressed.

Mrs. Pickford wrinkled her nose in distaste. "A Mr. Timmons and Sir Jergens."

"Do they possess similar tastes?"

"So it is said."

"Is there a particular location they could indulge their fantasies?"

"It is whispered there are…" The woman gave a nervous gasp as a log popped in the stone fireplace.

He grasped her hands, attempting to ease her distress. "What is it?"

The brown eyes darkened with a futile anger. "Secret auctions where the girls are offered to the guests who can pay the entrance fee."

An answering anger echoed in Dimitri. He was rarely shocked by the depravity that some men could sink to, but that did not lessen his desire to shoot them in the heart and leave them bleeding to death in a gutter.

"Do you know where the auctions are held?"

"It's never held in the same location." Her harsh laugh

filled the room. "Such men are too crafty to risk being caught."

"Not crafty enough." Reaching in the inner pocket of his jacket, Dimitri withdrew several coins and pressed them into her hand. "For your time."

Anxious to return to the Huntley town house and Emma, he had nearly reached the door when her soft voice halted him.

"Sir."

"Yes?"

He halted and turned to watch as Mrs. Pickford moved forward and quite unexpectedly tossed her arms around him in a fierce hug.

"I've been knocked about enough to figure most men ain't worth a bucket of spit, but I believe you might just prove me wrong."

A wry smile curved his lips. "Ah, if only everyone shared your kind opinion."

EMMA STUDIED HER reflection in the full-length mirror with a jolt of astonishment.

She had protested violently when Leonida, the Duchess of Huntley, had insisted she would have her dresser alter several of her gowns to fit Emma, but the beautiful woman with golden curls and blue eyes that were extraordinarily similar to those of Czar Alexander had insisted that it would take days, if not weeks, for a seamstress to create the proper wardrobe for Emma. And as for her determination to play the role of a maid…well, that been overridden with a gracious, but ruthless force by both Stefan and Leonida.

She smiled wryly. She had been initially overwhelmed when Dimitri had led her into the foyer of the Mayfair town house. Not even Vanya's beautiful home had prepared her for the double staircases that elegantly curved toward the formal landing with marble pillars and a Venetian chandelier that spilled light over the collection of Grecian statues.

The imposing entrance was only a taste of the luxury to be discovered in the vast house, and Emma had swiftly given up the effort to estimate what the oil masterpieces framed on the walls and the various objects of art spread throughout the home might be worth.

And then she had been introduced to the Duke and Duchess of Huntley.

Stefan, with his dark hair and lean, autocratic face that would cause any woman's heart to miss a beat. His dark blue eyes had held a cunning intelligence that seemed to pierce to her very soul. And at his side the lovely Leonida who had at first glance seemed as frigidly beautiful as the tundra in winter.

She would have fled in terror if Dimitri had not stepped close to run a comforting hand down her back.

Then, with a surprising laugh, the duke and duchess had moved forward, warmly welcoming her to their home and assuring her that they would do whatever possible to help retrieve her sister.

Leonida had whisked her away to her chambers where she had insisted on hours of fittings with her dresser while Dimitri had mysteriously disappeared with Stefan.

Now she gazed in the mirror in amazement at the transformation that Leonida had achieved.

The evening gown was a spangled crepe draped over a satin slip of shimmering silver. The bodice was cut off the shoulders with tiny puff sleeves and a silver velvet ribbon tied snuggly beneath her bosom. With her honey curls piled loosely atop her head and her cheeks flushed with pleasure she had never appeared more elegant.

Almost as if she truly were a proper lady, she acknowledged with a rueful sigh.

Hesitantly her hand reached to touch a diamond-crusted button.

"It is lovely, but—"

"No arguments," Leonida interrupted, turning Emma to meet her determined expression. "You look exquisite."

Emma grimaced. Since her mother's death she had precious little time to fuss over her appearance. Not that it truly mattered. She had more important concerns to occupy her attention.

"Hardly exquisite," she muttered.

Leonida shook her head in disbelief. "Emma, how can you not realize you are extraordinarily lovely?"

Discomforted by her companion's insistence that she might be more than passably pretty, Emma paced across the Persian carpet. She had fallen in love with the amber bedchamber with its canopy bed and lemonwood furnishings covered with English chintz the moment she had entered the room, but she was too restless to fully appreciate her surroundings.

She blamed her unease on being so far from her familiar village and in the home of an English duke. Any woman in her position would be unnerved.

A voice in the back of her mind, however, whispered that the skittish sensation was entirely due to Dimitri Tipova and his reaction when he returned to the town house to discover she had demanded separate bedchambers.

Chiding herself for allowing her thoughts to once again be distracted by the bothersome man, she turned back to meet Leonida's curious gaze.

"Anya has always been the beauty of the family," she admitted.

"No doubt because you were willing to disguise your own beauty and allow her to shine."

Emma shrugged. She never considered the sacrifices

she had made or allowed self-pity to embitter her. She was a great deal more fortunate than many people.

"Most would tell you I was born a tyrannical, ill-tempered spinster," she said ruefully.

Leonida smiled. "Well, there is no one who will mistake you for a spinster in this gown."

"Leonida speaks the truth, *moya dusha*," a dark, whiskey-smooth voice murmured. "There is not a man who will gaze upon you and not wish to possess you."

Sharp excitement jolted through her as Emma turned to discover Dimitri strolling into the room, his elegant ruby jacket and black waistcoat unable to disguise his raw masculinity.

"Dimitri," she breathed.

"You need not thank me for my efforts, Dimitri," Leonida drawled with obvious amusement. "It was a pleasure to assist Emma. She is a guest that I am glad to have in my home."

The smoldering golden gaze never shifted from Emma's wary face. "I will speak with Emma in private."

Leonida placed an arm around Emma's shoulders, making it clear she was willing to stand up to the dangerous cutthroat.

"Emma?"

"It is fine, Leonida," she assured her companion, wishing she felt as confident as she sounded.

Not that she feared Dimitri would hurt her. At least not physically. But that did not lessen the danger.

"I will be in my rooms just down the corridor if you have need of me," Leonida said, moving toward the doorway. She paused at Dimitri's side. "Take care."

Dimitri's lips twisted. "Your warning comes far too late, Your Grace."

Leonida chuckled. "Good."

"And I thought your husband vindictive."

"We are kindred spirits. It is a rare gift that Stefan and I were nearly too stubborn to appreciate." Leonida glanced toward Emma, her expression impossible to read. "I would hope you would be wiser."

With a cryptic smile Leonida left the room, closing the door behind her.

Alone with Dimitri, Emma swallowed the lump in her throat, shivering as his golden gaze seared over her body. Suddenly, she was acutely reminded of lying beneath him, his slender fingers tangled in her hair as he urgently made love to her.

"Is there something you need?"

He prowled forward. "You."

Instinctively, she backed away, her heart galloping at a mad pace as she bumped into the wall.

"Dimitri, no."

His hands slammed against the wall on either side of her shoulders.

"Why did you insist we have separate rooms?" he growled.

"I told you before we left your ship that our…"

"Affair?"

Absurdly, Emma found herself unable to say the word. As if by refusing to name the savage awareness that pulsed between them she could somehow banish the sensations.

"I told you it was at an end."

"And I disagreed." His eyes darkened as he buried his face in the curve of her neck. "Mmm. I missed you today."

Her hands lifted to his chest, her fingers grasping the lapels of his jacket as he nuzzled the hollow behind her ear.

"It was on your orders that I was forced to waste the entire day acquiring a new wardrobe," she complained, reminding herself of all the reasons she should be slapping this man's face rather than melting beneath his skillful touch.

"Never a waste." He pulled back to study her silver gown. "You are...breathtaking. Although I would prefer less of you on display. I suppose this was Leonida's notion?"

Before she could respond, he returned to his delicate caresses, his lips tracing a path of kisses down the line of her collarbone.

Her lashes fluttered downward, her body longing to press against him in silent invitation.

"Dimitri, we are expected downstairs for dinner," she forced herself to mutter.

He reached the edge of her bodice, her nipples tightening in anticipation as his warm breath brushed her skin.

"Huntley is besotted with his wife. It is quite likely dinner will be delayed."

She shuddered, a soft moan of surrender escaping her lips. Who was she trying to deceive? Her mind might be convinced that sharing Dimitri's bed was a dangerous notion, but her body was already aching for his touch.

Easily sensing her capitulation, Dimitri slid his arms around her waist, molding her to the hard muscles of his body as his lips continued their destructive path over the curve of her breasts.

Emma's breath caught in her throat, her hands trembling as she reached up to clutch at his shoulders. She briefly forgot her stern determination to keep Dimitri at a distance, and even that they would be expected to meet the duke and duchess for dinner within the hour. All that mattered was...

She abruptly stiffened as the unmistakable stench of cloying perfume assaulted her.

Fury exploded through her. How dare he? He had told her he was devoting the day to tracking down the gentlemen who might have purchased her sister.

Instead, he returned to her reeking of another woman.

Gritting her teeth, she shoved her hands against his chest, nearly toppling him backward as she stalked toward the door and yanked it open.

"Get out."

He scowled, a flare of color staining his high cheekbones as he studied her with a frustrated gaze.

"What is it, *moya dusha?*"

Her chin tilted. "You bastard."

"True enough, but you've known that from the beginning," he snapped. "Why are you so angry?"

"Do not ever kiss me when you stink of another woman."

CHAPTER TWELVE

THE LONG, FORMAL GALLERY was predictably ornate, with marble columns topped by gilded capitals that framed the shallow niches where the Greek statues were displayed and a grand fresco painted on the vaulted ceiling.

At the far end a string quartet struggled to be heard over the gathered crowd. The elegantly attired aristocrats were far too intent on preening for one another to pay heed to the entertainment.

Not unless one considered entertainment to be scandal and seduction.

In no humor to appreciate the absurdity of London society, or the irony of pretending to be one of the aristocrats he so deeply despised, Dimitri leaned against a marble column and glared across the gallery at the honey-haired woman who was currently surrounded by a bevy of eager gentlemen.

And why would they not be eager?

Even among London's most celebrated women she sparkled with a fascinating beauty that had nothing to do with the emerald gown embroidered with pearls and everything to do with the creamy perfection of her skin and mysterious shimmer in her hazel eyes.

He snarled beneath his breath as one particularly forward gentleman angled so he could have a perfect view of Emma's scooped bodice. The savage need to march across the marble floor and publicly claim the stubborn female was like a punch to his stomach. Unfortunately,

Emma was quite likely to slap him in the face if he dared to approach.

"Perhaps it escaped your notice, Tipova, but it took a considerable effort to procure invitations to this particular soiree," Huntley drawled, coming to a halt at Dimitri's side. "Should you not be taking advantage of your proximity to Sanderson rather than hovering in the corner and glaring at your faux wife?"

Dimitri's gaze never strayed from Emma. "You are a duke. Every door is open to you."

"Open for me, but not my unknown Russian companion who has yet to prove to London society that he is not a barbarian who lives among the wolves and gnaws on bones."

Dimitri snorted, well aware that most of England believed that Russia was a land of savages. Granted the puffed up peacocks were willing enough to welcome Russian armies as allies in defeating Napoleon, but they certainly didn't believe the people were civilized enough for an English drawing room.

"Pompous asses."

"Do you wish to be introduced to Sanderson or not?" Huntley demanded.

Dimitri shook his head. "No."

The duke scowled, his hand waving toward the crowd. "Tipova, if you forced me to this repulsive gathering as a punishment—"

"Compose yourself Huntley," Dimitri drawled, his pride pricked. He might be floundering when it came to Emma Linley-Kirov, but he was perfectly capable of devising the best means to ensnare Lord Sanderson. Which was precisely why he had requested that Huntley procure them invitations to Sir Jergens's soiree. And why he was lurking in the shadows rather standing next to Emma where he belonged. Or better yet, sweeping the aggravating woman back to his ship so they could have a few hours alone. "You admitted that you have never made a secret of your dislike for Sanderson. Do you not think it would be suspicious if you were to approach him for the simple purpose of introducing me, and then I begin questioning him on his most private affairs?"

Huntley shrugged. "Please yourself."

"I always do." Dimitri stiffened as he watched Sanderson head toward the doors leading onto the terrace. On the point of following the rotund nobleman, he abruptly turned to stab his companion with a flat glare. "Huntley."

"Yes?"

"My thespian skills are without equal, but I will kill any man who dares to be overly forward with Emma." There was no mistaking the lethal intent in his voice. "You might wish to stay close enough to ensure I have no need to demonstrate just how barbaric this Russian can truly be."

Expecting a mocking smile, Dimitri was relieved when Huntley instead nodded with understanding.

"Do not worry, Tipova. No one will trouble her."

With a last glance toward Emma, Dimitri strolled with seeming nonchalance across the gallery, his lean body shown to advantage in the black jacket and silver waistcoat. He ignored open smiles of invitation from the women and wary suspicion of the men. His attention was solely focused on the gentleman disappearing through the French doors.

Stepping onto the wide terrace, Dimitri searched the darkness, a predatory smile curving his lips as he watched the flabby nobleman lean against the stone balustrade and pour the contents of his crystal glass into the garden below.

"It would seem that I am not alone in my distaste for inferior champagne," he murmured, striding across the terrace as he withdrew a silver flask from the inner pocket of his jacket. "Allow me."

The round face with heavy jowls and a protruding nose already turning red in the chill night air turned in his direction, Sanderson's deep-set eyes lingering on the diamond stickpin the size of a quail egg Dimitri had tucked in his cravat before shifting to the extended flask.

"What is it?"

"The finest vodka to be found in all of London."

Taking the flask, the nobleman drank deeply of the potent spirits before handing it back to Dimitri.

"So you're the Cossack?" he sneered.

Dimitri peered down the length of his nose, deliberately sweeping a frigid gaze over the burgundy jacket stretched painfully tight over the man's expanding stomach and the hint of wear on the leather pumps.

"I am Russian, yes."

The sneer faltered, and Sanderson nervously cleared his throat.

"What brings you to England?"

"Huntley invited me for a visit during his stay in St. Petersburg. He assured me that I would discover a number of diversions. Unfortunately…"

"Unfortunately?"

Dimitri leaned casually against the railing, stifling a yawn as he cunningly dropped the bait to lure his prey into the waiting trap.

"I have discovered the pious duke and I have very differing notions of entertainment," he mocked. "If I wished to devote my days to stuffy gentlemen's clubs and my evenings to tediously escorting my wife from one ballroom to another I could have remained in Russia."

Sanderson inched closer, a gleam of interest in his pale brown eyes.

"You have my utmost sympathy. Huntley has always been a self-righteous prig."

Dimitri hid a smile. He had depended upon the lesser man's predictable envy of Huntley.

"A pity." He adjusted the cuff of his jacket, ensuring the large ruby in his ring caught and reflected the moonlight. "A gentleman is offered such a wide variety of opportunities it is nothing less than a sin to deny himself the full bounty of pleasures."

His covert glance witnessed Sanderson licking his thick lips, an unmistakable greed tightening his expression.

"Such pleasures can often be quite expensive."

"What is the purpose of possessing money if it is not to enjoy life?"

"It would seem we are gentlemen of a like mind."

Dimitri arched a brow. "Are we?"

"If you wish, I could perhaps escort you to those amusements that Huntley would never approve of."

Dimitri hid his stark satisfaction. He was a gambler who understood never to overplay his hand.

"That is a generous offer, but you cannot wish to escort a foreign stranger about town," he said, a hint of wariness in his voice. It would be unnatural for him not to be suspicious of such an offer.

Sanderson offered an unctuous smile. "I consider it my duty as an Englishman."

"Duty?"

He tugged on the cravat tied about his fat neck. "You cannot return to Russia assuming all Englishmen are as pompously dull as Huntley and his ilk. We do have a reputation to uphold."

"And?" Dimitri prompted, folding his arms across his chest.

"What do you mean?"

He paused, narrowing his gaze. "Forgive me, I am by nature a suspicious man. I prefer to have the cards on the table, as you English say."

Sanderson's smile widened with approval. Clearly he appreciated Dimitri's blunt acceptance that the offer of companionship was not without cost.

"Very well." He stepped close, lowering his voice to make certain they could not be overheard by the few guests strolling across the terrace. "I believe we can be of service to one another."

Dimitri gritted his teeth. He longed to wrap his hands around the nasty man's throat and choke the truth from him. A pity he could not be certain Sanderson had any connection to his father or the kidnapped girls. For now he had no choice but to remain patient and hope the man would lead him to the truth.

"I am prepared to listen."

Sanderson cast a nervous glance toward the light from the gallery windows that spilled across the terrace. Understandable. Wicked deeds belonged in the shadows.

"You wish your visit to London to be a memorable event and I am familiar with an assortment of establishments that are willing to cater to a gentleman's every need."

"*Every* need?"

The nobleman leered in anticipation. "Absolutely."

Dimitri pretended to consider the offer. "And what would you desire in return?"

"I share your love for adventure, but like so many noblemen my current finances are in straightened circumstances."

"Ah. I would of course be happy to finance any expenses we might incur."

Sanderson's loathsome chuckle echoed through the garden. "When do you wish to begin?"

No one could have been more astonished than Emma to discover herself a source of fascination among the elegant English ton. In truth, she had anticipated her charade being exposed the moment she stepped over the threshold of the town house. Instead, she had been surrounded by a bevy of curious aristocrats who vied to capture her attention.

Oh, she comprehended that a measure of their interest was stirred by her arrival in the company of the Duke and Duchess of Huntley. And, of course, by being on the arm of Dimitri, who appeared to terrify society with his ruthless beauty and hint of savage danger in his golden eyes.

But she was female enough to accept that had she not been so frantic to discover some hint of her sister, she might have taken pleasure in the soiree.

Instead, she stood at Leonida's side with a smile forced onto her lips and waited for Dimitri to covertly trail Lord Sanderson onto the terrace. The man had confessed what he had learned in the brothel, but had adamantly refused to allow Emma to be a part of the search for Anya.

Which meant Emma intended to take matters into her own hands.

Leaning close to Leonida, she whispered into her ear. "It is time."

The duchess covertly tugged Emma away from the crowd, her beautiful face creased with concerned.

"Emma, please take care."

Emma hid her smile, having heard the story of Leonida's frantic flight from England to St. Petersburg that had included a kidnapping and near-death experience. The woman was hardly in the position to lecture Emma on being careful.

"I intend to do nothing more than question the staff. I swear I will be discreet."

"And quick." Leonida glanced toward the imposing duke, who stood near a marble column, his remote expression keeping away all but the boldest encroacher. "If Stefan discovers you are missing, then he will most certainly come in search of you. And I know from painful experience he is a difficult man to avoid. And as for Dimitri…" She grimaced. "I shudder to think of what he would say should I allow you out of my sight."

Emma did a good deal more than merely shudder.

She was well aware that if Dimitri discovered she was executing her own search for Anya he would have her hauled back to his ship and sent to Russia.

"I shall return before anyone suspects I am gone," she swore.

Weaving her way toward the entrance at the far side of the gallery, Emma ignored the attempts to capture her attention. Then, moving down the corridor away from the near-deafening chatter of the guests, she slowed her pace as she peered into the various rooms. They were all opulently decorated with rosewood furnishings and richly painted ceilings. Her stomach clenched. Did Sir Jergens afford his lavish home by selling Russian children?

She had nearly reached the back of the house when she spied the maid who was stirring the fire in what appeared to be a small parlor. Pausing in the doorway she bent down to rip the hem of her gown before she entered the room and headed directly toward the servant.

"You there."

The maid, with a round face and fuzzy brown hair that escaped her white cap, hurriedly rose to her feet, wiping her hands on her apron.

"Aye, my lady?" she breathed, bobbing a hasty curtsey.

Emma summoned a kind smile, hoping to put the maid at ease. "I fear a clumsy oaf has trod upon my gown and torn my hem. Would you be kind enough to assist me?"

"Of course. If you will follow me?"

The maid led her toward a window seat where a basket of darning had been tucked out of sight.

"Is it very bad?" Emma demanded.

The maid knelt on the carpet, reaching to pull out a needle and thread from the sewing basket.

"Not at all," she assured Emma, "I shall be done in a trice."

"I know it is not your duty…"

"Maggie," the girl shyly offered at Emma's prompting.

"Maggie, but my maid was forced to return to her mother in St. Petersburg and I have yet to replace her."

"I am happy to oblige, my lady."

Emma allowed the maid to concentrate on threading the needle and begin stitching the hem before she pretended to be struck by a sudden thought.

"Do you know, it has just occurred to me that you might be just who I need to speak with."

The maid glanced up in puzzlement. "Me?"

"Yes, I shall have need of a servant during the remainder of my visit and while I am certain an English maid would be perfectly qualified for the position, I must admit that I would prefer a Russian girl. Do you know where I might hire such a maid?"

The color visibly drained from the plump face. "Russian?"

The woman was obviously alarmed, but it was impossible to know if it was a mere reaction to being questioned by a supposed noblewoman. Emma considered her words.

"Well, most London domestic services only offer English or French servants. I had hoped you might be acquainted with a suitable girl."

"I…"

"Have I said something wrong?"

Maggie abruptly ducked her head, concentrating furiously on sewing the ripped hem.

"No."

"I would be willing to pay for your assistance, Maggie," Emma urged softly.

"I'm sorry, my lady, I don't know any foreign girls."

Emma bit her lip, studying the rigid line of the maid's shoulders and the tremble of her finger as she tied off the thread. The poor girl was truly frightened. Did she dare press her further?

"Then perhaps one of your friends would be able to recommend someone?" she at last asked.

The maid surged upright, a hectic glitter in her brown eyes. "There you are, as good as new."

"Maggie?"

"I must be returning to my duties." Without warning Maggie was turning to rush out of the room.

"Wait."

Cursing her lack of finesse, Emma belatedly followed in the servant's wake, not entirely surprised to discover that the girl had already disappeared. She was certain Maggie must know something. But what? And how did she force the poor girl to confess?

Ten minutes later, Emma came to a halt and glanced about the warren of rooms and hallways that made up the servant's quarters. Maggie was nowhere to be found and the servants who scurried past her were sending her the sort of curious glances that inevitably led to gossip. The one thing that Emma was determined to avoid.

Accepting that she had done enough damage for one evening, she gave a shake of her head and turned to retrace her steps back to the ballroom. It was only then that she realized that an extremely large man with a dark complexion had crept up behind her. Her eyes widened as she realized he was oddly attired with a scarf on his head and a matching loose white robe wrapped with a black rope that held it in place.

Who was he? And more important, what was he doing creeping about the London town house?

Instinctively, her lips parted to scream, but before she could make a sound the man had clamped a hand over her mouth and firmly wrapped an arm around her waist, plucking her feet far enough off the ground so he could back toward a nearby door.

Emma struggled as a surge of fear exploded through her. She might be several pounds lighter and barely tall enough to reach the man's shoulder, but that did not keep her from scratching at the hand over her mouth or desperately swinging her legs in an attempt to connect a blow to his knee.

The brute flinched and muttered beneath his breath, but he never hesitated as he used his foot to kick open the door and hauled her down a narrow flight of stairs into the abandoned rose garden.

Emma stilled her futile struggles. The man was too powerful for her to battle. Her only hope was to conserve her strength and pray she would be offered the opportunity to escape once he released his painful grip.

She shivered as a breeze whipped around the side of the house, easily cutting through the thin fabric of her gown. English winters might not compare to the brutal ferocity of Russia, but this was no weather to be prancing about frozen gardens without so much as a cloak.

The stranger carried her down the narrow path, heading toward the small grotto in the center of the garden. Then, stepping through the opening, he roughly set her back on her feet, making no effort to assist her when she stumbled into the darkness.

A slender male hand grasped her arm, gently steadying her before she fell to her knees. Emma was aware of the potent scent of exotic spices and warm male skin before the hand was removed and the darkness was pierced by candlelight.

She blinked against the sudden change from dark to light, then as her eyes became accustomed, she studied the slender man standing directly in front of her.

Her first thought was that he was as exotically male as his scent had been.

Although attired in English clothing with a black jacket fobbed with gold and white satin pantaloons, there was no mistaking the foreign beauty of his finely carved features and the rich glow of his golden skin. His hair was as dark as the midnight sky and cut close to his head, emphasizing his wide brow and the black, deep-set eyes that smoldered with a restless intelligence.

She shivered. The stranger carried with him the lethal allure of the desert. Scorching days beneath the incandescent sun and cool nights by the oasis, wrapped in a man's arms.

Emma's heart slammed against her chest as the stranger studied her for a long, disturbing moment, then his dark gaze shifted over her shoulder and he spoke to a man still standing behind her in a strange language.

There was a shuffle as the robed man left the gazebo and Emma was alone with the strikingly handsome man who set aside the candle and strolled toward her.

"Forgive me," he murmured, his smoky voice feathering down her spine. "I requested that my servant bring you to me and apparently he took my command quite literally."

Emma licked her lips, not fooled by his polished manners. She did not doubt for a moment that the servant had been commanded to bring her to the garden by whatever means necessary.

"So it would seem." She clutched her shaking hands together, glancing about the marble grotto with its pastoral scenes painted on the walls and benches set beneath the slotted windows. It was surprisingly spacious, but to

Emma's mind the stranger's presence seemed to overwhelm the circular space. "Who are you?"

He offered a half bow. "Just as you, I am a visitor to this country."

Which told her precisely nothing.

"And you believe that gives you leave to have me hauled about as if I am a bit of rubbish?"

A small smile curved his lips, emphasizing his dark beauty. "I have apologized."

Emma remained wary, but her panic eased. Surely if the man intended harm he would not be chatting with her in a grotto near enough for someone to hear her scream?

"But you have not yet introduced yourself, or told me why you have brought me to this excessively cold garden," she pointed out.

The dark gaze swept over her upturned face. "For now I believe it is best that we both guard our true identities..." He deliberately paused. "Emma."

"How did you know—"

"There are more dangers in London than you suspect," he overrode her startled question.

She shivered at his odd words. Did he know why she was in London? Was he somehow involved with those who had taken her sister?

"Is that a threat?" she breathed.

"A warning for you to take care," he corrected, his hand lifting to cup her chin in a gentle grip. "It would be tragic if you were to be harmed."

Acutely aware of the warmth of his touch and the tantalizing brush of his breath on her cheek, Emma resisted the urge to struggle against him. Dimitri Tipova had taught her to recognize a predator when one had her cornered.

"What do you want of me?"

"I have told myself that we could be of assistance to one another, but now that you are so near I wonder if I was not deceiving myself." His voice roughened as his gaze deliberately rested on her lips. "You are quite beautiful."

"Please...do not."

He ignored her unsteady plea, his fingers tracing the delicate lines of her face.

"Such exquisite skin. And soft, silken hair. And eyes that are the precise shade of my beloved cat." His head slowly lowered. "Fascinating."

"No." Emma pressed her hands against his chest, her cheeks flushed. "I will scream."

With a rueful grimace, the man pulled back, the dark eyes glittering with a wicked promise that their kiss had merely been delayed.

"You have no need to fear me," he promised. "I only wish to let you know that you are not alone in your search."

Her heart skipped a beat. "My search?"

He frowned as he abruptly glanced toward the door. "Someone approaches." He grasped her shoulders, his expression somber. "If you wish my help you will tell no one of this encounter."

"Why not?"

"Because, like the scorpion, I prefer to remain in the shadows until the moment is ripe to strike at my enemies."

Emma studied the proud golden features. This was a man accustomed to giving commands and having them obeyed. Not that a position of power made him trustworthy, of course. The men who had kidnapped her sister were supposed noblemen.

But she could not deny there was a part of her that was certain he was someone she could rely upon.

"And what if I have need of you?" she husked. "How can I contact you?"

The dark eyes flared with satisfaction and before

she could stop him, he had leaned down to steal a brief, possessive kiss.

"Do not worry, I shall always be near," he whispered.

Not entirely reassured, Emma shivered as he silently slipped from the grotto and disappeared into the shadows of the garden.

She was not at all convinced he was a gentleman she wished to have keeping watch on her, she acknowledged as she followed him out of the grotto and headed back toward the town house. Then again, if he could provide assistance in rescuing her sister, then he could lurk in the shadows all he desired.

Avoiding the servant's door where she had been forced into the garden, Emma instead hurried toward the terrace at the far edge of the house. She climbed the steps and was headed for the French doors when a familiar form stepped into her path.

"Emma." Dimitri glared down at her with obvious annoyance. "What are you doing out here?"

Emma jerked in surprise, her raw nerves not at all prepared to deal with yet another overbearing male. What had she done to be plagued with such creatures?

"I…I needed a breath of fresh air."

"Fresh air?"

"Yes."

The golden eyes narrowed with suspicion. "And you had no intention of attempting to overhear my conversation with Lord Sanderson?"

She breathed a soft sigh of relief at the realization he had presumed she had followed him onto the terrace. She might be a fool, but for now she had no intention of telling Dimitri of her encounter with the strange foreigner.

Not when he was certain to use the knowledge as an excuse to keep her locked in the Huntley town house, or worse, returned to his ship.

Besides, who knew whether the stranger might eventually be of service?

"There is nothing nefarious in my presence on the terrace, Dimitri. I took a brief stroll through the garden and now I am returning to the ballroom."

"Alone?" he drawled in disbelief. "Where is Leonida?"

"No doubt in the company of her charming husband."

"Ah." His expression softened as he stepped close enough to wrap his arms around her waist. "And were you jealous, *milaya?* Did you perhaps wish to be in the company of a charming, clever, excessively handsome gentleman?"

She trembled at his familiar touch, her body tightening with a sharp-edged hunger. In the flickering torchlight, with his hair ruffled in the breeze and his eyes dark with desire, he appeared enticingly uncivilized.

The desire to have him sweep her off her feet and carry her into the shadows of the garden was terrifyingly potent. Instead, she forced herself to step back, meeting his smoldering gaze with a tilt of her chin.

She would not be manipulated. Not by Dimitri Tipova nor by the stranger in the grotto.

"Yes," she admitted with a taunting smile. "Unfortunately, I have yet to discover such a man."

CHAPTER THIRTEEN

DESPITE HIS BEST INTENTIONS, Dimitri found his thoughts drifting as Huntley discussed the various political implications from the recent Congress of Verona. It was not that he did not comprehend the dangers inherent in Spain's current instability, or France's proposed intervention. The mere fact that Alexander Pavlovich was offering to send one hundred and fifty thousand troops to Piedmont to dampen the uprising of Jacobins meant that there was a very real potential for war.

But on this winter afternoon, the squabbling between Metternich and Wellington and Chateaubriand seemed thankfully distant.

Instead, he gazed down at the terraced garden shown to full advantage by the row of floor-to-ceiling windows, his mood as dark as the threatening clouds.

At last sensing Dimitri's tension, Huntley rose from the heavy walnut desk and crossed the white marble floor of the library.

"How does your hunt go?"

"Slowly." Dimitri grimaced, reluctantly recalling the paltry entertainments he'd been forced to endure over the past days. Drunken boxing matches, seedy gambling halls, a dog fight and brothels that catered to any number of perversions. None, however, had offered the sort of young females he had demanded of Lord Sanderson. "I have hopes this evening I can convince my prey I am to be trusted with his secrets."

"It has only been a fortnight." The duke shrugged. "You cannot expect a miracle."

Dimitri's humorless laugh echoed through the vast room. The elegant library was large enough to house an army battalion.

"I cannot, but I assure you that is precisely what Emma expects."

"Understandable. It is obvious she is consumed with fear for her sister."

Dimitri clenched his hands. He fully sympathized with Emma's concern. He better than anyone knew the guilt that tormented her at Anya's continued absence, and her relentless determination to rescue her. No matter what the cost to herself.

Or to him.

But he couldn't deny his frustration at the impenetrable barriers she had surrounded herself with since arriving in London.

"I sympathize with her impatience, but I cannot allow her emotions to lead her to foolishness," he growled. "If she does not trust that I am capable of rescuing Anya, then she is most certain to take matters into her own hands."

Huntley smiled wryly. "I could have warned you of the dangers of entangling yourself with a headstrong female."

An icy dread gripped his heart as the haunting memory of his mother and her brutal death seared through his mind.

"There is no need for such warnings," he replied. "I am painfully familiar with the dangers. You are certain Leonida is keeping a close guard on her?"

Huntley arched a dark brow. "Why do you ask?"

With a sharp motion, Dimitri turned to pace toward a towering bookcase.

"I suspect Emma is keeping a secret from me."

"She is a woman. They are compelled by nature to keep a poor man baffled and suspicious."

"Not all women," Dimitri protested. And it was the truth. How many females had he taken into his care over the years? How many had eagerly allowed him to protect them from the cruel injustices that threatened them? "There are those who comprehend the need to depend on a man and to defer to him rather than constantly battling to assert her independence."

"If you say." Huntley at least made an effort to disguise his amusement. "Why do you believe she is keeping a secret from you?"

Dimitri continued his pacing, his brow furrowed with frustration. He had first assumed Emma's oddly furtive manner was caused by her annoyance at his refusal to allow her to chase about London in search of her sister. It was understandable she would desire to punish him.

But as the days passed, he was forced to accept that Emma was not a woman to harbor a grudge. If she were annoyed with him, then she would brazenly slap his face, not pout behind his back.

No. There was something occupying her mind. Something she was determined to keep hidden from him.

"It is those guilty glances when she thinks I am not looking," he muttered, acutely aware that he sounded a fool. "And those tiny flinches of surprise when I enter a room unexpectedly."

Huntley slowly smiled, crossing to regard Dimitri with an amused gaze.

"Have you considered her wariness in your presence is caused by the same affliction that has you pacing the floors and snapping at those foolish enough to cross your path?"

Dimitri tensed, not particularly pleased to be a source of entertainment for the duke.

"What affliction?"

"Desire."

"That is none of your concern," he growled, his voice edged with warning.

"I am not blind, Tipova," the man persisted. "It is obvious that the two of you have been intimate. Perhaps if you would return Emma to your bed then both of you could collect your composure and concentrate on your purpose here."

Dimitri gave a sharp crack of laughter. Did the duke believe that he was responsible for his enforced celibacy? Christ, he would sooner be tarred and feathered than spend another night alone in his bed.

"It was not my choice to have separate chambers," he proclaimed.

A hint of pity darkened Huntley's expression. "Ah."

Dimitri ignored the implication that it was his lack of talent that had driven Emma from his bed. He had no need to boast of his skill. Instead, he concentrated on making certain Huntley realized just how fragile Emma was beneath her facade of unshakable fortitude.

"Emma has been forced to take on responsibilities that would have crushed most women."

Huntley nodded. "I suspected as much."

"Then you must also have suspected that her unconventional choices have made her vulnerable to nasty gossip that has plagued her since her father's death. She would be deeply hurt if Leonida were to consider her less than a proper lady."

Huntley stiffened, obviously outraged by the suggestion they would deliberately harm their guest.

"Leonida is already extremely fond of Emma, as am I. We would never think less of her."

Dimitri shrugged. "Perhaps you could convince her. I have been unable to do so."

Huntley paused, studying Dimitri's guarded expression. "Why do I sense you have not made the attempt?"

Dimitri swallowed a sigh. The duke was annoyingly perceptive.

"Emma was a virgin before becoming my lover," he grudgingly confessed.

"You did not—"

"Force her? No," he snapped. "But in her mind I did seduce her. It appeased her conscience to tell herself that I took advantage of her innocence."

"And now?"

Dimitri shifted uneasily. What did the man want from him? A confession that his relationship with Emma had gone beyond a short tumble to ease his lust? That he needed her to be more than merely a reluctant lover?

"Now I wish her to accept her place in my bed because that is where she desires to be and not because I have lured her there," he muttered.

Huntley reached to clap him on the back. "Take the word of a man who has made his fair share of mistakes, Tipova, pride is a cold companion."

Dimitri headed toward the door, unwilling to discuss Emma and the baffling emotions that refused to leave him in peace.

"Sanderson will be waiting for me."

UPSTAIRS IN THE DUCHESS of Huntley's private parlor, the two women might have been poised for a painting.

Leonida was prettily settled on a brocade settee, her lilac gown a perfect complement to her golden beauty. Across the room decorated with painted mural scenes and boasting a coved ceiling, stood Emma attired in a blue-and-silver-striped walking gown with a blue velvet pelisse fastened with large silver buttons as she glanced out the bow window.

Neither woman, however, was remotely aware of the charming vision they created.

In truth, Emma was aware of nothing beyond the sight

of Dimitri striding through the back garden to the mews. Even at a distance he appeared absurdly handsome with his caped greatcoat emphasizing the width of his shoulders and the pale light slanting over the savage beauty of his bronzed face.

Her teeth clenched with a combination of unwelcome appreciation and sheer annoyance that he was once again spending the day hunting for her sister, while she was expected to remain quietly at home, awaiting his return like a well-trained dog.

"If the tea is not to your taste I could order you whatever you desire," Leonida murmured from behind.

Turning, Emma set aside her Wedgwood cup with a grimace. "Arsenic?"

"No man is worth dying for."

"Oh, I did not intend the poison for me."

Leonida tilted back her head to laugh with rich appreciation. "Oh, I do like you, Emma Linley-Kirov."

"Why did he bother to bring me to London if he meant to forget my very existence?" she growled, pacing across the Persian carpet to absently toy with the jade figurines that lined the mantel.

"If the burning glances he has been sending in your direction is any indication, he has not been capable of forgetting your existence for even a moment."

Emma could not contain her shiver. She was well aware of Dimitri's hot, lingering glances. How could she not be? The air itself seemed to catch fire the moment he entered the room. And she would be lying if she did not admit that she had spent more than one night aching for his touch.

But she had made her decision to bring an end to their affair. A decision that was only strengthened by the realization that she would never be capable of keeping her secrets hidden while sharing a bed with Dimitri Tipova.

How long would it be before the incorrigible man not only realized she was making her own inquiries throughout

London in an effort to locate Anya, but that there was a strange man supposedly keeping watch over her?

No. Whatever the temptation, she had to keep in mind that Dimitri had his own purpose in being in London. And if she, or Anya, had to be sacrificed to achieve that goal, then so be it.

"Desiring me in his bed and including me in his search for my sister is not at all the same," she said, her voice bitter. "He refuses to admit I might have some value beyond my body."

Leonida sighed. "Men are so sadly stupid."

"I doubt you would include your husband in your condemnation of the opposite sex."

"Of course I would," the duchess corrected. "Until I managed to properly train him, Stefan was as arrogant, insensitive and incapable of accepting a woman's ability to make her own decisions as Dimitri."

"Do you truly believe a man such as Dimitri Tipova could be trained by any woman?"

"You would not ask that question if you knew Stefan's brother, Edmond." Leonida set aside her teacup and rose to her feet. "I do not envy Brianna for the torment that man put her through before they wed. Of course now she is excessively happy."

Emma's heart twisted with an emotion perilously close to envy. She would be a fool to ever believe she shared more than a passing affair with Dimitri. Her destiny was a small coaching inn in Yabinsk. To yearn for more was only inviting disappointment.

"Enough of Dimitri Tipova," she snapped. "I am here for Anya, no other purpose."

"Certainly," Leonida calmly agreed. "How can I be of service?"

Emma sucked in a deep breath, regaining her composure. "Your maid was kind enough to discover that Lady

Sanderson enjoys a late morning stroll through Green Park."

"Good." With brisk steps, the duchess moved toward the door. "Then we should be on our way."

Emma hurried behind the woman as she headed down the long hall and then the marble sweep of stairs.

"There is no need for you to accompany me, Leonida," she protested. "You have done enough as it is."

"Nonsense." Pausing in the foyer, Leonida waited for a maid to scurry forward with a fawn cloak lined with fur and matching bonnet she settled on her golden curls. "I am going with you and there will be no arguments."

Hastily Emma pulled on a pair of warm gloves and a pretty bonnet trimmed with blue velvet ribbons.

"I cannot allow you to put yourself in danger."

"What danger can there be in a morning stroll through Green Park with two burly footmen to keep guard?"

Emma studied her companion's resolute expression, then she heaved a sigh of resignation.

"You are very stubborn."

Leonida chuckled. "So I have been told."

There was a brief wait as the groom scurried to bring around a black carriage with the Duke of Huntley's insignia painted on the side. But soon enough they were settled on the leather seats with blankets swaddled around them and warmed bricks beneath their feet.

Emma instinctively shifted to peer out the window as they rattled over the cobblestones, a sigh of appreciation escaping her lips as they turned onto Park Lane. Her gaze lingered on the palatial Grosvenor House with its stuccoed exterior and two-story bays that overlooked Hyde Park with aloof grandeur. And the less flamboyant Londonderry House that had been originally designed with a formal simplicity by Stewart and was in the process of lavish restorations. Leonida had whispered that Lady Londonderry was funding the alterations and desired to have a suitable setting to display her famous diamonds.

"London is perhaps not as elegant as St. Petersburg, but it has its own charm, do you not think?" Leonida murmured.

"I do," Emma readily agreed, a wistful smile curving her lips. "It is just as my mother described it."

"Yes, Dimitri mentioned your mother was English."

Emma nodded. The memory of her mother holding her tightly on her lap as she spoke of her homeland caused a bittersweet ache in the center of her heart.

"She often spoke of her home that she left behind to travel to Russia as a nanny. It made me long to visit." She grimaced. "Although not under such circumstances."

"Do you intend to contact your relatives while you are here?"

Emma shrugged. She had hesitated to contact her distant relatives after the death of her father. The last thing she desired was to be seen as a pathetic orphan in search of charity. And perhaps, if she were perfectly honest, she would have to admit that a small voice in the back of her head warned that there might be those among their relatives that might not consider her a suitable guardian for Anya. She would not take the risk her sister might be taken from her.

Utterly selfish of her, of course. And as she was discovering, utterly stupid.

Perhaps if she had allowed Anya to go to a traditional family with a stable home and a mother capable of devoting her time to her children, Anya might have outgrown her impulsive lust for attention.

"I might consider seeking them out once Anya is safe," she said, refusing to imagine the possibility that she would not find her sister. "It would be nice to meet our family. We have been alone a long time."

"You are not alone, Emma." Without warning, Leonida leaned forward to grip her hand. "Never again."

The warmth of Leonida's generous kindness helped to ease the icy dread that was lodged in the pit of Emma's stomach. It was odd. How often did the common folk in her tiny village complain of the cold disdain of the aristocrats, and how they cared for no one but themselves? And yet, her neighbors had done nothing to assist her when she needed help, while this woman who had been born into lavish luxury had not hesitated to extend a hand of friendship and to open her home to a perfect stranger.

"Thank you," she said, her voice brimming with sincerity.

The carriage rolled to a halt, a handful of grooms scrambling to open the door and pull out the steps.

"Here we are," Leonida announced, offering Emma a wink as they were carefully assisted from the coach and then discreetly followed by the burly guards as they passed through the gates.

A frown formed on Emma's brow as they strolled along across the frozen ground, her gaze skimming over the flat expanse of parkland that was surprisingly bustling with elegant pedestrians.

"Heavens! I had no notion it would be so vast," she murmured. "How will we ever find Lady Sanderson?"

"There are only a few paths that attract a lady of fashion." Leonida threaded her arm through Emma's and tugged her toward a line of trees. "This way."

"Where are we going?"

"The Queen's Walk. It passes by the basin." They walked in silence, both enjoying the sense of peace that was so rare in the bustling city, then Leonida turned to catch Emma's small smile. "What are you thinking?"

Emma sucked in a deep breath, acutely aware of the history that surrounded her. As beautiful as St. Petersburg might be, it had not yet acquired the centuries of stories and memories that shrouded London in mystery.

"My mother told me that Green Park was created by King Charles II and that it never was allowed to have flowers since his queen discovered him offering blooms to another lady while they strolled among the deer and temples."

Leonida chuckled. "Who is to say if it is true or not? I do know the temples were destroyed during the various celebrations over the years and, of course, there was a fireworks accident that caused a dreadful fire. Not that I am complaining. There is something very appealing in simple nature unmarred by man." Leonida leaned close to Emma's ear. "I believe the woman in the burgundy cloak with the yapping dog is Lady Sanderson."

Emma covertly glanced toward the woman who was struggling to maintain her grip on the leash holding a small, ill-trained dog. She stumbled in shock. Could that dumpy woman in a garish velvet cloak and matching bonnet be a lady of society? She looked more like the butcher's wife with her plump, ruddy cheeks and brown curls that escaped the limp bun at the nape of her neck.

"Truly?" she breathed.

"It is rumored she brought with her a considerable dowry, although Lord Sanderson has swiftly squandered her fortune. How do you intend to approach her?"

"I haven't the least notion." Emma ignored her companion's speculative gaze as they headed directly toward the woman who had halted to untangle her leash from a bush. It was not until Lady Sanderson had straightened and was watching their approach with astonishment that inspiration struck. "What a darling puppy," she cooed, squeezing Leonida's arm. "Is he not a darling, Your Grace?"

"Most handsome," Leonida readily agreed, managing to hide her grimace as the dog rolled in a patch of mud. "Wherever did you find him?"

The woman's mud-brown eyes widened with terrified shock at being approached by the elusive Duchess of Huntley.

"Your Grace, this is such a…" Lady Sanderson paused, making a visible effort to regain command of her shattered composure. "Lancelot was a gift from my father."

Leonida smiled graciously. "Lady Sanderson, is it not?"

"Yes. Yes, it is indeed."

"Sanderson?" Emma tilted her head to the side, pretending to be deep in thought. "Why is the name so familiar? Ah, of course. Your husband has kindly offered to escort Dimitri about town."

There was no mistaking the loathing that briefly flared through the older woman's eyes before she managed a stiff smile. Emma shuddered in sympathy. As difficult as her life had been, she at least had not been bartered off to a man she held in disgust. Not all the money, or exclusive parties or grand houses in Mayfair could compensate for that misery.

"Did he?"

"I believe they were also discussing some business or another."

"Business?" Lady Sanderson blinked in confusion. "I am sure you must be mistaken."

Emma giggled, ignoring the small pang of guilt at deceiving the poor woman.

"That is quite possible. Dimitri is forever scolding me for making a muddle of what I am told." She deliberately paused. "Still, I was quite certain that he mentioned Lord Sanderson was seeking a buyer for a piece of property that he wishes to sell."

"That is impossible. My husband's estate is entailed despite his efforts to have the will altered. He has no authority to dispose of his property."

"I do not believe it was a part of the estate. Indeed,

Dimitri implied it was a rarely used home or building," Emma pressed. The men had to be holding her sister and the other girls somewhere in London. And if Lord Sanderson was as stupid as Dimitri had implied then he was quite likely to have hidden them in a place of convenience rather than ensuring their presence could not cause him scandal. "Or perhaps it was a shop." She let loose another giggle. "There, you see? I am hopeless in recalling what I have been told."

"My father owns several warehouses in Cutler Street, but I can assure you they are not for sale." Obviously flustered by Emma's probing, the woman managed an awkward curtsey. "If you will excuse me, it is time for Lancelot's bath."

They watched in silence as the woman scooped up her dog and scurried away with surprising speed for a woman of her considerable girth.

"She is in rather a hurry," Emma said.

"So I noticed." Leonida stepped directly in front of Emma, reaching to grasp her hands with a worried frown. "Emma."

"Hmm?"

"I am willing to go to great lengths to assist you in your search for Anya, but you cannot search through warehouses on Cutler Street without protection." She squeezed Emma's fingers. "Do you understand?"

Emma forced a smile, silently apologizing to the woman who had offered her such kindness.

"Of course."

DIMITRI'S INSTINCTS that had been honed in the gutters of St. Petersburg were on full alert as the carriage pulled to a halt in the dark, narrow street.

The large, uninhabited buildings and maze of alleys were a perfect refuge for criminals. And an even more perfect location for a trap.

Discreetly, he shifted on the leather seat, slipping his hand into the pocket of his greatcoat. His fingers curled with an easy familiarity around the handle of his loaded pistol. He had also tucked a knife in a sheath at his lower back and another in his high, glossy boot.

If Sanderson were stupid enough to assume he was the typical effete nobleman, he was bound to be unpleasantly surprised.

"Are you certain you have the correct address?"

The nobleman lifted a bottle of brandy to his mouth, taking a deep swig. Dimitri curled his lips in the darkness. Only a simpleton would allow his wits to be dulled in such a neighborhood.

"Quite certain," Sanderson assured him, a hint of smug amusement in his voice as he shoved open the door to the carriage and blithely stepped onto the filthy street.

With a great deal more caution, Dimitri followed his gaze, searching the shadows even as he kept his fingers curled around the handle of his pistol. Sanderson might be stupid enough to get his throat slit, but Dimitri did not intend to be such a willing victim.

At last his gaze returned to the stark brick building, searching the narrow windows for an indication of danger.

"I have visited a number of brothels and none of them have resembled a warehouse that reeks of tobacco," he rasped. "I shudder to think of what sort of female would ply her wares at such a location."

Taking a last drink of the brandy, Sanderson casually tossed aside the bottle, swaying in the sharp breeze. Dimitri grimaced. He abhorred a man who could not hold his spirits.

"This is not precisely a brothel," Sanderson slurred.

"Yes, I had managed to surmise as much," Dimitri said dryly. "You promised this evening I should have the opportunity to taste of innocence. I do not appreciate being misled."

Sanderson wagged a fat finger moving to unlock a heavy wooden door.

"Have patience."

"Patience will not transform this decrepit building into an establishment worthy of my patronage. Nor will it offer me the sort of female I had hoped to ease my hunger."

Stepping through the doorway, Sanderson waited for Dimitri to join him before closing the door and lighting a gas lantern that had been set on a low bench. The dull glow revealed precisely what Dimitri had anticipated. A cavernous room filled with crates that had recently been unloaded at the East India Docks. The only thing that appeared to be missing was the guard that must surely keep watch on such valuable property.

Sanderson weaved a path through the stacked crates. "Now that is where you are mistaken."

"What do you mean?" Dimitri demanded, warily following in his wake.

"First I must swear you to absolute secrecy."

Dimitri snorted, coming to an abrupt stop at the man's ridiculous theatrical manner.

"There are gentlemen who might enjoy this pretense of mystery, but I am not one." An explosion of fury raced through him. He had wasted endless nights being led about London by this stupid clod. Nights that he could have devoted to Emma and returning her to her rightful place in his bed. And for what? To be dangled by vague promises of young girls just ripe for the plucking? "Nor am I foolish enough to be led into so obvious a trap."

Sanderson blinked, as if surprised by Dimitri's suspicions.

"'Tis no trap, I assure you."

"Then why are we here?"

Sanderson allowed a sly smile to curve his lips. "You

are not alone in your preference for tender young creatures. The more tender the better, eh?"

"As you say."

"Unfortunately, there are those in society who do not fully appreciate our choice of entertainment, so we must hide in the shadows."

"Understandable." Dimitri grimly squashed his surge of hope. The man had been making vague references to his ability to procure young girls for days. "It is best not to attract unwanted attention."

"Precisely." Sanderson leaned toward Dimitri, oblivious to the gas lantern that swayed dangerously close to a nearby crate. Ridiculous twit. "Which is why we have a number of young females transported from Russia to be auctioned for your pleasure."

Dimitri tensed. "They are Russian?"

"An odd coincidence, is it not?"

"Odd indeed." Dimitri's voice was hoarse, his mouth dry. Russian females? Could he at last be on the threshold of destroying Count Nevskaya and his accomplices? It seemed impossible after so many years of futile effort. "And they are to be auctioned tonight?"

"Actually, the auction is not until tomorrow eve, but with a generous offer I am certain I can convince my partners to give you first choice of the wenches."

"The females are in the warehouse?"

"They are." Sanderson offered a leering smile. "Would you care to meet them?"

"More than you could imagine."

CHAPTER FOURTEEN

UNAWARE OF HIS COMPANION'S tense anticipation, Sanderson led Dimitri through a series of locked doors, then down a set of stone steps to a narrow tunnel below. Dimitri was not surprised by the secret passage. In fact, he was intimately familiar with such hidden cellars. Any gentleman who imported goods knew that it was vital to possess a public warehouse where the officials could inspect your legally transported cargo, and a separate location for those goods you prefer to keep away from prying eyes. He had several such places scattered throughout St. Petersburg.

"Follow me," Sanderson whispered, weaving his way through the damp tunnel.

Still conscious that he might very well be entering a trap, Dimitri remained on guard.

"I must admit I am curious how you managed to acquire Russian maidens," he prompted.

"It is a profitable exchange," the nobleman readily answered, the top of his high beaver hat nearly brushing the wooden beams that lined the ceiling and his glossy boots splashing through the occasional puddles. "We provide suitable English virgins to be sent to Russia and in return we are offered the tastiest of Russian fruits."

Dimitri hid a grimace, wondering how much of the business his father kept hidden from Sanderson. Count Nevskaya could not be so stupid as to offer more than the barest information to the babbling buffoon.

He could only hope it would be enough to convince Alexander Pavlovich to prosecute the nobleman.

"Very clever," he murmured. "I presume you have a colleague in Russia, so you need not make such a journey yourself?"

"We do, but of course, we are sworn to keep our identities in the deepest confidence."

"Granted a certain measure of caution is required, but surely there is no need for secrets among friends?" he urged with a chuckle.

"I doubt Count Nevskaya would agree," Sanderson grumbled, drunkenly unaware he had just revealed what Dimitri desired to hear. "He is obsessed with disguising his participation in our little scheme. There is a rumor he possesses an enemy that has pledged to destroy him. It has no doubt made him a tad skittish."

Dimitri smiled with cold satisfaction. "No doubt."

They had nearly reached the end of the tunnel where a heavy wooden door blocked their path when Sanderson abruptly turned to face Dimitri.

"A moment, sir."

Dimitri scowled with impatience. "Why are we stopping?"

Sanderson awkwardly cleared his throat. "Forgive me, but I wish to be assured you have recalled to bring along your purse. We are forced to hire rather dangerous ruffians to ensure the women maintain their innocence during the long voyage and they would not take kindly to a gentleman seeking to despoil a maid unless he had paid for the pleasure."

"I have come prepared." Dimitri reached beneath his coat to pull out the folded bills from his pocket, then he pulled his other hand out of his pocket just far enough to reveal the ivory handle of his pistol. "Fully prepared."

"So I see." Sanderson blanched, his hands unsteady as he turned to pound on the wooden door. "Valik, it is Sanderson. Open the door."

The door cracked open a sliver. "First I will see the money," a male voice thick with a Russian accent demanded.

A flush stained Sanderson's fat cheeks. He might be slow-witted, but he knew when he was being humiliated.

"Do not seek to rise above yourself, Valik," he growled. "The women are my property to dispose of as I wish."

"It is my duty to protect my employer's investment."

"Stand aside or I will have you hauled to Newgate prison and left to rot."

There was the sound of foul Russian curses, then with obvious reluctance the man pulled open the door and stepped back.

"Bring the females," Sanderson commanded as he swept regally into the cramped cellar.

Dimitri made use of the man's generous girth to covertly slide into the shadowed chamber unnoticed. A swift glance assured him that the room was empty beyond the hovering servant, but his tension did not lessen.

There was something oddly familiar about the Russian's bluntly carved features and small, deep-set eyes that glittered with cold intelligence. Dimitri's gaze lowered to take in the man's rough clothing that did nothing to hide the thick muscles and the pistol he held with ease.

He silently slid his own pistol out of his pocket, his body coiled and prepared to attack as the man approached Sanderson with a fierce scowl.

"First I will have payment…" He began, only to cease in shock as he caught sight of Dimitri over the nobleman's shoulder. Using his sharp instincts, he had his gun lifted and pointed at Dimitri's heart. "You."

Sanderson squeaked in terror as Dimitri roughly shoved him out of his way, his gun aimed at the Russian's head. He had discovered when he was a youth trying to survive on the streets that a shot to the heart was not always a killing blow. A hole in the head, however, was deadly.

"Bloody hell, have you taken leave of your senses?" Sanderson shouted.

"Stupid bastard," the servant growled, his gaze never wavering from Dimitri's grim expression.

"What are you doing?"

"Attempting to keep us from the gallows," Valik hissed. "Unless it was your intention to betray the count?"

Sanderson backed away, wringing his pudgy hands. "Do not be absurd. There must be some mistake."

"There is no mistake. Your fine Russian nobleman is Dimitri Tipova, the czar of St. Petersburg's criminals and sworn enemy of my employer."

Accepting that his charade was at an end, Dimitri held his gun steady as he calculated the best means of escaping the cellars that did not include a coffin.

"Sworn enemy?" he taunted, hoping that the temperamental servant could be prodded into recklessness. "Very dramatic."

"Lord almighty," Sanderson wailed. "We must do something."

"You will collect the girls and transport them out of England," Valik commanded with a composure at complete odds with his employer.

Dimitri was under no illusion which of the two was more dangerous. Which was precisely why his gun remained trained on the Russian even as he cursed the possibility of Sanderson slipping from his grasp.

"Now?" the nobleman rasped.

"Of course now, you idiot."

"But surely there is no need to panic? If you—" Sanderson waved his hands in Dimitri's direction. "Properly dispose of the threat then we can continue with the auction as planned. We are all interested in ensuring we gain a measure of profit before we ship the cargo."

Dimitri laughed with mocking amusement. "My father must have been desperate to have entered into business with such a buffoon."

The Russian grimaced. "I did warn him that his English partners were fools destined to ruin our scheme."

"How dare you speak of your betters in such a fashion?" Emboldened by his greed, Sanderson took a step forward, his double chins quivering with outrage. "Valik, you will kill this traitor and be rid of his body. I will continue with the auction as originally planned. Do you hear me?"

Fury tightened Valik's brutish face, his eyes glittering with a deadly hatred.

"All I hear is a braying ass who is determined to destroy us all," he snapped. "Do you believe that Tipova told no one he suspected you were involved in selling children?"

"Who would he—bloody hell," Sanderson gasped, pulling a lacy handkerchief from his pocket to dab at the sweat beading his upper lip. "The Duke of Huntley. I am ruined."

"It is not only Huntley who is aware of your debauchery, but the prime minister," Dimitri admitted with a cold smile. He had met with the gentleman only days after his arrival in London, thanks to Huntley's insistence.

Sanderson turned a pasty gray, setting aside the gas lantern as he swayed in horror.

"Liverpool?"

"To be honest I was taken aback by his eagerness to have you arrested. But then I realized a public trial at the Old Bailey might be a perfect means of assuring the unsettled populace that the nobles are not above the law." Dimitri ruthlessly pressed. "Perhaps your worthless existence might have some purpose after all."

"Oh, my God. Liverpool has hated me since we were

at Oxford together. A damned shame those Cato Street conspirators did not manage to kill the humorless prude," the distraught Sanderson muttered, clearly too ignorant to realize that had the radicals managed to assassinate the cabinet members as they had planned, they intended to overthrow the entire government, as well. And to be rid of noblemen such as Sanderson and his chums. "What the devil am I to do?"

"You will take the women from this warehouse and find some means to get them out of the country," Valik demanded.

Sanderson shook his head in panic. "No, I cannot."

There was a tense pause as Valik considered his limited choices. Then, catching both Dimitri and Sanderson by surprise, he withdrew a matching pistol from the pocket of his dark wool coat and shoved it into Sanderson's hand.

"Here."

Sanderson cursed, fumbling to point the gun in Dimitri's direction.

"What the devil are you doing?"

"Attempting to keep my head attached to my body," Valik admitted, backing toward the door that led deeper into the catacombs. "I will see to the girls."

Dimitri's teeth clenched as Sanderson's fingers tensed on the pistol. It was doubtful the damned nobleman could hit a target at ten paces if he were aiming, but it would be just Dimitri's luck that the bastard would kill him by accident.

"What of me?" Sanderson shrilled.

"You will..." Valik paused with a cruel smile. "Dispose of the problem you have caused."

"Wait..."

The servant disappeared into the shadows, leaving behind a tense silence.

Dimitri covertly shifted forward. If he could distract

the nobleman, he might be able to overpower him before the dolt could squeeze off a shot.

"Well, Sanderson, it appears that you have been left to bear the punishment for the sins of others."

"I will not—" Sanderson gave a dangerous wave of the gun as he noticed Dimitri's slow advance. "Stay back."

"I could be of assistance."

"Aye, you truly do believe me to be an idiot."

"I have no interest in you or your lack of intelligence, Sanderson," Dimitri soothed. "My purpose in coming to England was solely to destroy Count Nevskaya. If you cooperate, I will speak to Alexander Pavlovich in your defense."

Sanderson licked his lips. "What would you have me do?"

"Return with me to Russia."

"Russia? Why?"

Dimitri took another sly step forward. Still too far away to strike, but ever closer.

"I want you to confess all you know of the count's involvement in the slave trade."

The man jerked, his eyes wide. "We have never been involved with slaves."

Dimitri could not hide his revulsion at the ridiculous protest.

"Did I offend your delicate sensibilities?" he mocked. "Do you perhaps choose to refer to your sordid business as kidnapping defenseless children and selling them to be abused by disgusting lechers?"

Sanderson frowned in puzzlement. "They are just peasants. What good are they except to become whores?"

Dimitri stilled, his finger twitching on the trigger of his pistol. Unlike his companion, he was a deadly shot. One bullet and the twit would be a rotting corpse.

Then, he sucked in a steadying breath, reminding himself

that the only means to bring an end to the trafficking of Russian girls was to ensure his father was exposed as a monster and driven from society. And for that he needed Sanderson alive.

"I doubt the good citizens of England would so readily agree," he warned. "In their current mood they might very well stir up a riot if they are not satisfied with your punishment. Have you ever witnessed a man ravaged by a mob? It is a nasty means to die."

Sanderson trembled, the sweat dripping from his ruddy face.

"And what would traveling to Russia achieve?"

"If you confess to the czar, he might be willing to offer you sanctuary in Russia."

"So I can live like a heathen in some frozen village far from decent society?" Sanderson looked as if Dimitri had threatened to geld him. "Never."

"So you would rather be the source of scandalous ridicule as you are paraded through the streets on the way to the gallows?"

"No."

Overcome with his terror, Sanderson stumbled backward, his hand tightening on the pistol. Dimitri leaped to the side as the deafening sound of a gunshot filled the small chamber, but it was a heartbeat too late as the bullet sliced through his upper arm.

Landing on the hard ground, he struggled against a tide of blackness as the shocking pain ripped through his body.

EMMA WAS FULLY AWARE of the foolishness of sneaking from the Huntley town house dressed in the rough clothing of a stable hand that she had stolen from the laundry room. And for taking a hack to the nasty warren of streets where the Sanderson warehouses were located. And for hiding in a narrow alley as the elegant carriage came to a halt in the dark street and two gentlemen stepped onto the damp cobblestones.

It would no doubt serve her right if she were to have her throat cut and her body tossed into the gutter, she had ruefully admitted. But she had made the decision that she would do whatever necessary to rescue Anya when she had left Yabinsk. Even if that meant putting her life at risk.

Remaining in the shadows, her heart gave a sharp lurch as she easily recognized Dimitri standing in front of the warehouse. Despite the darkness she would know the broad set of his shoulders and the proud, perfect lines of his profile anywhere. There was no other gentleman in England who could match his dark, ruthless beauty.

And, of course, there was that disturbing awareness that swept through her body like a tidal wave. She would know Dimitri was near even if she were blindfolded.

So did his presence mean that her desperate hope that Anya and the other girls might be hidden in the warehouse was not utter insanity?

Gathering her ebbing courage, Emma silently crept forward as the men entered, waiting until she heard them crossing the wooden planks of the floor before slipping through the door. Her heart thundered in her chest, her mouth dry with fear. Whether it was the terror of being murdered by a ruffian, or of being caught by Dimitri was impossible to say.

Either posed a fate she intended to avoid.

She stepped into the large storage room, her nose wrinkling at the overwhelming scent of dried tobacco and spices. In the darkness she could make out the silhouettes of wooden crates stacked in neat rows, and in the distance the unmistakable glow of a gas light that was rapidly disappearing down a flight of stairs.

Not giving herself time to consider the countless reasons

she should be fleeing the warehouse with all possible speed, Emma cautiously crept past the crates, lingering at the opening to the stairs. She paused, ensuring that the men were not about to make a sudden reappearance. Then praying the wooden steps did not squeak and reveal her presence, she forced herself into the narrow stairwell.

She stumbled as she reached the bottom, startled by the black shroud of darkness that surrounded her. Not that she should have been surprised. Underground tunnels were as a rule dark and damp.

Reaching out her hand, she hesitantly made her way over the uneven ground, her rasping breath the only sound to break the thick silence.

Then, just as she began to fear that she was hopelessly lost in the dark, she heard distant voices. She shuffled forward, relieved by the dim glow of light that spilled from an open door into the tunnel.

Reaching the edge of the pool of light, she paused and pressed herself against the wall of the tunnel, clearly able to hear the raised voices of the men. For a moment she struggled to understand the argument, then her heart gave a violent leap.

Dear God, Lord Sanderson was holding Dimitri at gunpoint. And just as alarming, Anya was hidden somewhere nearby and that horrid Valik was rushing off to take her away.

Emma knew she had to do something. She had to…

Her shocked mind was still struggling to decide on a course of action when the air was shattered by the sound of a gunshot.

"Dimitri," she whispered, sheer terror holding her prisoner as Lord Sanderson suddenly stumbled past her and disappeared down the tunnel. But as Dimitri's low moan reached her, she thrust aside her fear and rushed into the room, discovering Dimitri lying on the floor, his beautiful face twisted in pain. With a small cry she sank onto her knees, her hand reaching to cup his cheek. "Dimitri, can you hear me?"

"Emma?" The thick curtain of his lashes lifted, revealing golden eyes that were shockingly lucid considering he had just been shot. And smoldering with fury. "What are you doing here?"

"It does not matter." She ran a frantic gaze over his body, spotting the torn coat sleeve and the blood already staining the fabric. "You have been hurt, we must get you to a surgeon."

Muttering under his breath, Dimitri sat upright, studying the wound beneath the heavy layers of clothing.

"It is no more than a scratch," he concluded, forcing himself to his feet.

Emma straightened, reaching to grasp his arm as he swayed. "Must you be so stubborn?"

He cast a smoldering glance over her wool coat and male breeches.

"Be assured we will have a thorough discussion regarding who is the more stubborn later, *milaya,* but for now I have to capture Sanderson before he can escape."

Emma frowned in puzzlement. For a moment the thought that Dimitri had been seriously wounded had driven everything from her mind. Now, the memory of the argument she had overheard seared through her mind.

"Sanderson?"

"He cannot have gone far."

"What does it matter where he has gone?"

"With his confession to Alexander Pavlovich, my father will at last be exposed to society as a monster."

"But we must go after that horrible Valik. He said he was taking the girls out of England," she argued.

Dimitri made a sound of impatience. "They will not be allowed to escape."

Emma's lips parted to inform him that she would go after the man alone if necessary when they both turned toward the door and the unmistakable sound of approaching footsteps.

"Emma?" a familiar male voice called.

Dimitri sent her a startled frown. "You brought Huntley with you?"

"Nothing so polite," the duke drawled, appearing ridiculously out of place in his elegant black coat and glossy Hessians. His stark expression, however, perfectly mirrored Dimitri's. "She snuck away the moment my back was turned."

Indifferent to the nobleman's fierce displeasure, Emma regarded him with a pleading expression.

"Please, you must help me, Your Grace. My sister—"

Her words were rudely interrupted as Dimitri firmly shoved her into the grasp of the duke.

"Return Emma to your town house and have her locked in her rooms."

Stefan had her arm in a vice grip before Emma could escape. "Very well."

"No!" Emma futilely struggled to free herself. "I am going to find Anya."

The two men ignored her.

"What of you?" the duke inquired.

"I must stop Sanderson from fleeing." His golden gaze shifted to Emma's mutinous expression. "Then I will make certain the girls are found and taken to my ship. They will be safe there."

Stefan dipped his head in agreement. "My servants will assist you."

"Thank you." His gaze never shifted from Emma's face, his own expression bleak. "Do not let her out of your sight."

In disbelief, Emma felt herself being ruthlessly urged

toward the door she had so recently charged through. Precisely the opposite direction she was desperate to go.

"Let go of me." She glared at Dimitri as she was over-
powered by the large Englishman. "I will never forgive you
for this, Dimitri Tipova."

His jaw tightened. "Emma, these men are vicious. They
will kill anyone they believe threatens them."

"I do not care," she shouted. "Anya is here. I will not
leave without her."

Dimitri turned his attention to the duke. "Huntley."

"You are certain?" the duke demanded.

"Yes."

"Forgive me," Stefan muttered, then with one powerful
motion he had Emma tossed over his shoulder and was
rapidly heading back down the tunnel.

Emma cursed and screamed and kicked, but her efforts
to escape were ignored as she was hauled away like a bit
of unwanted rubbish.

Why had she halted to see if Dimitri were alive or dead,
she bitterly wondered?

Had she continued across the room and into the darkness
beyond she might even now be rescuing Anya from harm.
Instead, she had allowed her weakness for the captivat-
ing criminal to make her hesitate. And as punishment for
her vulnerability she was once again unable to save her
sister.

It was a mistake she would not make again, she
swore.

Attempting to gather her badly shredded dignity, Emma
ceased her struggles and allowed herself to be carried from
the warehouse and bundled into the elegant black carriage.
Stefan followed behind, settling his large body on the
leather bench opposite her.

"This is for the best, Emma," he assured her as the carriage jerked into motion.

She clenched her hands in her lap, cursing the day she had ever encountered Dimitri Tipova.

"And what if it were your sister being held captive by ruthless beasts who intend to auction her to the highest bidder? Would you meekly return to your home and hope she be rescued?"

Stefan's expression gentled in understanding.

"I have been forced to swallow my pride and accept that another might possess the skills I lacked to confront a particular danger." He reached across to lightly touch her cheek. "You must trust Dimitri."

She turned to glare out the window, her heart aching with disappointment.

She had already put her trust in Dimitri. Naive fool that she was. Even when she had sensed that his lust for revenge was greater than his affection for her.

"Dimitri is driven by his need to punish his father," she said tightly. "He will sacrifice Anya if it ensures the humiliation of Count Nevskaya."

Unable to deny the truth of her words, Stefan heaved a sigh.

"Then trust my servants. They will not allow the girls to be taken from London."

"I trust no one but myself."

"Emma—"

"Please, no more lectures, Your Grace," she warned in raw tones.

A tense silence filled the air as they rumbled their way through the London streets to Mayfair. More than once Emma considered the desperate notion of trying to leap from the carriage and make her way back to the warehouse only to dismiss such foolishness.

Not only was it quite likely that the fall would break her neck, but she would not be allowed to go more than a few steps before Stefan's burly grooms would have her captured.

Arriving at the imposing town house, Stefan kept a tight grip on her arm as he escorted her into the elegant vestibule.

"My staff will be warned that you are not to leave the grounds," he declared in rueful tones.

Emma tilted her chin. "Then I am your prisoner?"

"My guest who I intend to protect, with or without your blessing."

"You must do as you think best." Turning on her heel, she headed for the nearby stairs. "As will I."

CHAPTER FIFTEEN

THE BLUSH OF DAWN BARELY painted the sky when Emma heard the key being turned in her lock.

After being imprisoned in her bedchamber by the Duke of Huntley, she had spent the long night pacing the floor, dividing her time between cursing Dimitri Tipova for treating her as if she were a blundering idiot and praying that he swiftly returned with her sister.

How dare he send her away when she had traveled halfway around the world to find Anya? And how dare he put his need for revenge before the young girls who were at the mercy of those despicable animals?

As the hours had passed, her anger had swelled until she was trembling with the need to escape from her lavish prison. She had been taking care of herself for a number of years and she did not appreciate having her hard-earned independence snatched away.

So perhaps it was understandable that when the door slid open to reveal the foreign gentleman who had kidnapped her during Sir Jergens's soiree she did not scream. Or even attempt to race past him into the hall. Instead, she watched in weary curiosity as he offered a smooth bow.

"May I enter?"

"I…" She licked her lips, struggling to force her foggy brain to think clearly. A voice in the back of her mind warned that honest gentlemen did not sneak through a duke's town house and approach a maiden in her private chambers. But it was a voice she ignored as she met his steady black gaze. "Yes."

He hovered in the doorway, a faint smile curving his lips. "If you would be so kind as to close the curtains?"

"Why?"

"There are an inordinate number of servants lurking about the grounds. If they were to notice the shadow of a gentleman in your private chamber they would be certain to investigate."

Emma bit her lip, then gave a jerky nod. She understood the danger of allowing a strange man into her rooms, but she also knew that one scream and a dozen servants would rush to her rescue. The man had risked his life to seek her out in such an unconventional manner. Whatever he desired of her it had to be important.

"Of course."

She moved to pull shut the heavy curtains, inanely aware she was still attired in the rough breeches and linen shirt of a stable boy, her hair hanging in tangles and her face smudged from her adventure in the warehouse. The stranger, on the other hand, was elegantly dressed in a black jacket and satin pantaloons with a huge ruby twinkling in the depths of his cravat. As if he had just stepped out of an elegant ballroom.

Wrapping her arms around her waist, she watched as the darkly beautiful man entered the room and closed the door behind his slender form.

"What are you doing here?" she demanded.

Holding out his hands in a gesture of peace, he slowly approached her.

"As I suggested during our first encounter we have a mutual purpose in traveling to London."

"Surely it is past time for allusion and innuendo?" she snapped, her temper frayed and her nerves raw with concern for her sister. "If you have something to say, then please do so."

"Plain speech? Very well." He halted directly before

her, his exotic scent tantalizing her. "I know why you have traveled to England."

She stilled, wary he could be hoping to trick her into confessing her secrets.

"How could you possibly know?"

He reached up to pluck the hat off his head and tossed it onto a low table, the sable darkness of his hair glinting in the flames of the fireplace.

"With the proper enticement and enough patience a man can discover any information he desires."

She shivered, unable to believe that Dimitri's crew would be disloyal, no matter what the temptation. But then again, Dimitri had been forced to confide his purpose in coming to England to a number of government officials, including the prime minister. She doubted that their staffs would be above suspicion.

"And why would you be interested in my reason for traveling to England?"

His black gaze swept over her face, lingering on the lush curve of her lips.

"Beyond my fascination with your beauty?"

Her heart gave a nervous flutter.

"Please, do not," she breathed.

"Allow me to begin at the beginning." Pressing his hands together in a formal gesture, he offered a solemn dip of his head. "I am Caliph Rajih."

"Caliph?" Emma frowned, attempting to recall her studies of the near Orient—lessons that had been sadly vague when it came to foreign royalty. "You are a prince?"

"I am a leader of my people," he agreed.

The knowledge should perhaps have been shocking. After all, what sort of prince lurked in the shadows rather than take his place among the finest of London society? But Emma was more resigned than shocked. Had she not already suspected that he was accustomed to giving commands and having them obeyed? It was etched in the proud lines of his face and the arrogant carriage of his slender body.

"Where?" she demanded.

"Egypt."

Again, she was struck by thoughts of sunlight blazing over golden dunes and tents crowded about a small oasis. Men forged in the merciless desert were rumored to be as hard and unforgiving as the land that birthed them.

"You are a very long way from your home."

"As are you." His hand lifted to caress a stray curl resting against her cheek. "We are similar in many ways."

She hastily stepped away from his disturbing touch. "Why have you come to London?"

He studied her for a long moment, the dark eyes glittering with a wicked anticipation that sent a shiver of unease down her spine. Then, with a shrug, he paced toward the fireplace and leaned against the marble mantel.

"I will not bore you with the long and ofttimes tragic history of my country, but suffice it to say that we at last possess a powerful viceroy who is prepared to embrace the future rather than to smother us in the past," he said, reaching beneath his jacket to pull out a lacquered snuff box. His brows lifted as he caught Emma's sudden flare of amusement. "Why do you smile?"

Emma sank onto one of the sofas, weary after her endless night of pacing.

"You are obviously of the desert and yet there is something oddly English about you."

"Ah." With a practiced motion he flipped open the box and took a small pinch of the snuff, placing it neatly on his wrist before bending his head to inhale the perfumed tobacco. He returned the box to his pocket and met Emma's small smile. "My father sent me to school here when I was just twelve. He believed, as the pasha does, that a closer connection to the West is vital for our survival. I lived in this country until my father's death six years ago."

That certainly explained his ease with the English language.

"Then you are a diplomat?"

"When the occasion demands." He shrugged, his expression somber. "On this journey, however, my purpose is to bring to an end an ancient practice that has been a blight on my country's reputation."

"I fear I do not comprehend."

"The slave trade."

"Oh." She shook her head in confusion. "I thought..."

His eyes narrowed as she broke off her hasty words.

"You thought we were all savages who were so desperate for soft white flesh that we encourage the infidels to peddle their females in our markets?"

She wrinkled her nose, accepting she was very much in the wrong. How often she had to hide her outrage when she had overheard herself being referred to as a Russian savage? It was shameful that she would offer the same obtuse assumption.

"Forgive me."

He held up a slender hand, his expression rueful. "No, it is I who begs your forgiveness, Emma. For too long our corrupt officials have turned a blind eye to the traffickers. The pasha, however, seeks to improve our relationship with England as well as the Continent and he has made a vow to bar the peddling of females in our markets."

She nodded in sympathy. Despite the best efforts of the Romanovs, much of Russia still remained mired in the past. Change was never a simple matter for people to embrace, even when it might be for their own good.

"Does this have something to do with my sister?"

"I believe so. During the past few years I have noticed a number of Russian whores in the brothels of Cairo. I, of course, began my search for those responsible in Russia. You can imagine my frustration when I could discover no evidence of ships carrying unwilling females to Cairo."

Emma was quick to realize the truth. "Because they were traveling to England."

A pleased smile curved his lips, as if she had somehow fulfilled his expectation.

"You are intelligent as well as beautiful," he murmured. "Yes, the girls are taken from Russia to London and sold for the private pleasure of wealthy Englishmen. Eventually the men become weary of their trinket and wish to be rid of her with as little fuss as possible."

She ignored the sick dread in her stomach. If she allowed herself to dwell on all the horrible tortures that Anya might be enduring she would go stark raving mad.

Instead, she concentrated on the caliph's unexpected information.

It appeared that Dimitri had underestimated his father once again. They had assumed that once the Russian girls had been sold to the English roués that they would eventually be left in a local brothel. But if the caliph was right...

Dear Lord, she had to find Anya.

Emma surged to her feet, her hands trembling as she pushed back the thick curls that tumbled about her shoulders.

"You suspect they are taken to Cairo?"

His hooded gaze seared over her pale face before lowering to her slender body.

"They are no longer innocent, but there are a great many of my countrymen who harbor a lust for such pale, perfect beauty," he admitted, his voice low and husky.

Emma shivered, sternly refusing to allow her thoughts to stray from Anya and the beasts who held her captive.

"Do you believe the same men who have brought them to England also arrange to have them taken to Cairo?"

"Yes."

She pressed a hand to her heaving stomach. "Is there no limit to their depravity?"

"It would seem not." His dark features hardened, a lethal fury flaring through his eyes. "From what I have managed to discover, Count Nevskaya's servants remain in London until they collect the Russian females that have been returned to them, as well as the English girls that are their payment, and travel to Egypt. Once there, they sell the Russians in the markets before continuing back to St. Petersburg with the English maidens to pleasure the count and his friends."

"There is little wonder Dimitri was incapable of untangling their sordid business."

"Tipova," the caliph growled. "Do not speak his name in my presence."

She blinked at his fierce response. "Why?"

"I went to great trouble to prepare my trap only to have Tipova blunder into my snare and send my prey fleeing into the night." He straightened from the mantel and crossed to stand before her. "Along with your sister."

"Anya." Emma instinctively grasped his arm. "You know where she is?"

His warm hand covered her fingers, his male scent cloaking her in a musky spice.

"If she was among the females taken from the warehouse, then she is currently aboard a ship called the *Katherine Marie* and headed for Cairo."

The *Katherine Marie?* Emma would have fallen to her knees if he had not grasped her arms to keep her upright.

"Dear God, I failed her," she breathed, barely aware of being pulled into the caliph's arms and held against his chest. "It does not matter how I try, I always fail her."

Still holding her close, he bent his head to whisper in her ear.

"It is not too late, Emma."

She pulled back to meet the dark glitter of his gaze. "What do you mean?"

"My ship is being prepared as we speak. I intend to

sail for Cairo within the hour." He smiled with a blatant challenge. "Will you join me?"

A PRISTINE LAYER OF WHITE snow draped London as Dimitri wearily entered the Huntley town house.

In the distance a church bell tolled and the sound of the coal wagon rattled over the cobblestones, but a sleepy silence remained settled over the elegant neighborhood. It might be near ten in the morning, but society remained snuggled in their warm beds. It would be hours before they were primped and prepared to meet the day.

Worthless nitwits.

Allowing the waiting butler to take his outer garments, Dimitri shoved his fingers through his damp hair and climbed the steps.

His every instinct urged him to travel directly to Emma's chambers. The sight of the wounded fury burning in her eyes as Huntley had carried her away had plagued him the entire morning.

It was infuriating. He had only been protecting the stubborn minx despite her determination to get herself killed. God almighty, what sort of female would disguise herself as a stable boy and sneak about a neighborhood that would terrify the most hardened criminal? And then to attempt to charge after the Russian brute as if she were indestructible...

Obviously, Emma Linley-Kirov was in dire need of a man willing and able to restrain her dangerous impulses.

So why did he feel an overwhelming compulsion to seek her out and banish the shadow of betrayal from her eyes?

Climbing the marble steps, he was jerked out of his thoughts as Huntley appeared on the landing above him, clearly having lain in wait for his return.

"Tipova. At last." The duke wore a brocade gown with his dark hair tousled and his face unshaven, but his casual appearance did not lessen his imperious manner as he gestured for Dimitri to follow him into the book-lined study. He waved a slender hand toward the walnut desk as he crossed to toss another log into the fireplace. "The brandy is on the desk."

"I prefer my vodka," Dimitri said, pulling out his silver flask as he strolled to stand beside the bay window that offered a view of the snowy street below.

Stefan replaced the fire screen, then joined Dimitri at the window.

"You look like hell."

"Which is precisely how I feel," Dimitri admitted.

The duke's astute glance lingered on the bloody rip in Dimitri's coat.

"Shall I summon a surgeon?"

"I have recovered from far worse." He took a drink of the vodka. "Have you spoken to Emma this morning?"

"It is still early. She is asleep in her bedchamber."

Dimitri narrowed his gaze. Emma was frantic with her concern for her sister, not to mention anxious to stick a dagger in his heart, he would bet his last ruble she was pacing her floor as she awaited his return.

Assuming she had not found a means of slipping past Huntley's servants.

"Are you certain?"

Huntley grimaced. "I personally locked her in her rooms despite my wife's fervent protests. Any debt between us is now paid in full."

A sympathetic smile touched Dimitri's mouth. He had been subjected to Leonida's "fervent protests" during her stay in St. Petersburg.

"Agreed."

"Tell me what happened after I left," Huntley commanded. "Did you manage to locate Sanderson?"

Dimitri rubbed the aching muscles of his neck, still awaiting the sense of elation he had expected to feel. He told himself that he was too weary to properly celebrate his victory.

"I apprehended him as his carriage was leaving his town house. By the amount of luggage he had packed I assume he intended to be away from his home for a considerable length of time."

"Did he struggle?"

"He fell to his knees, weeping like a baby."

Huntley shook his head in disgust. "Spineless coward."

"He did manage one lucky shot," Dimitri muttered, his arm aching from the bullet wound. "The bastard."

"Where is he now?"

"Your message to Liverpool ensured the prime minister was prepared for my arrival with my captive. Liverpool swore that Sanderson would be well guarded until he could finish his confession to the king."

"And then?"

"Then he is to be given into my care to be taken to Alexander Pavlovich."

"What of the others?"

Dimitri shrugged as he turned to pace the floor. Despite the exhaustion that clung heavily to his body, he felt oddly restless.

Or perhaps not so oddly, he wryly acknowledged.

The incessant need to be with Emma was an itch that would not be dismissed. She was his to protect, a savage voice whispered in the back of his mind. Not Huntley's.

"The king's guards have been sent to capture Timmons and Jergens. They should be in custody by the end of the day," he muttered, unnerved by the primitive sensations that smoldered deep in his heart. "It will take weeks, if not months to gather the various servants involved."

"So it is done."

Dimitri turned back toward his companion, his expression grim.

"Not entirely."

"Ah." Huntley gave a nod of comprehension. "Anya."

"Your servants have been searching through the stews, but thus far they have found nothing."

"That is unfortunate."

Dimitri's sharp laugh echoed through the room. "It is more than unfortunate. Emma will hold me responsible if we do not find her sister."

Huntley offered a smile of sympathy, wise enough not to bother with absurd assurances that Emma would understand Dimitri was only doing what was best for her. They both knew the woman could not be reasonable when it came to her sister.

"They cannot hide forever, and I assure you that I have the roads leading from London being watched," he promised. "They will not slip past my guards."

"And the docks?"

With a shrug, the duke moved to pour himself a glass of brandy. "I have sent word that anyone seeking passage for a number of young ladies is to be detained."

Dimitri's brows snapped together. "Huntley, men who are in the smuggling trade do not purchase tickets."

"Perhaps not as a rule, but those men had no plans to flee London without notice. It is not a simple matter to arrange for a ship willing to sail with illegal cargo."

"True enough," Dimitri grudgingly conceded, still far from satisfied.

There were a large number of captains willing to turn a blind eye to smuggled goods with the proper incentive, but there were only a handful who were willing to dabble in the slave trade. It would surely take Valik a few days to arrange passage out of England.

Unless…

The flask dropped from his hand, the fine vodka spilling across the Persian carpet.

Huntley stepped toward him with a frown. "Tipova?"

"It is a simple matter if there is already a ship waiting," he gritted.

"What?"

"The *Katherine Marie*."

Huntley's eyes widened. "Bloody hell."

"Well, I hope the two of you are pleased with yourself."

As one they both turned to head toward the door, only to be halted as Leonida swept into the room, appearing remarkably beautiful in an ivory morning gown trimmed with sable and her golden hair artfully curled, but it was the angry flush on her cheeks and the tears glittering in her eyes that captured Dimitri's attention.

"Darling, now is not the best time…" Huntley began, then paused as his wife pointed a finger directly in his face.

"She is gone."

An icy dread sliced through Dimitri. "What did you say?"

Leonida turned to glare in his direction, her expression one of furious accusation.

"Since I refuse to starve my guests while they are being held as a prisoner beneath my roof I had a breakfast tray prepared," she hissed. "When I entered Emma's room I discovered her bed had not been slept in and that her belongings were missing. She is gone and you have no one to blame but yourself."

CHAPTER SIXTEEN

EMMA STOOD AT THE BOW of the ship, watching the dancing waves that shimmered the color of mercury in the sunlight. In the distance, the coast of Alexandria was drawing ever closer, making her shiver at the exotic silhouettes of domes and obelisks that stood starkly against the vivid blue sky. Dear Lord, had she been a fool to come here?

It was a question that had haunted her since she had allowed Caliph Rajih to lead her from the Duke of Huntley's town house to his waiting ship.

Not that Rajih had given her cause for alarm, she conceded. In truth, he had behaved as a perfect gentleman during the voyage, joining her only for dinner in her private cabin before placing a chaste kiss on her lips and disappearing topside.

Emma could not discern whether his restraint was because the rough seas had demanded his full attention among the crew or because his flirtations in London had merely been a means to lure her onto his ship.

Or perhaps he considered her a female worthy of more than a convenient affair that would make her a source of amusement among his crew.

Unlike some gentlemen of her acquaintance...

Her hands tightened on the brass railing, her teeth clenching at the unwelcome thought of Dimitri Tipova.

No, she would not waste her time thinking of the man who had sacrificed her sister for his own revenge.

"Imposing, is it not?" a soft male voice whispered in her ear.

She turned her head to discover Rajih at her side, her eyes widening in surprise at the sight of him standing in his traditional white robes. Accustomed to seeing him in European attire, she could not deny a faint shiver of appreciation at the sight of his sophisticated facade stripped away to reveal the ruthless man of the desert beneath.

Of course, what woman would not appreciate the striking beauty of his dark, austere features and black eyes that burned with a restless intelligence?

Disturbed by her unexpected reaction to his presence, she abruptly turned to regard the vast citadel that Rajih was pointing out with obvious pride.

Constructed of pale stone, the large fortress consumed most of the island where it had been built to defend the city of Alexandria. Her gaze obediently skimmed fortified walls and forbidding castles that no doubt had terrified potential invaders.

"Very impressive."

"Yes, however it is a pity that the famed lighthouse that once stood in that precise location was destroyed. It was said to possess a vast mirror that could offer glimpses of distant cities and could cause attacking ships to be consumed by flames."

A portion of her tension eased at his light tone. As was no doubt his intention, she acknowledged with a faint smile.

"A most astonishing mirror."

"It was. But now it is lost like so many of our treasures." He shrugged, the anguished regret she sensed deep inside him at the callous plunder of his country tempered by a grim determination to regain command of Egypt's future. "But enough of the past." He swept his hands toward the busy quay. "This is the future."

Emma's attention turned toward the docks, momentarily dazzled by the large crowd milling along the banks of the river. Men with turbans, veiled women, sailors, fishermen, hawkers and children in all hues filled the air with a near-deafening clatter.

It was confusing and strikingly foreign and for a moment, Emma breathed in the brilliant sights and sounds. How different this was from her cold, barren cottage in Yabinsk.

Never in her wildest fantasies could she ever have considered the thought of standing at the bow of a ship with a handsome caliph at her side as they arrived in Egypt.

With a shake of her head she sharply reminded herself of the reason for her to be so far from home.

"Exquisite, but far more crowded than I expected," she admitted, her brow furrowed with concern. "How will we ever find Anya among so many?"

"It is doubtful the men will linger in Alexandria. They will earn a far better price for their merchandise in Cairo. For now there is nothing to be done but to appreciate the charms of the city." Rajih stepped closer, a smile curving his lips as she gave a sudden exclamation of delight. "Tell me what you see."

She pointed toward the strange animals kneeling at the edge of the water.

"I presume those must be the camels I have read of?"

He chuckled at her amazement. "They are as necessary to my people as the horses are to yours, but I must warn you they can be as temperamental and stubborn as a female."

She narrowed her gaze. "Indeed."

Capturing her hand, he lifted it to press his lips to her knuckles, then before she could protest his intimacy, he was pointing toward the horizon.

"There. Do you see the dome?"

"Yes."

"That is the seraglio of the pasha."

"Seraglio?"

"The harem." He smiled at her predictable frown before

smoothly turning her attention toward the towering obe-
lisk. "And there is Cleopatra's Needle as well as Amud
el-Sawari, or as the French have called it, Pompey's Pillar."
His fingers brushed her cheek, his dark eyes lingering on
the curve of her lips. "Perhaps if we have the opportunity
I will take you to the catacombs. They are quite popular
among the tourists."

Her heart missed a tiny beat. Only a female in her grave
would fail to appreciate Rajih's potent attraction.

"But surely you do not intend to linger?"

"It will be morning before a boat can be arranged to
take us to Cairo."

Her hands tightened on the railing. She had been certain
they were gaining on the men who held her sister captive.
Now Rajih was suggesting she tour Alexandria as if she
were a silly tourist while Anya was taken ever farther away
from her.

"What about those camels?" she demanded. "There
must be a few we could—"

Rajih turned her to meet his somber gaze. "Emma, it
will be far quicker, not to mention considerably more pleasant to travel by boat."

She made a sound of impatience. "I am not a pampered
lady of society. I am accustomed to hard work and considerable discomfort when necessary."

"But it is not necessary." He laid a finger over her lips
to cease her objections. "And while I do not question your
fortitude you are not yet prepared for the unmerciful punishment of the desert. You must trust me."

Emma heaved a frustrated sigh. She did not want to trust
Rajih. Or Dimitri. Or any other man.

She wanted to find Anya and return home where they
both belonged.

Unfortunately, she had no choice but to depend upon the

caliph and to pray that he truly intended to help her rescue her sister from the monsters who had stolen her.

She returned to her cabin as they docked, pulling on a bonnet that was the precise shade of her pale orchid gown and arranged the veil to cover her face. Then, standing aside as her baggage was taken by a small boy wearing no more than a baggy pair of pants and sleeveless vest, she allowed Rajih to lead her off the ship and into a waiting carriage.

She settled on the leather seat, wincing at the turbaned servants who ran ahead of the vehicle, cudgeling the unwary who strayed in their path.

"Where are we to stay?"

"I own a house in Alexandria." Rajih waved a slender hand at the men who rushed to line the streets, shouting out what Emma presumed must be words of welcome. "It is far more modest than my home in Cairo, but it will offer a welcome comfort after such a rough journey."

On the point of demanding the precise nature of their living arrangements, Emma was distracted as their carriage was halted by a caravan of donkeys carrying men who beat small drums. Following them was a small crowd attired in silk robes trimmed with gold.

"Good heavens."

"Do not fear." Rajih placed a comforting arm around her shoulders. "It can be somewhat overwhelming for a visitor."

"Somewhat?"

"Customs and fashions, and even religion, might separate countries, but people are very much the same wherever you might travel."

She sucked in a steadying breath, her gaze skimming over the palm trees that lined the narrow lane and row of pale stone buildings that held shops, hotels and cafés where men sat around tables smoking tall pipes.

"I suppose that is true enough." Her gaze lingered on the

gentlemen wearing familiar tailored jackets and breeches strolling down the street as if they were royalty. "And to be honest, I am surprised to find so many Europeans."

Rajih shrugged. "It was not so long ago that the Sultan Kebir was in command of my country."

Sultan Kebir?

"Napoleon?" she deduced.

He nodded, the muscles of his jaw knotted. There was no need to ask his opinion of the French invaders.

"Yes."

"And you have yet to be rid of the infidel invaders?" she asked gently.

The dark eyes hardened in grim resolution. Caliph Rajih was a man who would sacrifice whatever necessary, including his pride, to resurrect his country from the ashes.

"For now we have need of their expertise," he forced himself to admit. "In ages past there was none who could compare with our scholars and engineers and scientists. We ruled without equal and none could stand in our path."

The carriage jerked back into motion, turning toward the outskirts of the bustling city.

"Do you intend to conquer the world?" she teased.

"Not this evening, but in time our glory will be restored."

Emma wrinkled her nose. Egypt had not been the only country to be invaded by Napoleon's forces, nor to have sacrificed the blood of too many good soldiers to be rid of his armies.

"Perhaps it is because I am a mere female from a forgotten Russian village, but I prefer peace to glory."

The merciless expression eased as he tugged a honey curl that had escaped from beneath her bonnet.

"As a *mere female?*" he drawled. "The crew of my ship was convinced you possessed the heart of a lioness with your golden beauty and fierce courage. You are as rare as the finest emerald."

His finger drifted down the curve of her neck, then scooped along the low cut of her bodice. She shivered, instinctively pulling away from the temptation of his touch. No matter what the caliph's attractions, she had given her heart to another.

Even if he was an ungrateful jackass.

"Rajih."

He smiled with a rueful resignation. "He is far away and yet still in your thoughts, is he not?"

A flush touched her cheeks as she attempted to feign indifference.

"He?"

"Your Russian thief."

"I have no desire to discuss Dimitri Tipova." She clenched her teeth against the jagged ache of loss. "He is a part of my past I wish to forget."

"And yet you carry his memory in your heart." Before she could guess his intention, Rajih grabbed her hand and pressed it to his lips. "Have no fear, beloved. I shall banish his ghost in time."

Having discovered it was impossible to argue with arrogant men, Emma sought to distract her companion instead.

"Goodness, why are those children darting into the road?"

The shimmer in his dark eyes revealed that he was aware of her ploy, but with a last kiss on her knuckles, he shifted to slide open the carriage window. At once a clutch of ragged boys ran forward, shoving tiny bundles into Rajih's outstretched hand. He tossed a handful of coins into the street before closing the window and turning back to Emma.

She watched in interest as he delicately unwrapped a fig leaf and revealed a small pile of dark fruit.

"Taste," he urged, lifting one of the delicacies toward her mouth.

"What is it?"

"Dates dipped in honey."

She took a tentative bite, sliding shut her eyes in appreciation as the sweetness exploded on her tongue.

"Mmm," she breathed, unconsciously licking her lips. "Ambrosia."

She heard Rajih's breath catch, his eyes darkening before he lowered his head.

"Allow me," he rasped, kissing the honey that clung to her mouth. "The sweetest of ambrosia."

His enticing scent cloaked around her, the exotic spice as heady a temptation as the strength in the hand that cupped her face. It would be easy to give in to Rajih's urging to replace Dimitri in her heart.

Not that she truly thought he could accomplish the impossible feat, but there would be undoubted pleasure in the effort.

Thankfully, she was a woman who learned from her mistakes.

She had allowed herself to depend upon Dimitri and had been betrayed. She would not allow another man the opportunity to disappoint her.

Pressing her hands to his chest, she pulled away from his kiss.

"We have halted."

His hand briefly tightened on her cheek, then with obvious reluctance he pulled back, a flush staining his cheekbones.

They said nothing as a servant in loose robes rushed forward to pull open the carriage door, and Rajih led her into the three-storied stucco home that was framed by palm trees and mimosa.

She noted the tiled floors and fountains surrounded by low divans as they moved through the foyer and into the inner rooms. She had no need for Rajih to tell her that the tapestries that lined the walls were ancient heirlooms or that the delicate pottery were priceless works of art. Even a peasant from Russia could recognize the exquisite craftsmanship of her surroundings, she wryly acknowledged.

They stepped through a set of towering doors into the square courtyard before Rajih at last came to a halt and turned to offer her a small bow.

"Welcome to my home, Emma Linley-Kirov," he said in an oddly formal fashion.

Her brows lifted as she studied the small stream of water that meandered through the dark greenery and the banks of flowers that filled the air with a thick perfume. In the center was a large fountain that sprayed water into the air and was surrounded by marble benches.

It was like a hidden jewel; all the more lovely because it was so unexpected.

"You consider this a modest home?" she demanded.

"It once belonged to my grandfather."

There was a sound overhead and she glanced up to discover birds of prey silhouetted against the brilliant blue sky. A small shiver feathered down her spine.

"Is there a harem?" she asked.

"Of course." His lips twitched as he deliberately stepped closer, his slender hand waving toward the profusion of brilliant blooms. "These gardens are a part of the seraglio. I believe you will find them suitably comfortable."

She licked her lips, belatedly aware that they were very much alone in the courtyard.

"Perhaps it would be best if I were to find rooms at a hotel—"

Rajih reached to tug off her bonnet, a heat flaring in his eyes as her honey curls tumbled about her shoulders.

"Do you fear I might lock you away as my concubine?"

"I would be a fool not to be concerned."

"Undoubtedly." He chuckled, brushing a light kiss over her lips before straightening to regard her with a steady gaze. "And I am a brute to tease you. Yes, Emma, during your stay our tradition demands that you remain in the women's quarters. It is for your own protection. But be assured that you will never be my prisoner."

DIMITRI PACED THE NORTH terrace of Windsor Castle, his gaze absently studying the frozen countryside spread beneath him. A servant had pointed out the Thames churning a path through the meadows, as well as the cluster of distant buildings he had proclaimed to be Eton College. He had also attempted to interest Dimitri in the history of the Round Tower standing in the middle ward that had been built by Henry II and the fine architecture of St. George's Chapel that he was assured possessed a fine stone-vaulted ceiling and a stained-glass window that was the finest in all the world.

At last accepting that the grim-faced Russian would not be coaxed into the warmth of the Grand Vestibule, nor impressed by the grand English castle, the servant had returned to his duties, leaving Dimitri alone with his dark thoughts.

He had not been offered an explanation as to why George IV had insisted that Lord Sanderson and Sir Jergens be brought to this castle to be held and questioned, although he suspected the portly king was anxious to suppress the revelation that proper English nobles were involved in the tawdry sex slave business. Such things were meant to be kept hidden from society.

But while Dimitri was anxious to be done with the royal formalities so that the men could be taken to Russia and their confessions heard by Alexander Pavlovich, that was not the reason he was restlessly pacing the frozen terrace.

No. The raw, gnawing fear that plagued him could be placed entirely at the feet of Emma Linley-Kirov.

His heart twisted in pain.

It had been three days since Emma had disappeared from Huntley's town house. Three days of futile searches through London. Of sending dozens of servants into the surrounding countryside, as well as to Paris and beyond to St. Petersburg to seek out any information of her whereabouts.

Of sleepless nights and endless bottles of vodka in an effort to dull the self-recriminations.

Perhaps he should accept that Emma had made her choice. He had done everything in his power to prevent her from her ridiculous habit of leaping into danger, had he not? If she were determined to get her throat slit, then there was nothing he could do to stop her.

Instead, he moodily vacillated between blinding fury that she would leave his protection and put herself at risk and a torturous knowledge that it had been his obsession to destroy his father that had driven her from his side.

Where the hell had she gone?

Was she alone? Had she found the trail of Valik and her sister? Had she been captured...?

The sound of approaching footsteps was a welcome distraction. Dimitri turned to watch Huntley's approach, hiding a smile as the duke irritably waved away the covey of servants attempting to straighten his caped greatcoat and wrap a cashmere scarf around his neck.

Dimitri had endured a similar battle when he had arrived at the castle, nearly forced to punch the aggressive footman determined to take his gloves and beaver hat. Thank God he would soon be back in St. Petersburg where he was never mistaken for a feeble nobleman incapable of putting on and taking off his own damned clothes.

Huntley's long stride never slowed as he headed toward the stone steps leading to the street below. Dimitri easily fell into step beside him, as eager as his companion to be finished with their business in Windsor and on their way back to London.

"It is done?" he demanded.

Huntley snorted in disgust, his breath visible in the chilled air.

"Between his bouts of wailing and pathetic pleas for forgiveness, Sanderson managed to confess the details of his sordid business."

"And Jergens?"

"He was equally forthcoming." Huntley shook his head. "A pity the guards did not discover Timmons until he had managed to take the coward's path."

Dimitri shrugged. Mr. Timmons had been discovered in his bedchamber with a bullet hole in his temple, obviously unable to face the sordid scandal that was about to spread throughout London.

"Did they reveal Count Nevskaya's participation in the nasty business?" he demanded.

"With glorious detail." Huntley's laugh echoed in the still air. "Indeed, they were both eager to claim that the count had approached them several years ago with the scheme and that they were no more than helpless dupes being manipulated by the evil Russian."

Dimitri waited for the torrent of exhilaration to overwhelm him.

This was the moment he had waited for since he learned of his mother's death.

The means to brand his father as a depraved fiend who preyed upon helpless children was in his hands. There would be none in society who would not turn their backs on him.

He would be an outcast. Alone in his shame.

Just as Dimitri had dreamed of for so long.

Any satisfaction he felt, however, was as cold and empty as his heart.

"I do not doubt the truth of his claim," he said, absently tapping his riding crop against his glossy riding boots as they moved down the steep incline toward the lower ward. "Sanderson does not possess enough wits to devise such a cunning plot. My father, however, has never suffered from a lack of intelligence."

"No, only a lack of morality."

"That is a rare commodity among noblemen."

Huntley lifted his brows at the less than flattering accusation. "I could say the same of thieves and scoundrels."

They followed the curve in the road, ignoring the snowflakes that drifted from the sullen clouds.

"Have you arranged with the king to have the men sent to Russia?"

"We are in..." Huntley paused, as if seeking the appropriate word. "Negotiations."

Dimitri muttered a Russian curse, his face hard with warning. "Huntley."

"Be patient, Tipova." Huntley slapped Dimitri on the back. "The king still harbors a bitterness at the perceived insults Alexander Pavlovich offered during his visit to England."

Dimitri's temper flared. He had not sacrificed so much only to have his opportunity for revenge threatened by a petulant peacock sitting on a throne.

"That was years ago," he growled.

Huntley lowered his voice, as aware as Dimitri of the numerous servants who scurried about the castle grounds. It never failed to astonish Dimitri how many nobles were blind to the people who served them. Such stupidity ensured that he was easily capable of discovering whatever information he desired.

And information was power.

"George might be king of England now that his father has died but that has not cured his unfortunate tendency to spiteful pettiness." Huntley grimaced. "As poor Brummell has learned to his regret."

"I do not care if Alexander Pavlovich pissed on your fat king's throne. I will not be denied my justice."

The duke grasped his arm and roughly hurried them both down the road to where their horses awaited them.

"Do not be a fool, Tipova," he muttered. "With a measure of diplomacy I will soon have the king convinced that the best means for him to be rid of a potential scandal is to send the men to Russia and lay the entire blame on Count Nevskaya. But not if you rile his temper. Be sensible."

Dimitri shook off the duke's hand, his expression sour. "I am in no mood to be sensible."

"Then be patient. It will be no more than a few days and you will have your revenge."

Dimitri gave a short laugh. "My revenge."

Huntley regarded him with a curious gaze. "It is what you desire, is it not?"

"So I have always believed." Dimitri glanced toward the moat that was filled with gardens rather than water. "For the past twenty years I have devoted my life to one purpose. The destruction of my father."

"No one can blame you for your hatred of the man who ruined your mother."

Dimitri winced. Would he ever be able to think of his mother without tormenting regret?

Regret that she had ever caught the vile attention of Count Nevskaya. Regret that she had been so stubbornly foolish as to attempt blackmailing him.

Regret that she had left him when he had needed her the most.

His heart gave another painful squeeze as he thought of another woman who had abandoned him when he needed her.

"No one but Emma."

"Ah."

"She holds me responsible for the loss of her sister."

The duke offered a sympathetic smile. "She was angry and not thinking clearly that evening. She is fully aware that you had no hand in the kidnapping of her sister."

"She might not hold me responsible for her sister's kidnapping, but she believes I allowed Anya to be shipped away beneath my nose." Dimitri's thoughts were jerked back to the night in the warehouse and his burning need to chase after Lord Sanderson before the fat fool could escape. "And she would not be wrong."

"They will be caught the moment they return to Russia," Huntley assured him, his imperious tone making Dimitri smile with wry humor. Huntley was one of the few noblemen that Dimitri did not wish had been drowned at birth, but the duke possessed the innate arrogance that allowed him to assume that his every wish would be granted. "Between Alexander Pavlovich's soldiers and your own servants there is nowhere they can hide."

"But they are not returning to Russia," a rough English voice broke into their conversation. With lethal ease, both Dimitri and the duke pulled their loaded pistols from the pockets of their coats and pointed at the man leaning against a low, stone wall. Swiftly, the stranger lifted his hands to reveal he was unharmed. "Here now, no need for guns and such. I'm a peaceable man."

Dimitri's aim never wavered. The man was small and wiry with the rough woolen clothing of a servant, but there was a cunning etched on the lean face and a hard glimmer of warning in the pale blue eyes that the man had lived the sort of life that made him dangerous. Dimitri had many such men in his employ—cold-blooded, ruthless and loyal to whoever was paying his salary.

"Who are you?" he rasped.

"Mr. Thomas Stroutt." He plucked the worn hat from his head and performed an awkward bow. "At yer service."

Huntley stepped forward, his pistol pointed directly between the man's eyes.

"I suggest you offer a compelling reason for eavesdropping upon a private conversation."

Thomas cleared his throat. "I believe I have information that will be of service to you fine gentlemen."

Dimitri sent his companion a glance that urged they hear the man out. He sensed Thomas Stroutt was too intelligent to approach the Duke of Huntley without a compelling reason.

"Speak quickly," Dimitri warned.

"I was hired by Mr. Peter Abrahams," the man said.

"Hired?"

"I am a man with a certain skill in discovering information others attempt to keep hidden."

Dimitri arched a brow. The man was a Bow Street Runner or a thief-taker.

In either case he was a man that Dimitri would wager missed very little.

"Who is Peter Abrahams?"

"He is the father of Lady Sanderson." Thomas replaced the hat on his dark hair. "A most powerful gentleman who is fiercely devoted to his daughter and her welfare."

"Why would Abrahams hire you?"

"The gentleman has become increasingly concerned that Lord Sanderson is connected to an unfortunate collection of shady characters."

"Shady is not the description I would have chosen," Huntley muttered in disgust.

Thomas turned to spit on the cobblestones, his expression dark.

"So we have discovered. Unfortunately, the information came too late to prevent poor Lady Sanderson from becoming a victim of the man's treachery."

Huntley gave a warning wave of his pistol. "You have yet to offer a reason I should not put a bullet in your brain."

The man shifted warily, wise enough to sense that the duke was not the usual coxcomb littering society.

"During my investigations I found that you were not the only men apart from Mr. Abrahams seeking the truth of Lord Sanderson's business."

Dimitri stiffened, far from pleased. He had spent a number of irksome hours in the company of Lord Sanderson. How was it possible he had been unaware there were others spying on the nobleman?

He was growing old and careless, he wryly concluded. Perhaps it was time he retired to his private estate and learn how to fish. Or were aging criminals expected to tend to their rose gardens?

With a shake of his head, he returned his attention to the man standing before him.

"Who else?"

"One of them Oriental sorts."

"Chinese?"

Thomas shrugged, revealing the predictable English contempt for foreigners.

"No, one of them Turks, I think."

"Do you have a name?"

"Caliph Rajih."

Huntley made a sound of disbelief. "You are certain?"

Thomas nodded. "Aye."

Dimitri turned to study the duke's shocked expression. "Are you acquainted with him?"

"We attended school together," Huntley admitted, his brows pulled together in a puzzled frown. "He is Egyptian, although he spent a good deal of his life in England and Europe until the past few years. From all accounts a favorite of Muhammad Ali Pasha."

Dimitri sympathized with Huntley's astonishment. "Why would he be interested in Sanderson?"

Thomas glanced about to ensure there was no one near. "When the females that Sanderson has been buying are no longer of value in London, they are taken to the slave markets in Cairo."

"Bloody hell," Huntley breathed.

A sudden chill arrowed down Dimitri's spine and, barely aware he was moving, he had reached to grab the woolen scarf wrapped around Thomas's neck, giving him a small shake.

"Where is the caliph now?"

With a practiced movement Thomas managed to free himself from Dimitri's grip, his expression knowing.

"He sailed away from London three days ago." The man rubbed his bruised throat, his eyes never straying from Dimitri's tight features. "Along with a female who looked remarkably like the woman posing as your wife."

CHAPTER SEVENTEEN

MUCH TO EMMA'S frustration the journey from Alexandria to Cairo was postponed for three days as Rajih had revealed a sandstorm was sweeping through the desert without warning.

Her patience wasn't improved once they were aboard the shallow sailboat that carried them along the yellowish water of the Nile. There was a beauty to be found in the stunning scenery that slid past. The stark, reddish carpet of desert on one side and the rolling green fields on the opposite side. And most impressive of all the looming pyramids that made Emma want to pinch herself and ensure this was not all some strange dream.

At last they landed in Bulak and traveled to Rajih's home on the outskirts of the old city.

Or at least, what he called a home.

To Emma the sprawling three-storied building with mosaic-tiled floors and delicate tapestries, as well as ornate chandeliers was more a palace than a simple home. She had counted three formal courtyards, a private mosque and a domed pavilion before being hurried into the private gardens surrounding the women's quarters.

Behind the towering doors guarded by armed servants, Emma had found herself surrounded by a series of elegant apartments that framed the private baths. The floors were tiled with a lovely blue-and-ivory pattern while the walls were painted with frescoes that portrayed women bending at the feet of a long-forgotten caliph. Next to the vast gardens there was a charming room with low divans and gold-framed mirrors that reflected the vibrant colors from the blooms that spilled through the open archways.

Emma waited only long enough for Rajih to brush a light kiss on her cheek and warn her to stay out of the afternoon heat before sneaking out the back of the gardens.

Rajih was without a doubt a charming, well-educated companion who had treated her with tender care. In truth, he was precisely the sort of man she had dreamed of as a young girl in Yabinsk and if not for the aching concern for her sister, and of course, Dimitri Tipova...

She shut off her futile thoughts and quickened her step.

She was in Cairo for one purpose, and one purpose only.

Anya.

Clad in a traveling gown of pale lilac and a bonnet that possessed a thick veil to cover her face, she adjusted the small pistol she had brought from London that was tucked in the full sleeve of her gown.

She was not stupid. She understood that a woman traveling the narrow, dirt streets alone was foolishly dangerous, but what other choice did she have?

Rajih might be handsome and attentive and willing to indulge her in many ways, but to his mind she was a mere female who should bend to his will. He would conduct his search for Anya in his own manner and in his own time.

That was unacceptable.

Searching for the bazaars, Emma ignored the leers from the passing men as well as the shrill laughter from the women who leaned over wooden balconies to reveal their lush bodies barely hidden by the gauzy robes. In truth, she was more unnerved by the large dogs that darted among the crowd and the young men on donkeys who seemed intent on riding down hapless pedestrians.

A drop of sweat trickled down her back as she turned a

corner, reminding her of Rajih's warning that she was not yet prepared to endure the afternoon sunlight. Abruptly, she halted as she caught sight of the open gate that offered a glimpse of the covered bazaar beyond. Her heart gave a small leap as a potent perfume wafted through the air.

Was it possible?

Her scream went unheard as a hand was shoved over her mouth and an arm wrapped around her waist from behind. She struggled, but she was unable to halt herself being pulled back toward the street. Then, thankfully, she recognized the musky scent of Rajih's cologne.

"I believe that will be enough sightseeing for today," he drawled, bundling her into the waiting carriage with barely leashed anger. Settling her on the seat next to her, he yanked off her bonnet and tossed it on the floor. "I begin to sympathize with your poor Cossack. Do you possess no sense of self-preservation whatsoever?"

She folded her hands in her lap, attempting to hide her unease.

"I am here to search for my sister, not to be hidden away in your harem," she said, her chin tilted.

His dark, beautiful features were rigid with anger. "And you do not trust I am doing my best to make certain she is found?"

She shifted to glance out the window, seeking the words that would make Rajih understand the relentless need that burned deep inside her.

"Anya is my sister and my responsibility. I could not bear thinking I did not do everything in my power to protect her." Her hands curled into tight fists of frustration. "Is that so very hard to understand?"

There was a brief silence, then slender fingers cupped her face, gently turning her back to meet Rajih's dark, searching gaze.

"Do you know, *habiba,* I find myself quite envious of your sister," he said, his voice husky.

"Envious?"

His fingers tightened on her cheek. "You love so fiercely. Any man would be honored to have earned such a rare gift."

She grimaced, considering the few men who had bothered to pay her attention.

"Thus far the gentlemen I have known are not particularly interested in earning a place in my heart," she said, deliberately meeting his smoldering gaze. "Only my bed."

His thumb brushed her lower lip. "There are many men who can be extremely stupid."

"So I have discovered."

"And there are those men who find it far easier to reveal the desire of their bodies rather than confess the secrets of their hearts."

Her own heart gave a treacherous leap, warning her that a small part of her still longed to believe that Dimitri had considered her more than a convenient body in his bed. Which simply proved just how foolish she could truly be.

"It does not matter." She shrugged. "I have no interest in offering my heart to another."

"No?"

"My place is at Yabinsk, tending to my business and caring for my sister."

His gaze lowered to her lips, his thumb continuing to tease at the corner of her mouth.

"You do not truly believe you can return to such a mundane existence, do you?"

Emma shied from the thought of her small coaching inn and cramped cottage.

"What is my choice?"

"You could remain with me."

"As your concubine?"

He brushed a soft kiss over her lips. "Are you proposing a more formal arrangement?"

Heat flooded her cheeks at his teasing. "Certainly not. In fact, I presume you must wed for political gain."

Without warning his hand dropped from her face and his expression became guarded.

"I will bow to the pasha's will."

Emma regarded him with a frown, sensing that she had touched a source of distress.

"Does the thought of marrying for political gain trouble you?"

His smile was forced. "I have known I was to be a pawn from the moment my father sent me to England to be groomed as a diplomat."

"That does not answer my question."

The dark eyes narrowed, as if caught off guard by her persistence. And perhaps he was. Rajih was obviously unaccustomed to sharing his feelings. No doubt the burden of being born a caliph.

For a moment she could easily imagine Rajih as a young boy, forced to watch as his country was overrun with infidel invaders, and then the pain of being sent to England where he must have felt alone and terrified by his strange surroundings.

What man would not have learned to guard his emotions?

At last he offered a slow nod. "Yes, Emma, it troubles me greatly that my life is not my own to arrange as I would desire, but I accept my duty." His expression softened as his gaze swept over her upturned face. "And more important, I have discovered the importance of embracing happiness when it makes its rare appearance."

She ducked her head, unwilling to encourage his flirtations. She suspected that his gentlemanly restraint would be tossed aside with the slightest encouragement.

"Have you discovered nothing of my sister?"

Rajih heaved a faint sigh, then he pulled a curtain across the carriage window, thankfully blocking out the relentless sunlight.

"I have learned the *Katherine Marie* docked two days before we arrived at Alexandria and that the crew remained at least one night in the city."

Emma was torn between relief that she was still on her sister's trail, and the frustration that she continued to remain just out of reach.

"And when they left, did they come to Cairo?"

"That was their intention."

She stiffened as she heard the edge in his voice.

"What are you not telling me?"

"The Russian who was in charge of the girls was determined to flee Alexandria," he said. "Perhaps he sensed he was being followed."

She grabbed his arm, wanting to shake the truth from him.

"Rajih."

"As I told you, the most convenient means to travel is by boat, but it is also the most noticeable." He grimaced. "A smuggler could not risk attracting the attention of the pasha's guards."

His words made sense. The men responsible for kidnapping the girls had proven an undeniable talent for remaining invisible.

"So how did they travel?"

"By caravan."

Emma frowned. Since arriving in Egypt she had often seen the long line of camels and occasionally horses as they moved over the distant hills. It had not appeared a particularly comfortable means of travel, but it was not unusual.

"I do not understand—" Her words came to an abrupt

halt as she was hit by a sudden realization. "Oh, dear Lord. The sandstorm."

He gave a sharp nod. "Yes."

"Were they—"

"Nothing is known of their fate, Emma," he gently assured her. "It is quite possible they were disoriented by the storm and remain in the desert. I have sent word among the Bedouin tribes to search for them."

She bent forward, covering her face with her hands as her stomach clenched with a dread that was becoming all too common. Last night she had dreamed that Anya was still a baby and that she had gone to her cradle only to find it empty. She had raced about the dark cottage, screaming for help that had never come.

Had it been a premonition?

Was it possible that Anya was dead?

Without warning, the obstinate belief that she would rescue her sister and return them both to their home in Yabinsk wavered.

"It is almost as if fate is determined to keep me from Anya," she choked, tears filling her eyes.

She felt Rajih's strong arm circle her shoulders, pulling her against the hard muscles of his chest.

"They will be discovered," he murmured.

Her hands lowered as she tilted back her head to meet his concerned gaze.

"So I have been assured over and over, and yet I am no closer to Anya than when I left Russia."

He frowned, his thumb brushing away her tears. "Come, Emma, it is not in your nature to lose hope."

She shook her head, potently aware of the heat filling the carriage and distant chanting from the mosque. Never had Russia, and the life she had fought to build, seemed so far away.

"It is not so much a matter of losing hope as it is

accepting I do not have the skills necessary to be useful to my sister."

The carriage came to a halt, and with care, Rajih led her through the gardens to the seraglio, the whisper of his robes melding with the tinkle of the fountains in an oddly soothing sound.

"You are tired and hungry," he assured her. "By morning you will have regained your spirits and no doubt will have some new means to terrify me."

Emma nodded, realizing he was right. She could not recall the last time she had slept through the night.

"Yes, I am tired."

Halting at the arched entry into the harem's private gardens, he motioned toward a slender woman covered in veils who hurried forward.

"Put yourself in Samira's hands." He brushed his lips over her forehead. "She has a magical touch."

With an uncharacteristic sense of weariness, Emma allowed herself to be led into the cool shadows of the harem. Perhaps it was the heat, or the weeks of gnawing anxiety, or the long journey, but suddenly Emma felt in dire need of a few hours of peace.

Reaching the inner apartments, Emma allowed Samira to help remove her gown and undergarments. She sighed in pleasure as the heavy fabric slid away and she understood the logic of the loose robes and silken trousers preferred by the local women. It was far too warm for European clothing.

Once naked she allowed the servant to lead her into the sunken baths, stretching out her body and leaning her head against the tiled edge to study the glass dome that loomed above her.

Slowly the tension drained from her muscles and she cleared her mind of Anya and Dimitri and Caliph Rajih. For a few hours she desired only to forget her troubles.

A delectable hour later she left the baths and wrapped herself in a thin towel. Samira gestured for her to follow her into a shadowed alcove where velvet pillows had been piled in the center of the tiled floor. Arranged beside the pillows was a silver tray with various bottles of oils and burning pots of incense.

There was another flurry of gestures and Emma awkwardly lowered herself facedown onto the pillows, hiding her face in the velvet softness as she felt the towel being tugged aside. She was not a noblewoman accustomed to having servants seeing her naked, and certainly not touching her with such intimacy.

She heard a shuffle of feet and the clink of bottles before she sensed someone kneeling at her side. Warm oil was poured over her bare back, the intoxicating scent teasing at her nose and sliding sensually over her skin.

Still adjusting to the strange sensations, her breath caught in pleasurable surprise as warm male fingers stroked down the curve of her back. It felt…sinful. Decadent. And utterly wonderful.

"Rajih," she breathed, not needing to turn her head to recognize his scent.

"Does my touch please you?" he murmured softly.

"You should not—"

"Shh." He spoke directly into her ear, his fingers lingering on the rigid muscles at the base of her spine. "Allow me to ease your tension."

"I thought men were forbidden to enter the women's quarters unless they were…."

He chuckled as she stumbled over the word. "Eunuchs?"

"Yes."

"But I am not just a man," he said, his innate arrogance threaded through his dark voice. "I am caliph. I go where

I please. And it pleases me very much to be here with you."

She shivered, knowing she should send him away. "I will not become your concubine."

"Perhaps you should wait until you are asked to fill such a position, Emma."

"But you..."

Baffled by his reprimand, Emma shifted so she could glance over her shoulder, her words faltering at the teasing smile that curved his lips.

Rajih was always handsome, but with his robes loosened to reveal a glimpse of his golden chest and his carved features softened, he was near irresistible.

"I am offered the finest beauties to be found throughout the world," he reminded her, his slender fingers wielding their magic as they moved up her back. "Women with hair of fire or as dark and glossy as a raven's wing. Women who have been trained in the fine arts of pleasing a man or those who have been sequestered since they were babes to ensure their purity."

Despite the mocking shimmer in his eyes, Emma knew he was not boasting. He was a prince among his people, not to mention extraordinarily attractive, and she was quite certain any woman would consider it an honor to capture his attention. And, of course, in this part of the world, it would be very likely that the various sheiks and clan chiefs would offer the most beautiful of their women for his pleasure.

She smiled, astonishingly indifferent to her shameless lack of clothing and his brazen touch as she followed his lead.

"Some of them princesses, no doubt."

"Certainly."

"Hmm." Her gaze swept around the shadowed alcove. "And yet your harems remain empty."

Without giving her time to anticipate his intent, he bent down to brush his lips along the line of her shoulder.

"As you know, I have been away from my home for several weeks."

Her hands clenched the pillows, her body reacting to his skillful touch despite her reluctant heart.

"And your females managed to escape during your absence? How unfortunate."

He nibbled a path to her neck. "Do not fear, I have only to reveal my interest in seeking companionship to have the seraglio filled with graceful females, all eager to please their master."

She made a sound of disgust even as her body threatened to melt beneath his warm caresses.

"Master?"

He nipped the lobe of her ear, the heady scents of incense and precious oils making it difficult to think clearly.

"But of course. At heart I am still a savage."

"Then it is convenient I am not destined to be a member of your harem. No man shall ever be my master."

The moment her brave words echoed through the still air, Emma knew she had made a mistake. Rajih sucked in a sharp breath, his hands sliding into her damp curls and arching her neck so his lips could create havoc along the line of her throat.

"You challenge me to prove you wrong, *habiba*," he husked.

"I—" A burst of heat exploded in the pit of her stomach as he reached the sensitive spot at the juncture of her neck and shoulder. "Oh. That is not fair."

His laughter feathered over her skin. "Are there rules to our game?"

"You think this is a game?"

"A most delightful diversion."

Her toes curled as she struggled to think clearly. "Am I the prize to be won?"

"If you prefer, I am willing to be your reward," he chivalrously offered, shifting until his hard arousal pressed against her thigh. "Tell me what you desire."

Belatedly realizing that matters had progressed beyond what was comfortable, Emma stiffened.

"Rajih…"

She was not certain what she intended to say, but in the end it did not matter as there was the rustle of robes and a veiled servant was suddenly kneeling in the doorway of the alcove.

"Master," the woman murmured.

Swearing at the intrusion, Rajih wrapped Emma in the towel and shifted to block her from the view of the servant.

"I requested that we not be interrupted."

"Forgive me, Caliph, but your steward insisted you would wish to speak with Girard Bey." Her head was pressed to the tile floor. "He has information that is of interest to you."

For a moment Emma could feel the tension coiling through Rajih as he battled with the urge to send the servant away and his obvious curiosity about his unexpected guest.

At last he thrust his fingers through the dark satin of his hair and accepted the inevitable.

"Offer him coffee and assure him I will join him shortly," he commanded.

"Yes, Caliph."

In silence, the servant rose and vanished from the alcove. Rajih turned to offer Emma a tight smile, his eyes smoldering with a frustrated desire.

"Forgive me." He rose to his feet in an elegant motion,

straightened his robes. "I fear our entertainment will have to be postponed until later."

"Wait." Clutching the towel about her body, Emma rose and grasped his arm. "Please."

He covered her hand with his own, his eyes smoldering with promise.

"So eager, Emma? I promise not to keep you waiting for long."

She ignored his sensuous words, her thoughts returning to Anya.

"Does this man have information concerning my sister?"

His lips twisted, as if chagrined by her response, but his voice was gentle.

"No, Emma. Girard Bey is very much a gentleman of the city. I must depend upon those who consider the desert their home to locate the missing caravan." He lifted her hand to his lips before heading out of the alcove. "Return to the baths. I will join you as soon as I am able."

Emma forced herself to count to one hundred before she scurried to her private chambers and hurriedly pulled on the loose satin robes in rich blue and trimmed in gold that had been left on the low bed. It was odd to feel the cool satin brush her bare skin with no undergarments to act as a barrier, but she was in too great a hurry to consider modesty.

With quick steps she moved through the harem, ignoring the guards who stood at the doors and the numerous servants who gawked as she headed toward the formal quarters of the house. She was not certain whether or not females were allowed beyond the seraglio, but she was determined to follow Rajih.

It was not that she suspected he would deliberately lie to her, she assured herself. But she sensed he would be quite willing to hide information. Even if it concerned Anya.

It was the sound of voices that led her toward the large saloon on the opposite side of the house. Halting at a side door, she peered into the room, absently admiring the mosaic on the floor and the soaring ceiling that was painted with a lovely scene of a desert oasis. The low divans were crimson velvet with gold satin pillows and the high windows were shuttered against the sun, leaving the area bathed in welcome shadows. On one divan a middle-aged gentleman in a pale green, European-cut jacket and black breeches was settled, his thin face and small eyes reminding Emma of a rodent.

"Caliph," he was saying, his thick French accent revealing his heritage. "Forgive my intrusion."

Emma pressed against the door frame as Rajih appeared through an archway, a silver tray in his hands. A faint smile touched her lips. While the Frenchman was obviously dressed in the latest fashion, and possessed the air of a well-pampered nobleman, he was easily overshadowed by Rajih who was wearing what many men would consider little more than a dress and carrying a tray as if he were a common maid.

There was something harshly masculine about the Caliph that would cast any other man in the shade.

Well, any man but Dimitri Tipova.

She scrubbed the treacherous thought from her mind as she watched Rajih set the tray on a low table in front of the divan.

"My doors are always open to you, my friend," he said, reaching for the crystal decanter. "Sherry?"

The stranger leaned forward to grasp a small glass, and then—to Emma's shock—tucked a tidy pile of francs into the inner pocket of his jacket.

"You know my weaknesses too well," he said with an oily smile.

Rajih shrugged, seemingly accustomed to offering money along with his sherry.

"Pleasures are not weaknesses and it is my honor to ensure your stay in my country is one of comfort."

The man sipped his sherry. "So kind."

"I presume that you have information for me?" Rajih prompted.

"*Oui.*" He set aside the empty glass. "You requested that I send you notice if I learned of any Russians arriving in Cairo."

"And?" Rajih demanded.

"I have reason to believe the Russian ambassador has just welcomed a small party into his home."

Emma frowned. Was it possible that the Russian ambassador was involved in the slave trade? And if he was, could he truly be so shameless as to have the girls brought to his home?

It seemed a needless risk when the pasha was so adamantly opposed to the barbaric practice.

"Do you have a name?" Rajih asked.

"Dimitri Tipova," the Frenchman said, unaware as Emma pressed a hand over her mouth to muffle her shocked cry of disbelief. "So far as I can determine he has no title, but it seems as if he is being offered a gracious welcome so he must be a favorite of the Romanovs. Is that the man you seek?"

Rajih dipped his head, his expression resigned rather than astonished. Almost as if he had been expecting Dimitri to travel to Cairo.

"It is."

The Frenchman grimaced. "It will not be an easy matter to have him removed from Cairo if he is under the protection of the ambassador."

"Do not trouble yourself, Girard," Rajih smoothly assured him. "I will deal with Dimitri Tipova."

CHAPTER EIGHTEEN

DIMITRI WAS WELL AWARE that his ability to blend into any surrounding was his greatest talent.

He could move as easily through the gutters of Moscow as across the glittering ballroom of the Winter Palace. And with the proper clothing, no one would suspect he was an imposter.

Such a skill had allowed him to rise from a lowly pick-pocket to the Beggar Czar.

Now, however, he felt distinctly disturbed.

It was not the Turkish robes he had donned in favor of his tailored clothing, or the small boys who stood at his side waving palm leaves in an effort to stir the stifling heat that filled the low brick house with its arched entryways and tiled floors. He had traveled through the near Orient on several occasions and had become accustomed to their traditions.

No, his unease was caused entirely by the fat gentleman sprawled on the low divan across from him.

Dimitri wasn't privy to Alexander Pavlovich's reason for offering Baron Koman the position of Ambassador to Egypt, but he suspected the czar had been anxious to rid himself of the vile man's presence. Why else would he send him to the most distant post possible, regardless of the fact he was utterly incompetent?

Dressed in loose robes and puffing on a water pipe, the rotund Russian lounged on his cushions, waiting for the pretty maid to refill his plate. His blond hair was thinning and his heavy features already red and swollen from his years of dissipation.

He reminded Dimitri of the decaying ruins outside of Cairo that were being swept away by the desert sands. He could only wish the same fate for Baron Koman.

Oblivious to Dimitri's seething dislike, Koman waved his full plate in Dimitri's direction.

"Oxtail?"

"Thank you, no." Dimitri hid a shudder as he rose from the divan and paced toward the fountain in the center of the floor. The heat and smoke from Koman's pipe were making his stomach churn. "I prefer to avoid a heavy meal so early in the day."

"Which accounts for your fine figure while mine..." The Baron laughed. "Well, it sadly reveals my love for my fine chef and my distinct distaste for bestirring myself. I blame the damnable heat. Only a savage would be foolish enough to dash about when a sensible man would seek the shade."

"The natives would probably be equally shocked to witness us tunneling a path through the snow."

"True enough, my boy." The baron licked his fingers, eyeing Dimitri with a curious gaze. So far as he knew, Dimitri was a favored friend of Alexander Pavlovich, as well as of the Duke of Huntley, who had come in search of Russian girls being sold in the slave trade. There was no need to explain that he was also a hardened criminal who was under threat of death in a number of countries... although not Egypt. At least not yet. "And there are benefits to living in a place that is not entirely civilized," Koman continued, a lecherous gleam in his eyes. "When you have finished your meal, we will travel to the bath where a man may find whatever pleasure he might desire."

Having visited a number of baths in Cairo, Dimitri was unfortunately aware of what pleasures were offered.

"An enticing invitation, but I am anxious to speak with the caliph."

"My dear Tipova, as I warned you last eve, a man cannot simply demand an audience with the caliph," the baron protested. "There is very rigid protocol that must be followed."

Not for the first time, Dimitri regretted his decision to call upon the ambassador. On the journey to Egypt it had seemed a reasonable decision to seek out the baron and request his hospitality for the duration of his stay. Huntley had warned Dimitri that rampaging like a madman through Cairo in search of Emma would not only make enemies of the locals, but would embarrass the woman he had come to claim.

Now he accepted that he had sadly miscalculated. The fat buffoon was never going to stir himself. Besides, Dimitri was in no mood for diplomacy. The need to find Emma was like a savage fire burning in his gut. He did not care if he had to sift the damnable country sand grain by sand grain to find her.

"I have a letter of introduction from the Duke of Huntley," he growled. "What more could I need?"

"Who is to say with these heathens? Best for me to approach the caliph when the timing is appropriate." The baron's tone was patronizing. "Until then I promise to keep you suitably entertained. You mentioned an interest in the local brothels? I know of a female who can dance the—"

"My only interest lies in finding the Russian girls who were stolen from St. Petersburg," he interrupted.

Koman heaved a deep sigh as he struggled to lift his considerable bulk off the divan.

"I would expect such a tedious lack of appreciation for the exotic pleasures from Alexander Pavlovich," the older man mourned. "But I had expected better from you, Tipova."

Dimitri smiled wryly. "It seems I am destined to be a disappointment to all I encounter. Have you heard rumors of Russian girls being sold in the markets?"

With a flick of his hand, Koman sent his servants scurrying from the room, leaving them alone to speak in privacy.

"In truth, Muhammad Ali Pasha's disapproval of the slave trade has made the traffickers meticulously cautious. The females are no longer paraded through the bazaar for a gentleman to purchase." The baron pulled a handkerchief from the sleeve of his robes, his gaze sliding uneasily away from Dimitri's. "You must receive an invitation to the private auctions."

Dimitri tensed. The bastard. It was obvious the man was intimately familiar with the slavers and their delicate wares.

"I am certain a gentleman of your standing could swiftly procure the necessary invitation," he said.

"Undoubtedly, but it would be such a bother. Far better to allow the officials to tend to such affairs." With a forced smile, the baron backed toward the entryway. "Ah. If you will excuse me?"

"Of course."

Dimitri made no effort to halt the idiot as he scurried out of the room.

Why bother? The baron was a worthless idiot who Dimitri was embarrassed to claim as a fellow Russian. But there had to be at least one person in the house who could be of use.

With that thought in mind, Dimitri left the smoke-filled room and dredged up memories of the brief tour he had taken of the house last eve. There was a separate counsel building near the pasha's citadel, but Dimitri recalled Koman waving a dismissive hand toward an office before leading him to his private quarters.

Passing the stairs that led to the upper rooms, Dimitri turned down a short hall and entered the large chamber that held a traditional desk and chair. Tall shelves lined with leather-bound books consumed the walls and a Persian carpet covered the floor. The double doors leading to the inner courtyard had been left open and Dimitri sucked in a deep breath of the fresh air. Although his profession meant he spent many nights in dark gambling houses filled with smoke and sin and lust, he found it increasingly unpleasant to mingle among the desperate souls.

Yet another warning he was growing old, he wryly accepted.

Stepping over the threshold, Dimitri halted as a thin gentleman with a thick mane of brown hair, dressed in a modest gray jacket and black waistcoat, rose to his feet. At first glance he appeared a somber man with unremarkable features and retiring demeanor. But Dimitri was accustomed to seeking the worth of a man beyond his outward appearance.

He, better than anyone, understood that a man could create any guise he desired.

"Stanislav, is it not?" he asked. "Baron Koman's secretary?"

Stepping around the desk, the man offered a deep bow, his brown eyes filled with a shrewd intelligence.

"Yes, my lord?"

Dimitri waved a dismissive hand. "Please call me Tipova, I am no gentleman."

"May I be of assistance?"

"That is my hope." Dimitri folded his arms over his chest. Stanislav was young, but there was an air of tidy efficiency about the office otherwise absent throughout the rest of the house. "There must be one person on the baron's staff who possesses the skill and ambition to ensure that Alexander Pavlovich is unaware that his Egyptian ambassador is a fat, lazy letch with no interest beyond his enormous appetites. I am betting that person is you."

The man paled, his gaze darting toward the door. "Sir—"

"Any deception came to an end the moment I stepped over the threshold," he warned his companion. "Now it is your decision whether my recommendation to Alexander Pavlovich includes the removal of the entire household or merely the baron."

Stanislav froze, his expression revealing his flurry of emotions—suspicion that Dimitri was attempting to lure him into a trap; fear that he might be tarnished with his employer's incompetency; and a burgeoning hope that his secretly nourished ambitions might at last be fulfilled.

It was the hope that at last triumphed, and with a small gesture, the secretary headed toward the private chamber attached to the office.

"If you will follow me?"

"You are a gentleman destined for a fine career," Dimitri murmured.

"I can only hope I survive to reap my just rewards." Once they were in the small chamber that held nothing more than a narrow bed and wooden armoire, Stanislav closed the door and turned to face Dimitri. "What do you desire of me?"

"You know why I am in Egypt?"

"I heard rumors that you seek a female who was taken from St. Petersburg by slavers and that you believe she was brought to the streets of Cairo."

Dimitri nodded in approval at the concise response. "What do you know of the woman?"

The man folded his hands behind his back, his expression clouding as he considered the question.

"There have been several Russian females sold in the slave markets over the past years." He shook his head.

"Unfortunately, the poor creatures are so broken by the time I can find them that they dare not speak of the men who have abused them. A pity. I can think of nothing I would enjoy more than having the animals drawn and quartered."

Dimitri smiled. "Do not fear, Stanislav, soon enough those men responsible for the theft of the girls will be brought to justice. If not by Alexander Pavlovich's hand, then by my own."

The young man arched a brow at the cold, lethal intent that was threaded through Dimitri's voice.

"I have heard that angering Dimitri Tipova is more dangerous than crossing paths with a wolf. Now I realize the rumors did not exaggerate."

He gave a sharp laugh. Certainly he had cast himself in the role of a dangerous wolf, stalking his prey with patient cunning. Only Emma had made him realize that he had been little better than those he hunted, willingly sacrificing young girls to sate his personal lust for revenge.

"A pity the rumors did not also claim I was man of intelligence."

The secretary frowned. "I beg your pardon?"

"Before I could detain those responsible they fled to England with several Russian girls."

"Ah." If Stanislav sensed that Dimitri was not being entirely forthcoming, he was wise enough to keep such thoughts to himself. "And you believe they were traveling to Cairo?"

"Yes. Can you discover if they have arrived?"

"Do you have the name of the slavers?"

"Valik."

"Russian." The secretary nodded, his absent expression revealing he was already considering the best means of acquiring the information Dimitri demanded. "That should narrow my inquiries. I will begin immediately."

"Stanislav?" Dimitri called as the man opened the door and prepared to leave the room.

"Yes?"

"I prefer discretion, but do whatever necessary to locate the girls."

"If they are in Cairo, they will be found, that I can assure you," the younger man promised without hesitation.

Dimitri smiled. "Czar Alexander is fortunate in his choice of diplomats."

DIMITRI WAITED UNTIL THE sun was setting before he made his way on foot through the crowded streets of Cairo to Caliph Rajih's palace.

With his dark coloring and traditional robes, he easily blended with the natives, capable of moving through the pedestrians without attracting attention. Not that his robes made him invisible. Unfortunate, since he had not had the need to sneak past guards since he was a lad.

Trusting his youthful skills, he slid along the high wall surrounding the palace, using the shadows to conceal his presence from the numerous guards. Then, reaching the back mews, he climbed over the wooden gate and dropped onto the cobbled yard near the stables.

A wry smile touched his lips as he realized he had managed to knock over a small marble statue, a mistake he would never have made as a lad, but at least he hadn't broken his fool neck. And for the moment, he hadn't alerted the entire household to his intrusion.

Aware his luck could change at any moment, he made his way to the gardens. His visits to Cairo taught him the women's quarters would be placed at the back of the house and surrounded by yet another wall. Egyptian men were fiercely protective of their females.

Actually, he had always considered them well beyond

protective. They were insanely obsessed with keeping their wives secluded.

He was dedicated to keeping women safeguarded, but why would a man desire a harem? The various females who drifted in and out of his life were enjoyable enough, but he had never felt compelled to lock them in his home. He had enough duties without adding a large number of wives he would have to tend to for the rest of their lives.

No, he had no urge to keep a female as his prisoner.

Not unless that female was Emma Linley-Kirov, a treacherous voice whispered in the back of his mind.

Clenching his teeth, Dimitri crushed the fury that threatened to overwhelm him.

From what he could discover Emma had gone willingly with the caliph aboard his ship. In fact, the dockhands they had questioned in London had been adamant in their assurance that the female in Rajih's company had not only been a willing companion, but had frequently urged him to hurry.

She would not be at all pleased if he intruded upon the household, tossing about demands and hauling her away from the palace.

For now he had no choice but to try and convince Emma that he was far more capable of assisting her in retrieving Anya than the caliph.

Hardly an easy task considering she held him responsible for allowing her sister to be taken from London.

Circling the shallow pond surrounded by lotus plants, Dimitri had just caught sight of the grilled gate that separated the women's quarters when a rustle had him spinning toward the fountain in the center of the courtyard.

His gaze narrowed as a dark, slender man with black hair and matching eyes stepped into view. Dimitri knew at once that it was Caliph Rajih. What other man would wear robes so richly trimmed? Or carry himself with the sort of arrogance that made Dimitri long to pummel his too-handsome face?

A mocking smile tugged at the man's lips as he offered a low bow.

"Welcome, Dimitri Tipova, I have been expecting you."

Swallowing a curse, Dimitri folded his arms over his chest and hid his frustration behind a mask of polite indifference.

"How very disappointing. I had not realized I was so predictable."

"Do not be too disappointed." The caliph strolled forward, his utter confidence warning Dimitri that he had several guards hidden nearby. "Most men are predictable when a beautiful woman is involved."

"You have Emma?" he asked, needing to be certain.

"She is an honored guest in my home," Rajih confirmed.

Dimitri struggled between relief that Emma was near and an irrational rage at the knowledge she had chosen to abandon him and place her trust in this man.

"Guest?" he gritted.

"Of course." Rajih chuckled. "Do you prefer to believe she is a prisoner that I forced to Egypt against her will? Perhaps you have imagined rescuing her from my harem and earning her undying gratitude?"

Dimitri made a sound of disgust. "You know nothing of Emma if you believe she would express any gratitude at being rescued, even if that was what she desired. She is more likely to blacken my eye and demand to know why I had not arrived sooner."

"Yes." The dark eyes flared with a genuine emotion that made Dimitri grit his teeth. "She is quite spirited."

"A polite means of saying she is willful, stubborn and

happy to toss herself into danger in the pursuit of her sister?" he demanded.

"I would never be so ungentlemanly."

Dimitri offered a sardonic laugh. "Thankfully, I was raised upon the streets of St. Petersburg and not the hallowed halls of Eton. I have a peculiar habit of speaking my mind."

Rajih waved a slender hand toward the gates of the harem. "If she is such a bother, I question why you would have traveled such a distance, not to mention risking my wrath by intruding into my home without permission, in pursuit of her."

"Because she is mine."

Silence filled the gardens at his stark words. Then, without warning, the caliph tilted back his head to laugh with rich amusement.

"I do not believe she would agree with your claim."

Dimitri stepped forward, shocked by the primitive sense of possession thundering through his blood.

What was the matter with him? He was a man who prided himself on his cold cunning and ruthless logic. Only fools allowed themselves to be ruled by their passions.

But there was nothing cold in his urgent desire to bury the dagger he had hidden beneath his robes in Caliph Rajih's heart.

"For now, I am more interested in ensuring that *you* recognize my claim," he growled.

"It would be a good deal more believable if she had not eagerly fled your company to be with me."

Dimitri's breath hissed through his teeth. "Emma is desperate to rescue her sister. She would bargain with the devil if she thought it would bring her closer to Anya."

"Yes, I am aware of the guilt and fear that haunts my beloved's heart," Rajih murmured. "And unlike you, Tipova, I am willing to do whatever necessary to ease her pain."

Dimitri winced, despite the knowledge the man was being deliberately provoking. It was true. He had failed Emma. Oh, he could claim any number of reasonable excuses for his decisions, but all that mattered was that Emma had turned to another man rather than believing he could be trusted to offer her what she most desired.

"What do you want of her?" he asked.

"Is that a jest?"

"Do you intend to keep her as your concubine?"

The caliph glanced toward the harem, his expression unwittingly soft with yearning.

"That would, of course, be the reasonable choice. She is beautiful and highly desirable, but she is also a foreigner with no connection to power and wealth. Even worse she is opinionated, ill-tempered and impulsive."

"Do not toy with me."

"Very well." Rajih turned back to meet Dimitri's fierce gaze. "The thought of taking her as my wife has become a near unbearable temptation."

His heart nearly stopped. "Never."

"You were given the opportunity to earn the fair lady's heart, but you cared more for your revenge," Rajih challenged.

"You know nothing of the matter."

"I know that Emma believes you betrayed her trust as well as her heart. She will never forgive you."

"That is for Emma to decide."

"Her decision was made when she stepped onto my ship." Rajih shrugged. "Accept your loss as a gentleman and walk away."

"I seem to waste an inordinate amount of time reminding others I am no gentleman," Dimitri snarled. "Emma will never be your bride."

"You have no means to stop me."

"I will see you in hell before I allow you to take Emma from me."

"I already have taken her," the caliph reminded him.

"Not for long."

Dimitri charged forward, fully intending to kill the bastard with his bare hands. Emma was his. No man, powerful prince or not, was going to steal her away.

He had taken a handful of steps when the garden was filled with burly servants dressed in robes and armed with curved swords that gleamed with a deadly promise in the torchlight. Still he continued forward, his calculating intelligence for once overwhelmed by primitive emotion.

Thick, muscular arms grabbed him from behind, then a large fist slammed into his jaw from the side, briefly making him lose consciousness. When he awoke it was to discover that he was framed by two of the servants, his arms held in iron grips as he was being roughly hauled through the back gate and tossed onto the street.

Rising to his feet, Dimitri dusted off his robes and lifted his head to discover Rajih standing just inside the gates.

"A small warning, Tipova," he drawled. "The next time you enter my home uninvited I will have you beheaded."

Dimitri narrowed his gaze. "You will regret standing in my path."

EMMA HID IN THE MIMOSA, watching the gates being slammed in Dimitri's face and Rajih leading his servants back toward the inner courtyard.

The sound of raised voices disturbed the night air, luring her from her private rooms, but by the time she had pulled on her robes and made her way out of the house, the servants had Dimitri in their hands and were tossing him out of the palace.

Now she stood in shadows, watching the man she had assumed she would never see again.

She had been shocked last evening when she had over-heard Rajih's conversation with the Frenchman. He had sounded as if he had been expecting Dimitri's arrival in Cairo. Which was absurd, was it not?

Dimitri had achieved what he desired. He had the wit-nesses he needed to stand before Alexander Pavlovich and swear that Count Nevskaya was involved in the slave trade. Why would he travel to Egypt rather than St. Petersburg?

The question badgered her throughout the sleepless night and restless day.

Now she watched as Dimitri slammed his hand against the sturdy wrought-iron gates, his face shrouded in shad-ows. Not that she actually needed to see his face to sense he was infuriated at having been so rudely tossed from Rajih's home.

He was a man who gave the commands and expected others to obey them.

A wry smile touched her lips as her heart fluttered and her blood heated. Despite the velvet darkness and the dis-tance between them, she could feel the tug of his compel-ling presence. It did not seem to matter that she was furious with him. Just the very sight of Dimitri was enough to make her tingle with awareness.

Waiting until Rajih had disappeared into the inner court-yard, Emma moved toward the gates, ignoring the tiny voice that whispered she was being a fool.

No doubt it would be far more sensible to return to her quarters and pretend that Dimitri had never arrived in Cairo. Surely she had enough troubles keeping Rajih at a proper distance and finding her sister?

But her curiosity would not allow her to simply walk away.

Or at least she told herself that it was curiosity.

Any other explanation was too dangerous to ponder.

"Why are you here?" she rasped, stepping into the pool of light from the nearby torch.

"Emma," he breathed, his expression impossible to read as his golden gaze swept over her. "Unlock the gate."

"No." She wrapped her arms around her waist, feeling oddly vulnerable in the loose silk robes, her hair tumbling about her shoulders. "Please answer my question."

"You know why I am here, *moya dusha*." His husky voice brushed over her like a caress, shivers of unwelcome pleasure racing through her. "I came for you."

"Then you have made a wasted journey."

"I would travel twice as far to be near you."

"That would be quite charming if I did not know you so well, Dimitri."

His lips twisted. "Somehow I do not think that a compliment."

"You did not follow me. If you are here, then it is for your own purpose." She took a step closer. "Did Sanderson manage to escape from your grasp?"

"So far as I know he is still in the custody of King George and his guards, although Huntley promised he would be taken to St. Petersburg to be questioned by Alexander Pavlovich."

She frowned, unable to accept he would allow Sanderson out of his sight before he was certain Count Nevskaya had been publicly humiliated.

"Then…" Her puzzlement disappeared as she was struck by a sudden thought. "Ah. Of course."

He narrowed his gaze, as if sensing he was not going to be pleased with what she had to say.

"Of course?"

"You will have need of Valik." She shrugged. "He is the obvious liaison between your father and Lord Sanderson. With his testimony there is no one who can doubt Count Nevskaya's guilt."

"It is true I intend to locate Valik." He lifted a hand to halt her angry words. "But only because he can lead us to Anya."

She stiffened. Did he truly believe she was so gullible?

"It is too late to feign concern for my sister. You could have rescued her in London, but you chose your obsession for revenge."

His expression hardened at her accusation. "I could defend myself by pointing out that by exposing my father, as well as Lord Sanderson and his cronies, I prevented a number of innocent girls from suffering the same fate as your sister."

Emma glared, not willing to listen to his arguments.

"Just go away, Dimitri."

His grip tightened on the gate, his eyes flashing with a warning that sent a chill down her spine.

"You will never be rid of me, Emma," he swore. "It does not matter where you go or how far you run, I will always be near."

CHAPTER NINETEEN

EMMA SPENT THE NEXT DAY pacing through the harem, torn between the fear that Dimitri might actually storm the palace and attempt to take her by force, and a treacherous disappointment when he did not so much as make an appearance.

She was clearly losing what few wits she had left, she told herself. Dimitri Tipova had made his choice in London. Just as she had made hers.

There was nothing left for them to say.

As night began to fall she pulled on a silken robe in a soft shade of ivory that was richly embroidered with silver thread and tiny emeralds. Her curls were still damp from her bath and she left them loose to flow down her back. Then, with a dab of the jasmine oil that Rajih had sent to the harems that morning, she stepped into the gardens.

She was weary of her sense of isolation.

As lovely as her surroundings might be, she was accustomed to being endlessly occupied with one task or another and, of course, being among others. There was no privacy to be found in her coaching inn, or even the cottage with Anya and her friends constantly underfoot.

The hours of peaceful silence allowed her far too much time to imagine the horror and fear Anya must be enduring. Or worse, to ponder the memory of Dimitri as he stood at the gates of the palace, his presence still calling to her with irresistible force.

Entering the garden, she paced toward the fountain, pleased to discover the air had already cooled as dusk began to spread across the sky in dazzling shades of pink, peach and a vivid fuchsia.

She glanced in appreciation toward the distant sand dunes that appeared purple in the fading light. A line of camels stood silhouetted in the gathering shadows and the sound of exotic birds chirping filled the air. It was a vision out of a dream.

She bent down to run her fingers through the water pooling at the base of the fountain.

"Good evening, Emma."

Recognizing the rich, masculine sound of Rajih's voice, Emma straightened, her brows lifting as she caught sight of his lean form fitted in a dark uniform with gold braiding and several medals pinned to his chest. She had seen him in elegantly tailored clothing and the loose robes of his people, but the sight of him in full military dress was a sharp reminder of his power and position.

"Oh." She pressed a hand over her racing heart. "You startled me."

"Forgive me." He bowed before drawing closer to study her with a blatant sensuality. "As exquisitely beautiful as ever."

She smiled. "While you appear quite forbidding. Is there a special occasion for such finery?"

"Much to my dismay I have been commanded to make an appearance at my uncle's home."

An edge to his voice warned Emma there was more to his annoyance than the invitation to dinner.

"Has something happened?"

"My uncle indicated that he was entertaining several foreign dignitaries."

Her smiled widened. "Ah, so he wishes you to be at hand to charm them?"

"That would be my assumption under normal circumstances."

She tilted her head to the side, studying him with a searching gaze.

"Are these not normal circumstances?"

He stepped close, his hand cupping her chin and his thumb lightly stroking her lower lip.

"Not so long as Dimitri Tipova remains in Cairo."

"Dimitri?" She hid the sudden pounding of her heart, pretending nonchalance. "Is he in Cairo?"

The dark face was unreadable. "He is."

"And…" She licked her dry lips. "He is to be a guest at tonight's dinner?"

"I think it is more likely he arranged for my uncle to host the dinner and insist upon my presence."

She jerked in astonishment at the accusation. "How could he possibly have such influence among your family?"

"Tipova may not possess a title, but he has a vast fortune and he has made certain that the knowledge of that fortune is well-known throughout Cairo." Rajih grimaced. "Including those members of my family who are always eager to attach themselves to wealth."

Emma rolled her eyes. Of course. Dimitri was talented in the art of manipulation. Whether it was via money, power or sex.

"Even presuming that he was capable of arranging a dinner with your uncle, what would be the purpose?" she demanded.

"Obviously he wishes to keep me occupied."

"Why?"

Rajih shifted his hand to run his fingers through her hair, his touch gentle and yet possessive.

"To steal you away, of course."

"Absurd."

"There is nothing absurd in his determination to have you as his own." The dark eyes flashed with annoyance. "Nothing will deter him."

Emma folded her arms across her waist. Why was her senseless heart fluttering with excitement? She was still far from convinced that she was the reason that Dimitri had traveled to Cairo. Or that if he had followed her it was anything more than wounded male pride.

She would lay odds that the man had never had a woman willingly leave his bed. Not, at least, until he was done with the affair. And it would only make it worse that Emma had left with another man.

"If he is foolish enough to believe he can simply carry me off I shall soon disabuse him," she muttered.

He gently tugged her hair, his gaze scrutinizing her pale face. "Will you?"

"So far as I am concerned Dimitri Tipova is no better than any other man," she snapped. "He is willing to use me for his own pleasure without concern for my needs."

"Do not condemn all men, *habiba*."

She wrinkled her nose at the realization she had been excessively rude to the man who had offered her nothing but kindness.

"It is not a matter of condemning men, Rajih, but an acceptance that I would be a fool to depend upon anyone but myself." She touched his arm, a sadness settling in her heart. "I have been disappointed on too many occasions to offer my trust."

A silence settled over the gardens, filled only by the splash of the fountain and the soft flutter of wings as a bird settled on a nearby sycamore branch. Emma shifted uneasily, unnerved by his steady gaze. It was almost as if Rajih was attempting to see into her very soul.

"A reluctance to trust does not mean you have managed to banish Tipova from your heart," he said softly. "Your vehement reaction suggests that you still harbor feelings for the man."

Heat stained her cheeks. "I harbor a desire to have him carried into the desert and eaten by the jackals."

Rajih's lips twisted. "Ah, *habiba,* I regret I am incapable of inspiring such passion."

She frowned at his words. Had he not just heard her claim that she desired Dimitri to be eaten by jackals?

"Anger and passion are not at all the same."

"You are very innocent."

Anger sliced through her at his patronizing tone. With a sharp movement she brushed aside his lingering hand and stepped back.

"If that is a kind means of saying that I am stupid I readily agree."

Rajih shook his head. "I mean precisely what I said. There's a genuine purity about you that will remain untarnished no matter what happens in your life." He shrugged, his gaze skimming down her slender body. "Unfortunate for you, of course."

"Why unfortunate?"

"Because it is destined to attract the worst sort of bounders and scoundrels." Then he reached for her, pulling her hard against his sculpted torso. "You are irresistible to those of us with jaded hearts."

"Rajih."

He pressed a finger to her lips, sensing her reluctance.

"I will not press you, *habiba,* but I do demand a promise."

"A promise?"

"That you will not leave my home without first discussing your departure with me."

Emma considered before agreeing to Rajih's request. She would not give her word lightly. Not when she expected others to fulfill their vows.

"I promise," she at last agreed.

He brushed his lips over her forehead. "Thank you. I must go."

"Wait." She grasped his arm. "Have you heard nothing of my sister?"

"Not as yet," he said, genuine sympathy in his dark eyes. "But hold on to hope, Emma. They will be found."

She remained standing beside the fountain as Rajih bowed and turned to leave the garden.

Hold on to hope...

Such simple words, and yet they were increasingly difficult to cling to.

Lost in thoughts of her sister's torment, Emma did not hear the sound of rustling among the mimosa, or the soft tread of footsteps on the paved pathway. It was not until a pair of arms circled her waist and hauled her back against a hard chest that she realized the dangers of her distraction.

Her heart lodged in her throat as she instantly recognized Dimitri's warm scent. Not that she needed more than his touch to know who held her. There was no other man who could send thrilling quivers through her body at the mere brush of his hand.

It was wretchedly unfair.

No, there was no need to question that the man holding her captive was Dimitri. Nor to wonder how he had managed to enter the enclosed harem surrounded by guards. Dimitri could no doubt slip into the citadel and steal the pasha's jewels if he desired.

Splaying his fingers against her stomach, Dimitri bent his head to whisper directly in her ear.

"You play a dangerous game, *moya dusha,*" he warned. "If I ever witness you in the arms of another man again I will kill him."

Emma struggled to breath, telling herself it was anger, not desperate longing, that made her tremble.

"So Rajih was right."

His arms tightened. "Do not speak his name."

"I will speak whatever name I might choose. You have no authority over me."

He tensed, then surprisingly, she felt his grip ease, his lips brushing the curve of her ear.

"Such courage, and yet you tremble," he taunted. "Do I frighten you?"

Excitement fluttered in her stomach, her toes curling as heat flowed through her veins.

It had been so terribly long since she had allowed herself to enjoy Dimitri's touch. Now her entire body ached with unfulfilled need.

Not that she was about to admit as much to the infuriating demon who was kissing a path of fire down the side of her neck.

"What woman would not be frightened when a man creeps into her private quarters and speaks of his intent to kill?" she accused.

"You must know I would never hurt you, Emma."

"But you did hurt me, Dimitri." The words tumbled from her lips before she could stop them.

Dimitri tensed, his warm breath teasing the delicate skin of her neck and sending jolts of pleasure down her spine.

"That was never my intention."

Angered as much by her reaction to his touch as by his ridiculous words, she arched away from the potent heat of his caressing lips.

"Yes, it was. You have always known you would allow nothing to come between you and your revenge," she hissed. "Certainly not me or my poor sister."

"And if I tell you that I regret my choice? That I would make a different decision if we were back in that warehouse in London?"

She shook her head, refusing to consider his words

sincere. "I would say that it is very convenient to claim such regret now that you have what you desire."

His grip tightened and with relentless determination he turned her in his arms to meet the blazing gold of his eyes.

"But I do not have what I desire," he rasped, his hands gripping her hips and pressing her against the swollen thrust of his arousal.

Dangerous warmth pooled between her legs. "Stop now."

"Emma, have you no regrets?"

She turned her head, unable to think clearly when he was so near.

"Of course I do," she muttered.

He placed a hand against her face, firmly turning her face to meet his tense expression. For the first time she noticed the shadows beneath his remarkable eyes and the pronounced jut of his cheekbones, revealing that he had lost weight since she had last seen him. An annoying pang of sympathy tugged at her heart.

"Then surely you can find it in your heart to forgive me?" he asked.

"I do not wish to forgive you," she said, as much to convince herself as Dimitri Tipova. "All I want is to find my sister and return home."

"Your home is with me."

Her heart faltered at the sheer certainty in his voice. "No."

The golden gaze blazed over her face. "Yes, *moya dusha*."

She pressed against his chest. It was so simple to swear she was done with Dimitri and his persuasive kisses when he was far away. But when he held her so close against him...

Emma shook her head in denial. "I have no need of you."

"Perhaps I have need of you."

Her sharp laugh echoed through the gardens. There was only one reason Dimitri would need a woman.

"To warm your bed?"

"I will not deny I am desperate to have you in my arms. But it is more than mere lust. You are meant to be at my side."

"For as long as I please you."

"For so long as we please one another." In one fluid movement, Dimitri swept her off her feet, cradling her against his chest as he carried her toward the arched entrance of the women's quarters. "Allow me to please you, *milaya*."

Her heart raced with a combination of anger and searing need.

"No. Rajih…"

Her words were brought to a shocking halt as he covered her mouth with a tempestuous kiss that stole her breath.

He tasted of vodka and male desire. A heady combination that made her entire body clench with an aching hunger.

"I warned you not to speak that name," he muttered against her mouth. "The only man on your mind or your lips will be me."

She would have denied his stark claim of possession if he hadn't kissed her again, her barely restrained desire flowing through her like molten lava. Instinctively, her arms lifted to circle his neck, her lips parting in silent invitation.

Distantly, she was aware they had entered the seraglio and he was headed toward the private apartments. She could smell the burning incense and the precious oils beside the baths, but she made no effort to struggle from his grasp.

Why bother?

She wanted Dimitri.

Desperately.

Finding her apartments with unnerving accuracy, Dimitri stepped into her bedchamber where a fire already burned against the chill of the approaching night. He shut the door behind them and slid her down his body until she was standing directly in front of him.

"You have plagued my every dream, *milaya*," he rasped, a flush staining his cheeks and his eyes glittering with a hectic fire. "I have never wanted a woman as I want you."

A renegade warmth flooded her heart. Dear Lord, how many nights had she cried herself to sleep after being treated as if she were little better than a leper by the men in her village? Or scurried from the local shops after overhearing her neighbors laughing at her threadbare gown and haggard appearance?

To the world she had offered an impervious composure allowing her to tend to her business and protect Anya from the censure of others. But inside…

Inside she had hidden the wounds that never healed.

Not until Dimitri, a tiny voice whispered.

He had been the first to see beyond her ugly wool gowns and prickly independence to the vulnerable woman beneath. And more important, the first to make her feel as alluring and desirable as any other woman.

It was a rare gift she would always treasure. Even after he was gone from her life.

She thrust aside the jagged pain threatening her heart.

In this moment she did not want to think of the inevitable loneliness in her future or the past betrayals. Tonight she would accept the pleasure Dimitri offered.

"This means nothing," she muttered, more for herself than for her companion.

Then, before she could falter, she reached to pull the silken robes over her head, tossing the heavy fabric aside to reveal she wore nothing but slippers beneath.

Dimitri's breath hissed through his teeth, his body so stiff he looked as if he had been transformed into a statue. Although no statue had eyes that blazed with a pure gold fire.

"Emma," he rasped, his voice thick with longing. "You have missed me, have you not?"

"No."

A sudden smile curved his lips at her refusal to admit her inner emotions, and with hands that were not entirely steady, he hastily rid himself of his own robes before tugging off his soft leather boots.

"Your body tells me otherwise," he husked, his gaze on her beaded nipples as he prowled toward her.

She shivered, already anticipating the feel of his hands on her bare skin.

"I do not deny that I desire you." She bravely met his smoldering gaze. "But there is nothing more."

Dimitri cupped her face in his hands, a hint of pique tightening his features. Almost as if he were disturbed by her indifference.

Which was ridiculous, was it not? What interest did he have in her beyond the use of her body?

"Do you wish me to beg for your affections?" he asked in a rough voice.

"You beg?" She laughed at the mere thought. "You would not know how."

"You wrong me." He leaned downward, softly teasing her lips with his. "It was one of my finer talents before I was sent to school. All I had need of was a cane and a rag to tie over my eyes and I could make a small fortune."

She squashed the thought of Dimitri as a small boy

struggling to survive on the streets of St. Petersburg. She was already far too vulnerable.

"Do not remind me how talented you are in deceiving others," she husked.

He swore at her stubborn resistance, then parting her lips with the tip of his tongue, he plundered her mouth with unrestrained passions.

Emma's pulse raced as his tongue slipped into her mouth and, arching against the hardness of his chest, she shoved her fingers into the thick satin of his hair. He groaned, wrapping her in his arms as he urged her backward. Still holding her mouth captive, he tumbled them both onto the wide divan.

All thoughts were lost as he landed on top of her, his heart beating a rapid tattoo against her tender breasts.

He should have been too heavy, too overwhelming, too… male. Instead, she savored the feel of being pressed into the velvet cushions and the rough scrape of his hair against her skin.

This was no gentle seduction. No sweet love play.

This was a raw craving that refused to be denied.

"Emma…" Breathing heavily, he brushed heated kisses over her face, his hands outlining the curve of her hips. "It has been too long."

It had been too long. Far too long, she admitted to herself, arching beneath him in a silent plea for relief from the need clawing deep inside her.

"Then why are you wasting our time together with conversation?" she demanded, her voice strained.

He growled, his mouth trailing down her throat and over the upper curve of her breasts. Emma had no notion where her brazen manner was coming from, but she was too impatient to worry over it. She had spent too many nights dreaming of being in Dimitri's arms to squander a moment.

"As you wish, *moya dusha,*" he rasped, his hands shifting to cup her breasts so he could ravage them with his lips and tongue and teeth.

She cried out in pleasure, her legs parting so he could settle between them. The hard length of his arousal pressed against her inner thigh. She shuddered, already damp with longing.

"Dimitri."

"Patience," he urged, his lips moving down the soft swell of her stomach, his hands slipping beneath her backside to lift her to his seeking mouth.

"Dear...Lord," she breathed, trembling beneath the onslaught of sensations.

He was wicked, decadent and as beautiful as a bronzed god in the flickering firelight.

What woman could possibly resist?

Certainly not Emma.

Biting her lower lip to keep her moans from filling the harem, she felt Dimitri shift until his mouth could nibble on the flesh of her inner thigh, his hands holding her still as she squirmed in pleasure.

His lips stroked ever higher, at last finding the very source of her desire. She closed her eyes in appreciation, her fingers clutching his hair as he stroked his tongue through the heart of her femininity.

Her head spun and her soft pants filled the air. That exquisite pleasure was beginning to build in her lower belly and still he continued with his caresses. Over and over he teased the tiny nub, seeming to take delight in her muffled groans.

At last she tugged at his hair, hovering on the edge of pure bliss.

"Please," she begged, her voice barely recognizable.

His head lifted to meet her dazed gaze, his eyes glowing with a fierce craving.

"What would you have of me, Emma?"

Your love.

The words whispered through her mind only to be roughly shoved aside.

She would not ruin this night with impossible dreams.

"I need you," she whispered.

"Yes."

Surging upward, he entered her with one smooth thrust.

Emma sucked in a sharp breath, her hands sliding down the rigid muscles of his back as he set a relentless pace that had her soaring toward the stars.

CHAPTER TWENTY

TUCKING EMMA AGAINST HIS side, Dimitri breathed deep in an effort to slow the thundering pace of his heart.

A task that would have been considerably easier if his potent awareness of her was not still rampaging through his body and urging him to take advantage of their rare moment together.

It had been too long.

Far too long.

And the need to drown himself in the pleasure of her sweet desire was nearly overwhelming.

Unfortunately, he could not ignore the manner Emma's body was stiffening as sanity returned, her tiny hands reaching to press against his chest.

"I have missed you, *milaya,*" he whispered, pressing his lips to her hair as he sought to temper the palpable regret in the air.

"This was—"

"Exquisite?" he interrupted. "Astonishing? A miracle?"

"A mistake."

"No, Emma, the only mistake was attempting to leave me. We belong together."

Her eyes shimmered like the finest emeralds in the firelight.

"I did not leave you, Dimitri."

His fingers stroked the satin skin of her shoulder, his body already stirring at the feel of her warm curves pressed against his body.

"No?"

"No." She shifted to meet his gaze with a somber expression. "I followed my sister. Something you attempted to prevent me from doing."

His grip unwittingly tightened. "My only desire was to keep you safe."

"That was not what I wanted of you."

"I understand your need to rescue Anya," he said. "I even admire your courage."

"And yet you locked me in Lord Huntley's house while you allowed Anya to be taken from London."

He swallowed a sigh. How many years had it been since he had explained his decisions to anyone? Quite likely it had not been since his mother's death.

And most certainly he did not apologize. Not ever.

At least, not until Emma Linley-Kirov.

"For how long do you intend to punish me for my impetuous decision?" he asked, his voice low.

She shifted on the cushions, a faint color staining her cheeks.

"I am not attempting to punish you. I am merely explaining why we cannot possibly be lovers."

His brows lifted as he swept a glance down her naked form.

"And yet we are."

She arched away, her features hard with a frustrating denial.

"No."

"Emma, I have apologized for not putting Anya before my revenge scheme, but I truly believed we would easily be able to find the girls once Sanderson was captured." He struggled to maintain his patience. Why did she have to be so damnably stubborn? "What more would you have of me?"

She tilted her chin. "Your promise that you will let me

make my own decisions even when you do not agree with them."

"You mean I am to turn a blind eye when you wish to charge into danger?"

"It is my right."

"It is madness."

With a sudden surge, she wiggled out of his grasp and slid off the bed, grasping her satin robe and pulling it over her beautiful body before he could halt her. His lips twisted as he rose to his feet and pulled on his own clothing.

With her exotic surroundings and strange garb, she looked moons away from the prudish spinster who had entered his coffee shop in St. Petersburg. He wondered if she realized just how much she had transformed over the past weeks?

"You comprehend how impossible this is?" she was demanding, tying her hair in a braid with shaking hands.

His brows snapped together at her husky words. "Dammit, Emma, you seek to unman me."

"Because I will not become a meek, biddable creature who is grateful to obey your every command?"

Biddable? He swallowed his instinctive laugh. He had never encountered a woman less biddable than Emma Linley-Kirov.

"Because you will not allow me to protect you."

"I do not want your protection. I want—"

He stilled as she hastily bit off her words, a hint of panic in her eyes as if she had nearly revealed something she was determined to keep hidden from him.

"What do you want?"

She turned away, pacing toward the towering Oriental vase that was set in the corner of the room.

"It does not matter."

With three long strides he was at her side, grasping her upper arm and turning her to meet his searching gaze.

"Tell me, *moya dusha*. What do you want of me?"

She shook her head, her eyes dark with an unreadable emotion.

"What you cannot offer."

Dimitri refused to be bothered at the conviction in her voice. He would regain this woman's fragile trust. Eventually, she would put the past behind them and look toward a future together.

He would accept no less.

"Do not be so certain." He skimmed his hand up her arm, cupping the back of her neck in a possessive motion. "I have not traveled such a distance to return home without you."

She shivered, the pulse at the base of her throat fluttering with an unmistakable reaction to his touch.

"The choice is not yours."

He allowed a wicked smile to curve his lips. "Perhaps not, but there is nothing to curb me from convincing you that your place is at my side."

She studied him, her delicate features troubled. "Why?"

Dimitri paused, sensing the question was important to Emma.

"What are you asking?"

"You have had lovers before me."

"Do you wish me to apologize for them?"

She grimaced, and Dimitri harbored the hope that she was bothered by the thought of him with another woman. God knew that he had been tortured by Caliph Rajih.

"Of course not," she denied. "But I find it difficult to imagine you are always so reluctant to end an affair."

He shrugged. It was true enough. He had never sought to prolong an affair. There was always the danger that his lovers would begin to hope that they could claim more than a temporary position in his life.

Of course, he had never before had a woman who continued to stir his interest, not to mention his desire, long after he should have tired of her companionship.

A part of him was terrified at his need to keep her near.

Any man instinctively understood that the moment a female became as necessary as breathing that he was in deep trouble.

The larger part, however, didn't give a damn if he were in trouble or not. The mere thought of his life without Emma was unbearable.

He brushed his lips over her forehead. "None have ever been like you."

He heard her breath catch, but she obstinately pulled away from his touch, her expression set in grim lines.

"No doubt because they did not resist your need to be their savior," she accused. "If I were foolish enough to give in to your urgings and return to St. Petersburg, you would soon grow weary of me."

His anger stirred. Perhaps because there was a hint of truth in her words? He could not deny he made a habit of rescuing damsels in distress. And that he took pleasure in their feminine gratitude. It eased his guilt at his inability to save his mother.

But Emma had long ago transformed from a female in need of rescuing to the one female who could fill his heart with joy.

"Savior?" He shook his head, refusing to let her believe for a moment he considered her anything but a beautiful, desirable woman that he was determined to have in his life for all eternity. "Not even my dearest friends would believe I am anything other than a selfish pirate who takes what he wants and damn the consequences. And I assure you, I never intend to grow weary of you."

She backed away, her arms wrapped around her waist. "It would not be a matter of whether you want to or not.

Once I am safely in your care you would have no reason to consider me as anything other than a burden you would be anxious to be rid of."

Dimitri studied her guarded expression, sensing the hollowness of her words. Her fear went deeper than him losing interest in her.

"Do you know, Emma, I believe I at last begin to understand you," he said slowly.

She touched the tip of her tongue to her upper lip. "I very much doubt that."

"You are afraid."

"Certainly, I am," she hastily admitted. "I have been afraid since I discovered Anya missing."

"You are afraid of your feelings for me." He brushed a stray curl off her cheek. "That is why you continue to devise ridiculous reasons to keep me at a distance."

Her face paled in the flickering firelight, the scent of incense nearly overwhelming.

"Your arrogance truly is astonishing," she rasped.

His fingers lingered on her cheek, savoring the warm satin of her skin.

"Listen to me. You can trust your heart to my care. I will not abandon you as others have done."

He felt her tense beneath his fingertips, her eyes wide and dark with wounds that she struggled so hard to keep hidden.

"Why would you say such a ridiculous thing?"

A dangerous tenderness swept through him. He desperately longed to scoop her in his arms and take her someplace where she could never be hurt again.

"Because those you loved and depended upon died, leaving you alone to shoulder burdens that have been far too heavy." His thumb outlined her lower lip. "It is little wonder you protect your heart with such ferocity."

For a brief, breathless moment Emma swayed toward

him, as if he had at last managed to convince her of his sincerity. Then, with a frightened shake of her head, she again stepped back, her spine stiff.

"Please just go away."

Dimitri muttered a curse, fully intending to remain precisely where he stood until he had exhausted Emma's arguments. For all her protests he had not missed the brief glimpse of yearning he had seen shimmering in her eyes.

Emma might claim she wanted nothing more than her independence, but he had seen the truth of her heart.

It was the appearance of a robed servant who gestured at him from the arched doorway that ruined his plan.

Hurriedly hiding his disbelief behind a resigned expression, he brushed his lips over her cheek before stepping back and smoothing his tousled hair.

"Perhaps you are right," he said.

She blinked, her defensive anger faltering beneath his unexpected capitulation.

"I beg your pardon?"

"This is not the time or place for such a discussion," he forced himself to say.

"You are leaving?"

He smiled despite his annoyance at the ill-timed interruption. Emma could not entirely hide her disappointment at his announcement.

"It is what you desire, is it not?"

She hunched her shoulders. "Of course it is."

With a chuckle, he leaned down to lightly kiss her lips. "Dream of me."

He had reached the door when a delicate porcelain figurine went sailing past his head to smash against the stone wall.

"You are...impossible," she shouted after his retreating back.

His smile remained as he followed the retreating servant toward the back of the harem.

It was odd that he had known dozens of beautiful women who were not only compliant, but eager to please him, and yet none had stirred more than a passing interest.

Perhaps fate had decided to punish him after his years of sin.

Only it did not seem like punishment. He stifled a groan as he recalled the explosive pleasure he had so recently enjoyed. For all the irritation that Emma offered, being with her was as close to paradise as a man could possibly find.

The servant slipped through a narrow door into the gardens beyond, and with an effort Dimitri shoved aside his thoughts of Emma and concentrated on the servant who slid to a halt in the shadows of the high wall surrounding the harem.

At a glance there was nothing about the veiled servant to capture his interest. There were at least a dozen females attired in precisely the same manner throughout the palace, although this particular servant was taller than most.

It was only Dimitri's familiarity with Josef and his willingness to go to any length to slip about unnoticed that allowed him to recognize the slender Russian man. And, of course, his ugly countenance that no veil could entirely disguise.

Reaching up a hand, Josef tugged aside the thin veil, and headdress, a taunting smile curling his lips.

"Yet another satisfied lover, eh, Tipova?" he mocked. "You have a remarkable talent with women."

"My talent does not extend to appearing as one," Dimitri teased in return, allowing his gaze to skim down the robes his servant wore with remarkable ease. Joseph was a magnificent actor who could play any role required. "You are exquisite."

"Take care, Tipova. I have several daggers hidden beneath these robes," the scar-faced man warned.

They both tensed as the distant sound of voices echoed through the gardens, reminding Dimitri they were standing in the gardens of a man who had only yesterday threatened to have him beheaded.

As if reading his mind, Josef silently turned toward the wall, running his hands over the smooth stones until there was a faint click and a portion slid open.

"Through here," the man urged.

Ducking through the opening, Dimitri glanced about the dark street that ran beside the palace, abruptly realizing that Josef had managed to discover a secret entrance through the ancient walls.

"You never cease to amaze me, Josef," he muttered as his companion joined him.

With swift, efficient motions, Josef rid himself of his robes to reveal a rough tunic and loose breeches worn by Turkish servants.

"I prefer a more tangible reward than mere amazement."

"What of my heartfelt appreciation?" Dimitri laughed as his servant grunted his disapproval. "Do not fear, you will be properly rewarded." His amusement faded as he glanced up and down the narrow street, ensuring they could not be overheard. "What have you discovered?"

"There was a man who resembled Valik's description who was seen in a café near the citadel."

It was precisely what Dimitri had hoped to discover when he requested Josef make contacts among the natives of Cairo. After all, a man involved in an illegal trade might do his best to avoid soldiers or those in authority, but he would never notice the thousands of commoners who filled the markets and cafés and public baths. Such people always made the best spies.

"Have you visited the café?"

"I went there earlier to enjoy a small pastry."

"Did your pastry include any information?"

"Not so much as I would have desired." Josef's grimace was barely visible in the wash of moonlight. "There were several patrons who recalled a large man, possibly Russian, who briefly visited the café, but he left long before I arrived and no one knew where he was staying."

Dimitri swore. "So we are still in ignorance."

"Not entirely. I made a search of the neighborhood."

"And?"

"I discovered three brothels within walking distance of the café."

Dimitri shrugged, not willing to leap to conclusions that might blind him to other possibilities. He had already allowed Anya to slip through his fingers once. It would not happen again.

"The auctions needn't be offered at a brothel. It is quite possible that the girls are being held in a private residence."

"It is possible, but with the pasha's current disapproval of the slave trade there are fewer citizens willing to risk the citadel's dungeons by being so intimately associated with the traffickers," Josef reasoned. "If they are hidden in a brothel then all involved could plead to have no knowledge of the auction. Besides, we must begin somewhere."

"Yes," Dimitri readily agreed, sensing there was something his companion was keeping from him. "Is that why you intruded on my private evening with Emma?"

Josef discreetly shifted back, a certain indication that he had been indulging his love for daring gambles.

"I made a brief sojourn to each of the brothels to discover the various pleasures offered."

Anger jolted through Dimitri at the grudging confession. Damn, the obstinate fool. After Josef had risked his neck to bring an end to a foul murderer who had kidnapped the Duchess of Huntley, Dimitri had decided his old friend had reached an age when his lust for adventure needed to be curtailed. He had brought him to England and then Egypt for his cunning, not to charge recklessly into danger.

"You entered the brothels alone?"

Josef jerked a head toward the nearby harem. "As you just mentioned, you were otherwise occupied."

"You should have waited until I could accompany you," he growled. "I did not bring you to Cairo for you to have your throat slit and your body tossed into the Nile."

"If I desired a mother hen, Tipova, I would find one considerably more attractive than you."

Dimitri glanced toward the pile of robes that Josef had so recently shed.

"You are hardly in a position to toss about insults."

The slender man snorted, his lips twitching with amusement. "Do you wish to know what I learned or not?"

Dimitri heaved a sigh. What was the point in chastising the man? Josef had spent a lifetime tossing dice with the devil. It was going to take a more than a lecture from Dimitri to curtail his dance with death.

"I do," he admitted.

"Two of the brothels were eager to welcome me inside and introduce me to their females. They even allowed me the opportunity to search the establishments."

"I thought we agreed not to stir unnecessary curiosity?"

A smug smile spread across his face. "I explained that I was seeking a respectable brothel for my wealthy employer and that he suffered a peculiar fear of fleas. What could I do but inspect the rooms?"

"I assume you found nothing?"

"Fleas."

"Charming." Dimitri shuddered. He was far too familiar with the filth and squalor to be found in cheap establishments. "And the third brothel?"

"Oddly enough they claimed that they could not accommodate my employer for the next week."

Dimitri's interest was instantly piqued. "Did they offer an explanation?"

"I was told that there had been a fire in the private chambers and that they were making repairs."

Dimitri gave a decisive shake of his head. "There is no brothel that would turn away a potential customer even if the place was *still* on fire."

"My thoughts exactly."

A thick silence descended as Dimitri glanced down the empty street and then toward the looming palace.

On the other side of the thick walls Emma was no doubt still cursing his name and tossing priceless artifacts at the door, and yet he desired nothing more than to return to her private quarters and drag her into his arms.

But if there were even a slim possibility that he could discover Valik and the innocent females he was holding prisoner then he had no choice but to put aside his personal desires and pursue the bastard.

"Damn."

Josef smirked, seeming to enjoy Dimitri's reluctance to leave Emma.

"If you want to return to the lady I will search the brothel," he taunted. "At your age you really should avoid situations that demand agility."

"The traffickers are not the only ones who can toss you into the Nile, my friend." He pointed down the dark street. "Lead me to the brothel."

CHAPTER TWENTY-ONE

EMMA WAS INFURIATED.

She told herself that it was Dimitri Tipova's intrusion into Rajih's palace and his brazen seduction that made her long to toss every breakable object in the vast palace. Had she not made it clear the last time they met that she wanted him to leave her in peace? He had no right to force his company on her.

But while she might be in a temper, she was not utterly unreasonable.

If she had truly been disturbed by Dimitri's arrival then surely all she need have done was call for one of the countless servants? Dimitri was a dangerous, even lethal, adversary, but not even he could fend off a half dozen large eunuchs.

Besides which, there was no means to convince herself that the seduction had been anything but mutual.

A shameless excitement jolted through her body. She had wanted Dimitri with such fervor that nothing could have kept her from his arms. And if he had not so rudely abandoned her, then she would no doubt be willing and eager to be seduced again.

And that was the cause of her anger, she ruefully acknowledged.

Not because Dimitri Tipova had intruded into the harem grounds, but because he had left them.

Stepping out of the seraglio that suddenly threatened to smother her, Emma breathed deeply of the perfumed air, glancing up at the sky spattered with twinkling stars.

She was a fool, of course. She had been adamant that she would never forgive Dimitri for his betrayal, and yet, he had only to kiss her for her to toss aside all common sense and melt in his arms.

She shivered, startled by the bittersweet pang of yearning that pierced her heart without warning.

She wished she was home in her shabby cottage.

Perhaps it was not so surprising.

Since her mother's death her life had never been easy. Not only had she faced the duties of the household and caring for Anya, but she had been forced to toss aside her own dreams of a future. But for all her sacrifices, she had never felt as...lost as she did now.

In Yabinsk she knew what each day would bring.

Now she felt as if she were floundering through a blizzard with no notion of where she was headed, or what was awaiting her at the end of the road.

Consumed by her disturbing thoughts, Emma welcomed the soft sound of slippers on the path. Turning her head she watched as the veiled servant hurried toward her.

"There you are, mistress," the girl said, her voice soft but edged with surprising urgency.

"Samira." She stepped toward the servant. "Is there something you need?"

"Yes. The caliph is waiting for you."

"He has returned?"

"He is waiting in a carriage behind the seraglio."

Emma frowned in confusion, disturbed by the odd chill that crept down her spine.

"I do not understand. Why would he be waiting in a carriage?"

"His message merely said that I was to request you join him." The woman cast a furtive glance around the garden, as if fearful of being overheard. "Do you wish me to inform him that it is inconvenient?"

"No. I..." She shook her head. There was no reason to be uneasy. Rajih would never harm her. And it might very well be that he had discovered information that could lead them to Anya. "Of course I will join him. Thank you, Samira."

There was the briefest hesitation before the servant bowed, then she turned to lead Emma through the banks of mimosa.

"This way."

They traveled through the garden in silence, Emma occasionally glancing over her shoulder to ensure that Dimitri was not lurking among the shadows.

Against her will she wondered where he had gone and why he had left so abruptly.

Had he somehow been alerted to Rajih's return and left before he could be discovered? Or had he simply achieved what he wanted with her and was now seeking fresh entertainment?

She stumbled, shocked by the pain of the thought of Dimitri enjoying the pleasures of another woman.

No. She would not think of Dimitri or the manner he could infuriate her one moment and send her pulse fluttering the next. Not when such a task did nothing but leave her with an aching head.

Far better to concentrate on Rajih and his mysterious request.

Samira paused to unlock the back gate, motioning Emma through with a wave of her hand.

Emma absently smoothed her hands down her robes, acutely aware of her mussed appearance. Would Rajih suspect the reason for her wrinkled robes and flushed cheeks?

Her brief flare of unease was forgotten as she stepped past the high wall of the palace to discover the dark carriage waiting for her.

Another chill trickled down her spine.

Rajih had a stable full of carriages as well as the strange contraptions that were placed atop a camel to ride through the desert. But his vehicles were all sleek and elegant and noticeably expensive.

Nothing at all like the black, bulky carriage that was built for function rather than beauty.

Emma paused, unwilling to deny her prickling sense of alarm. She might not understand the strange premonition plaguing her, but she was not going to ignore it.

She turned on her heel, intending to rush back into the safety of the harem. Instead, she discovered a large man with thick features and small, terrifyingly cold eyes waiting for her.

Her lips parted to scream, but before she could make a sound the stranger had his beefy hand wrapped over her mouth and a heavily muscled arm wrapped around her waist.

"So kind of you to join me, Emma Linley-Kirov," he muttered in Russian.

Emma's heart froze in fear. The man had to be one of the slave traders. What other Russian would be staying in Cairo and dare to attack a guest of Caliph Rajih?

But how had he found her? And more terrifying, what did he intend to do with her?

As if reading her mind, the brute tightened his arm around her waist, hoisting Emma a few inches off the ground to haul her toward the nearby carriage. Emma struggled, her legs flailing and her arms reaching over her head to yank at her captor's hair.

He ignored her pitiful efforts, easily bundling her into the carriage and forcing her onto the worn leather seat. Then, with an efficiency that spoke of years of practice, he jerked her arms above her head and snapped the steel manacles that were attached to the roof around her wrists.

Once he was certain she was securely imprisoned he took the seat opposite her and gestured to a servant hovering outside the carriage. The door was slammed shut and Emma realized there was no handle on the inside of the door just as the vehicle jerked into motion.

Her heart painfully began palpitating, slamming against her ribs as she accepted she was completely at the mercy of her kidnapper.

Forcing her horrified gaze from the manacles that bit painfully into her flesh, she regarded the man seated across from her.

The sight of him did little to ease her terror.

Not only was he large and thickly muscled, but there was a lack of emotion on his broad face. He was a man obviously accustomed to holding women as his hostages. And no amount of tears or pleading would sway him.

All she could do was pretend a confidence she was far from feeling.

"You will regret this," she warned.

He appeared remarkably unconcerned. "This is what you have wanted, is it not?"

"It most certainly is not."

"Then why have you been chasing after me for weeks?"

His mocking words stole any hope that this was nothing more than a terrible misunderstanding.

"You are Valik?"

His small eyes glittered in the faint torchlight that slipped through the barred windows of the carriage as they turned onto a crowded street and slowed to a mere crawl. Emma could hear the chatter from busy cafés and the call of the vendors, but she knew that she might as well have been alone in the world with the man seated across from her.

For now there was no escape.

"Obviously we have no need for introductions."

"Where is my sister?"

"Have no fear." A cruel smile touched his lips. "The two of you will soon be reunited."

Emma ignored the threat, more concerned with Anya's welfare than her own.

"Has she been hurt?"

"She is alive." He shrugged. "Which is all that concerns me."

"You—"

"Careful," he growled, revealing his first hint of emotion. "You don't want to say something you might regret."

Emma deliberately tilted her chin, sensing the hideous man took pleasure in intimidating women. She would be damned before she gave him the satisfaction.

"You are a fool, you know," she said tartly. "Lord Sanderson has already made his confession to King George and even now is traveling to Russia to appear before Czar Alexander."

He regarded her with an unnerving intensity. "Which is why I decided to have you join your precious sister."

"I do not understand."

"It is fairly simple, kitten." He leaned forward, wrapping Emma in the stench of stale vodka and unwashed body. "I might have been born in the gutters, but I've always had a preference for a more luxurious life."

She wrinkled her nose, wishing his preference included a bath and change of clothing.

"By kidnapping and selling children?"

He settled back in his seat, his leer sliding over her with a repulsive thoroughness.

"It happens to be a career that pays quite well," he boasted. "Far better than begging for a handful of coins on the frozen streets of Moscow."

"There are honest professions," she rasped.

"Not for a bastard serf." His short laugh echoed through the carriage. "So far as the empire is concerned we have no use but to be conscripted to the army or buried in the mines of Siberia. Neither fate appealed to me."

Unfortunately, Emma could not argue. Those in Russia who were born into poverty were rarely given the opportunity to better their lives. In truth their existences were often grim, brutal struggles for survival.

"You implied you had a reason for kidnapping me." She diverted the conversation back to more important matters.

"Beyond the charm of your companionship?" he mocked.

"Yes."

"You, kitten, are to be my revenge."

"Revenge?"

The beady eyes flared with shocking hatred. "Dimitri Tipova has ruined my very lucrative arrangement and that's not a thing a man forgets. I had to give thought to a proper punishment."

Emma's breath caught in her throat. Absurdly, she had never considered the possibility that the demented brute would seek to hurt Dimitri. After all, it didn't take a great deal of intelligence to realize that a man did not rise to be the czar of the criminal world without the ruthless skill to defeat any opponent.

Now she struggled not to allow a wrenching surge of fear to overwhelm her.

"You have no idea what he is capable of," she warned. "He will destroy you if you do not flee before he discovers you are in Cairo."

"Oh, I intend to flee," he drawled. "Once I am certain that Tipova knows that I have stolen his lover and intend to share her with the most depraved men to be found in Egypt."

She shifted on the seat, her arms aching from being held above her head. Her mind, however, was racing. This horrid man would not be allowed to hurt Dimitri.

The mere thought of him being injured, or worse, was unbearable.

"You are mistaken."

"Am I?"

"Yes." She cleared her throat, forcing herself to meet his malevolent gaze. "I hired Dimitri Tipova to help in my search for Anya, but he is no more than my employee."

"The Beggar Czar a mere employee?" He snorted in disbelief. "Don't treat me as if I'm an idiot."

She managed a disdainful sniff. "Obviously he had his own motives for assisting me, but they had nothing to do with being my lover. I am a proper lady."

"Even a proper lady becomes a tart when given the opportunity."

Heat stained her cheeks. "You are offensive."

"And you are a liar." He reached to grab her chin, his fingers bruising. "I saw the two of you together in that warehouse in London. The man is so besotted with you that he will go stark raving mad at the thought of you being used as a common whore. I might even let my guards have a turn or two. They so rarely get the chance to taste the wares."

Despite her best intentions, her brittle courage faltered beneath his vile threat.

"Do you have no conscience whatsoever?" she husked.

"None. You would do well to remember that." The carriage came to a halt and reaching beneath his jacket, Valik pulled out a pistol. With a grim expression he pointed it directly in her face. "We have arrived. I would suggest that you not fight my servant. I prefer to savor my revenge, but I will shoot you if I must."

"I hope you rot in hell, you monster."

"Bitch."

THE HOUSE WAS BUILT IN a narrow street and nearly hidden behind the large palm trees. On the front a balcony hung over the street with grilled windows, no doubt used for the girls to lure potential customers. In the back a wooden pavilion was swiftly falling to ruin and a narrow alley was filled with rubbish.

It appeared to be like any other brothel in Cairo if not for the guards posted at every entrance. And, of course, the pack of mangy dogs that had nearly mauled him when he first approached the building. Dimitri had taken refuge on the side terrace, leaving Josef to deal with the savage curs.

Nearly twenty minutes later the wiry servant shimmied up the trellis to join him, his bare feet barely making a sound as he crossed the wooden terrace.

"You disposed of the dogs?" he demanded, his voice a low whisper.

Josef nodded. "The kitchen of the local café was stocked with a nice supply of meat. They were easy enough to lure away." He gestured toward the narrow window that Dimitri had already used to enter the house and search for the girls. "What did you discover?"

"The bottom floor has four rooms. A front parlor, an office, the kitchens and a pantry. The second floor has six small bedchambers." He grimaced. "The upper floor contains the attics, but the doors and windows are barred. I assume that if the females are here that is where they are being held."

"Interesting." Josef glanced over the edge of the terrace to the shadows below. "Guards?"

"Far too many for a mere brothel. I have counted five so far."

Josef rubbed the tip of his nose, considering their few options.

"A dangerous situation. Perhaps we should wait until later in the evening. The guards will eventually seek a place to hide from the employers and enjoy a bottle of raki together."

Dimitri chaffed at yet another delay. He wanted to expose the slavers and rescue the females so he could concentrate on Emma. Surely once he had her sister she would agree to leave the damnable harem and return to St. Petersburg where she belonged?

But he was not a fool.

If he acted too hastily he risked sending the bastards fleeing before they could be captured. Or worse. He could stumble into a trap.

Still undecided, Dimitri shifted toward the edge of the terrace as he heard a noise in the alley.

"What is that?"

Josef peered into the shadows. "A carriage."

They both tensed, knowing that a vehicle would never willingly choose to travel through the filth of the alley unless there was a need for secrecy.

Was it possible the auction was already beginning?

He scowled, debating how long it would take to convince the authorities to send soldiers. It would be far more efficient to gather his own servants and attack the brothel. Unfortunately, he was not certain that the pasha would approve of a foreigner shedding blood on the streets of Cairo.

Not when the gentlemen attending the auction were quite likely wealthy citizens who could create any number of political difficulties.

Dimitri bent down as a servant hurried toward the carriage, opening the door and reaching inside. His eyes narrowed as he heard the low sound of male voices, then the unmistakable shriek of a furious female.

Had they been keeping the women at another location and were only now bringing them to the brothel?

That complicated matters since he couldn't know if Anya had yet arrived.

Leaning forward, he watched as the servant stepped back from the carriage, his arms wrapped around a furiously struggling woman. For a moment he was distracted by the sight of the large Russian who stepped from the carriage, instantly recognizing him as the man from the London warehouse. Then, as he heard Josef suck in a shocked breath, he returned his attention to the female who continued her futile fight for freedom, the moonlight shimmering over her honey curls and delicate features.

"Emma."

All logical thought ceased as he vaulted off the terrace, overwhelmed by his savage need to gut the man who dared to put his hands on her.

God, he had to reach her. He had to…

Without warning, he was tackled from behind, landing awkwardly on the hard ground. He cursed as Josef grasped his arm and wrenched it to a painful angle behind his back, effectively holding him captive.

"Damn you, Tipova, do not force me to hurt you," the servant hissed.

Dimitri struggled, but the smaller man had the leverage to keep him trapped, not to mention enough force on his arm to threaten to snap it in two. Something Dimitri was quite certain his friend was prepared to do if necessary.

Turning his head, he spit out the dirt and watched in the distance as Emma was hauled into a side door of the brothel, followed by the hulking form of Valik.

Any hope of a hasty rescue was slipping away.

"Let me up," he commanded.

"You promise you will not do anything stupid?"

He trembled with fury. "Josef."

"You may release him," a soft voice ordered. "I promise to shoot him if he takes a step toward the brothel."

Josef leaped off his back, his gun pointed at Caliph Rajih as he appeared from the shadows of the pavilion. With less grace, Dimitri surged upright, his hands clenched at his side as he glared at the slender man in a dark uniform, a curved sword in his hand.

"I should have suspected you were involved in this vile business," he rasped, his body rigid with a combination of anger and anguish. Emma was in the hands of slave traders, and while his blind thirst to reach her was being tempered by the realization he might very well endanger her by barging into the situation without considering the consequences, he was still tormented by his frantic urgency. "Your presence in London, not to mention your interest in Emma, was far too convenient."

Ignoring Josef's pistol pointed directly at his heart, Rajih stepped forward, his expression hard.

"You ever again accuse me of being involved with the slave trade and I will have your head on a pike," he warned, the sharp edge of his sword glinting in the moonlight. "Believe me, that is not an empty threat."

Dimitri stepped forward, his hands clenched with the fierce need to strike out.

"You think we are stupid enough to believe your presence here is a mere accident?"

"I could ask the same of your presence, Tipova. What are you doing at this brothel?"

The two men glared at each other, both seeking to prove their dominance. Like dogs snarling and snapping at one another. At last it was the realization he was wasting precious time that Dimitri swallowed his pride.

He would sacrifice whatever necessary to save Emma.

"My servant heard rumors that a large Russian man was seen in the neighborhood," he confessed, his tone pitched so it would not carry on the night air. "He investigated and found that this particular brothel had supposedly suffered a fire."

Rajih glanced toward the building that was shabby, but unmarred by flames.

"A fire?"

Josef shrugged. "So I was told."

"Not a particularly convincing lie," Rajih said.

Josef rolled his eyes. "The servants did not impress me with their swift wits."

"I have explained my presence, Caliph." Dimitri folded his arms over his chest. "Now I will hear your story."

"There is no...story." The dark eyes narrowed. "I returned to my home after enduring a tedious dinner party, which I believe I have you to thank for my invitation."

Dimitri could not halt the cold smile from curling his lips. He had considered himself quite clever in arranging Rajih to be absent from the palace so he could spend the evening in Emma's arms.

"I sent no invitation," he protested.

"We will settle that debt at a more convenient moment."

He waved aside the threat. "You said you returned home."

"Yes, and when I discovered Emma was missing I gathered my servants so I could question them."

"What did you learn?"

"I learned that I had more than one uninvited guest during my absence," Rajih said, his tone promising retribution. "Yet another grievance I intend to settle with you later. For now it only matters that one of my female servants confessed to accepting a bribe to lead Emma to a carriage waiting near the stables."

"Perhaps you should take greater care in hiring your staff."

Something like remorse flared over the dark face. "Samira was jealous of my obvious affection for Emma. She now deeply regrets her behavior."

"Not so deeply as she will regret her behavior if Emma is harmed."

The caliph moved the sword just enough to remind Dimitri it was in his hand. A subtle warning.

"I am capable of punishing my own servants."

"Tell me precisely what she said."

"She knew very little." Rajih shook his head. "A Russian man approached her in the bazaar earlier in the day and urged her to join him at a local café. Samira knew it was wrong, but she was angry and agreed to his request."

"Valik," Josef muttered.

"Whoever he was, he offered Samira several drachmas if she would lead Emma to the carriage at precisely ten o'clock," Rajih continued. "He told her that Emma was his sister who had fled from home and he was anxious to return her to Russia and her family."

Dimitri glanced toward the house, every passing moment grating against his nerves.

"That still does not explain your presence here," he snapped.

"The carriage left only moments before my arrival. Once I had a description of the vehicle, it took little effort to catch up with it in such heavy traffic."

"This makes no sense." Josef interrupted the conversation without warning.

Dimitri glanced at his servant in surprise. "What do you mean?"

"Why would Valik kidnap her?"

"Obviously, he discovered Emma had followed him to

Cairo and was afraid she would reveal his sordid business to the pasha."

"If he had managed to find out that Emma was in Cairo, then he most certainly knew you were here," Josef reasoned. "After all, you have made no effort to hide your presence while the woman has been hidden in a harem. Considering you pose the far greater danger to him, Valik would be a fool to hazard stealing Emma from the caliph's palace when he could quite easily shoot you in the back."

"Not to mention the pure satisfaction," Rajih murmured.

Dimitri shot him a dark scowl before returning his attention to Josef.

"Just say what is on your mind, Josef."

"The only reason a man is willing to risk his neck is for love or—"

"Hate," Dimitri finished for his companion, his thoughts racing.

Josef's words made sense. He better than anyone understood the effectiveness of manipulating others with threats to their families. A man might refuse to pay a gambling bill even after a savage beating, but he would beg, borrow or steal the necessary funds to protect his wife.

And if you wanted to sincerely hurt a man…

Well, you threatened his lover, not him.

"He no doubt holds you to blame for interfering in his profitable affairs," Rajih pointed out the obvious.

"Yes." His gut twisted in icy fear. If something happened to Emma he would be destroyed. "What better revenge?"

Josef stepped forward to grab his arm, his face tight with concern.

"Or trap."

"Yes," Dimitri slowly agreed, his gaze shifting toward the brothel as a plan began to form. As much as he might long to charge into the house and shoot anyone who might stand in his path, he had enough sense to know that Emma would be killed before he could ever reach her. No, he had to convince the damnable Valik to release her unharmed. And there was only one means of persuading such a man.

"Of course, it ceases to be a trap once you recognize it for what it is," he husked.

"Damn," Josef muttered. "You're going to do something stupid, aren't you?"

Dimitri turned back to meet his companion's accusing glare.

"Yes, and you are going to assist me."

CHAPTER TWENTY-TWO

"Ow." EMMA GLARED AT the large servant who carried her through the filthy brothel, his expression stoic despite the fact he had just smacked Emma's head into the door frame of the parlor. "If I must be carried then could you at least not ram me into the walls?"

Leading them past the low divans and stacks of pillows tossed about the bare floor, Valik glanced over his shoulder with a mocking smile.

"You are wasting your time if you hope for a response from my servant. I cut out his tongue when I hired him."

Emma fought to control her panic. "My God, you are demented."

"Cautious." The large man shrugged, angling toward the narrow staircase. "No matter how much I might be willing to pay a man to keep my secrets I can never be certain of his loyalty. It is far more effective to make certain he can't speak at all."

The man carrying her through the dark room with a low ceiling and heavy scent of incense appeared indifferent to being discussed as if he were no more than an animal. Perhaps his spirit was too broken to care.

"The world will be a far better place when Dimitri hunts you down and kills you," she hissed.

Valik chuckled, pausing at the base of the stairs to turn and regard her with a smile of evil anticipation.

"If he is reckless enough to seek me out, then he will quickly discover that he is the prey, not the hunter."

"You are…" Realization hit with shocking force and

Emma felt her stomach clench with an icy dread. "Oh, my God. You are hoping he will come after me."

The man's smile widened, his hand waving about the seemingly empty room. No doubt he had a dozen guards hidden about the place.

"Let us just say that I am prepared should he choose to rescue his woman. And if he doesn't...well, I at least have the satisfaction of knowing that for the remainder of his life he will blame himself for your painful and degrading destiny."

She struggled to hide her fear, knowing that was precisely what he desired.

"You know nothing of Dimitri. He will kill you and there is nothing you can do to stop him."

"Such faith in your lover," he taunted. "It's heart-warming."

"I have faith in the knowledge you are not half the man that he is."

Fury flashed through the beady eyes, and turning on his heel, Valik stomped heavily up the stairs.

"It's no wonder your sister was so eager to flee your sour nature," he growled. "I would have smothered you in your sleep."

"Anya? Is she here?"

"You wish to join her? It is my pleasure," he muttered, continuing up a second flight of stairs to the attics. He paused to unlock a heavy door, pushing it open to climb yet another short flight of stairs. At the top there were two doors on either side of the narrow hallway. He unlocked the one on the right-hand side, thrusting it open with a grim smile. "Enjoy your reunion. It is to be of a short duration. You are both to be sold tonight."

Emma cursed as the servant dumped her over the threshold, slamming the door shut and locking it before she could react. Rising to her feet, she rubbed her bruised hip and glanced around the cramped room.

There was not much to see.

The ceiling was low and flat with a small ladder that led to a narrow opening in the roof. There were a few pillows scattered over plank wooden floor and an oil lantern billowing smoke and a grudging light on an upturned barrel in one corner, but no furniture and nothing to ease the bleak emptiness. Across the narrow room a piece of fabric was hung in a doorway, concealing the room beyond.

Where were Anya and the girls that Valik was holding hostage? If they were near she should surely hear something from them?

Were they bound and gagged? Were they being forced into silence by guards?

Were they…

She squashed her increasingly panicked thoughts, stepping toward the center of the room.

"Anya?" she called softly. "Anya?"

There was a rustle of fabric and Emma watched as the curtain across the door was thrust aside and her sister stepped into the room.

She sucked in a sharp breath, her anxious gaze running over her sister's loose curls that were several shades lighter than her own and the pale face with a pair of large blue eyes that Emma had always envied.

Despite being clad in odd baggy trousers and a small embroidered vest that left her stomach exposed, she looked precisely as she did the morning she had disappeared and Emma felt a pang of surprise tug at her heart.

Perhaps she had expected Anya to look…different.

As if her terrifying adventure should have altered her in some visible manner.

Instead, she regarded Emma with a familiar petulant expression, her chin jutted to a stubborn angle.

"Emma?" Her voice was sharp. "What are you doing here?"

Emma blinked back her tears of joy, telling herself that Anya's less than welcoming reaction was merely shock at her unexpected arrival.

"It was my intention to rescue you," she said, her voice choked with emotion. "Unfortunately, it would appear that I am to be hoisted on my own petard."

"Hoisted on a what?"

"It does not matter. Where are the other girls?"

Anya shrugged. "They are being prepared for the auction in the rooms across the hall."

Unable to reign in her need to touch her sister and assure herself that she truly was unharmed, Emma rushed across the room, wrapping her arms around the startled Anya. "Oh, dear Lord, it is so wonderful to see you."

"Emma, release me," Anya commanded. "I cannot breathe."

"Forgive me. I am just so relieved to know you are alive. You cannot imagine how terrified I have been." Emma pulled back, her hands running over her younger sister as she had done when she was little and had taken a tumble from a tree. "Come, let me look at you. Are you hurt? Have they..."

"For God's sake, Emma, would you just stop your tugging on me?" Anya snapped, shoving away from Emma's lingering touch with obvious impatience.

Emma bit her lower lip, wondering if Anya was fearful that she was about to be scolded on being so foolish as to have run off with virtual strangers. Her sister resented being in the wrong and tended to strike out in defense.

"Of course," Emma said, gently tucking one of her sister's curls behind her ear. "At least assure me that you are well."

"I am perfectly well." Anya pushed Emma aside. "Or I would be if you would stop fussing over me."

Emma wrapped her arms around her waist, attempting to hide her pain at Anya's dismissive manner. She did not expect her sister to gush in delight that she had risked her life to come in search of her. Or even to offer a simple gesture of gratitude.

But should Anya not be at least a tad relieved she was no longer alone with the bastards who had kidnapped her?

"I cannot help myself," Emma said slowly. "I have been frantic to find you since you left Yabinsk."

"Well, as you can see, I am fine."

"Yes, I suppose so." Emma shook her head, accepting her sister's words. Which allowed her to turn her thoughts to the question that had plagued her since she had discovered her sister missing. "Anya, why did you…"

"You know why I left, Emma," Anya interrupted the hesitant question, pacing the small space with jerky steps. "You might have been content being an eccentric spinster who everyone mocks behind your back, but I would rather die than be cursed with your fate."

Emma winced at the brutal description. "I never expected you to share my fate. There is no reason you cannot wed a decent man and have a home and family of your own."

"A decent man?" Anya tossed her head, her golden curls shimmering in the lamplight. "You mean Boris Glavori who buried his first wife after forcing a dozen children on her? Or perhaps the butcher who came to call on me with blood beneath his nails?"

"Surely anything would be preferable to being taken captive by slave traders?"

"You know nothing."

Emma shook her head in growing confusion. "Then explain it to me."

Anya hunched her shoulders, refusing to meet Emma's gaze. "It is true that Count Tarvek and his brother proved to be hideous creatures who should be beheaded without delay. I do not comprehend how they could ever claim to be gentlemen."

"I assure you they will soon reap their just rewards," Emma promised.

"But not all the men in their employ are evil."

Emma froze, a sense of dread lodging in her heart. "What are you saying?"

With a sudden movement Anya turned away, heading back toward the curtained doorway.

"You should never have come after me."

"But you must have known I would." Emma followed in her sister's wake, baffled. This was not going at all as she had imagined it would. Where were the other girls? And why was Anya behaving as if Emma were an unwelcome intruder rather than a savior? "You are my sister. I love you, Anya. I would protect you with my life."

They entered a room barely as large as a closet with a narrow cot and a chipped washstand. Bending down, Anya yanked a leather satchel from beneath the bed and clutched it to her chest.

"Well, it is because of you that Mikhail and I have not yet managed to escape," she said. "I can only hope that you have not yet again ruined our plans."

"Who is Mikhail?"

"One of the guards." Anya's chin tilted at Emma's horrified expression. "He happens to be desperately in love with me."

"He is a trafficker?" Emma rasped.

Anya sniffed. "I should have known you would find fault without even knowing him."

Emma itched to grab her sister and give her a violent shake. As relieved as she might be to have at last found her, there was no doubt Anya had not changed a wit. She was still stubborn, impulsive and utterly selfish.

"Have you taken leave of your senses?" she gritted. "My God, he is responsible for kidnapping children and selling them to monsters."

"He has kept me safe when others would have harmed me and he intends to take me to his home in Austria."

Emma swallowed her angry words. Why bother? Anya had never listened to anything she had to say before. And perhaps she should try and consider what her sister had endured.

After all, she must have felt scared and alone when she realized she had fallen into the hands of slave traders. If this guard had shown her a bit of kindness and had sheltered her from the others, then it was perhaps not surprising that she would have attached herself to him.

"My dear, you are not thinking clearly," she said gently. "Only to be expected after all you have endured. Once we have returned home—"

"Never." Anya stepped backward, a sulky pout tugging at her lips. "I will never return to Yabinsk and you cannot force me."

"Perhaps we can visit England before returning to Russia," Emma coaxed, refusing to acknowledge the possibility they might not find a means to escape from Valik's clutches. "We do have family there, after all."

Anya stomped her foot. "You have not listened to a word I have said."

"Certainly I have listened, but you cannot expect me to allow you to remain at the power of a slave trader. It is insanity."

"He is a good man."

"Even if I could be persuaded to believe he is a saint I would not let you be with him." Emma grasped Anya's shoulders, willing the foolish girl to recognize common sense. "You are a child, Anya, and you belong at home with me."

The moment the words tumbled from her lips she wanted to call them back. Over the past months Anya had become increasingly sensitive to being seen as a girl rather than a woman.

Whirling on her heel, she stormed back into the larger room, her cheeks stained with color.

"You always ruin everything."

"Anya, this is ridiculous." Emma clenched her hands, following behind her sister. "I have traveled from St. Petersburg to London to Cairo to find you. Once we find a means to escape then we will discuss your future."

Anya never slowed as she headed to the back of the attic. "I no longer have to obey you, Emma Linley-Kirov."

"Did you ever?"

"I am a grown woman and I will make my own decisions." Reaching the small ladder, Anya turned back to glare at Emma. "I will never return to that horrid cottage."

Emma faltered, her heart twisting with distress. Had she not sacrificed everything to ensure her sister could have a stable home?

"Was it truly so bad?" she rasped.

"It was horrible. Like being caught in a poacher's trap." Anya shuddered, her pretty features hard with disgust. "God, there was nothing but snow and mud and ignorant villagers who had nothing better to do with their days than to make life a misery for others."

"But we had each other."

"Each other?" Anya's shrill laugh grated against Emma's tender nerves. "No, I was just another cross that St. Emma had to bear."

"Anya," Emma breathed, studying her sister as if she had never seen her before. And perhaps she hadn't. Before their father's death he had warned Emma that she was spoiling

little Anya and that it would be better for the young girl
to take on a few of the responsibilities around the cottage.
Emma, however, had wanted to protect her sister from the
tedious chores. Now it seemed that her effort to help Anya
had only created resentment in the younger woman. "That
is not true."

"Of course it is." The blue eyes darkened with a simmering antipathy. "You have reveled in your role as martyr
since mother died. Do you know how often I was scolded
to be properly grateful that you had sacrificed yourself for
me?"

"Would you have preferred that I had abandoned you?"
Emma wrapped her arms around her waist, as if she could
protect herself from Anya's cutting condemnation. "Or
taken you to an orphanage?"

Anya sniffed. "You could have sought help from our re-
lations. There had to have been at least one family member
who would have offered to provide us with a decent allow-
ance so we did not have live as though we were no better
than serfs."

Emma grimaced. "I could not beg for charity from complete strangers."

"Only because your pride was more important than my
happiness. If you had considered my feelings at all then I
would never have allowed the count to lure me away from
home."

Emma shifted uneasily. How could she deny the charge?
She had allowed her pride to prevent her from seeking assistance from the family she had never known. Of course,
she could hardly have suspected that Gerhardt Herrick
would be so kind. Or that he would have been so willing
to acknowledge a distant relative.

At the time she had only known that it was her responsibility to find the means to support her sister and she had
done the best she could.

"Anya..." Her soft plea was interrupted by the sound of a slamming door from below and the rumble of male voices. Emma stiffened, an icy fear flowing through her veins. Valik had warned that the auction would be held tonight. Was it beginning? "What is that?"

"Yet more trouble. No doubt because of you."

With a last glare, Anya turned to climb the stairs.

"Where are you going?" Emma demanded.

"I told you that Mikhail intends to take me to his home."

"How do you intend to escape?"

"He promised he would tend to the details." Reaching the top of the ladder, Anya reached up to push open a trap door. "I am to meet him on the roof."

Emma tilted back her head, unable to believe after all that had occurred that her sister could still behave in such a reckless fashion.

"You are placing your trust in a slave trader who has not even shared his plan of escape?" she rasped, reaching to grab the skirt of Anya's gown. "For God's sake, he will have you completely at his mercy."

Anya kicked out, dislodging Emma's hand. "Let go of me."

"Please, Anya, listen to me."

"No."

Anya shoved her satchel through the small opening before scrambling behind it, pulling herself out of the attic and onto the roof.

Emma grabbed the ladder and prepared to climb after her sister. "Wait."

Anya peered through the opening, her curls tumbled about her pale face.

"I am sorry, Emma, but you cannot come with us."

Emma's eyes widened in stunned disbelief. "You intend to leave me here to be sold in a slave auction?"

"You should never have followed me."

"Anya."

The trap door was slammed shut and Emma listened in amazement as there was the sound of scraping, as if something were being shoved over the door to keep it from opening. Still, Emma remained poised on the ladder, refusing to believe her sister would actually abandon her in the attics while she made her own escape.

No matter what happened in the past, Anya could surely not be so heartless?

It took nearly a quarter of an hour for Emma to accept that her sister could indeed be that heartless. She had climbed the ladder, pounding on the trap door that would not budge and futilely calling for her sister who refused to answer.

At last she had been forced to accept defeat.

"Dear God," she muttered, laying her head against the wooden rung of the ladder and closing her eyes in weariness. "I have been so stupid."

WITH AN ANNOYED impatience, Dimitri allowed the two guards to roughly drag him through the brothel, at last shoving him onto a low divan in the parlor.

It had taken three attempts to at last be caught by the ridiculous fools. He had all but approached them and requested a waltz before they had noticed him pretending to pick the lock of a side door. He could only assume that the men had grown weary of guarding females who had yet to earn a single ruble for them.

Now, he turned his head to watch as Valik entered the room, his hair tousled, as if he had run his fingers through it more than once. The expression on his beefy face, however, was smug. No doubt he was preening at the mistaken belief he had accomplished something no other man had managed.

"Ah, Dimitri Tipova," the Russian drawled, halting directly before the divan. "You cannot know how I have longed for you to pay a visit."

Dimitri settled more comfortably on the cushions, stretching out his legs and crossing them at the ankle.

"I should have visited you much sooner if you had not been fleeing from me in terror." He flicked a glance toward the two guards who both stood like mindless statues. "Not that I am surprised. Those men who peddle in the flesh trade are by nature spineless cowards who skulk in the dark and prey on the weak."

"You dare to lecture me?" Valik gave a sharp laugh. "You command every criminal in St. Petersburg, including a dozen whores. Christ, you chop off the hands of anyone who irritates you. And you look down your nose at me?"

Dimitri shrugged. "I do not force anyone into a life of sin, I only demand that they obey my particular laws, and in return I offer them my protection from those predators who are without honor."

"Arrogant bastard."

"So I have been told."

"You may think you are better than me, but I am the one who came out the victor. I captured the notorious Dimitri Tipova."

Dimitri lifted a mocking brow. "Surely you cannot believe that I stumbled into such an obvious trap? I did not rise to my current position by being stupid...." His gaze returned to the hulking guards. "Or careless."

The sneering smile faltered and Valik waved a dismissive hand toward his companions.

"Leave us," he commanded, waiting until the men had lumbered from the parlor before returning his attention to Dimitri. "You cannot fool me. You are desperate to rescue your lover."

Stark, brutal fury speared through Dimitri at the

realization that Emma was even now in the filthy brothel, being held against her will and no doubt terrified.

"Oh, I fully intend to rescue Emma," he said, his soft voice only emphasizing his lethal intent. "It is in your hands whether you end this encounter with enough wealth to begin a new life. Or as a corpse."

Dimitri hid a smile as the man took an instinctive step backward.

"You are in no position to threaten me," he snarled, obviously angered by his display of cowardice.

"You think not?" Dimitri smiled. "I assure you that you have only moments to decide whether you wish to conduct a profitable business arrangement with me or be escorted to the pasha's citadel by Caliph Rajih's guards."

Dimitri watched in satisfaction as Valik paled at the threat.

Rajih had not been pleased when Dimitri had insisted that he enter the brothel alone, insisting that they wait until he could call for his servants and they could surround and attack the brothel in a coordinated effort. And Josef had treacherously agreed with the bastard. But Dimitri had refused to yield.

There would be no guards, no attacks and no shots fired until Emma was safely in his hands.

"You are bluffing," the large man rasped.

"If you have heard anything of my reputation then you should know that I never bluff."

Valik clenched his hands, suspicion tightening his features as he paced the floor.

"The caliph knows nothing of me or this brothel."

"How do you think I found you?"

He shot Dimitri a skeptical frown. "You want me to believe he sent you here?"

"Do not be an idiot," Dimitri retorted. "The caliph dared to steal Emma away from me while I was occupied in

London and brought her to this godforsaken country." He did not have to pretend his surge of annoyance. "I intend to punish him, not become his lackey."

The beady eyes narrowed. "I did wonder why the woman was in the caliph's harem."

"A mistake I had every intention of correcting."

"So if you are not friendly with the caliph, then how would you know he is planning to send his guards to this brothel as you claim?"

"I called upon the palace earlier in the evening." Dimitri allowed a faint smile to touch his lips. "Of course, I took the precaution of slipping in unnoticed."

Valik snorted. "Of course."

"Why trouble the servants?" Dimitri lifted his shoulder in a nonchalant movement. "I am perfectly capable of opening a door. Or window, if necessary. It allows me to discover information that might otherwise have remained a secret."

Valik returned to his pacing, his expression hard as he sensed his opportunity for revenge slipping away.

"What information?" he growled.

Dimitri unconsciously tapped his fingers on the cushions of the divan. It was one thing to be cautious, but did the fool intend to spend the entire evening chatting?

Rajih's patience would not last for long, and as for Josef... well, if the fiercely loyal servant became convinced that Dimitri was in danger, he would do whatever necessary to rescue him.

Including putting Emma at risk.

"The most interesting was the tearful confessions of a female servant who spoke of a Russian man who bribed her to lure Emma into a waiting carriage behind the harem," Dimitri said, coming straight to the point.

"Bitch."

"It was then the caliph sent a servant to trail your

carriage through the heavy traffic while he gathered his guards and prepared an assault on those who had dared to kidnap his favorite concubine." Dimitri leaned forward, not bothering to hide his smoldering frustration. "I followed the servant so I could arrive before Rajih and slip Emma away."

Valik shoved his fingers through his hair, his expression harassed.

"Are the two of you demented?" he muttered. "The woman is a sharp-tongued vixen who any man with a thimble of sense should be delighted to be rid of."

Dimitri's hand instinctively slid up the sleeve of his robe where he had a dagger strapped to his forearm. He had another dagger tucked in his soft leather boots and a pistol in the holster beneath his left arm. The guards had been fools not to search him more carefully for weapons.

Unfortunately, he was not yet in a position to slice Valik open and leave him for the jackals. That particular pleasure would have to wait until he was certain Emma and the other girls were well away from the bastard.

"If that is true then you will be relieved to give her into my care."

"No." Coming to a halt, the Russian scowled in frustration. "You have destroyed my life, you smug bastard. Now you shall witness your woman used by every male who attends the auction this evening before I put you out of your misery." He paused, his expression gloating. "Perhaps I should warn you, some of the men can be excessively rough. I doubt Emma will survive the experience."

Dimitri slowly rose to his feet, refusing to react to the taunt despite the savage fury churning in his heart.

He had discovered as a youth on the streets of St. Petersburg that it was the man who refused to be goaded who survived.

Cold logic was always superior to mindless anger. Just as intelligence was always superior to brute strength.

He would eventually have the opportunity to make this man suffer. The sort of slow, agonizing suffering that could only end in death. But for now he had to convince the bastard that there was only one means for his survival.

"Are you deaf?" he taunted. "There will be no auction, Valik. Already the caliph is preparing to attack."

Sweat bloomed on the man's forehead, his breathing heavy. "Then I will kill you both and escape."

"Escape to where?" Dimitri pressed. "You are in a foreign country and I will bet my last drachma that you have little money. And worse, your wealthy associates are too consumed with their own survival to lend you assistance." He glanced toward a grilled window where the sound of braying donkeys and the distant howl of jackals were poignant reminders of how far from home they were. "A pity."

"I will sell the females," he stubbornly insisted.

Dimitri gave a bark of laughter. "You can sell a pack of terrified young women while fleeing from the caliph's guards? I doubt that even you are that talented."

Valik's bravado faltered beneath Dimitri's ruthless prodding, his hand swiping at the sweat that dripped down his brow.

"What do you offer?" he demanded at last.

Dimitri folded his hands over his chest. "You will allow me to leave the brothel with Emma and the other females. In return I will give you five hundred rubles."

"Five hundred?" The man licked his lips. "A paltry sum for a man in your position."

Dimitri had deliberately chosen a sum that would be large enough to tempt the man without being overly excessive. Valik was too cunning not to suspect a trap if Dimitri were willing to offer a fortune.

"It is what I have at hand and certainly it is enough to purchase a ticket upon a ship leaving Egypt," he said. "It offers you hope."

"You have the money with you?"

Dimitri narrowed his gaze. "I did just tell you that I was neither stupid nor careless. My servant is waiting at the Al-Hakim mosque. He will give you the money once he is certain I am safe."

Valik was shaking his head before Dimitri finished, his expression hard with suspicion.

"I am not a fool, either. What is to keep your servant from simply shooting me in the heart?"

Dimitri shrugged, already prepared for Valik's refusal. He preferred to issue commands and have them obeyed, but he could barter with the skill of a merchant when necessary.

"Then we will travel to the mosque together," he offered. "With me as your hostage my servant will not dare harm you until I am released."

Valik frowned, silently pacing and weighing the undoubted danger of accepting Dimitri's offer against the potential benefits.

Dimitri held his tongue, realizing if he pressed too hard the man might give in to his primitive desire to simply shoot him in the heart. He did, after all, hold Dimitri responsible for destroying his very profitable business.

Besides, Dimitri had little more to offer. His plan had been hastily conceived with none of his usual attention to details.

At last the man came to an abrupt halt, a fevered color staining his face.

"No."

An icy dread lodged in the center of Dimitri's gut. "No?"

"No." Valik moved to grab Dimitri's upper arm in a bruising grip. "I have a better idea."

CHAPTER TWENTY-THREE

WITH HER HARD-EARNED ability to put the latest disaster out of her mind and concentrate on the troubles at hand, Emma efficiently searched the attics for a means to escape, and then when it was obvious she was trapped, she searched again for a potential weapon.

What was the point in giving in to her disappointment at Anya's betrayal? Or to allow herself to be consumed by the fear of being brutally raped?

Neither would help change her situation.

Instead, she had to keep her thoughts centered on the best means of escaping.

Unable to find any sharp object, she settled for breaking off one leg of a stool she had discovered beneath Anya's cot and moved to hide behind the door. Eventually someone would come to get her, and she intended to be prepared.

She did not know how much time passed before she heard the heavy sound of approaching footsteps. Ignoring her cramped muscles, she gripped the wooden stool leg. She did not believe for a moment she could overpower a man twice her size and weight, but she hoped to catch the monster off guard. All she needed was enough of a distraction to dart through the door before the man could catch her.

And then...

Well, her plan didn't extend beyond the door, but for now that was enough.

Lifting the weapon above her head, she held her breath

as the door was pushed open. Then, as the large form of Valik entered the room, she launched herself at his back.

The stool leg shattered as it hit the man's broad shoulder, but it did not have the impact she hoped for. Instead of sprawling to the ground, the man whirled on his heel, his face an ugly shade of puce as he lifted a meaty hand to hit her.

"Damn you, bitch."

Braced for the impact, Emma was unaware of the second man who entered the attic. It was not until strong arms wrapped around her from behind and clamped her to a wide chest that she realized the danger.

"No," the man rasped, surprisingly turning to protect Emma from the blow.

Instantly recognizing the voice, Emma glanced over her shoulder in shock.

"Dimitri?" she breathed, wondering if he were a mirage. Rajih had warned her that the desert was a treacherous place, offering her heart's desire only to reveal it was all no more than an illusion. Still, he seemed real enough. If he were a figment of her imagination, surely he would not be scowling at her as if he were infuriated by her attack on Valik, or his arms would not be holding her so tightly she could barely breathe? "What are you doing here?"

The golden gaze shifted to Valik, who was angrily pacing through the attic.

"A discussion for later, *milaya,*" he muttered.

Valik ripped aside the curtain that separated the two rooms.

"Where is your sister?" he growled.

Emma licked her lips, hastily conjuring a lie to cover Anya's absence. Whatever Anya had done, she was still her sister. Her only family. And Emma would protect her with her dying breath.

"A guard came by a few minutes ago to take her from the room."

She ignored Dimitri's searching gaze as Valik stepped toward them.

"What guard?"

"How would I know? It is not as if we were in a position for introductions."

Perhaps sensing Emma was hiding the truth, Dimitri shifted until he was standing between her and the slave trader.

"You have no time to linger, Valik," he warned. "Not if you want to keep your head attached to your body."

"Fine." In one smooth motion, Valik reached into the pocket of his jacket to remove a pistol he promptly pointed at Emma. "Do not forget for a moment that your lover's life depends on you. You attempt something foolish and she dies."

Dimitri's expression hardened, but he said nothing as he tucked Emma close to his side and led her down the stairs. Too terrified to protest, Emma barely noticed as they moved through the silent brothel.

She had no notion if Dimitri had followed her to the brothel or if Valik had captured him. She didn't know where they were headed, or what was going to happen when they arrived. And for the moment, she did not care.

All that mattered was that Dimitri was in danger and it was entirely her fault.

Sick with dread, Emma stumbled through the narrow door that led to the back alley. A strange prickle made the hair on the nape of her neck rise, as if she were being watched from the shadows, but she dared not glance around with Valik pressing the pistol to the center of her back.

"The carriage," Valik growled, steering them past the pavilion to the waiting vehicle and yanking open the door. "Get in."

Already suspecting what was about to occur, Emma grudgingly climbed into the dark interior, her mouth dry as Dimitri settled on the seat opposite with a grim expression. She sensed that it would take very little to prod him into a foolish bout of heroism.

Her fear was confirmed when Valik reached inside the carriage, yanking her hands over her head to lock them in the dangling manacles.

"No," he snapped, surging forward.

A pistol pressed against her temple. "I warn you, Tipova, sit back."

Emma tensed, not out of concern for herself, but the horrifying fear that Dimitri would be injured.

"Dimitri...please," she whispered between lips that were stiff with foreboding.

His eyes flashed with golden fire, but with a grudging motion he settled back on the leather seat and turned his glare toward Valik.

"That is not necessary."

"We play this game by my rules, Tipova." Valik stepped back with a humorless smile and slammed the door.

Dimitri muttered a few of the more foul Russian curses as he noticed the lack of a handle, accepting that they were well and truly trapped. Then, he cursed again as they felt Valik climb onto the driver's seat and with a jerk, they were rattling down the narrow alley.

"How did you find me?" she demanded, as much to distract her dangerously infuriated companion as to ease her curiosity.

Dimitri's jaw knotted as he waged a battle to maintain his composure. He had ruthlessly devoted the past twenty years to carving a place for himself in the world where he was always in command of the situation.

To be at the mercy of another had to be worse than torture.

"I didn't," he said, his words clipped. "I was at the brothel before you arrived with Valik."

Emma narrowed her eyes, forgetting the painful steel biting into her wrists and the jarring sway of the carriage. Discovering that Dimitri had already been at the brothel was not at all what she had expected.

"Why would you be there?"

"It was not for the reason you are so clearly imagining," he retorted, shifting so he could peer out the narrow window. "Josef learned that a large Russian man had been seen in the neighborhood and he suspected he had some connection to the local brothel. He wished me to join him so we could investigate."

"Is that why...?"

His gaze flicked back to study her wary expression. "Why?" he prompted.

She blushed, wishing she could call back her impulsive words.

"Why you left the harem?"

The golden eyes warmed, as if he were savoring a particularly pleasant memory.

"I certainly did not leave willingly, but I could not ignore the potential to find Anya," he husked, his handsome features somber in the light that flickered from the torches that lined the streets. "I have learned my lesson."

Bittersweet misery settled in her heart at the unwelcome reminder of her sister. For all her relief that Anya seemed safe in the care of the guard, Mikhail, it would take time before she could think of her without the aching sense of loss.

"Anya," she breathed, lowering her lashes to hide the pain.

She heard the creak of leather as Dimitri shifted forward. "You managed to speak with her, did you not?"

"Yes."

"Has she been hurt?"

The manacles holding her captive rattled as she shrugged. "She claims she is unharmed."

"Do you fear she is trying to spare you the truth of her injuries?"

"Sparing me?" Emma's sharp laugh filled the carriage. "No, that certainly was not her intention."

There was a short pause, then Dimitri's hand cupped her chin and tilted her face to meet his piercing gaze.

"Emma?"

She tried to be angry with him. Her relationship with Anya was a private matter. What right did he have to press her?

But his gentle touch was sending comforting warmth through her that eased the pain of Anya's treachery, and she found the words tumbling from her lips before she could prevent them.

"I should have listened to your warnings."

"You begin to worry me, *milaya*." A faint smile curved his lips, but his expression was troubled. "Have you taken a blow to the head?"

"I simply realize that my efforts to care for Anya have done nothing but push her away." She blinked back the hot surge of tears. "As you said, I have no one to blame but myself for being abandoned by those I love."

His fingers tightened on her chin, his brows pulling together in a frown.

"Halt that."

"Why? I would think you would be pleased to know you were right."

He studied her for a long moment, his unnerving stare seeing far too much.

"Tell me what happened."

"Does it matter?"

"Please, Emma." His warm breath brushed her cheek. "Tell me."

She briefly closed her eyes, savoring the sensation of having him near. She was horrified he had put himself in danger, but a weak part of her wanted to wrap herself in his arms and be surrounded by his strength.

Where was her proud sense of independence now?

"Anya was in the attics when I was brought to the brothel," she confessed, grudgingly opening her eyes to meet his smoldering gaze. "Let us just say she was not pleased by my attempts to rescue her."

"Why not?"

"She already had planned to escape with one of the guards. I was an unwelcome interference to her elopement."

A dangerous tension filled the carriage, sending a shiver down her spine.

"A guard?"

Emma hesitated, still reluctant to reveal Anya's perfidy. Perhaps because she feared it would reflect on her failure to instill proper morals into her sister, she ruefully conceded. Then she winced as they turned a sharp corner, the manacles biting into her flesh as a reminder of their dire situation.

Dimitri had risked everything to rescue her. He deserved the truth.

"She swears that he is in love with her," she muttered. "He promised to take her to his home in Austria."

His fingers stroked over her cheek, his tone cautious, as if he were afraid of causing her more distress.

"I assume that you attempted to convince her of the stupidity in trusting such a man?"

Emma's lips twisted, remembering how she had pleaded with her stubborn sister.

"Of course, but she refused to listen to reason. She is

quite convinced that there is no worse fate than returning to Yabinsk with me."

Sympathy briefly softened his features. "She is very young, *milaya*. If you are patient, she will eventually come to appreciate all you have sacrificed."

Emma shook her head. It had taken Anya's agonizing rejection to force her to accept that she had been willfully blind over the year.

There was nothing she could do, nothing that she could offer, that would be enough for her sister.

Nothing.

"No, she is lost to me."

"Emma, listen to me," he urged, his voice lowering to ensure it did not carry past bars that blocked the windows. Not that it was likely Valik could overhear anything over the clatter of the crowds that filled the streets. How late was it, she inanely wondered? Midnight? Certainly Cairo was still bustling. "Caliph Rajih is waiting outside the brothel. As soon as he is certain you are safe he will rescue the girls and capture the remaining guards," Dimitri assured her. "As much as I might hate the bastard, you can trust Anya to his care."

Emma felt a surge of relief that girls being held captive would at last be safe, but shook her head at Dimitri's belief that Anya would be among the rescued women.

"You do not understand, Anya is already gone."

He stilled, his eyes narrowing at her words. "I remember you said that a guard had come to take Anya from the attics," he said slowly. "I sensed then you were lying."

"It was all I could think of to keep him from going in search of her."

His hand cupped her cheek. "Where is she?"

"I had only been in the attics for a few moments when she gathered a satchel and escaped through a trap door in the roof. She claimed that her beloved was awaiting her."

"And you remained behind?"

She turned her head, unable to watch the dawning comprehension in the golden eyes.

"Obviously."

"Why?"

"Surely we should be discussing how we are to escape?" she demanded, watching the light flickering beyond the carriage window. How much farther to the mosque? Surely they had to be close?

Dimitri firmly turned her face back to meet his ruthless scrutiny.

"Why did you remain in the attics, Emma?"

"Because Anya locked the door behind her," she snapped. "Are you satisfied?"

Emma was not surprised by the furious outrage that rippled over his beautiful face. Dimitri Tipova might be considered a criminal by most, but he possessed an unwavering sense of honor and a loyalty to those who depended on him. He would consider Anya's abandonment the worst sort of treachery.

"No, I am damned well not satisfied," he growled, a violent anger glittering in his eyes. "Do you mean to tell me that the ungrateful brat not only deserted you so that she could flee with her lover, but that she blocked a means for you to escape even knowing you were to be sold as a whore?"

Emma shrugged, weary of the bitter disappointment that spilled through her heart like acid.

"It no longer matters."

"When I manage to capture that bitch—"

"Please, Dimitri," she husked, unwilling to hear his opinion of Anya.

"I do not care if she is your sister or not, if she ever hurts you again, she will answer to me."

"She was my family," she reminded him, telling herself

that his fierce threat did not send a jolt of satisfaction through her. She could surely not be so petty. "Now I am alone."

The raven brows lifted at her husky words. "Is that a jest?"

"It is the truth."

His jaw tightened, revealing an unexpected annoyance. Why? With both her parents dead and Anya gone, there was no one left in her life.

"Then you must inform Herrick Gerhardt who has publicly claimed you as his cousin, as well as Vanya who considers you a beloved friend." His voice held a sardonic bite. "Ah, yes, and there is Leonida who threatened unmentionable harm on my manhood if I did not return you unharmed to the Huntley town house."

"It is not the same as—"

"I suppose I should also include Caliph Rajih, may his soul rot in hell, who is willing to risk the displeasure of this pasha to make you his wife," he relentlessly overrode her protest.

Her cheeks burned. A part of her accepted that Dimitri was not merely offering false comfort. Since leaving Yabinsk she had discovered that there were truly good people in the world willing to offer her assistance. Still, after so many years of having no one but herself to depend upon, it was difficult to put her trust in others.

"He is not thinking clearly," she said.

"No, he is not." The golden eyes flashed with an unnerving determination. "If he was, then he would know that you belong to me."

Her heart slammed against her ribs as she jerked away from his lingering touch.

"I do not belong to you, Dimitri Tipova."

"Of course you do." He settled back in his seat, his arms

folded across his chest. "You are not alone, Emma. Not ever again."

A perilous yearning tugged at her heart. He could so easily make her weak when she needed to be strong.

Stronger than she had ever been in her life.

"Do you have a plan for our escape or not?" she rasped.

His frustrated sigh filled the carriage. "It is more of a bargain than a plan. Josef is waiting for us at the mosque with money that I will offer to Valik for our freedom."

She frowned, wondering if he were disguising his true plan.

"You intend to bribe him?"

His lips twisted at the unmistakable disbelief in her voice. "It seemed the best means to ensure you were not harmed."

"And after you give him the money?"

He shrugged. "We shall hopefully never again be forced to endure his unpleasant company."

"You will allow him to flee?"

He caught and held her suspicious gaze. "If it means that you are safe."

She studied his somber expression, unable to stay her flicker of distrust.

"What of your revenge?"

"How often must I tell you that there is nothing more important than you?" He leaned forward, claiming her lips in a punishing kiss. "Nothing."

She forgot the discomfort of having her arms trapped above her head and the fact they were both at the mercy of a heartless slave trader. Instead, she sank into the persuasive demand of his kiss, needing the reassurance she was not to be betrayed and abandoned once again.

It was only when the sway of the carriage lessened that she pulled back, her heart squeezing with a surge of fear.

"We are slowing."

He swore, unable to hide his concern.

"Emma, I have no means to make certain that Valik will not attempt something desperate."

"What do you mean?"

The carriage halted and Emma heard the sound of Valik leaping to the ground and striding around the vehicle.

"As soon as Valik has released you I have told Josef to put you in the carriage and leave." He glanced toward the window before turning back to stab her with an urgent gaze. "No matter what might happen."

"You believe Valik intends to betray us?"

He paused, clearly caught between the desire to reassure her and the knowledge that she would prefer the truth.

"For the moment he is desperate to escape, but once he has the money in his hands, he will recall that I am to blame for all his troubles," he admitted. "At such moments men tend to toss aside good sense and allow their emotions to rule them."

Her eyes ran a lingering glance over his beautiful face, drinking in every line and curve that was indelibly engraved on her mind.

"Men such as you?" she asked softly.

"I never let my emotions rule me."

A sickening dread welled through her heart as she heard Valik's approaching footsteps.

"If that were true you would not have tried to rescue me. And you most certainly would not be in this carriage."

He shrugged. "It was a logical decision."

"It was insanity." Her voice was thick with emotion. "Dimitri, if something were to happen to you—"

"Emma, I command hundreds of cutthroats, thieves and pickpockets, all of whom are far more dangerous than Valik," he reassured her. "So long as I know that you are out of danger I am capable of besting a mere slave trader."

She bit her lower lip. "You are not so invincible as you believe."

"Of course I am. You will not be rid of me so easily."

They both stiffened as the door to the carriage was slowly pulled open.

"Dimitri," she breathed, her mouth dry with fear.

"Remember," he urged harshly. "You are to go directly to Josef and do not leave his side."

Valik stood beside the open doorway, his pistol pointed directly at Dimitri.

"Out, Tipova. Slowly." The large man watched Dimitri climb out of the carriage, his expression wary and his large face damp with sweat. Then, he lifted his hands to unlock the manacles holding Emma captive. "Now for you."

"Valik, if you leave a mark on her skin I will make certain your next profession is being a eunuch," Dimitri drawled, the lethal edge in his voice unmistakable.

The man made no response as he grabbed Emma's arm and roughly hauled her from the carriage. She could hear the rapid rasp of his breath and feel the tremble of his body. Valik was near a state of panic. Which could only mean disaster.

Feeling as if her heart were being crushed by a giant fist, Emma sent Dimitri a frantic glance, silently willing him not to do anything that might startle the growingly desperate fool. Dimitri, however, ignored her silent warning. Instead, he was watching Valik with the eyes of a predator preparing to strike.

Maintaining his bruising grip, Valik jerked Emma around the end of the carriage, allowing her a glimpse of the nearby mosque.

Constructed of bricks with a stone facade, the mosque had been built by Fatimid Caliph al-Aziz in 990 and, according to Rajih, it had recently been used by Napoleon as a fortress despite the insult to the faithful citizens of Cairo.

From her vantage she could see the central portal and the two corner minarets that marked the entrance to the courtyard framed by open arcades, but it was too dark to fully appreciate the beauty of the ancient structure.

And of course, it did not improve matters that she was currently being held captive by a dangerous lunatic.

"Where is your servant?" Valik demanded.

Dimitri paused, perhaps sensing Valik's growing apprehension, then, turning toward the mosque, he gave a low whistle.

There was a tense moment before a black carriage turned the corner and rolled to a halt on the opposite side of the street. A slender servant in a linen shirt and loose trousers leaped from the driver's seat and tied off the reins. He had reached the middle of the street when Valik lifted a warning hand, perhaps unnerved by the sight of the man's hard face marred by a scar running along his cheek, or the barely leashed violence that glittered in his eyes.

"Do not come any closer."

"Josef." Dimitri shifted to stand beside Valik. "You have the money?"

"I do." The servant held up a leather purse.

"Give it to me," Valik commanded.

"No," Dimitri snapped. "We will do this exchange by my rules."

Emma felt the slave trader stiffen in outrage, the rasp of his heavy breathing and the sour scent of his fear sending a prickle of warning over her skin.

"You may command the streets of St. Petersburg, Tipova, but I do not take orders from you," he said, his voice thick with hatred.

"You will if you want your money."

"What do you want?"

"Release Emma. Once she is in the carriage, Josef will toss you the purse."

"I don't trust you."

"Josef, open the purse," Dimitri ordered. On cue, Josef loosened the leather drawstrings and opened the purse so the torchlight could flicker over the silver rubles inside. "You see?" Dimitri said. "It is just as I promised."

"And as soon as you have the female you will have me shot," Valik muttered, jerking Emma against his foul body and wrapping a thick arm around her waist. "No. Give me the money and I will leave the woman near the citadel."

CHAPTER TWENTY-FOUR

DIMITRI SWALLOWED HIS curses and struggled against the pounding fury that beat through his body at the sight of Emma being manhandled by the filthy creature.

His instincts dictated a leap forward and wrench her away before gutting the bastard. Instead, he was forced to grit his teeth and wait until Valik was properly distracted. He could not risk Emma being injured because of his primitive urges.

The plan, after all, had been nothing more than a hasty prayer that he would rescue Emma from the looming auction, hopefully without provoking the nervous Russian into killing them all.

"Calm yourself, Valik," he soothed. "We had a bargain."

Valik shifted away from him, pointing the pistol against Emma's temple.

"I am negotiating a new bargain."

Dimitri tensed, fighting to contain his raging emotions behind icy composure. There had never been a moment more vital to think with a calm detachment.

Calling upon the brutal discipline that he had honed after his mother's death, he cast a discreet glance toward Josef. This was far from the first dire situation he had shared with his servant, and over the years they had developed an unspoken ability to know precisely what the other was thinking. At times it was almost frightening.

"You are not stupid," he said, his voice as cold as a

winter's night in Siberia. "You know I will not let you leave with Emma."

Valik licked his lips, his beady gaze shifting to Josef as the slender man deliberately strolled forward, his hand reaching into the pocket of his jacket to remove a pistol.

"Take another step and I will kill her," he rasped.

"Josef," Dimitri pretended to chastise his servant, using Valik's distraction to shift a step closer.

"I wager I can put a bullet between his eyes before he can shoot the woman," Josef taunted.

"There will be no need," Dimitri drawled, taking yet another step. "I am certain Valik intends to be reasonable, do you not?"

As expected, the agitated man did not allow his gaze to waver from Josef, or the gun he was currently pointing in his direction.

"Give me the money."

Josef held up the purse and allowed it to dangle from the tips of his fingers.

"This money?"

"Tipova, I would suggest that you command your servant to give me what I want," Valik snarled. "Otherwise your lover is going to suffer a very nasty fate."

Dimitri could barely hear over his thundering heart, but his hands remained steady as he reached beneath the sleeve of his robe to retrieve his dagger.

For the moment, he was utterly focused. The scent of the perfume makers, the sway of the palm trees, the bray of a nearby donkey and the chill of the night breeze all faded away as he gripped the handle of the dagger. All he needed was the smallest opportunity. Just a breath of a chance.

And he would strike.

"Josef rarely listens to me," he said. "It is only because he amuses me that I allow him to remain in my employ."

Josef waved his pistol, keeping Valik's attention without being overly threatening.

"I thought it was because of my talent for disposing of the corpses you leave behind?"

"Not all those corpses were my doing," Dimitri protested.

"Yes, but I tidy my own messes." There was another wave of the pistol. "I suppose I will be expected to dispose of this fool, as well?"

"It is not as if we are in St. Petersburg where you must dig through layers of ice. You can toss him into the desert and leave him for the vultures."

Josef ran an assessing glance over Valik, his expression sour.

"Perhaps you have failed to notice that he is as large as an ox? You'll have to hire me help to drag him out of the gutter."

"There are a number of monkeys scurrying about who might be of assistance."

Valik nervously shifted. "You cannot fool me into believing you do not care about the woman."

Realizing that the slave trader was about to turn and discover how close to his back Dimitri had moved, Josef gave a wild laugh as he stumbled toward him.

"I don't," he called. "And since I am the one with the pistol…"

Startled by the sudden movement, Valik allowed his fear to overcome him. Removing the pistol from Emma's temple he instead pointed it in Josef's direction.

"I told you to stay back."

A cold smile curved Dimitri's lips as he attacked.

The bastard had made two mistakes. The first was assuming that Josef was the more dangerous adversary. And the second was turning his gun away from Emma. It

SCOUNDREL'S HONOR

had been his one guarantee that Dimitri would not dare
to strike.

Plunging the knife deep in Valik's back, Dimitri wrapped
an arm around his throat and yanked him to the side, effectively dislodging Emma from the man's grasp. Only
then did he drive the larger man to the dirt road, digging
the knife deeper into his flesh.

Valik grunted, briefly caught off guard. Dimitri was
swift to take advantage, jerking the dagger free only to
slam it low in the man's back, experienced enough to avoid
the ribs so the blade could dig deep into his body.

Dimitri felt warm blood rush over his hand, cursing
Valik's massive size and ruthless thirst for survival. A lesser
man would have conceded defeat, realizing he had been
mortally wounded.

Valik, however, refused to accept fate without a fight and
with a sudden roar he swung out a beefy arm. His elbow
connected with Dimitri's chin with shocking force, briefly
blinding him with pain.

Dimitri cursed, his hold on his opponent loosening. It
was enough for Valik to roll away, shrieking in pain as
Dimitri grimly held on to the dagger while it was ripped
from Valik's flesh.

For an odd, timeless motion the two of them lay on
the road, face-to-face with the spectrum of death hovering
between them. Valik's eyes glittered with demented fury,
flecks of blood visible on his lips. In contrast, Dimitri was
coldly determined, quite willing to die if it meant saving
Emma.

Then, as one, they both moved to put an end to the
violent encounter.

Pulling back his arm, Dimitri swung it in an arc, surprised when Valik made no effort to deflect the blow. It
was not until the explosive sound of a firing pistol nearly
deafened him that he realized the man was still holding his

gun. And that he had shifted to aim the weapon directly at him.

He oddly felt no fear. Only a wry acceptance that he was at last to be punished for his wicked ways. And regret. A sharp, biting regret that he would be leaving Emma far too soon.

Of course, if he were going to hell, he had no intention of going alone. Putting the full force of his body behind his strike, Dimitri drove the dagger directly into the center of Valik's heart.

He felt the blade slide easily through Valik's chest and at the same moment he felt as if a large, very angry horse had just kicked him in the shoulder. The breath was jerked from his body as the bullet slammed into his flesh, the force of the blow sending him rolling across the road.

Distantly, he heard the sound of Josef's curses and Emma's screams, but it was difficult to think through the sudden fog that was clouding his mind.

There was pain. Red-hot, searing pain. And a frustration that his body refused to respond to his commands, so that he could make certain Valik was dead as he was supposed to be and not preparing to shoot again. But there was also the shocking realization he was not about to make his inevitable journey to hell.

How many times had he been shot in his lifetime? A half dozen? Certainly often enough to recognize a flesh wound from a mortal injury.

He wasn't going to die.

Well, at least not in the next few moments.

The relief had barely passed through his mind when there was a flurry of footsteps and Emma sank to her knees at his side. Welcome warmth filled his heart at the sight of her pale face leaning over him.

Surely that was terrified concern for him simmering in her beautiful green eyes?

"Dimitri, damn you," she choked, her gaze shifting to the blood staining his robe. "I knew this was a ridiculous plan."

He smiled at her, savoring the feel of her fingers gently smoothing the hair from his brow, even as her knee pressed against his arm to send a blaze of agony through him.

"I told you it was a bargain, not a plan," he reminded her.

"It was still ridiculous."

"My sharp-tongued vixen." His gaze skimmed over her delicate features framed by a halo of honey curls. "Should you not be offering a kiss to ease my pain rather than lecturing me on my botched rescue? Which was highly successful despite your complaints."

"Successful?" She regarded him as if he'd taken leave of his senses. And perhaps he had. He was lying flat on his back, bleeding onto a dirty Cairo street from a gunshot wound to his shoulder—his second gunshot wound in the past month—with his assailant only a few feet away, but all he could think of was the wonderment that his time with this lovely woman was not yet at an end. "You have been shot."

"But you are safe," he said softly.

She frowned, shaking her head in frustration. "You are the most aggravating—"

She was interrupted as Josef appeared at her side, a pistol held loosely in his hand.

"What of Valik?" Dimitri demanded.

"Dead," the servant assured him. "What do you want me to do with the body?"

"Leave him for the jackals to enjoy," he muttered, his pain making it difficult to think clearly. "For the moment I am more interested in bleeding somewhere other than a filthy street."

"We must find a surgeon," Emma breathed.

Dimitri shuddered. Any man who had traveled through the world knew one of the greatest dangers was putting his health in the care of the local doctors.

They inevitably caused more damage than they cured.

"Are you so anxious to see me dead?" he rasped.

She frowned in confusion. "Of course not, but you have just been shot."

"I wouldn't take my dog to the local surgeon," Josef muttered.

"But—"

"Josef is experienced in stitching my wounds." Dimitri headed off her arguments.

She grimaced, casting a jaundiced glance at his servant. "I suppose he has had a great deal of practice?"

"Enough," Josef readily admitted.

"It is nothing to be proud of." She returned her harried attention to Dimitri. "What if the bullet is still in your shoulder?"

Josef shrugged. "Then I will dig it out."

"And risk it becoming inflamed?"

Ignoring his pain, Dimitri reached to grasp Emma's hand. She was stubborn enough to go in search of a damnable doctor if she thought it best for him.

"I needn't worry," he said, his voice strained. "I will have you to nurse me back to health, *milaya*."

Her eyes narrowed at his teasing, but the stroke of her fingers on his brow was exquisitely tender.

"How can you be so certain I will not leave you for those vultures you spoke of earlier?" she demanded.

"Because it is in your nature to care for others, even when they do not deserve your concern."

Misery flared through her eyes and he silently cursed his thoughtless words.

The last thing he desired was to remind her of her worthless sister.

"Perhaps I have learned that caring for others is a dangerous emotion that is not worth the pain," she said, her voice so low he barely caught her bitter words.

"Emma—"

"Guards are coming," Josef snapped, his hand tightening on the pistol and his slender body tense as he prepared for trouble.

Dimitri ignored Emma's protest as he struggled to lift his head.

"The caliph's?"

"The pasha. And they do not look pleased."

He managed to sit upright despite the agony that jolted down his arm.

"Damn."

Seemingly indifferent to the approaching soldiers who were fully armed with both rifles and swords, Emma carefully shifted to put a bracing arm behind his back. Dimitri swallowed a rueful sigh. The ridiculous woman would always be more concerned with the welfare of others than her own safety.

Which was precisely why he intended to devote the rest of his life to protecting her.

"Surely that is good?" she asked. "We have done nothing wrong."

Dimitri battled against the wave of dizziness, his gaze taking in the determined approach of the five soldiers. His heart sank at the sight of their military precision and obvious ease with their weapons.

This was no ragtag group of mercenaries.

They were trained fighters who had tasted war.

"We have shed blood on the streets of Cairo," he absently murmured. "I doubt the pasha will approve."

"Valik is…" Emma caught her words, glancing toward Valik's unnaturally still body. "He was a slave trader. A criminal."

"And what am I?" he demanded wryly. He turned to meet Josef's calculating gaze. "Can we flee?"

"You can." He nodded toward the nearby carriage. "I will distract them."

"No." Dimitri's tone was commanding. He would not risk his most loyal servant. "I doubt the pasha's mood will be improved if we were to kill his soldiers."

He heard Emma suck in a sharp breath. "You are going to allow yourself to be captured?"

"There does not seem to be much choice." He swiftly considered his severely limited options. There was no avoiding the soldiers. Not without putting Emma in danger. He could only hope that the pasha would offer a reasonable hospitality until he could find the means to escape. "Josef, slip away and gather the men. Take them out of the city and if we have not been released within the week—"

"Wait," Emma interrupted, her expression grim. "You will need Josef. I have a better plan."

His brows snapped together. "Emma."

"Trust me."

Without giving him the opportunity to stop her, Emma surged to her feet and darted toward the nearby palm trees before becoming lost among the shadows.

Dimitri gritted his teeth, and Josef muttered his vile opinion of females who were too stubborn for their own good. Neither, however, were foolish enough to risk drawing the approaching soldiers' attention toward the fleeing woman.

Instead, they exchanged a resigned glance and prepared to be arrested by Muhammad Ali Pasha.

EMMA RAN THROUGH THE streets of Cairo like a mad woman, utterly indifferent to the drunken men and roaming packs of dogs that threatened her. All she could think of was finding help before Dimitri could be taken by the approaching guards.

A futile hope, she discovered as she at last reached Rajih's palace only to be told he had not yet returned.

Not knowing where else to turn, Emma allowed herself to be escorted into the harem to await his arrival.

It was not as if she could approach the pasha and demand that his soldiers release Dimitri.

Could she?

Pacing the tiled floor, she impatiently counted the passing minutes. For once the soft tinkle of the fountain and the faint scent of incense did nothing to soothe her frayed nerves. Nor did the expensive wine that was left near the baths on a silver tray.

It seemed like an eternity before she at last heard the sound of voices in the inner courtyard. With a small cry of relief she darted from her private rooms, only to be forced to halt as she realized Rajih was not alone.

Standing behind one of the carved-marble columns, she watched as Rajih directed his servants to care for the five young girls huddling together in obvious fear.

She was briefly distracted as she studied the pale, dirty faces of the poor females who were dressed in gauzy trousers and tiny vests that revealed more of their shivering bodies than they concealed.

They looked so terrified. As if they could not allow themselves to believe they were actually safe in Rajih's care.

And who could blame them? They had spent weeks being held hostage, forced from one place to another with the constant threat of being raped, or worse, hanging over their heads. It might very well be they would never again be able to trust in others.

Her heart constricted with unbearable pity, fiercely glad

that Dimitri had managed to put a dagger in Valik's black heart.

It was only a pity that the other men involved in the hideous business were not destined for a similar fate.

She waited until the robed servants had led the wary girls toward the back of the harem before she stepped from behind the column.

Sensing her presence, Rajih spun on his heel, his eyes widening in surprise as she launched herself forward, straight into his welcoming arms.

"Emma."

"Oh, Rajih, thank God," she husked.

He brushed his lips over the top of her head before pulling back to study her with a searching gaze.

"Should I be delighted by such a fervent greeting or alarmed?"

"Are those the girls from the brothel?"

His dark eyes shimmered with regret. "They are."

"What will happen to them now?"

"Tipova implied that the current Russian ambassador is not to be fully trusted with young, vulnerable girls, so I will have my personal servants return them to St. Petersburg."

She managed a small smile. If not for Dimitri Tipova, she was quite certain she would have lost her heart to this man.

"That is very generous," she said. "You are a good man, Caliph Rajih."

He shook his head, his fingers tucking her tangled curls behind her ear.

"You might wish to withhold your kind opinion," he warned. "I fear I have unfortunate news."

She pulled back, belatedly recalling he had put himself in danger to rescue the girls. Who knew how many guards Valik had left behind at the brothel?

"You were not hurt, were you?"

His dark features softened at her impulsive concern. "No, I am fine."

"Then what has happened?"

He paused, clearly reluctant to reveal what was upon his mind.

"Emma, your sister was not among the girls I rescued from the brothel," he at last disclosed. "I questioned the females but they claimed that Anya has been kept separate from them since they left England and they have no knowledge of where she is." His arms tightened around her, as if fearing she might suddenly bolt into the night. "I have servants searching for her, but for the moment it seems that she has simply disappeared. I am sorry, I should have been quicker to send in my guards."

Emma grimaced, regretting that Rajih was torturing himself with guilt at having failed her.

"No, Rajih, Anya fled before you were able to enter the brothel," she swiftly reassured him. "All that matters is that you managed to rescue the other girls."

"She fled?" Rajih frowned in confusion. "Alone?"

Emma shook her head, hunching her shoulders against the tide of sick betrayal.

"She was with one of the guards," she said. "They are supposedly on their way to Austria."

Rajih stilled, clearly sensing her distress. "Do you want me to send my guards after them?"

"No, she had made her choice."

"Emma—"

Swallowing the lump in her throat, Emma pulled out of his comforting arms and tilted her chin. Now was no time to fret over her sister's astounding selfishness. Not when Dimitri was depending upon her.

"Please, Rajih, I do need your assistance, but not for Anya," she pleaded softly.

"What do you need?"

"Dimitri has been taken captive by Muhammad Ali Pasha's guards. We must free him."

A thick silence filled the courtyard as Rajih considered her confession, then slowly he folded his arms over his chest.

"Tell me what happened."

As concisely as possible she revealed their carriage ride from the brothel to the mosque and Valik's refusal to release her. She briefly faltered as she described Dimitri's attack on the horrid man. There would not be a night when she was not haunted by the vivid image of Dimitri being shot, not knowing for an agonizing moment whether he was alive or dead.

With effort she gathered her composure and finished explaining Dimitri's dire situation, emphasizing the very large and heavily armed guards who had been rapidly approaching.

Once she was finished, Rajih turned to pace through the perfumed shadows of the courtyard, his expression impossible to read.

"How badly is he injured?"

"The shot was to his shoulder, but I fear the bullet may still be in the wound and he lost a great deal of blood."

"Do not fear," he muttered absently. "The pasha has a number of healers."

She snorted. "If Josef will let them near."

Rajih halted, turning to regard her with a warning gaze. "The choice will not be his to make."

A shiver inched down Emma's spine. There was an edge in his voice that sharply reminded her that they were in a foreign country with its own laws and traditions. For the moment, Dimitri and Josef were at the complete mercy of the pasha.

"Is Dimitri in danger?"

"I am not entirely certain." Rajih thankfully knew her well enough to speak the truth. In this moment she could not bear to be treated as if she were a mindless, shrinking violet in need of tender care. "The pasha will not be pleased that a foreigner committed murder on the streets for all to see."

"But Valik was a slave trader, not to mention he was holding me hostage," she protested.

"True, but the officials prefer that such matters be dealt with discreetly." Rajih grimaced. "The pasha possesses a dislike for explaining violent deaths of the foreign consuls."

Emma possessed a small measure of sympathy for the ruler. His country was too often at the mercy of invaders. He could not risk offending potential allies.

That did not mean, however, she would meekly stand aside and allow Dimitri to become a sacrifice to his political weakness.

She stepped forward and laid a hand on Rajih's forearm. "Can you speak with the pasha and convince him that Dimitri is innocent?"

The dark eyes lowered to study her fingers that lay against the fine fabric of his jacket, a mysterious smile curving his lips.

"I could, but it would hardly be to my benefit," he murmured.

She frowned. "Rajih?"

"If I am not mistaken, Tipova intends to take you away from Egypt."

An uncomfortable sensation tugged at her heart. Something that might have been regret.

"With or without Dimitri I intend to return to Russia."

His eyes lifted to stab her with a relentless gaze. "Why?"

"It is my home."

With a gentle care, Rajih covered the fingers that rested on his arm, his gaze sweeping over her upturned face.

"No, Emma, Russia is the place you were born," he corrected. "Your home is where you choose to be."

A dim, nearly forgotten memory of her parents seated before the fireplace in the cottage rose to mind. There had been nothing special about the evening. At least nothing that she could recall. But the image of her mother and father snuggled closely on the sofa, their hands entwined and their faces soft with love, had created a warmth in her young heart.

That was what created a home.

"I suppose that is true."

As if sensing her bittersweet memories, Rajih shifted to cup her face in his hands, his expression somber.

"I want you to stay with me."

"As your concubine?"

"As my wife."

Wife. She blinked, regarding him with disbelief.

For goodness' sake, was he touched in the head?

He was, after all, a shockingly handsome man with a ruthless virility that would make any female weak in the knees. She had seen how women fluttered when he stepped onto the streets of Cairo.

And of course, there was the tiny matter of him being a wealthy caliph with a number of estates spread throughout Egypt.

The mere notion he could desire an aging spinster with an evil temper and sharp tongue was…

Without warning, her laughter was spilling through the dark courtyard.

"This is absurd," she choked.

His brows drew together, his pride obviously offended.

"You find my proposal amusing?"

"I find it astonishing. I..." She bit her bottom lip, struggling to regain command of her fragile composure.

He stepped forward, grasping her shoulders in a firm grip. "Emma?"

"For most of my life I have either been the source of pity or amusement," she confessed, anxious to assure him that she was deeply honored by his proposal. "It is not a simple matter to accept that a gentleman could consider me worthy to be his wife. Certainly not a gentleman who is offered the most beautiful women in the world."

His expression eased at her words, his hands stroking a warm path down her back.

"You are a woman of rare courage and loyalty," he said. "These are qualities that I would desire for my sons."

Her heart missed a beat, and she sharply turned away. She had never allowed herself to consider the possibility of children. Not when she knew she was destined to be an old maid.

It was simply too painful.

"That is why you wish to marry me?"

"You know why I want you as my wife," he husked, his arms wrapping around her slender waist and his head lowering to bury in the curve of her neck. "The question is what do you want, Emma?"

CHAPTER TWENTY-FIVE

DIMITRI HAD A VAGUE memory of being surrounded by angry soldiers and roughly carried to the citadel. Thankfully, he had lost consciousness only moments after passing through the great round towers built into the walls guarding the fortress.

He preferred to stay unaware of his humiliation of being hauled to the dungeons as a common criminal.

Unfortunately, there was no means of remaining senseless when his servant was using a large dagger to dig out the bullet that remained in his shoulder. Hell, that sort of pain would have awoken him if he were dead.

Wrenching open eyes that felt as if they were filled with a good measure of desert sand, he glared at the slender man kneeling beside the low divan that Dimitri was stretched across.

"Damn you, Josef," he said, annoyed when the words came out as a thin whisper. "That is my shoulder you are poking and prying, not a slab of meat from the butcher."

With a last brutal twist of the dagger, Josef sat back on his heels, a smile touching his scarred face as he held up the bullet he had just removed.

"The pasha did offer one of his numerous females to tend to your injuries." Setting aside his tools of torture, the servant grabbed his silver flask and poured a generous measure of brandy into Dimitri's wound. "No doubt they would be gentle enough for your delicate nerves."

Dimitri ground his teeth against his shout of agony.

Why was it that a bullet always felt worse coming out than it did going in?

Sensing the encroaching darkness that threatened to overwhelm him, Dimitri grimly tried to focus on his surroundings.

Above him the vaulted ceiling was magnificently decorated with blue-and-white tiles, the superior craftsmanship unmistakable. Far too exquisite for the dungeons. Which was an improvement on this rotten day.

With a small movement, he turned his head far enough to sweep a glance over the large room filled with the divans and large pillows that were preferred among the natives, covered in yellow-and-green silk. The walls were covered with finely carved wooden panels, and there was a massive fireplace with a green-marble mantel. At last he shifted his attention to take in the arched windows where the early morning sunlight tumbled through the grilled screens.

He grimaced, realizing he had been unconscious more hours than he initially suspected.

Where was Emma? And most important, was she safe?

"They would certainly be preferable to gaze upon," he absently muttered.

Packing the wound with clean linen, Josef efficiently wrapped a narrow strip of fabric around his shoulder to hold it in place.

"Do you want one fetched?" he demanded.

With his thoughts still on Emma, Dimitri managed a painful laugh.

"You just dug a bullet out of my flesh, in an unnecessarily painful fashion I might add. I do not relish the thought of having another removed."

Josef snorted, washing his hands in the ceramic bowl filled with water.

"I doubt any of the females in the pasha's harem carry loaded pistols."

"No, but Emma would be eager to put another in my tender backside should she discover I allowed a beautiful female to put her hands on me."

A completely unexpected fondness flickered over his servant's narrow countenance.

"She is too honorable to shoot you from behind. She is far more likely to stab you in the heart with a dagger."

"That is most reassuring." Bemused, Dimitri struggled to sit upright, relieved to discover that the worst of the fiery pain seemed to be fading from his shoulder. Of course, he did not protest when his servant helped him slip on a pale blue robe and pressed a flask into his hand. "You surprise me, Josef," he admitted, drinking deep of the fiery spirits.

"Why?" Josef gathered the bloody rags and dagger, dumping them on a silver tray. "I have stitched you back together more times than I can recall."

"No, I am astonished that I am not forced to endure a lecture on the stupidity of men who fall victim to a female's snare."

Josef straightened, carrying the tray to set it on a low table inlaid with bronze.

"You know my opinion."

"Then why are you not scolding me as if I am a witless idiot?"

"If you must dangle on some female's leash then you could do much worse than Emma Linley-Kirov."

Dimitri was genuinely shocked. He had known Josef since they were both scrawny youths, struggling to stay alive in the gutters of St. Petersburg. In all that time the man had never revealed more than a bitter distrust for the opposite sex.

The predictable result of a boy beaten nearly to death by his mother and left in the rubbish to die.

"Good Lord, surely you cannot approve of a mere female?" he teased.

Josef turned to meet Dimitri's amused gaze. "She is different from most."

Dimitri's lips twisted. "True."

"Did you see her standing in the street as cool as you please, while Valik held a pistol to her head?" Josef smiled. "I could not have done better myself."

A stab of remembered terror made his heart forget to beat. "It is a vision engraved on my mind, I assure you."

"Most women would have swooned or at least been sniffling and begging for their life. But not Emma."

Dimitri nearly rolled his eyes at the admiration in his companion's voice. It was all very well for Josef to approve of Emma's impulsive courage. He was not the one who lived in constant fear she would plunge into some disaster he could not save her from.

"No, not Emma. She would spit in the eye of the devil," he admitted wryly. "Just like my mother."

"That is surely a good thing?"

"I had convinced myself that I preferred females who understood that it was a man's responsibility to offer her protection. Not a woman who—"

"A woman who would make a man proud," Josef finished with a lift of his brows.

Dimitri attempted to appear resigned, even as a smug satisfaction flared through his heart.

Yes, he would always be proud of Emma.

She was utterly unique.

"It is a pity she is destined to put me in an early grave."

"It is not too late to walk away."

"It was too late from the moment she arrived in St.

Petersburg." Dimitri lifted the flask to his lips, wincing as the bandages tugged at his injury. "Damn."

Josef moved back to the divan, scowling down at his employer.

"How does it feel?"

"As if I have a hole in my shoulder, but I will no doubt survive." Dimitri raised the flask in a toast. "Yet another fine job, old friend."

Josef grimaced as the faint sound of voices penetrated the large double doors at the far side of the room.

"Let us hope that I did not remove the bullet so that the pasha could have your head removed," he muttered.

Dimitri struggled off the divan, grasping Josef's arm as a wave of dizziness threatened to buckle his knees. He would meet his fate on his feet.

"We haven't yet been taken to the dungeon, which means we are still considered guests and not prisoners."

"Do not be so certain," Josef muttered. "There are two very large guards on the other side of the doors. It will not be easy to escape."

"For now I prefer to avoid insulting our host," he said, a hint of warning in his voice. It would not take long before Josef decided he had wearied of the pasha's hospitality and took matters into his own hands. "It is quite possible we will be released once I have the opportunity to explain to the pasha why there is a dead Russian in his gutter."

Josef grunted. "Or he might decide we would make a tasty meal for his pet tiger."

Dimitri hid his sudden smile, not bothering to correct his servant's odd belief that Egypt was filled with tigers and lions and any number of other dangerous animals.

"Highly doubtful."

"So you say."

Dimitri's hand tightened on Josef's arm as the doors were pushed open to reveal two slender female servants attired in nearly transparent robes with tiny jewels dangling from their noses.

"Patience, Josef."

SIX HOURS LATER, DIMITRI had managed to forget his decision to behave as a rational, law-abiding gentleman.

It was not that he had been ill-treated. Quite the contrary, in fact.

The females that had led them to the baths had been beautiful and anxious to please. Rather too anxious, he wryly admitted, recalling their shock when he had refused to allow them to wash him with their scented oils. And when they had returned to their room, it was to find a sumptuous feast had been left on trays.

Once he had eaten, Dimitri forced himself to lie back on the pillows and rest. His shoulder was rapidly healing, but it would take some time to regain his strength.

As the hours passed, however, his attempt to calmly await his fate evaporated like wavering mists of a mirage. He might be in luxurious comfort, but he had no assurance that Emma was not in trouble.

She had run into the night alone, traversing the dangerous streets of Cairo with nothing but luck to protect her.

The worry was like an aching thorn in the center of his heart.

Pacing the floor, he at last moved to stand beside the grilled window overlooking the southern enclosure of the citadel, his gaze lingering on the massive green dome of the Hall of Justice. Beyond it was the black-and-yellow marble palace built by An-Nasir Muhammad where the pasha conducted his daily business of ruling his empire.

Surely the pasha had to be near? How difficult could it be to send for him and demand an explanation for the death of Valik?

With a muttered curse he turned on his heel to glare at Josef, who was busy with his own pacing.

"Where the hell is the pasha?" he burst out.

Josef flashed him a jaundiced frown. "You were the one to counsel patience."

"I need to know that Emma is safe."

"Do not worry, Dimitri Tipova," a voice drawled from the door. "Emma is under my protection."

Dimitri jerked his head to view Caliph Rajih strolling across the delicate carpet. His gaze skimmed over the man's white robe heavily embroidered with gold trim and the matching turban, a scowl marring his brow as he lingered on the curved sword belted to his waist.

It was more than an ornamental weapon. That was obvious from the well-honed edge and worn leather of the hilt. There was also an ease in the manner Rajih wore the sword that suggested he was familiar with using the lethal tool.

Dimitri, on the other hand, had awoken to discover his pistol and knives had been taken while he slept. And even the dagger that Josef had used to cut the bullet from his shoulder had disappeared.

He did not like feeling vulnerable.

Or perhaps it was the smug smile curving the man's lips that he did not like.

All he knew was that he had a sudden urge to wrap his hands around the bastard's throat and squeeze the life from him.

"Where is she?" he snapped.

"She is visiting the pasha's seraglio."

Dimitri's stark relief that Emma was indeed safe warred with his outrage at the thought of her being within the pasha's harem.

"You brought her to the citadel?"

"Do not hold me accountable." Rajih shook his head.

"She refused to remain at the palace and threatened to come on her own if I did not allow her to accompany me."

"Ah." Despite his annoyance, Dimitri smiled at the man's obvious frustration. "You have my sympathy."

"I should no doubt have chained her to her bed, but I feared yet another of your enemies might be lurking about to snatch her while I was gone."

Dimitri refused to react to the deliberate taunt. Soon enough he would be whisking Emma back to St. Petersburg, and his newly constructed town house, where she belonged.

"My supposed enemies will be fleeing Cairo like rats from a sinking ship."

"Do not be so certain."

Dimitri tensed, not missing the edge of warning in the man's voice.

"What do you mean?"

"Despite my preference that you remain conveniently locked behind these walls, Emma was quite insistent I make a personal plea for your release."

Dimitri grinned. "She must have been quite persuasive."

"She is aware that I would do whatever necessary to please her."

"And what pleases her is my release? That must be a painful disappointment for you."

Rajih waved a dismissive hand. "Emma has a tender heart and she blames herself for your situation. She will eventually see the error of her ways and accept that I offer far more than a Russian criminal can, no matter how great his wealth."

There was enough truth in the caliph's accusation to send an unwelcome chill down Dimitri's spine.

He took pride in what he had accomplished over the

years. Why not? How often did a ragged beggar boy actually manage to create his own empire?

But for all his accomplishments, there was no denying that he was the bastard son of a whore and worse, a ruthless criminal who was, for all his fine estates and vast fortune, no better than a common serf.

What woman with the least amount of sense would not prefer a handsome caliph who could not only offer her wealth, but an opportunity to mingle among the finest of society?

Then, squaring his shoulder, he dismissed his unnerving doubt.

Most women would indeed leap at the opportunity to become Rajih's bride, but not Emma.

She desired many things; a family, a sense of independence, a home, but never wealth and certainly never social standing.

Those were the things that he could offer.

"She will never be yours," he grated, his hands clenched as he stepped toward the damned intruder.

"Tipova, perhaps you can postpone your urge to challenge the man who is here to plea for our release?" Josef stepped between them, poking Dimitri in the chest. "At least until we are away from this place? There are few prisons I cannot escape from, but this is a fortress."

Dimitri growled low in his throat, his predatory nature fully aroused. Unfortunately, he could not dismiss Josef's warning.

For the moment, he had to swallow his pride and accept whatever assistance Rajih was willing to offer.

"Have you spoken with the pasha?" he asked between gritted teeth.

The Egyptian smiled. "I have."

"You explained that Valik was in this country to auction young girls?"

"Yes."

Dimitri narrowed his gaze, sensing that Rajih had not come to announce he was at liberty to leave.

"And?"

Rajih moved to the tray on a side table, pouring a drink from the decanter of brandy.

"Unfortunately, I was not the only petitioner to approach the pasha concerning your presence in Cairo."

"Petitioner?" Dimitri stiffened in shock, wondering if the word had a different meaning in Egyptian politics. "What precisely does that mean?"

Rajih emptied his glass in one swallow. "When I was brought before the pasha to proclaim your innocence another arrived to swear to your guilt."

So, it was precisely what he feared.

But how could anyone possibly know he was currently being held captive by the pasha? And why would they come as a petitioner to proclaim his guilt?

"Who?"

"Baron Koman."

"The Russian ambassador?" He frowned, a fury exploding through him. "Damn his black soul."

Rajih smiled, not bothering to hide his amusement at Dimitri's frustration.

"I assume the two of you are acquainted?"

"Unfortunately." Dimitri paced across the floor, brooding on the unexpected complication. "The bastard must have discovered my intention to speak with Alexander Pavlovich to have him removed from his position."

Rajih made a choked sound of surprise. "You have such influence with Czar Alexander?"

"It is not a matter of influence. The man is an incompetent fool."

"Not entirely incompetent," Rajih countered. "He made quite a compelling argument that you are an infamous

Russian criminal who had recently decided to take command of the slave trade."

Dimitri came to a sharp halt, unable to dismiss the sensation that there was far more to his current troubles than an indolent, half-witted Russian nobleman.

"If that were true then why would I have killed Valik and allowed the girls to be released into your care?"

"It was suggested that it was a battle for power." Rajih shrugged. "You would, after all, need to destroy the current business before establishing your own."

Dimitri paused, his suspicions becoming certainty. "Koman made this suggestion?"

Rajih set aside his glass, sensing the sudden danger that prickled in the air.

"Why are you so surprised?" he asked. "You admitted the man has reason to wish you harm."

Dimitri prowled forward, his expression hard. "Yes, but he is a lazy, stupid man who is barely capable of summoning the ambition to leave his divan."

An age-old bitterness flared through Rajih's dark eyes. "He resembles every other foreign diplomat in Cairo."

"The crux of the matter is that Koman might pout and complain and even threaten retribution, but he would never summon the initiative or the temerity to approach the pasha," he growled, fiercely regretting his lack of weapons. "And he most certainly does not possess the intelligence to devise such a clever means of implicating me as a slave trader."

The dark eyes narrowed. "I assure you that it most certainly was the baron I just witnessed testifying to your guilt."

"I do not question his presence, only his motive," Dimitri replied, his voice cold. "There has to be more than revenge that compelled him to the citadel."

With a glare at Dimitri's bristling manner, Josef attempted to ease the rising hostility in the room.

"What could be more powerful than the desire for revenge?" he demanded.

Dimitri folded his arms over his chest. "Fear."

Josef absently stroked a finger over the scar marring his cheek.

"You believe he fears the loss of his position as a diplomat?"

"No," Dimitri readily denied. Koman was a self-indulgent pig who cared for nothing beyond his own pleasure. "It has to be a greater threat than his career."

"His wealth?"

Dimitri nodded. "Or his life."

Rajih made a sound of impatience. "You make no sense, Tipova. What possible gain could be in forcing Koman to testify against you?"

Dimitri's attention snapped back to the caliph, his suspicions a hard knot in the pit of his stomach.

"Tell me what the pasha has decided."

"Obviously, he has been put in an awkward situation." Rajih paused, as if carefully considering his words. "He has long considered me a trusted advisor, but he cannot be seen to ignore the accusations of the Russian ambassador who also happens to be a powerful nobleman."

A cold, humorless smile curved Dimitri's lips. His cunning mind was already devising various plans of escape that did not include the pasha or Caliph Rajih.

"I sympathize with his dilemma, but that does not reveal what he intends to do with me."

"Or me," Josef muttered.

"He has sent an advisor to St. Petersburg to speak with Czar Alexander before a decision is made."

Dimitri exchanged a startled glance with Josef. Was his mysterious enemy unaware that Alexander Pavlovich owed him several favors and assumed the czar would be happy to leave Dimitri rotting in a foreign prison? Or was this simply a delaying tactic?

He had first assumed that Koman's petition to the pasha was an attempt to punish him. It could be an opponent who desired him to be distracted for some nefarious purpose.

And he knew precisely who would desire him to be distracted.

"A tidy means of avoiding responsibility," he mocked.

Rajih silently studied Dimitri's forbidding expression, his hand instinctively reaching to curl around the hilt of his sword.

"You should be grateful. It was within his power to have you executed."

Dimitri was in no mood to be appreciative. "Am I to remain a prisoner while the advisor is in Russia?"

"A guest."

"A guest who is unable to leave the citadel?" he growled.

Rajih shifted his weight, his fingers tightening on his sword.

"An unfortunate necessity."

Dimitri refused to be intimidated, regardless of the stupidity of confronting an armed man with nothing more than his bare hands.

"It is also a predictable response."

Rajih narrowed his gaze. "Predictable?"

"The pasha had little choice but to insist I remain under guard after a prominent ambassador accused me of trafficking and murder."

Josef cleared his throat, his gaze nervously darting between the two men.

"Who would want you trapped here?"

Dimitri's gaze moved with a slow deliberation over Rajih's poised body.

"There is one gentleman who comes to mind."

With the elegant ease of a trained swordsman, Rajih had the sword pulled from his belt and the tip pressed beneath Dimitri's chin.

"If I wished to be rid of you, Tipova, I would not bother with such an elaborate scheme," the Egyptian warned. "The desert is littered with the bones of my enemies."

Dimitri was vibrantly aware of a faint breeze wafting through the grilled windows, the perfumed oils that clung to his robe and the trickle of blood that ran from his chin down his neck.

One misstep and he would be skewered.

"Perhaps you did not want me dead, but merely unable to return to Russia with Emma," he snapped. "With me locked in the citadel, you will be at liberty to offer her..." His jaw tightened. "Comfort."

The sword dug deeper, making Dimitri flinch, but he ignored the pain. Instead, he concentrated on the outrage that smoldered in Rajih's dark eyes.

That was not the expression of a man attempting to hide his guilt.

No. He was clearly offended.

Dangerously offended.

"You insult both Emma and myself," Rajih gritted. "I am not so desperate that I need to trick a female into my arms, and Emma is not so weak she must cling to whatever gentleman happens to be at hand."

With a grudging reluctance, Dimitri accepted that Rajih was not responsible for his current dilemma.

A pity.

He would have enjoyed wreaking vengeance on the arrogant son of a jackal.

"You are right," he managed to mutter. "I apologize."

"Are you taunting me?"

"No." Dimitri grimaced. "My particular business

demands that I be able to discern when someone is lying or telling me the truth. You cannot feign wounded pride."

With obvious annoyance he would not be allowed to remove Dimitri's head, Rajih lowered his sword and stepped back.

Josef moved to pour a large glass of the brandy, his expression revealing he held Dimitri entirely responsible for the near disastrous encounter. He downed the liquor in a single swallow.

"If it's not the caliph, then who?"

Rajih shrugged. "There are others who would wish you to be...indisposed."

Actually, there was an endless list of potential enemies. He had not achieved his position without cunning, treachery, coercion and a vast amount of brute force. But how many of them knew he was in Cairo? Or in the custody of the pasha?

And how many were powerful enough to force Baron Koman to do his bidding?

He gave a frustrated shake of his head. There was still something he was missing.

"Who do you suspect?"

"Valik's guards bolted the moment he left the brothel," Rajih offered. "They would be delighted to have you locked away while they attempt to make their escape from Egypt."

"It is possible."

"Or perhaps it is an unknown adversary who is manipulating matters from the shadows." Rajih smiled. "You seem to have a talent for creating enemies."

Josef set aside his empty glass. "We can discover the identity of the enemy once we are away from this place."

Dimitri paused before giving a discontented nod. "How long before you can convince the pasha to release us?" he demanded of the caliph.

"There is nothing to be done until Czar Alexander has responded to the pasha's request for assistance."

Dimitri's brows snapped together. "Impossible."

"There is no choice."

"Then I will find my own means of disappearing."

"Do not be a fool, Tipova." Rajih deliberately lifted his sword, his warning unmistakable. "If your servants are caught attempting to slip into the citadel they will be put to death immediately. Just as you will be killed if you are caught trying to escape."

"You cannot expect me to remain trapped here like a rat...."

Dimitri bit off his words as he was struck by a haunting reality.

Trapped.

Yes, that was precisely what he was.

Trapped and all but helpless.

If he were the mysterious enemy why would he want his prey trapped and helpless?

Rajih stepped toward him, regarding him with a suspicious expression.

"What were you saying?"

Dimitri forced a grim smile to his lips. "Very well."

Josef swore, reaching to grasp Dimitri's arm in a punishing grip.

"Tipova—"

"Josef, it is obvious we must wait for Alexander Pavlovich to demand our release." He overrode his servant's protest.

Josef glared at him with a sour disapproval. "You are assuming he won't tell the pasha to have us fed to his tiger."

"Tiger?" the caliph asked in confusion.

"It is of no importance," Dimitri muttered, swallowing

his pride as he contemplated the most pertinent dangers of his situation. "I must demand a favor of you, Rajih."

Dimitri had to appreciate the manner in which the man hesitated before offering his promise. He might never be friends with Rajih, but he did respect his integrity.

"That depends upon the favor," he admitted.

"I assure you that it does not include storming the citadel."

Rajih heaved a resigned sigh. "I am listening."

"I wish for Emma to be returned to the safety of St. Petersburg."

The other man stiffened, a stubborn expression settling on his lean face. Not that Dimitri was surprised. Rajih made no secret of his desire to keep Emma for himself.

"That is her decision."

"No, you must be firm with her," he insisted. "We both know how stubborn she can be. She will remain so long as she fears I am in danger, regardless of the fact that my enemies might very well use her to punish me."

"You do not believe me capable of keeping her safe?"

Dimitri crushed his possessive instincts. For now all that mattered was that Emma was whisked far away from Cairo.

"Once she is in St. Petersburg, she will be under the protection of Herrick Gerhardt, the czar's most trusted advisor. And more important, she will be too far away to be an effective pawn. That is the only true means to keep her safe."

There was a pause as Rajih considered Dimitri's request, then with a wry smile, he offered a dip of his head.

"I will do my best, but I do not perform miracles."

"That is all I ask."

The caliph turned to walk across the floor, pausing as he reached the heavy doors.

"It has been many years since I visited your country,"

he murmured, his voice filled with a blatant anticipation. "It will be delightful to spend a few weeks at the Summer Palace."

Dimitri clenched his hand, watching as the caliph stepped out of the room and the door closed behind him.

He should have stabbed the bastard with his own sword.

Indifferent to Dimitri's brooding desire for blood, Josef moved to stand directly before him, his hands planted on his hips.

"Have you gone completely mad?"

CHAPTER TWENTY-SIX

THE SERAGLIO WAS TRULY a place of wonderment.

Although recently refurbished, it maintained the charm of ages past with a domed ceiling decorated with blue-and-gold tiles to form a night sky slumbering above a large fountain carved into the center of the marble floor. The inner wall was covered by fine tapestries with a doorway that opened to the private gardens, while the arched windows on the opposite wall were covered by golden grills.

The furniture, however, was surprisingly European with several scrolled settees and an applewood writing desk situated beneath a framed mirror.

It was all very beautiful, but Emma was acutely aware of the heavily armed eunuchs patrolling the spiderweb of corridors and private rooms. It would be all but impossible for a person to slip unnoticed out of such a formidable fortress.

A knowledge that weighed heavily on her heart.

Ignoring the various refreshments served to her by veiled servants, Emma anxiously paced the floor, awaiting Rajih's return.

Not that she was particularly reassured when she was at last led to the lower stables where Rajih hurried her toward the waiting carriage. Not after he revealed that Dimitri was to remain a guest of the pasha until Alexander Pavlovich could be convinced to demand his release.

"No." With a jerk she freed her arm from Rajih's grasp, her chin jutted to a stubborn angle. "I am not leaving until I am certain that Dimitri is safe."

Regaining his grip on her elbow, Rajih steered her around the edge of the black carriage and away from the numerous servants milling about the stable yard.

"I promise that he is at considerably less risk as the guest of Muhammad Ali Pasha than in St. Petersburg where he no doubt possesses any number of enemies," he said.

"But he is not a guest," she hissed, "he is a prisoner."

Rajih grimaced, casting a covert glance toward a passing groom.

"Emma, I beg that you keep your voice down unless you wish both of us to share his fate."

She bit her lower lip, well aware she owed this man a debt of gratitude that could not be repaid.

Not only had he risked his life to rescue the poor girls from the brothel the previous evening, but he had sacrificed his pride to request Dimitri's release, even though he would as soon cut out his tongue.

And there was no escaping the knowledge that he had done so for her.

Just as so many others had suffered to assist her.

"Forgive me, Rajih, I never intended to put you in this awkward position," she said. "I have caused enough trouble for others."

Rajih frowned, cupping her chin to lift her face so he could study her suddenly subdued expression.

"None of this is your fault, *habiba*."

She could only wish that were true. Perhaps then she would not be plagued with a relentless guilt.

"If I had not been so stubbornly determined to chase after Anya, then Dimitri would be enjoying his life in St. Petersburg and you would not be forced to jeopardize your friendship with the pasha to plead for his release."

"The fault lies with the men who kidnapped the girls to sell like animals, not you."

"Still—"

He placed a finger across her lips, his gaze sweeping over her face with an odd yearning.

"Emma, the past cannot be altered. We must consider the future."

She sucked in a deep breath, ignoring the stench of horses and unwashed body that tainted the air. Her regrets would have to wait until she had the time and opportunity to make amends. Instead, she grabbed Rajih's hand and regarded him with a determined expression.

"You are right, of course, but that does not mean I am willing to abandon Dimitri."

The dark eyes simmered with something that might have been disappointment before he had smoothed his features to an unreadable expression.

"I am not suggesting that you abandon him, but rather that you use your own influence to ensure that he is found innocent," he said, his voice smooth.

She stepped back, suddenly wary. "You want me to speak with the pasha?"

His brows lifted at her impetuous words. "No, as charming as our leader would no doubt find you, this is a country that believes a woman should remain silent behind the walls of the seraglio. He would not allow you to testify on Tipova's behalf."

"Barbaric."

"It is the way of my people."

"Then how can I help?" She twisted her hands together in frustration. She detested the sense that she was helpless to rescue Dimitri. "You just admitted that Baron Koman has proven to be a traitor."

"Yes." Rajih's expression hardened, warning that Koman could expect to be punished for his treachery. "A most unexpected complication."

"Does Dimitri know why the baron would claim he is guilty?"

Rajih shrugged. "He says he does not."

"Maybe he is a part of the trafficking and now hopes to deceive others into believing Dimitri is responsible," she absently mused.

"It would be a convenient means to make another pay for his sins," he agreed. "But Dimitri is convinced there is another forcing the baron to do his bidding."

She snorted. "Dimitri is not always so infallible as he wants others to believe."

His lips twisted. "I will readily agree with Tipova's bloated arrogance."

Emma glanced toward the looming citadel, shivering despite the heat of the late-afternoon sunlight and the heavy ivory-colored robe that was richly embroidered with pearls.

"If I am not to approach the pasha or Baron Koman, then who am I supposed to influence?"

"Czar Alexander."

Emma's mouth dropped open in disbelief. Had Rajih just suggested that she blithely call upon the emperor of Russia and demand that he have a notorious criminal released from the prisons of Muhammad Ali Pasha?

"Are you jesting?" she breathed.

"Not at all."

She shook her head, swallowing her urge to laugh. "I fear you have a mistaken notion of my importance, Rajih."

His expression softened as he lifted a hand to brush a stray curl from her cheek.

"That is not possible."

"But it is," she insisted. "You met me in London in the companionship of the Duke and Duchess of Huntley, but that is only because they owed Dimitri some mysterious debt. I am not the lady of society I pretended to be."

Amusement smoldered in the dark eyes. "For which I am

eternally grateful, considering you were posing as Tipova's wife."

She ignored his teasing, determined that he would know the truth of her.

"What I mean is that I am not the person I pretended to be."

"Then who are you?" he asked, his voice soft.

"I am..." With a sharp motion she turned away, hiding her troubled expression. "Nobody."

Rajih's hands settled on her shoulders. "Emma."

"No, it is true." Her gaze absently lingered on the stunning sight of Cairo spread below. "I am a mere commoner from an unremarkable village in Russia. And even there I am a source of mockery. I have no influence."

She was not certain what she expected, but it was not his breathy chuckle as he lowered his head to speak directly into her ear.

"You could not be more mistaken, *habiba*. I am quite certain that within moments of being in your company, Alexander Pavlovich would be willing to demand the release of every prisoner in Egypt." He deliberately allowed his lips to brush her cheek. "But that will not be necessary."

"What do you mean?"

"Tipova mentioned that you are related to Herrick Gerhardt."

Caught off guard by the unexpected words, Emma stepped from his lingering touch. Turning, she regarded him with a wary frown.

"He is a distant relative," she admitted, "but we had never met until I came to St. Petersburg to seek his assistance in finding Anya."

"Distant relative or not, he is a well-respected advisor who has the ear of the czar."

"Herrick has been very kind, but I am not certain he

would be willing to speak with Czar Alexander on my behalf."

Rajih frowned, sensing her hesitation. "What is it Emma? Do you find it difficult to ask others for help?"

She was briefly distracted by his perceptiveness, even if it was misplaced on this occasion.

"To be honest, I used to find it impossible." She wrinkled her nose, all too easily recalling her stiff-necked refusal to seek out those distant relatives who might have been of assistance. "I considered it essential that I be able to survive on my own. After all, what could possibly be more important than my independence?"

"Anyone who has endured your loss would seek to gain a sense of control over their lives." He glanced up at the birds of prey circling overhead, his jaw clenched with suppressed emotions. "I understand better than most."

"Of course." Sympathy tugged at her heart. "You have lost both your parents."

His gaze shifted to the distant outline of the pyramids that stood with ageless splendor among the sand.

"And my country," he murmured. "Now I would do whatever necessary to protect it."

A bittersweet smile arched her lips. Until her sister had left her stranded in that brothel, she had believed that there was no sacrifice too great to keep her family safe.

"You do understand," she murmured. "A pity Anya was not so forgiving."

His expression hardened at the mention of Anya. "You cannot continue to punish yourself for the failures of your sister. You have done all that was possible to offer her a stable home. Her future is now in her own hands."

"Yes."

"So, will you overcome your reluctance and ask for Herrick Gerhardt's assistance?"

She paused, unconsciously shifting her feet. "Of course. I will do whatever possible to help."

"And yet you hesitate."

A wry smile curved her lips as she met his deliberately bland gaze.

"Because I am not utterly stupid," she said, her eyes narrowing in warning. "I know very well that Dimitri demanded that I be rushed away from the dangers of Cairo and returned to Russia."

His lips parted, as if he were debating the ridiculous notion of lying to her. At last he reached to take her hand in a comforting grip.

"Emma, there is nothing you can accomplish by remaining here. A female, especially an unwed female, has no power or freedom in Cairo." A suddenly wicked promise smoldered in the dark eyes. "Unless you prefer to remain hidden in my harem?"

Conceding that she had been neatly outmaneuvered, Emma gave a rueful shake of her head.

Rajih spoke the truth.

What could she possibly achieve if she lingered in Egypt? It was not as if she had a small army at her disposal to overrun the citadel. Or even the skills to slip past the guards and secretly free Dimitri.

And while she was far from convinced her plea to Herrick Gerhardt would be more than a waste of breath, she was willing to make the attempt.

"I am beginning to suspect you are attempting to be rid of me," she teased.

With a mysterious smile, Rajih lifted her fingers to his lips.

"Quite the contrary.

"What do you mean?"

"I intend to escort you to St. Petersburg."

WAITING UNTIL THE DINNER trays had been removed and the servants had finished preparing the beds for the night, Dimitri gathered several pillows from the outer chamber and arranged them beneath the silk sheets.

"This is a very bad plan," Josef muttered as he stuffed his own bed with pillows.

Dimitri smiled wryly. His servant had been grumbling and moaning for hours. Not that he blamed his companion. They were very much the pasha's prisoners, even if they were not locked in the dungeons. But, Dimitri was familiar enough with his long-time friend to know it was not being held in the citadel that was causing his foul mood, but fear that Dimitri's suspicions might not be as stupid as he wanted to believe.

Josef would stand before the firing squad without batting an eye, but the thought of someone he cared for in danger nearly unmanned him.

"It is not a plan at all," he pointed out. "Merely a hasty attempt to avoid being murdered in my bed."

Josef snorted. "I still don't understand why you believe we are going to be attacked."

"It is the only explanation that makes sense."

"Sense?" Josef straightened from the bed, throwing his hands in the air. "What sense is there in trying to keep you locked behind this fortress if someone wants you dead? It is much easier to shoot you in the back if you are walking down the street."

"Yes, but the benefit is knowing my precise location."

"So would kidnapping you."

Dimitri smiled, recalling numerous traps meant to destroy him that he had efficiently avoided. There were many on the streets of St. Petersburg who would swear he possessed magical powers.

"I am not so easily captured, as many men have discovered over the years."

Josef grunted, unable to argue with his logic. Not that he was satisfied. The servant would be snarling and snapping until they were far away from Egypt.

"But how could any enemy know you would kill Valik and that the pasha's guards would bring you to the citadel? Do you think they are fortune-tellers?"

Dimitri stepped back, regarding the narrow bed. At the moment it appeared to be a sheet pulled over a line of pillows. But in the dark and at a distance, the lumps beneath the sheet should give the impression of a body.

Or at least that was his hope.

All he needed was for his enemy to be distracted for a few moments to launch his ambush.

Dimitri returned his attention to Josef, accepting he had done all that was possible with no weapons, no notion of who or how many might attack, and a wounded shoulder that still ached like the very devil.

"No fortune-tellers, merely a man swift to take advantage of the situation," he said. "After all, no one attempted to have me arrested before now—"

"That we know of," Josef interrupted.

"That we know of," Dimitri conceded. "But now that I am trapped at the citadel, it obviously occurred to someone that they could use my confinement to their advantage."

"To kill you?"

Dimitri restlessly paced to blow out the candles that burned in the candelabras. The light from the fireplace should be ample enough to see any intruder without revealing his bed was empty.

"Who is to say?" he muttered. "It could be for the simple enjoyment of watching me suffer, or an attempt to flee before I have the opportunity to interfere in their plans, or any number of plots…including the desire to put me in my grave." His jaw clenched. "I intend to be prepared."

Josef's lips parted to continue his arguments, then

recognizing Dimitri's stubborn expression, he heaved a resigned sigh.

"What do you want of me?"

"It appears that the doors are the only entrance to the room, but I prefer not to take a risk of being caught off guard." He waved a hand toward the elaborate gilded-iron grills he had inspected earlier. So far as he could determine they appeared to be firmly attached to the stone of the citadel, but he had not survived so long without a good deal of caution. "I want you to remain near the windows."

Josef grimaced, but he readily moved to crouch near the edge of the windows.

"This is going to be a tedious night."

Dimitri extinguished the rest of the candles and moved to stand beside the door.

"It is preferable to listening to you snore."

They fell silent as they waited.

And waited. And waited.

As the minutes, and then hours, passed, however, he did not abandon his post or ease his vigilance. He was accustomed to thieves, cutthroats and pirates who did their business at night and on their own schedules.

Besides, if there were an assassin, he would want to wait until he was confident that Dimitri was asleep before entering the room.

Shifting his weight from foot to foot to keep alert, Dimitri froze at the sound of the door being slowly pressed open.

A fierce satisfaction jolted through him. Not at the sight of the slender man who slipped into the room and crept toward the bed with a pistol in his hand. In truth, it was unnerving to witness his potential murder from a distance. But at the knowledge his suspicions had been justified.

His instincts remained honed to razor sharpness, even if his lust for his career had begun to wane.

Waiting until the intruder had nearly reached the bed, Dimitri slid silently forward, approaching the man from behind. With one swift motion, he had plucked the pistol from the intruder's hand and pressed it to his temple. His other hand he wrapped around the man's neck, jerking him against his chest to cease his struggles.

There was the faint sound of shuffling from across the room before Josef was lighting the candles to show that the intruder was an Egyptian attired in a European-styled uniform that revealed he was one of the pasha's guards.

"Do you speak English? Russian?" Dimitri's fingers tightened on the man's throat, grimacing at the sour stench of fear that clung to him. Whoever he was, he most certainly was not a hardened criminal. "Answer me or I will crush your throat."

"I can discover the truth." Josef prowled forward, bending downward to uncover the knife strapped to the man's ankle. Then, with an evil grin that emphasized his scar, he pressed the tip of the knife to man's groin. "Answer the question."

"Bastards," the man spat in a thickly accented English.

"Who are you?" Dimitri asked.

"Fawzi."

"Well, Fawzi, perhaps you would not mind explaining what you are doing in this room?"

Fawzi shuddered, his breath a heavy rasp and his heart thumping so hard that Dimitri could actually feel its pounding beat.

"Please."

Sensing the fool was about to become hysterical, Dimitri glanced down at his servant.

"Josef, I believe our companion is prepared to be reasonable."

"Yes, yes." Waiting until Josef had removed the knife

from his most tender parts, Fawzi swallowed heavily. "It is nothing more than an unfortunate mistake."

"I will agree with unfortunate, but it was no mistake," Dimitri mocked.

"No, no. A big mistake. I thought I heard a noise and I entered to make certain you were not ill."

"How very considerate."

"The pasha was insistent you be comfortable during your stay at the citadel."

With a sudden movement, Dimitri shoved the man until he was turned to face him, pointing the pistol at his heart. He needed to see a man's face to know when he lied.

"Then perhaps we should join the pasha," he suggested. "He will be pleased to know how dedicated you have been to my welfare."

Fawzi licked his lips, his eyes darting toward the distant door.

"He will be in his bed."

"I do not mind awakening him."

Beneath his bronzed skin the man paled. "No."

A hard smile curved his lips. He was at least reassured that the nefarious plot to see him dead had not come from the pasha.

"Josef, would you discreetly discover what has happened to our guards?"

With a silence few men could match, Josef glided across the room and after a covert peek into the hallway, he disappeared through the door. A handful of minutes passed before he returned, his expression unreadable.

"They are both on the ground."

"Dead?"

"Drugged."

Dimitri returned his attention to Fawzi, his finger tightening on the trigger.

"It would be a simple matter to drug the dinner sent

from the kitchens." His gaze bore into the man's wide eyes. Fawzi was terrified at being caught, but Dimitri sensed a desperate cunning beneath his fear. He was like a rat, all the more dangerous for being cornered. "Especially if the tray was delivered by a fellow guard."

"Yes, I think we really must wake the pasha."

"Please." Fawzi held out his hands in a pleading motion. "What do you want of me?"

Dimitri studied the narrow face with its sunken black eyes and scraggly black beard.

"Why did you drug the guards and sneak into this room?" He gave a deliberate wave of the gun. "The truth."

The man hesitated, clearly weighing the danger of being caught in a lie. At last he grimaced.

"I came here to kill you."

Dimitri's lips twisted. That was certainly blunt.

"Is there a particular reason you wished me dead or do you simply hate all infidels?"

"A man approached me on my way back from a visit to my mother and offered me a fortune if I would put you in your grave."

"What man?"

"I don't know." Fawzi pressed his hands together in a gesture of entreaty. "No...wait. He called to me from a carriage as I was about to enter the citadel. He kept the curtain across the window so I never saw his face."

Frustration settled in the pit of his stomach.

Of course Fawzi never saw the man's face. Why would discovering the truth become a simple matter at this late date?

"Was he an Egyptian?"

"No, a foreigner. Like you."

"Russian?"

Fawzi shrugged. "Maybe."

"What did he say?" Dimitri took a step closer, his expression hard with warning. "I want every word."

"I can't remember every word."

"Try very, very hard."

Sweat dripped from the man's face as his gaze lowered to the pistol a short distance from his heart.

"He asked if I was a guard at the citadel and if I had the means to enter the room of the pasha's two foreign prisoners. When I admitted I could move freely about the citadel he promised me a purse filled with silver."

Dimitri lifted his brows in astonishment. "And you believed him?"

"He gave me a few coins to prove his sincerity," the man muttered, his expression sullen. "He said I could have the rest when I brought him proof that you were dead."

"What proof?"

The man nervously cleared his throat. "I was to cut out your eye and bring it to him."

"God almighty," Josef breathed.

"He claimed he would recognize it, so I was not to try and fool him," the man hurriedly explained.

Dimitri was forced to swallow a sudden lump in his throat. His life had been one of upheaval and violent survival. He had assumed that nothing could shock him.

Now, however, he was stunned by this ruthless confession. Who could hate him with such passion?

"Did he give a reason he desired my death?" he rasped.

"No."

Dimitri regarded the bumbling assassin with distaste. "You were willing to kill a man in his sleep and cut out his eye for no other reason than a purse of silver?"

An unctuous smile curved his lips as he pressed a hand to his chest.

"My mother is ill. I need the money for her medicine."

"Of course. Your poor, sick mother," Dimitri drawled, his eyes narrowing as he realized the pathetic louse might actually be of worth. "Then we had best go and collect your reward."

Without warning Josef moved to grab his arm.

"Have you lost all sense?" he demanded.

"We shall soon enough discover." Dimitri's gaze never shifted from Fawzi. "Where were you to meet your mysterious patron?"

CHAPTER TWENTY-SEVEN

DIMITRI WAS CAREFUL TO keep the pistol prominently displayed as Fawzi led them through the sleeping citadel. It seemed wise to remind the man just what would happen should he be foolish enough to attempt an escape or to alert the guards that prowled through the dark corridors.

Depending upon Fawzi's familiarity with the maze of rooms, they were soon out of the main building and moving through the servants' quarters. Dimitri demanded that they pause long enough for Josef and him to change into the rough linen tunics and loose breeches of stable hands before they were leaving the main building and heading toward the massive tower that guarded the nearest gate.

There was a tense moment as they were halted by the sentry, his expression skeptical as Fawzi babbled in Arabic. Unable to follow the conversation, Dimitri could only trust that the knife Josef had discreetly pressed to the man's back would discourage any attempt to attract unwanted attention.

At last they were through the thick walls that surrounded the citadel and moving down the hill to the city below.

Dimitri sucked in a deep breath, astonished that they had truly managed to escape the fortress.

Of course, if he were thinking clearly he would knock Fawzi senseless and flee Cairo with all possible speed. Instead, he poked the slender man in the back with his pistol and urged him toward the clump of palm trees.

Once they were lost in the thick shadows, he grabbed

Fawzi's arm and yanked him close enough he could whisper in his ear.

"Is that his carriage?"

He pointed toward the black vehicle that was parked before an abandoned building. At a glance he could determine no more than it resembled nearly every other carriage in Cairo and that there was one burly Egyptian groom standing next to the horse, lazily smoking a cheroot.

A closer glance, however, revealed the occasional twitch of the curtain that covered the carriage window, as if whoever was inside was growing impatient, and the slouched inattention of the groom.

His sheer negligence was a silent invitation to be hit over the head.

Obviously, whoever was plotting his death clearly had no military training and few skills necessary to survive the streets.

"Yes," Fawzi said. "I recognize the servant."

Josef moved to stand at his side. "Do I need to remind you that this is perhaps the most stupid decision you have ever made, Tipova?" he growled. "Including the night you dueled with three swordsmen at the same time."

A reminiscent smile touched his lips. Over the years his authority had often been challenged. His polished manners and preference for elegant attire convinced some fools that he could not possibly be as dangerous as his reputation implied.

In the past, he had enjoyed proving his worth.

Thankfully, he had reached an age where he was ready to put such reckless stupidity behind him.

No doubt because he now had something, or rather someone, to live for.

"I won, did I not?"

Josef narrowed his gaze, clearly not amused by his teasing.

"Damn you. We have escaped. Allow me to gather the others and we can be far away from Cairo before the pasha realizes we are no longer his guests."

Dimitri shook his head, his attention returning to the carriage across the road.

"Not until I discover who is so anxious to see me dead."

"What does it matter so long as they do not succeed?"

"Because they will quite likely try again." His gaze shifted to the nearby buildings, searching for hidden dangers that might be lurking in the shadows. "I do not intend to spend the remainder of my life in fear."

"You always have enemies wishing you harm," Josef muttered. "It has never troubled you before."

Dimitri turned to meet his servant's frustrated glance, his expression somber.

"I now have another's welfare to consider," he said, his tone suggesting that he would not compromise when it came to protecting Emma. "I will not leave here until I have brought an end to the threat."

"But…"

"My decision is made, Josef," Dimitri interrupted. "Fawzi."

"Yes?"

He pointed across the street. "I want you to approach the carriage and pretend that you have accomplished your mission."

"No, I have done all you have asked of me," Fawzi whined in alarm. "If I go to the man without the proof he demanded I will be shot."

Josef waved his knife in front of the man's face. "If it is an eye you are wanting then I can make certain you have what you need."

Not surprisingly, Fawzi fell back with a squeal, his face drenched with sweat.

"Josef." Dimitri sent the servant a warning glare. "I have need of him."

"Why?"

"He can provide a distraction while you dispose of the groom."

"And what of you?"

"I intend to join our mysterious lurker."

Josef clenched his jaw, his disapproval etched on every line of his face.

"Don't be a fool," he gritted. "We have no notion how many men might be in the carriage."

Dimitri grimaced. That was an unfortunate risk. But what choice did he have?

"No, but I will have the element of surprise."

Josef snorted. "Surprise will not halt a bullet to your heart."

"Trust me."

The men exchanged glares, then at last accepting that nothing would prevent Dimitri from confronting the unknown enemy, Josef heaved a frustrated sigh.

"Damn you, Tipova."

Keeping his firm hold on the Egyptian, Dimitri urged him toward the edge of the palm trees.

"Fawzi, I want you to count to twenty and then approach the carriage."

"And when he asks if you are dead?" the man rasped.

"Use your imagination. Just keep him occupied." His grip momentarily tightened, biting into Fawzi's arm with a warning pressure. "Oh, and Fawzi?"

The Egyptian swallowed heavily. "What?"

"If you attempt to reveal our presence, I will not only shoot you, but I will have you chopped into pieces and delivered to your poor, sick mother." He smiled with a cold cruelty that had frightened men far more courageous than Fawzi. "Do you understand?"

It took a moment for Fawzi to regain enough composure to give a shaky nod.

"Yes."

"Good." Dimitri gestured toward his servant. "Josef, the guard."

Muttering curses in various languages, Josef silently disappeared and headed down the street so he could approach the groom from behind. Dimitri followed several steps behind him, waiting near the corner for Fawzi to stumble and sway his way across the street.

Dimitri grimaced at the man's craven lack of discipline, but at least his peculiar manner had attracted the attention of the guard who remained oblivious as Josef approached and whacked the back of his head with the hilt of his knife.

With a grunt, the man tumbled to the ground, and Josef smoothly took the reins of the horse, keeping it from jarring the carriage. At the same moment, Dimitri moved forward, his gaze locked on Fawzi who was leaning toward the curtained window, speaking softly to whoever was inside.

He took a moment to make certain his pistol was primed, then with one smooth motion he had the door open and was surging into the carriage to press his gun against the chest of the man seated near the window.

"I suggest you sit very still and lift your hands so I can see them," he commanded, waiting until the stranger had raised his arms over his head before he used his free hand to search the man for weapons. Predictably he found an ivory-handled dueling pistol in the pocket of the caped greatcoat and a smaller gun tucked in the top of the glossy Hessians. He suspected there might be more hidden about the carriage, but for the moment he was satisfied that there were none near at hand. Keeping the pistol pointed at his companion, he settled in the opposite seat and offered a small smile. "Now, I believe introductions are in order."

There was a tense silence before the man slowly reached up to grasp the brim of his high beaver hat and toss it onto the seat beside him.

"While I would say they are superfluous," he drawled.

Dimitri stiffened, an icy shock momentarily halting his heart and squeezing the air from his body.

Although the inside of the carriage was dark, the curtain had been pushed aside to allow a spill of silver moonlight to wash over the man's gray hair and the elegantly carved features. Features that were heavily lined from a life of self-indulgence.

No. He grappled to make sense of what he was seeing. It was not possible.

And yet...

And yet, it could be that this moment had been destined since the day Count Nevskaya had forced the innocent child of a local cobbler to his bed.

The golden eyes that were a mirror image of Dimitri's flashed with a familiar hatred, jerking him out of his fog of disbelief.

"Father," he drawled, his voice cold and perfectly steady. Despite his shock, he had developed the ability to confront any situation with utter composure. Besides, he was beginning to suspect that fate had offered him a rare opportunity he would be an idiot to squander. "What an unpleasant surprise."

"I heartily return the sentiment," the count sneered. "You were supposed to be dead."

"While you were supposed to be rotting in Czar Alexander's prison."

With a tight smile, Nevskaya adjusted the signet ring he wore on his pinkie, seemingly indifferent to the gun pointed at his heart.

And perhaps he was.

Dimitri had devoted years to governing his feelings. It

had been a necessary skill to survival. He suspected his father, however, was not disguising his emotions. Count Nevskaya was simply devoid of all but anger and hatred.

How else could he have tossed his pregnant lover into the gutter? Or abused children without remorse?

"Clearly we are both doomed to disappointment," he murmured.

"What are you doing in Cairo?"

"Valik sent a messenger to St. Petersburg to warn me that Dimitri Tipova had followed him to London and was busily destroying the business I worked for years to create."

Dimitri's lips twisted. "Do you expect an apology?"

Nevskaya wrinkled his nose as if there were a foul smell in the air.

"I expect you to tend to your criminal activities and leave me in peace."

"But I do not wish to leave you in peace," he informed his father, his gaze never wavering from the face that had haunted him for too many years. "I want you to suffer exquisite agony each and every day of your miserable existence."

"Such melodrama." The count waved a dismissive hand. "You are so regrettably like your mother."

Dimitri's finger tightened on the trigger of his gun, only distantly aware of the sound of footsteps as Fawzi grasped his opportunity to escape.

How satisfying would it be to put a bullet in the reprobate's black heart?

"I happen to consider that a compliment," he gritted. "My mother was a beautiful, courageous woman who was destroyed by a disgusting letch." He flicked a contemptuous gaze over his father. "You are not worthy to speak her name."

"She was a peasant who was fortunate to have won my attention."

Oh, yes, definitely a bullet straight into his heart.

"Quite fortunate," he snapped. "She was raped, impregnated and then tossed into the gutter to die. I cannot fathom why she was not overwhelmed with gratitude."

"Bah."

Dimitri bit back his angry words. He was wasting his breath if he hoped to make his father suffer the least amount of guilt. The only means of truly wounding him was to attack his insufferable pride.

He forced himself to lean back in the seat, his expression sardonic.

"Of course, she did manage to outwit you."

"Absurd."

"How furious you were when she arrived on your doorstep and demanded that you pay for your son's education." Dimitri chuckled, genuinely enjoying the memory of his mother's boldness, her spine stiff and her head held high as the count threatened any number of vile retributions. "But she would not be bullied or cowed."

"I should have had you both disposed of like the vermin you were," his father bit out.

"Yes, it is a pity you were a pathetic coward who allowed yourself to be manipulated by a mere whore."

Fury flared through his father's golden eyes as an ugly color crawled beneath his skin. Dimitri braced himself, willing the man to attack. He might have qualms about shooting an unarmed man, no matter how deserving of death he might be, but he would not hesitate to defend himself.

Then, with an obvious effort, the count wrapped himself in his haughty composure.

"She soon enough regretted her temerity," he taunted. "I heard that she died in the gutter."

Dimitri smiled, grimly refusing to react. "And now you are about to share her fate."

Nevskaya's gaze covertly shifted toward the gun before returning to Dimitri's face. It was no more than a flicker. But it was enough to convince Dimitri that his father was not quite as impervious to the dangers of his situation as he would have him believe.

"You think I fear death?"

"Yes, I think you fear it very much," Dimitri said slowly. "But who could blame you? Men who prey on children are destined for the deepest pits of hell."

"I am a nobleman," he announced with cold disdain. "I am above tedious morals."

Dimitri grimaced. He might have laughed if not for the knowledge Nevskaya truly believed his social position gave him liberty to commit any sin with impunity.

And worse, he was not alone in his arrogance.

Despite Alexander Pavlovich's best attempts to rid Russia of its barbaric reputation there remained a blatant belief among the nobles that they possessed the God-given right to treat serfs however they pleased. Indeed, it was rumored the czar's own military advisor had recently beat to death one of his peasants.

Still, there was a growing disapproval toward such outlandish behavior as the czar became increasingly pious, filling his royal court with his more conservative supporters.

He shook his head, turning his thoughts to more important matters.

"You have not yet explained why you are in Cairo."

The older man shrugged. "Once I discovered that Sanderson had been arrested I knew it was only a matter of time before the idiot revealed my part in the—"

"Trafficking of children?" Dimitri supplied.

"Arrangement."

"I do not understand." Dimitri tilted his head to the side, a goading smile on his face. "If noblemen are above morals, then what do you care if your sins are exposed to the world?"

"Unlike his proud ancestors, Alexander Pavlovich is a weak, ineffective ruler who has allowed himself to become a tedious prude." His words echoed Dimitri's earlier thoughts. "His father would have been ashamed to know he had spawned such a spineless bore."

Dimitri shuddered. Czar Paul had been a brutal, stupid man, and a notoriously corrupt leader who had been increasingly unstable before his timely demise.

But then again, it was predictable that his father would prefer the man who had repealed Catherine's laws intended to protect the peasants.

"Hardly spineless." He settled more comfortably on the leather seat. "Alexander Pavlovich did, after all, manage to take the throne when he was still little more than a lad. A bold stroke."

"A knife in the back is the behavior of a coward."

"A rabid dog has to be put down by any means necessary."

The count made a sound of disgust, typically more concerned with his perverted sense of honor than the most basic morality.

"*You* would certainly think so. Peasants have no notion of honor."

Dimitri studied the man seated across from him, shifting through the confusing emotions that battered him.

For so many years Count Nevskaya had been the demon who haunted his life. The choices he had made, the sacrifices he'd suffered and the ruthless hunger to achieve a place in the world where he could never be a victim had all been due to his father.

Now as he sat across from the blackguard, he wondered why he had ever given him such power over his existence.

Not that he didn't still hate him with a violent passion. Or wish him into the fiery pits of hell.

But he was beginning to realize that Count Nevskaya was a cold, insignificant fool who had condemned himself to a life of lonely misery years ago.

A man who no longer had the power to hurt him.

A heady sense of relief raced through his blood. As if a heavy weight had been taken off his shoulders.

Or perhaps it was his heart.

"Do you truly believe yourself superior to me simply because of an accident of birth?" he demanded.

His father sniffed, offended by the mere question. "I am Count Nevskaya, an ancient and noble title. The blood of royalty flows through my veins."

"And yet, for all your grand titles and royal blood you have squandered your fortune and have become a common beggar, pleading to your wife's brother to keep your roof from tumbling onto your head." Dimitri took pleasure in reminding the pompous twit. "And of course, you are forced into kidnapping helpless children with the assistance of ridiculous buffoons such as Sanderson to support your debauchery." A cold smile curved his lips. "I, on the other hand, have amassed a vast fortune and purchased more than a dozen estates that are all fully staffed with loyal servants."

"You are an uncouth savage," his father snarled.

"And yet, I am welcomed at the Winter Palace while you have now become a source of embarrassment," Dimitri pressed. "No one in society would allow you across their thresholds."

Nevskaya flinched before he could stop the revealing movement, his gaunt face unnaturally pale.

Satisfaction warmed Dimitri's heart. For a man with his father's bloated pride it was unbearable to be shunned by his peers.

"This scandal will pass in time," the older man muttered.

"Not if you are locked in Czar Alexander's prison. Which is precisely why you fled when you discovered that Sanderson was revealing your sordid secrets."

"You know nothing."

Dimitri shrugged. "It is true I am confused why you would choose to flee to Cairo."

"It is none of your damned business."

The sound of a cart rattling down the dirt road filled the carriage as Dimitri considered the various possibilities.

Egypt was a convenient country to disappear in.

So long as a man had money he could live in comfortable seclusion. Still, he could not imagine the fastidious Count Nevskaya choosing to live among the savages.

He regarded his father with a frown. "Did you hope that Valik would take you in like a poor stray?"

"Those females belong to me."

Of course. How had he been so stupid?

"You were hoping to locate your servant so you could auction the girls and claim the full profit before you attempted to disappear." He shook his head in sheer revulsion. "Where did you hope to go once you had your money? The Indies? America?"

"Does it matter?"

"No, I do not suppose it does." Dimitri breathed in deeply, reminding himself the girls were safely out of the reach of this vile creature. "Not after I managed to ruin your scheme yet again," he taunted, his voice thick. "How very frustrating it must be for you to be constantly outwitted by your bastard son."

Fury darkened his father's golden eyes. "You may have escaped the pasha's guards tonight, but you will never be allowed to leave Egypt. Eventually you will be returned to the citadel."

Being returned to the citadel was the least of Dimitri's concerns at the moment, but the threat did put in mind a nagging question.

"That reminds me. However did you force Koman to crawl off his divan and petition my guilt before the pasha?"

There was a moment of sullen silence, then the older man absently smoothed the folds of his cravat, his fingers lingering on the ruby stickpin that shimmered like a drop of blood on the crisp white linen.

"The baron possesses a young daughter who resides with her mother in St. Petersburg."

"And?" Dimitri prompted.

"And I pointed out that such a gently reared female would be worth a fortune in the slave market."

Dimitri's breath hissed through his teeth. Whatever his dislike of the fat, indolent baron, no man deserved to have his daughter threatened with rape.

"And *I* have been branded a coldhearted bastard. Have you no conscience whatsoever? Ah…" His lips twisted in a sneer. "Of course. I was forgetting that noblemen have no need for common decency."

His father waved away Dimitri's mocking criticism. "I merely made a suggestion. It was Koman who assumed that it was a threat."

"You are truly remarkable. Do you take responsibility for nothing?"

His father leaned forward, his eyes glittering with a cold hatred.

"You are in no position to judge me," he hissed.

"Why? Because I am the son of a whore?"

"Because you are not so different from me."

Only years of rigid discipline kept Dimitri from pulling the trigger of the pistol.

"You compare us again, and I will yank out your tongue,"

he said, his frigid tone revealing he was prepared to follow through on his threat.

The count's lips twisted in an ugly smile, taking obvious pleasure in Dimitri's outrage.

"But we are. You have devoted your life to plotting your revenge upon me. And we both know you would have committed any sin, no matter how evil, to destroy me." He leaned forward. "I have done nothing less."

In the moonlight Dimitri could see the haunting likeness between them.

The wide forehead, the aquiline nose, high cheekbones and full lips.

He had always assumed that those physical similarities were all he had in common with Count Nevskaya. After all, the man was a depraved monster who had destroyed countless children. How could he bear to think they were related by more than blood?

But a tiny voice whispered that he had nearly allowed himself to become as empty and bitter as his miserable father.

His dark crusade for revenge had consumed his life. And the count was not mistaken when he claimed that Dimitri had been willing to do whatever necessary to destroy the man who he held responsible for his mother's death.

He had almost sacrificed his own heart.

In the end, it had been Emma who rescued him.

She filled his heart with love, banishing the hatred that had nearly destroyed him.

He allowed a smile of smug satisfaction. "The difference is that my revenge has succeeded whereas yours has failed miserably."

A malignant anger twisted the count's lean features. "Do not be so certain. You have not yet escaped Egypt."

Dimitri shrugged. "Even if I were to be captured and returned to the citadel it will be no more than a momentary inconvenience. We both know that Alexander Pavlovich will soon demand my release."

"Until he does, however, you will be trapped." The older man narrowed his gaze, a muscle in his jaw twitching. "And I can assure you that Fawzi was not the only man I hired to see you dead. Eventually one will succeed."

Dimitri had to admire his father's tenacity. Even when he had to realize his plot for revenge had been ruined, he continued to search for a means to salvage his pride.

"I do not believe you."

"Why would I lie?"

"If there were truly more assassins you would have kept them a secret," Dimitri countered. "To reveal them to me would steal away their greatest power."

"Power?"

"The power of catching me off guard." Dimitri shook his head. He had played chess often enough to know when he had his opponent in checkmate. "No, you are defeated, Father. Utterly and completely defeated."

His father abruptly stiffened, his icy composure crumbling as he at last accepted that he had been bested by his own son.

In that moment he was not the sophisticated Count Nevskaya. Or the cunning power behind the slave traders. Or even the father who had glared down his nose when Dimitri's mother had hauled him to the elegant town house.

No. This was a man facing ruin.

The golden eyes smoldered with a demented fire and spittle formed at the corners of his mouth.

"You will pay for this," the count spat, his hand fumbling toward the door of the carriage.

For a moment, Dimitri assumed his father was attempting to escape.

He was not, after all, the sort of man who would face his guilt with dignity. Had he not fled St. Petersburg like a gutless deserter, leaving behind his comrades to be charged with his crimes?

Then, he realized that Nevskaya was instead digging into a side pocket.

The world slowed as Dimitri watched his father with an odd detachment.

He knew what the man was searching for. He had similar pockets sewn into his own carriages to make certain he had a loaded pistol conveniently at hand. The streets could be a dangerous place. Who knew when you might have need of a hidden weapon?

His finger tightened on the trigger, but still he hesitated. So far as Dimitri was concerned, his quest to destroy his father was at an end.

What did the past matter when his future promised to be a glorious adventure with Emma Linley-Kirov?

As long as Dimitri made certain that the pasha knew the count was in his country and that he was responsible for the traffickers, eventually his father would be served his just rewards.

But even as he shoved himself toward the far door of the carriage, the count had the gun in his hand and was swinging it in Dimitri's direction. Dimitri had a brief moment to wryly accept his father had possessed none of his qualms as he swiftly fired a shot, the bullet grazing his already wounded shoulder.

Dimitri instinctively returned fire, his own shot far superior as it hit his father directly in the center of his chest.

It had been years since he had missed his target.

The stench of gunpowder filled the carriage and with a sense of inevitability, Dimitri watched as his father sprawled across the seat, the gun dropping from his lifeless fingers.

He knew that he should feel something.

Triumph. Sorrow. Relief.

Instead, his only thought was that he hoped his newest bullet wound was healed before he reached St. Petersburg. Emma would not be pleased if she discovered he had managed to be shot once again.

His inane musings were interrupted as the door to the carriage was yanked open and Josef stuck his head through the opening, his knife clutched in his hand.

His gaze darted about the carriage, settling on the motionless form of Nevskaya even as he reached down to snatch the pistol from the carriage floor.

"Damn you, Tipova, you nearly frightened me into my grave," he growled, waving the gun at the count. "Is he..."

"Dead," Dimitri said in clipped tones, waving his friend from the door so he could climb out of the carriage.

Once he was standing on the street, he sucked in a deep, cleansing breath.

He was vaguely aware of the Arabian jasmine-scented air and the distant passage of guards returning to the citadel, but he paid them no heed.

He was anxious to put the exotic splendor of Egypt behind him.

Moving to his side, Josef nodded his head toward the carriage.

"What do you want done with the body?"

Dimitri shrugged. "Leave it for the vultures."

"Fawzi disappeared, of course. Vile little rat," Josef muttered. "Did you want him tracked down?"

"No, I am done with revenge."

There was a short silence as Josef studied him with a narrowed gaze.

"Now what?"

"Now, Josef, we go home."

CHAPTER TWENTY-EIGHT

St. Petersburg

WITH A BREATH OF RELIEF, Emma slipped into the blessed silence of a small breakfast room at the back of Vanya Petrova's town house. A brief glance revealed walls covered in green damask panels with birchwood furnishings, but it was the view of the sunken rose garden that attracted her attention.

The hem of her ivory gown richly trimmed with gold lace brushed the parquet floor as she walked and her hands absently stroked the lovely fabric.

Vanya had surprised Emma with the dress earlier that morning. Obviously, the wily noblewoman had already suspected that Emma intended to use the excuse of having nothing appropriate to wear to her wedding to hide in her rooms.

A faint smile curved Emma's lips. She was, of course, delighted that Vanya was at last exchanging vows with her devoted lover, Richard Monroe. And deeply touched that the older woman had gone to the trouble of postponing the ceremony until Emma had returned to St. Petersburg.

After all, it was not as if she were a part of her family. Or even a close friend. She was simply a common peasant who imposed herself on the poor woman.

The realization had nagged at her with growing persistence over the past few days.

What reason did she have to linger in St. Petersburg?

Without warning, the image of a dark, lean face with

golden eyes seared through her mind. Dimitri. The damnable man who had yet to make his glorious arrival.

A savage pain sliced through her heart before she was ruthlessly thrusting aside the worthless emotion.

Although she had heard from Herrick that Dimitri had managed to escape from the pasha, and had been forced to kill his evil father, she had received no more than a terse note that might have been sent from a stranger.

Which was perfectly fine with her, she told herself.

Had she not already decided that she and Dimitri Tipova were utterly unsuitable?

Now if she could just convince her traitorous heart.

Ignoring the distant sound of laughter floating from the formal parlor, Emma studied the garden that slumbered beneath the pale February sunlight. Absently, she rubbed her bare arms, a strange chill crawling over her skin. No doubt it was a mere reaction to the cold after the heat of Cairo.

It was not as if she believed in premonitions.

The stern warning had barely passed through her mind when the sound of footsteps had her spinning about, her heart lodged in her throat.

For a breathless moment she expected Dimitri to step through the door. Ludicrous, of course. Even if he had returned to St. Petersburg there was no reason for him to make an appearance at Vanya's home.

No reason whatsoever.

Thankfully unaware of Emma's stupid sense of disappointment, the Duchess of Huntley entered the room, appearing stunningly beautiful in a pale blue gown that perfectly matched her eyes with silver netting that was sprinkled with a king's ransom in sapphires.

"What a beautiful wedding," she said, moving toward Emma with a determined smile.

Emma did not have to be told that Leonida had been

the one chosen to seek her out and ensure that she had not sunk into a fit of melancholy.

Over the past few days, she had been acutely aware of the worried glances from Herrick and Vanya, and even the haughty Duke of Huntley had chided her for the shadows beneath her eyes and the pallor of her skin. As if she were to blame for her sleepless nights.

"Yes." She managed a smile, knowing that Leonida only had her best interests at heart. "And Vanya made an exquisite bride."

"It makes one wonder why she tortured poor Richard for so many years by refusing to be his wife. It is obvious she adores him."

Emma shrugged. She was only vaguely familiar with the complicated courtship between Vanya and Richard, although she had heard several stories of Vanya's cunning plots over the years to protect Alexander Pavlovich's claim to the throne.

"Perhaps she was not yet prepared to sacrifice her independence."

"True. She is a remarkably intelligent woman who has led a most fascinating life." Leonida chuckled, the sunlight shimmering in her pale golden hair. "I hope someday she will be inclined to confess a few of her more thrilling adventures."

Emma glanced toward the delicate vases that Vanya had acquired on her journey to China.

"I deeply admire her."

"As do I." Leonida paused, a speculative glint in her eyes. "Still, a woman does not necessarily have to sacrifice her independence when she weds."

Even suspecting the conversation was destined to be shifted in the direction of Dimitri, Emma tensed.

"You say that only because you were blessed with a husband who is devoted to your happiness." She absently brushed aside a curl that had come loose from the elegant knot on top her head. "Most women have little choice but to bow to a man's will, regardless of her desires."

"Which only means that a woman must take care in choosing her husband."

Emma shook her head. A woman might be able to choose her husband, but she had little control over who she fell in love with.

"If only it were that simple." She sighed.

With a frown, Leonida reached to take her hand. "What is troubling you, Emma?"

"Nothing." Emma determinedly squared her shoulders. "In fact, my life is at last settled. I shall soon be returning to my cottage in Yabinsk."

"Oh." A frown tugged at Leonida's brows. "So far away?"

"I have promised both Vanya and Herrick Gerhardt that I will return to St. Petersburg to visit."

"And what of Dimitri?"

Emma tugged away from Leonida's grasp, spinning on her heel to pace to the ceramic stove set in the corner of the room.

"I do not know what you mean."

"I am not blind," Leonida said. "He loves you. And I am fairly certain you return his feelings."

Emma bit her lower lip, knowing it was futile to lie. Despite being a pampered lady of society, Leonida was far from stupid. And it was not as if Emma were skilled in disguising her emotions.

Unlike others.

"What if I do?"

"Love is a rare gift, Emma." Leonida moved to her side, her expression troubled. "Why would you turn your back on Dimitri?"

"I am not turning my back on Dimitri. I am…"

"Yes?" Leonida softly prompted.

Emma hunched her shoulders, wishing Leonida would rejoin the other guests. As much as she enjoyed the woman's charming friendship, Emma was unaccustomed to sharing her emotions with anyone.

"We could never be happy together," she muttered.

Leonida hesitated, as if carefully considering her words. "Does it trouble you he was forced to become a criminal?"

"Oddly enough, no." Emma smiled ruefully. Perhaps if she were a more righteous person she would be shocked by Dimitri's past, but life had taught her not to judge others. Not when she had endured the endless censure of her neighbors. "Oh, I am not naive. I know that he has suffered a brutal life and that he has profited from the sins of others, but I also know that he has a kind and generous heart and that he would give his life to protect those he considers his family."

"He also happens to be superbly handsome and indecently wealthy," Leonida teased. "What more could you desire?"

"It is not what I desire, but what Dimitri desires," she said, her brows lifting as Leonida suddenly laughed. "What is so amusing?"

"Dearest Emma." Leonida reached to pat her arm. "You need only see Dimitri's expression when you enter a room to know that it is taking all his restraint not to toss you over his shoulder and haul you away like the pirate he is."

A hot flush stained her cheeks. Not at the knowledge Dimitri had been so blatant in his passion for her. What woman would not be pleased to have such a handsome gentleman regarding her as if she were the most beautiful woman in the world? Instead, it was the memory of the vivid dreams that had plagued her.

She awkwardly cleared her throat. "I was not referring to Dimitri's lust."

"No?"

"I meant his passion for protecting those he loves."

Leonida wrinkled her nose, as if intimately familiar with domineering males.

"Ah, it is unfortunate, but there is no man who does not possess the urge to protect others," she admitted, a glimmer of sly humor shimmering in her blue eyes. "A wise woman allows him to fuss and then do precisely as she pleases."

"That might be well enough for most men, but not Dimitri." Emma wrapped her arms around her waist as she shivered with an aching sense of loss. "He blames himself for his mother's death."

Leonida sucked in a sharp breath. "How dreadful."

"The belief has tortured him his entire life."

"Which is all the more reason he needs you to help heal his wounds," Leonida urged gently, unaware her words were like a dagger to Emma's heart.

"No." She shook her head. "What he needs is a woman who is happy to depend upon him without question and does not mind having her life controlled by another."

"Actually, I think I should be allowed to decide the sort of woman I prefer, Emma Linley-Kirov."

A shocked silence filled the room as both women slowly turned to watch the handsome, raven-haired gentleman stroll toward them.

Her gaze slid down his slender form that was shown to advantage in a Persian-blue jacket with silver waistcoat and black pantaloons. His cravat was precisely knotted with a diamond stickpin tucked among the folds and his hair smoothed into a queue at his nape.

Emma's heart squeezed with a painful excitement. He was so splendidly, dangerously beautiful.

"Dimitri," she breathed.

At her side Leonida cleared her throat, a mysterious smile curving her lips.

"If you will excuse me, I promised Stefan I would save him a waltz."

Emma barely noticed the woman's discreet departure. In truth she was not certain she would have noticed if the ceiling had tumbled onto her head.

Not when her knees were threatening to give way and her breath annoyingly elusive.

He halted directly before her, his golden eyes watching the emotions rippling over her face with unnerving intensity.

"Did you receive my message?" he demanded at last.

His words helped to shatter the odd sense of unreality, reminding Emma that she had waited day after painful day for this man to reveal that he had not forgotten her existence.

"*Wait for me* is not a message," she informed him stiffly. "It is a command."

His lips twitched. "What I have to say to you could not be put into a letter."

Emma lowered her gaze, belatedly realizing she was giving away more than she had intended. Hurriedly, she sought to turn the conversation.

"Herrick revealed that you…"

Her words stumbled to a halt as she struggled to find a delicate means to offer her sympathy.

"Shot my father through the heart?"

She lifted her gaze to study his guarded expression, her tender heart rebelling at the thought he might blame himself for his father's death.

"That you were forced to protect yourself," she corrected.

A rueful smile curved his lips, his hand reaching to tuck a stray curl behind her ear.

"You would, of course, assume the best of me."

"If you wished to kill your father you could have done so anytime in the past twenty years." She paused, wondering if he were truly as calm as he wished her to believe. "Did he follow you to Cairo?"

The golden eyes darkened with a sudden impatience, his hands cupping her face as he regarded her with a sudden determination.

"Count Nevskaya no longer matters. Indeed, nothing matters but you."

Emma scrambled away, her heart fluttering as she sought to confront him with a measure of composure.

"Wait," she husked. "There is something I must tell you."

He stilled, his eyes narrowing as he watched her nervously tug at the sapphire ribbon threaded beneath her bodice.

"Why am I certain I am not going to like what you have to say?"

She licked her dry lips. "I am leaving in the morning for Yabinsk."

Emma braced herself for a furious response. Dimitri, after all, was a man who expected to make the decisions for others and have them obeyed.

Which made his rigid control all the more frightening.

"Why?"

"It is my home."

"You intend to spend the rest of your life alone in your cottage?"

With an effort, Emma hid her flinch at the stark truth in his accusation.

The rest of her life alone...

It was her worst fear, but what choice did she have?

"I have my coaching inn to keep me occupied and Anya might come to her senses and—"

"Anya will never return to that cottage and we both know it," he overrode her, shifting to block her path to the door.

How had he suspected she intended to flee?

"There is no need for you to be so cruel."

Frustration flared through the beautiful golden eyes. "Obviously there is every need. You are stubborn beyond reason."

Her chin tilted as she regarded him with a hint of outrage. Deep inside she knew it was foolish to hope that Anya would return to the cottage. And in truth, she was not certain if she could ever fully forgive her sister for her betrayal.

But Dimitri Tipova had no right to criticize her decisions.

"If that is what you believe then you will be pleased to be rid of me," she muttered.

Dimitri stepped forward, his hands lightly grabbing her upper arms as his features softened with regret.

"*Moya dusha,* please forgive me, but you must realize that returning to the cottage will not bring back your family."

A familiar pain tugged at her heart. "I am well aware that my family is gone. You have no need to remind me."

"Then why are you leaving?"

She heaved a resigned sigh. This man dared to claim that *she* was stubborn.

"I cannot remain in St. Petersburg."

"Have you developed a dislike for the city?"

"Really, Dimitri," she snapped with impatience. "You must be aware that Vanya was wed earlier today."

He grimaced with rueful amusement. "I could not fail to

notice since she devoted the past quarter of an hour lecturing me on my ill manners in missing the ceremony."

"Then you must realize it would be impossible for me to remain beneath the roof of newlyweds."

"They are not precisely the traditional newlyweds," he pointed out. "They have been lovers for the past twenty years or more."

Emma refused to be swayed. Vanya's wedding was, after all, no more than a convenient excuse to leave St. Petersburg.

"I am still intruding."

They glared at each other for a tense moment, then a slow, worrisome smile tugged at his lips, his brooding gaze gliding over her wary face and down to the scooped line of her bodice.

Emma shivered, her skin prickling as if she could feel the heat of his gaze.

"Vanya would not agree, but it was never my intention that you should reside here."

"*Your* intention?" She stiffened at his nonchalant tone. "You have no say in where I live..."

With his typical arrogance, Dimitri ignored her stern warning, his hands tightening on her arms as he yanked her against his chest. In the same motion his head swooped downward, claiming her mouth in a kiss of brazen possession.

Tiny jolts of pleasure raced through her, heating her blood and causing her toes to curl in her ivory slippers. He tasted of champagne and untamed male as he teased his tongue between her lips, his grip easing so his fingers could lightly caress her bare arms.

Emma shuddered as anticipation fluttered in the pit of her stomach.

She had ached for weeks for this man's touch. His hard, lean hands exploring her body, his seeking mouth stirring a wicked need, his low voice whispering encouragement in her ear.

Now she was forced to swallow a whimper of disappointment when he pulled back to study her flushed face.

"If you prefer the country I have an estate near Moscow and another just beyond Kiev," he murmured.

She blinked, struggling to follow his words while her body trembled with desire.

"You want me to live with you?"

"Of course." He peered deep in her eyes. "We belong together."

She shook her head sadly. "I cannot be the woman you want."

"No," he readily agreed, "you are the woman I need."

She paused, uncertain. "Need?"

"Before you came into my life, I thought it was enough to surround myself with those in need, filling the emptiness in my heart with a hatred for my father."

"You should not dismiss what you have accomplished," she chided. "Herrick has told me of those you rescued from the streets."

"I am a sinner, not a saint, Emma." He gently brushed her cheek with the back of his hand, his expression somber. "And I have begun to realize that a part of my need to be the savior is because it allows me to keep others at a distance."

"I do not understand."

With a sigh he dropped his hands and turned to pace toward the center of the room. Emma frowned, startled by the hint of vulnerability she had glimpsed in his eyes.

"When people depend upon me, all I need offer them is my protection. There is no danger to my heart," he confessed. "But you refused to accept my rules."

"Which is why we are so unsuited."

He swung back to meet her puzzled gaze. "No, it is why we are so perfectly matched."

"You are making no sense, Dimitri. We are forever squabbling with one another." She shrugged. "How could we possibly be suited?"

He hesitated, considering his words, then squaring his shoulders he peered deep in her eyes.

"The simple answer is that I love you, Emma Linley-Kirov."

Emma stumbled backward, her hand pressed to her chest in a futile effort to still her racing heart. Obviously, the heat of the desert sun had damaged Dimitri's mind.

"No," she breathed. "It is not possible."

Dimitri arched his brows, smiling wryly at her less than joyous response to his declaration of love.

"Not possible?"

"No."

He prowled forward, not halting until she was backed against the wall.

"Perhaps you should explain, since I am quite certain of my feelings," he said, the very softness of his tone conveying his sincerity.

Astonishing.

She shook her head, her mouth dry. "We have nothing in common."

"I suppose that is true enough," he readily agreed. "You are a proper lady while I am a notorious criminal and the son of a whore. I have no doubt that you are far above my touch."

She gasped. Surely he could not believe such nonsense?

"You must know that was not what I meant at all."

"Then what did you mean?"

"I am not beautiful or sophisticated or fascinating."

"Emma—"

"No." She placed her hand across his mouth. Did he know how desperately she wanted to toss aside all reason and accept his pledge of love? It was only the fear that she could never truly offer what he needed to heal his wounds that made her hesitate. "I am a simple woman who desires a quiet life. I have had quite enough adventure."

Pressing his lips to her palm, Dimitri gently tugged aside her hand, his eyes glowing with a near feverish light.

"Oddly enough, I have recently developed a taste for a quiet life, as well."

The mere thought was enough to bring a grudging smile to her lips.

"You?"

"I must admit that I am as shocked as you, *milaya*," he teased, aimlessly rubbing his thumb over her inner wrist. "I never imagined that one day I would hand the reins of my empire to another."

"You mean—"

"As of today Josef is now the Beggar Czar," he proudly announced. "While I am a mere gentleman who is unencumbered by such vast responsibilities."

She shook her head in bemusement. It certainly seemed the day for surprises.

"Why would you do such a thing?"

He leaned down to brush a soft kiss over her lips. "Because I intend to devote myself to my wife and children."

CHAPTER TWENTY-NINE

DIMITRI PRESSED HIS THUMB to the rapid flutter of Emma's pulse at her wrist, wryly aware that she appeared closer to swooning than leaping for joy.

How was it possible that a woman who had confronted scoundrels and kidnappers and slave traders without flinching was in a near panic at his marriage proposal?

"Dimitri," she at last managed to rasp. "What are you saying?"

"I am asking that you become my wife."

"Your...wife?"

His lips twisted. Perhaps he should have rehearsed his proposal. It was obvious he was making a botch of it.

"Am I not speaking clearly?"

She shook her head, her expression wary. "I comprehend the words, but I cannot accept that Dimitri Tipova, the scourge of St. Petersburg, could ever be satisfied spending his days seated in front of a fire in some remote estate."

"Ah, but I intend to keep myself fully occupied."

Her wariness deepened. "Occupied with what?"

His gaze lowered to the temptation of her scooped bodice. She was exquisite in the beautiful ivory gown, but she would be even more beautiful with it stripped away to reveal her own ivory glory.

He swallowed a groan as his body stirred in anticipation. "There are a few pleasant activities that come to mind."

"You cannot remain forever in bed," she muttered.

He chuckled at her ridiculous accusation. "You should never underestimate my desire for you."

"I am not jesting."

He felt her pulse leap, but she remained uneasy, as if afraid that she might shatter if she lowered her guard.

That knowledge tugged at his heart with a small pang of tenderness.

He cupped her cheek in his hand. "Neither am I, but I do have other plans."

"What plans?"

"To begin with I must learn the duties expected of a gentleman farmer." He pretended to be offended when she regarded him as if she feared he'd taken leave of his senses. "You need not smirk, I have no intention of brandishing a hoe or mucking among the pigs, but I never acquire a new business without discovering the means to make it a profitable enterprise." A determined grin curved his lips. He was astonishingly eager to begin his life on his country estate. There was nothing he loved more than a new adventure, and beginning a family with Emma would be the greatest adventure of all. "Before I am done I will know the cost of each and every seed that is planted, where to purchase the latest farming implements and which of the staff have been stealing the silver."

A grudging amusement shimmered in her eyes. "That will indeed keep you occupied."

"I shall also need to learn how to perform the typical pastimes of a gentleman of leisure."

"I am almost fearful to ask."

"I might be a master at tossing dice and picking a pocket, but I have never learned to hunt or fish or play snapdragons."

She frowned, clearly puzzled by his ramblings. "Why would you wish to play snapdragons?"

Dimitri faltered, his palms suddenly damp and his mouth dry.

He had never before been so nervous. Not even

when he had been taken hostage by a particularly nasty highwayman.

Of course, nothing before had ever been so important.

"So I can teach our children," he said, his voice thick.

Her mouth opened, but nothing came out but a tiny squeak of shock.

"Oh."

"You do want children, do you not, Emma?" he asked, gently.

"Yes." She blinked back sudden tears. "Yes, I want children very much," she husked.

He grimaced, gazing into her hazel eyes and knowing that he would never truly deserve this beautiful, courageous woman.

"I know I would not be the man that most females would choose to father their children."

Her brows snapped together, her chin tilting. She was always determined to see the best in others.

Which was no doubt one of the reasons he found her so endearing.

"You are wrong, Dimitri."

"Impossible, I am never wrong," he teased.

"I cannot imagine a more worthy man."

He shook his head. "I was raised on the streets, hating the man who raped my mother. I know nothing of how to be a decent father."

Her wariness faded, her hand lifting to cover his hand that was pressed to her cheek.

"You have been protecting and caring for others since your mother's death," she said. "Besides, there is only one thing a father truly needs to offer his children."

"And what is that?"

"Love."

With a groan he wrapped her in his arms and hauled her tight against his body.

"If I love them half so much as I love their mother, then I shall be the greatest father in all of Russia."

"Oh...Dimitri." Arching back her head, she regarded him with all the emotion she had been hiding behind her brittle composure. "I love you, too."

His heart swelled, the years of bitterness forgotten. Never had he thought to ever feel such overwhelming joy.

Certainly not with a headstrong, spirited, independent woman who refused to leave him in peace.

"I always suspected that you were a woman of intelligence," he retorted with a smug smile.

She rolled her eyes. "So modest."

"You still have not answered my question, *moya dusha*." He paused, his smile fading. "Will you marry me?"

Breathlessly awaiting her response, Dimitri was unaware of the elegant, silver-haired gentleman who stepped in the room in a claret jacket with a black waistcoat trimmed in silver buttons.

At least he was unaware until the man had the audacity to interrupt the precious moment.

"You might wish to hear what I have to say before you give your response, Emma."

Easily recognizing the male voice, Dimitri weighed the pleasure of pulling his pistol and shooting the intruder against Vanya's annoyance at having her wedding so rudely interrupted.

At last it was the embarrassed pink that brushed Emma's cheeks that had him turning to confront the damnable man, his arm keeping her tucked protectively against him.

"Gerhardt," he growled. "This is a private conversation."

The older but still-handsome man strolled across the room, deliberately ignoring Dimitri's warning. Not surprising. Herrick Gerhardt was perhaps the second most powerful man in all of Russia.

"Am I intruding?" he murmured.

"Yes," Dimitri snapped. "Go away."

"Dimitri." Emma flashed him a chiding glance at his rudeness, reminding him that Herrick was one of the few people she could claim as family.

Herrick smiled, easily sensing Dimitri's smoldering frustration.

"I do have a reason for thrusting myself into such an obviously private moment."

"A desire for an early grave?" Dimitri muttered.

The older man's smile widened, stirring Dimitri's suspicions. What was the devil playing at?

"Actually, I have just finished a most intriguing conversation with Alexander Pavlovich," Herrick drawled.

"And why would your conversation with Czar Alexander be of interest to us?" Dimitri demanded.

"He was most delighted to learn that you have seen the error of your ways and have turned away from your life of sin."

Dimitri hissed in surprise. He would have bet his last ruble that no one beyond Josef was aware of his intent to leave his position.

"How did you discover my plans?"

Herrick adjusted the lace that peeked from the sleeve of his jacket.

"We all have our little talents."

Dimitri shuddered, amazed by the man's uncanny ability to discover even the darkest secrets. If he were not so rational, he might suspect the man of being a mystic.

"You are a frightening man, Herrick Gerhardt."

Emma stepped away from his tight grip, her expression confused.

"You came here to tell us that the czar approves of Dimitri becoming a proper gentleman?"

Again there was that worrisome smile.

"Not entirely."

Dimitri narrowed his gaze. "Perhaps we should speak in private."

"No, I suspect that Emma will be interested in the czar's decision," Herrick chuckled. "Do not glare at me, Tipova. You are not about to be hauled before the firing squad. Although in time you might prefer such a fate."

"Herrick, please." Emma reached out to place her hand on Herrick's forearm, her voice not entirely steady. "What has happened?"

Immediate regret chased the amusement from Herrick's face as he patted her hand in comfort.

"Forgive me, I did not mean to worry you, my dear. That was never my intention," he ruefully apologized. "I am an old man who must take his pleasure where he can, and I have been savoring the image of Tipova's expression when I reveal that Alexander Pavlovich has made the decision to create a new title."

Dimitri took an instinctive step backward, a sense of dread lodging in his gut.

"Title?"

"Baron Voglevich." Herrick offered a formal bow. "I hope it suits you?"

Perhaps for the first time in his life, Dimitri was struck speechless.

He was aware that Alexander Pavlovich could be unpredictable, and certainly Dimitri had performed several dangerous tasks to protect the czar from potential uprisings, not to mention the information he acquired on the streets that he provided to the Winter Palace.

Still, he had never expected to receive a title.

Hell, he never *wanted* a title.

In his mind the men of society were worthless buffoons fit for nothing more than to provide easy plucking at his gaming houses.

It was Emma who at last filled the shocked silence. "Do you mean—"

"I mean that when you wed, you will be the Baroness Voglevich," Herrick gently completed her faltering words.

Dimitri clenched his hands, forcing himself to take a deep, calming breath.

"Why?"

"He is aware of the numerous services you have performed for the empire," Herrick explained. "This is his means of offering his gratitude."

Dimitri grimaced. "I would have preferred a large donation of rubles."

"You have all the wealth you will ever need and, to be honest, the royal coffers are notoriously bare." Herrick deliberately glanced toward the stunned woman at Dimitri's side. "And now you have a bride to consider."

Emma snatched her hand away, her eyes wide. "I have no desire for a title."

"Nonsense." Herrick regarded her with a stern expression. "You shall soon become accustomed to being a member of society. And your children, of course, will be grateful for the opportunities offered by their positions."

Dimitri heaved a rueful sigh as Emma struggled against Herrick's sly manipulation.

Clearly, they had been outmaneuvered.

Emma at last offered a reluctant laugh. "You do not fight fair."

"Never." Herrick clapped his hands together, a satisfied expression settling on his gaunt face. "We should toast your good fortune."

"I have a better notion." Dimitri pointed toward the door. "You will return to Vanya's lovely party and I shall concentrate on pleasing my wife-to-be."

Having achieved his goal, Herrick readily strolled across the floor.

"Of course. Oh, I suppose I should also mention that Czar Alexander has begun the arrangements for your wedding. He thought June would be a suitable month," he murmured, his footsteps never slowing despite Dimitri's and Emma's protests. "And, Emma, I have requested that our English relatives travel to Russia for the ceremony. I had no notion there would be so many. Let us hope they will leave once the wedding is over."

He swept from the room, leaving the two of them shaking their heads in disbelief.

"Good Lord," Emma muttered.

"It would seem you shall soon have all the family you ever desired," he said dryly. Then, noticing her pallor he pulled her into his arms, his hands running a comforting path over her back. "Emma?"

"Baroness." She blinked, her hands lifting to grasp his shoulders for support. "My head is spinning."

He brushed a soft kiss over her mouth. "Do you still love me?"

"Of course."

"Then nothing else matters."

He returned for a much more lingering kiss, his tongue dipping between her lips to taste of her sweetness.

At last pulling back to study her upturned face, he was gratified to discover the color had returned to her cheeks and a glow of excitement in her eyes.

A slow smile curved her lips. "Well, Dimitri Tipova, how does it feel to be a respectable gentleman?"

His hands curved over her hips, tugging her against the stirring muscles of his thighs.

"At the moment it feels astonishingly wonderful."

"Just so long as you do not become entirely civilized."

She lifted onto the tips of her toes, trailing a path of kisses along his jaw. "I would miss my wicked pirate."

Desire exploded through him and without giving her the opportunity to come to her senses he was across the room locking the door. Then without pause he returned to sweep her off her feet.

Headed for the nearby sofa, he glanced down at the woman who had stolen the heart of the greatest thief in all of Russia.

"Perhaps I should demonstrate how wicked I can be."

* * * * *